Author's Notes

This novel takes inspiration from real-life people. Any reference to real-life events, or people, have had their names changed to keep anonymity and to sustain these people's memories with fictional additives to progress the plot.

Please enjoy, dear reader.

Да благословит вас Бог.

(May God bless you.)

Prologue

I was trapped in that foreign country. I see a shanty town swept away from a sandstorm. My vision is blurred through my goggles, and the storm worsens. The loose rags we wore offered some protection from the storm but not too much. Only four of us were left out of ten with a sole drive guiding us:

Find the mosque.

"Of all the places to be led to, we were led into a fucking storm!" cries Vasya, his voice being drowned by the ferocity of grains. "Unless you see someone, shut your fucking mouth!" I bark in return. I am exhausted. My body aches. Slava... our leader was wounded. The mountain of muscle stopped moving thirty minutes ago... I know what happened, but I didn't want to believe it. The blood from the bullet hole had coagulated and stopped flowing over his striped shirt. His skin was raw and shredded. The makeshift sled I was dragging along had suddenly got heavier; hard to tell with its occupant's legs gone.

"There!"
"Where?!"
"I see an open building..." Cries Arseny, the boy soldier. "We need to get inside! Out of this godforsaken storm!"
"How do you know nobody's inside?"
"Stay out here then! I'll let the storm save me the effort of killing you!" Vasya bellows.
"Someone take Slava!" I order with what little energy I have.
"I'll take him Fedor, GO!"

My lower back is bleeding from the shrapnel wound reopening. I feel a comforting pat on my shoulder, permitting me to drop the sled. It gives me solace until despair hits my chest. Vasya slammed his hand into my flak vest hard enough to almost wind me... if I wasn't winded already. Probably did me a favour and cleared any sand in my lungs. *"You better know what you're doing!"* he whined.

4

Still feeling the shock in my chest and my body failing, I bring my last efforts to move to the open building... well... less a building and more a shithole. But we needed this shithole. We were down to four men of ten and I was not going to let the others die in that fucking storm. And after that ambush, we needed something to help us. God had spat on us enough! I'm making my way to the building, barely able to breathe or walk and I will myself to cut through the storm and push my broken body against the wall. There was no door, no windows, just holes cut out of brick. What might have been there, the storm took it away. My heart races, beating with fear, courage, and hope; hope that I might find this place empty. I clutch the prayer rope around my neck, and I ready my AK, hoping that this piece of shit would not jam, and I BURST! I throw myself into the doorway and I hear my lucky sound...

CLICK

The sound went off on my right as I entered. I turn *ready* to kill this fucker... and I stop. A boy... no more than five or six, holding a jammed Makarov pistol. As soon as he realised what he had done, tears flowed from his eyes. Tears of fear, not from his own life but from what he was guarding.
The body of a man.
Too young to be a father, but old enough to be a brother. "Ey, ey! It's OK. No danger, see?" Fear is in my voice, but I do my best to be calm. I slung my rifle over my shoulder in hopes of calming him, but it was clear that this boy needed more assurance. To him, I am some fucking invader that just killed his brother. So, I throw my hands up, bloodied as they are in a sign of peace. He cowered behind the body lying on the floor, looking for protection but there was none he could offer. "I'm not here to hurt you, OK? We're just here to..."

*Bang*Bang*Bang*Bang*

"NOOOOOOO!!"

I turn to see where the shots came from and I see Vasya, looking proud at what he had just done. Venom was in his voice when he said, "What are you screaming at? I saved your life!"

I collapsed there… horrified at what I had just seen. Still taking it in. Four shots… two to each. "I'm getting the others! Help drag Slava in here since you wanted to keep him."

My eyes felt like bulging saucers in my skull. I felt like a helpless goldfish out of water, gasping for its last breath. I woke up from that hell with a sudden jolt. My body now aged was in shock, and I saw my son clinging onto my leg.
My body remained in a pew, at the front of the church I led. My son being the same age as that child who was murdered.
"It's ok Dad. I'm here." My boy whispered.
I cradled him with my black bandaged hands… my hands…
The source of my pain and torment. I watched this boy tighten his death grip like he was clutching onto a precious piece of glass. My back couldn't stop rocking on the pew.
"I know Grigori. I know."

My Boy Bern

Bern
10:42am
Exam Day

Eighteen minutes were left on my exam, but I was already finished and was only watching the clock to see how much time I had left before I was able to leave. This wasn't too bad although I had the feeling that somehow, I felt wrong. Not the typical kind where I was panicking about the wrong answers or the school invigilators watching over my shoulder but the kind where I felt empty. This was different yet familiar at the same time, every ticking second felt like a scream, and the silent room felt like a void. I compulsively checked to see if my writing was neat enough or if my answers made any sense.

'Time surrenders itself… Wars are fought and lost with the victor proving to be the fool.'

"Good enough," I whisper to myself.

10:55am

I find my hands shaking, something feels wrong. I almost don't want to leave the exam hall, but I know I must. Looking around I see rows and columns of students in their desks. Some are panicking, calm, and negligent.

"Get yourself together," I said to myself, thinking I was one of the students panicking.
"Three minutes! Use your time well!"

Shit! I don't want to leave. I can't! Some of these students look apprehensive at the thought of leaving as well. This may only be a practice exam, but I feel intense, terrified even.

11:00am

7

"Time! Everyone, please stop writing and we will have our kind invigilators collect your papers." Cried the Head.

Kind is one way to put it, I know some of these pensioners will try to look up a girl's skirt if they have the chance. Probably chalk it up to see if they have answers written on their legs. Sitting there, I waited impatiently for the invigilators to collect the papers whilst moving at a grand speed of negative Mach four and I swear this old guy with a comb-over gave me the dirtiest look ever when he collected my paper. Unfortunately, I had to wait a while longer before the Head could say those magic words, "Thank you all for participating. You may leave in an organised fashion". He didn't of course; he made some long-winded speech about how he was proud of us, and how generic praise was making his generic life filled with generic joy. How... well generic.

God only knows how many times he said those words to previous years.

"Row seven. Please leave in an organised fashion."

"Thank god!" I thought to myself.

I leaped out of my chair like it was on fire and blazed a fiery yet orderly trail behind me, speeding my way toward the exit of the exam hall. As I was closing in on the exit, I assumed the typical guilty position. You know: Head down, hands in pockets, shoulders slumped, be invisible. I was quickly trying to get away from my crime scene until I got stopped by my first copper.

"How did you find the practice exam Bernard?" said the copper.

Oh yeah... that's my name as well. Bernard "Bern" Owen. I am Seventeen years of age, nearly Eighteen. Struggling student. Working extremely hard for my family. Half German. Half British. Short blonde hair, blue eyes, and skinny as a pole. But still unfortunate enough to attract attention even through my efforts to escape.

"Fine Mr Manto", I told the copper. "Just want to get out of here".

"Understandable, I think after being here you want to get home as soon as you can."

"Yeah… I guess." I whispered.

"I'm sorry, could you say that again?"

"It's fine sir, I'll be on my way". I blustered out clearly.

Soon my trail blazing turned into an inferno, and I ran. I got looks of course, but I think the other students just thought I was weird or just trying to get the hell out of there. Both of which, I wasn't going to hear the end of. I ran through the doorway, into the atrium, and then finally into the boys' toilets. I slammed my weight through the door, sprinted into the cubicle, and locked it, pretending it was my fortress. Then I collapsed, holding back the tears to quench my trail. My heart was ready to burst out of my chest and my hands couldn't stop shaking.

"It's not gone… Why do I feel this way?"

Old Man in Memoriam

Sidorovich
13:51

The prayer hall was unusually empty. The fog had taken the reflective sunlight from the opulent stained windows, taking the shine from Jesus's halo. Little light was offered to the little old church as if we were swallowed from the world. I paced these old halls that were far before my time as part of my tradition. Column after column, I step slowly towards the altar dragging along my decorated black robes, signifying my respect to the lord of the temple. Pew after pew of dark stained and chipped mahogany sitting atop a dusty cobbled floor, compulsively checking to find any imperfection that would render me a poor guest.

Until I found his message left on the front pew.

Adorned in black chipped leather with withering gold edges and an Orthodox cross cresting it. With it was its partner, a prayer rope hanging from its spine. I approached this treasure and grasped it as if it was porcelain.

I don't know why I kept this thing for so long, especially with the memories it leaves but it offers me some comfort of a past I do not wish to forget. I open this old bible and find an old photo buried between the pages, sitting atop a liturgy. I hold these memories in my black bandaged hands and remember the smell of the sand. The laughter. The music. The heat... And the screams. I went into that hell with nine brothers. Nine of the finest were immortalised in a black and white photo that was hidden in a bible like a dirty secret with the whisper of a cursed voice crossing my mind.

"Get up!" The voice demanded, "I can't fight them off without you!"

"Fedor? Is that you?" says the comforting voice.

"That depends Samara, can you still see from your height?" I joke.

Angelo Samara is my fellow priest in this church. Hailing from Greece, specifically, he comes from Heraklion. A little five-five fat man with the demeanour of an age-long friend. He comes in our order's black robes but without the bandages of my attire. He looks good for his age especially with alcohol being in his blood most of the day. He only started to finally lose the brown colour in his balding head.

"I don't need to see you to know you're here, your Russian ass never leaves this church." Get out there, get laid, I know I'm still doing it when you were at my age." He jokes as he walks towards my pew.
"But I am not your age anymore. I'm sixty-one. What kind of babushka will I be getting?" I say in confusion.
"I don't know… hard to say. Maybe it's the Turkish tobacco. Even then, Maggie might fall in love just looking at those bright sparkling eyes." He mocks.

I roll my 'bright sparkling' eyes in amusement with a smirk cracking my cold exterior. "Samara you idiot" I chuckle.
"I'll save that fun for you and your wife and your drinks cabinet." I joke back.

He slams his body onto my pew, sitting next to me. I can smell the alcohol on his breath.

"Now tell me, what are you doing here you miserable shit? It's your day off!" He asked in his own strange way.
"I'm just here…"
"You're looking at that photo again, aren't you?" he says with pain in his voice, and his eyes open wider than a crater, as if it was an insult passed by.
Caught in the act, I nod my head in shame. Samara gives me the look of a disappointed parent about to scold his child for a little infraction until it is challenged by his compassion. He renders his verdict with his kind words.

11

"You need to let go, revelling in the past with ghosts won't make it any easier." He sighs.

I feel torn between the two. The photos in my possession and the man who sat beside me. I want these memories, but they were painful ones. Ones that shaped me to my being and experiences that brought a man of grief and sorrow.
How could I let them go?

He places his meaty hand on my bony shoulders. "You know where to find me if you need anything but take your mind off it. Go find something in the office to do. Please, I need to prepare for the Friday sermon." he says in his comforting tone.

I sink my head. This battle was lost, and I knew my opponent was too good for me. So, I relented to his terms.

"OK…" I say in defeat.
I turn my head to look my adversary in the eye and give him my final demands before withdrawing my forces. smiling at him with the respect he deserves.
"But I'm only getting my gun to shoot you." I joke.
"Do it! You'll get me away from the wife at last." My advisory counterattacks.

We both laugh at him and his stupid joke. I get up off the pew and take my bible with me. I'm getting slower in my age and frailer. This time my hands hurt and struggled to pick up the bible, but I am used to the pain. I make my way to the left of the altar and go into an ancient wooden door as old as the church. I grab its twisted iron ring handle and open it. As I am about to leave the hall, I hear Samara.

"Fedor." He calls. I turn to respond to my surname and show my attention by facing him through the doorway. "If you do shoot me and we're both wrong, does that mean I lose my seventy-two virgins?" He jokes childishly. I roll my eyes in acknowledgment and close the door to the prayer hall.

12

The office is a mixture of military and mess. The small twenty-by-twenty office holds two wooden desks with drawers, two small bookshelves, two wooden chairs, and two crosses. One on each side. Like a mirror of itself with each showing a different life. His side had the prizes spirit cabinet. It was tall, old, possibly more than a hundred years old. It contains an assortment of alcohol some older than the cabinet itself, locked behind its dark mahogany and a diamond pattern glass window. I hunkered down in my side, my shelter, sat my weary bones on the chair, and lit up my pipe with my Turkish tobacco. I breathe in the earthy aroma, lean back, and breathe out.

Disabled

Bern

2:47pm
Exam Day

I sat on the cold floor, waiting for the dark, and suffering the slow loss of reality from my grasp. I didn't know how long I was on that floor. An hour, maybe two… Nobody came looking and nobody asked why there was one cubicle that was locked for however long. It seemed like an eternity and yet time felt incomplete or abstract. The longer I sat on that tiled floor, the longer the smell of urinal cakes and teenage boys from all backgrounds sank into my clothes.

Eventually, I got a call. My ringtone echoed in the bathroom, cracking free of the silence. It was my dad and for some reason, I felt hesitant.

"Hello?" I said meekly.

"There you are, how did you do in the exams?" He asked with enthusiasm.

My dad was a working-class man, He worked as a bailiff and was an officer of the courts and this man knew his shit. He had an unusually rough cockney accent even though he was brought up middle class.

"I don't know." After I said that my confidence was spiralling further down.

"What do you mean?" He asked.

There was a long pause before I answered, trying to figure out what was the most pleasing answer to disarm the situation.

"I feel like I did OK." I said with unnatural fear.

"Well… If you feel like you did OK then that's all anyone can ask, isn't it?" He nonchalantly dismissed.

"I guess."

"Look, how about you come home, and we'll talk about it properly, alright?"

"Yeah… alright."

He gave me some affirming words and then we said our goodbyes. Then I had to leave the cold floor. I dust off my school uniform and brace myself to open the cubicle door and then the bell rings.

3:00pm

"Shit!" I groan to myself.
Realising that time had slipped away again, I slinked through the cubicle door, hoping not to be seen by anyone too familiar. Crowds of schoolchildren were flooding out of the exits and through the atrium, desperate to get home. Eager to get home after a hard day's work or a hard day's torment.

I planned to blend in with the crowd all wearing white dress shirts, navy blazers, and black trousers. Head towards the gate. Then hike towards where my commander would be waiting for me. The briefing played over and over in my head as if I were a naval officer prepping my team for exfiltration.
"Ok fella, you can do this," I whispered to myself.
I braced, locked my shoulder to breach the door to the battlefield, then...
"There you are! I've been looking all over for you!"

My plan's been compromised, I need to reassess. My ally has me at a disadvantage. I must not show signs of vulnerability.

"Hey, Ava." I said meekly.
"How come you're red? I didn't make you jump, did I?" she said snarkily.
"No, no you didn't"
"Well, if I did then it's good that you were just in the toilets. Saves you shitting yourself again." she jokes. Her enthusiastic grin is up for show. I cracked a smile and felt less embarrassed.

Ava is lovely, she's the same school year as me, with dark brunette hair, 5'6, slim; so slim she was almost a walking skeleton, with the complexion of a ghoul, and came from a family of coal miners. She wore the typical black trousers and

15

navy-blue uniform, and you could tell she was rough around the edges but that could be because of her upbringing. Still, she was my girlfriend, and I loved her.

"Do you want to tell me what you were doing there then?" She cracked.

I looked down at the tiled floor as if my forehead was attracted to the floor. I must have been radiating ennui since my slump was broken by a light tug on my school blazer.

"Do you want to go home, or do you want to stay around mine for the night?"

"No, I promised I'd get home. I need to look after my brother". I lied of course. I didn't need to this time.

Her eye roll was practically audible. "You always need to look after him. Let your dad handle it for once."

I looked at her as if I was trying to wrestle my forehead from the pull it had to the floor.

"Fine, I can see you don't want to talk about it if you're giving me the eyes. At least let me walk you to your house."

"That's fine, thank you." I said with as much gratitude as I could.

What a fuckin' life yeah?

Michael
Half four-ish

"Here I am sat with me lad on the sofa, waiting for the other one to come round from school and I'm being flooded with fuckin' work! Look, David, it's not the life I want, but it's the life I got."

So, I'm having a right go at this lad from the black country over the phone cuz he's not pulling his weight.
"I'm sorry mate but I can't help ya. For some reason, people aren't paying their bills, and I got my *own* pile of work to do."
Oh, he's getting right cheeky with me now.
"Listen 'ere don't you *fuckin'* tell me…"

Right as I'm about to lay into this lad, Bern walks in the door. I take a massive breath and do me best to calm down. "We'll talk about it at the office tomorrow". Then I just hang up the phone and take a swig of me beer.
"I'm sorry if you saw me like that lad." I sighed "Work just gets the better of me, unfortunately."
I saw my skinny lad with his blonde crew cut just give me a massive sigh, then he said those words that honestly, just gave me so much purpose.

"It's ok, I know you're trying your best Dad."

That boy has done a wonder to my life.

"Listen, mate, I've gotta head back into the office. I'm dead sorry about this but I gotta get more work done."

There's just too much happening around in my life. Call this my confession if you would but I was doing fuckin' everything I could for my two boys. Bernard is a good lad, but he barely got himself into sixth form. He's a good lad. I *know* he's a good lad! But I always got the feeling that something was going on in this

17

boy's head and I couldn't put my finger on it. But right now, he was nearly out the door and into the bigger world, and as fucked as it sounds, my priority was the little 'un. Josh was ten. I love both boys but one's nearly a man.

"Again?" he winged.
"I gotta go otherwise I'll not be able to keep the house".
"But couldn't you...?"
"No!" I hate to admit it but I'm getting a little frustrated. I take a deep breath, close my eyes, then try again.
"Just... I can't, I'm sorry mate but I gotta go."

I don't know what it is, but the fuckin' stress is getting the better of me. I felt like I'm just going in fuckin' circles but I don't know what else to do to support these two.

I grabbed me stab proof, black fleece with the HM courts and tribunals logo, and got gone through the door, into the boiling heat, and into my black Skoda work car. After that... I need a word with David.

Bern

After whatever he said, my Dad just left. You know the type:

- 6'2
- Mid forties
- Julius Caesar haircut
- Caucasian
- British
- Twenty years of takeaway showing on their body

We lived in an old Victorian house. Although the house wasn't as well maintained as it should have been. It had been modernised recently although the project was half finished, leaving it a mess of ancient architecture and late 2000's interior design. I pushed my worn-down school shoes off my exhausted feet and left them in the crimson and emerald-tiled hallway, although the names were the prettiest things about it.

18

I wanted to be alone, I had enough of it all at this point. My little brother was left alone in his room, playing on his Xbox. He was on the latest game he found in fashion and most likely was screaming at it like a banshee and swearing like a sailor. I dragged myself up the wooden stairs and into my room. This was my haven, or as safe as it could be without fear of being invaded by my family. My room was next to my brothers which left little for noise reduction. Even from downstairs I could hear everything he was saying and was being allowed to get away with it. Although, it was likely from my dad's constant working state. I pushed open the white battered door that led to my haven. The door was damaged from years of neglect with the lock on the wall being broken, or should I say, broken off. Even a gust of wind could enter my room without much effort. I closed my door and put my bag against it as a doorstop and collapsed on my bed. Less bed, more of a bare mattress on the floor. I slammed my head into my pillow; however, I was disturbed by my window which had the blaring sunshine's blinding light on me. This was due to my shutters being not only wooden but missing chunks from years of abuse which gave me little privacy from the world as well.

"Bernard!" My brother's voice yelled. "Could you get me a drink?"

Here we go again.

Michael
Half five-ish

Even trying to get here as fast as I could, traffic was a nightmare. Travelling is always a nightmare especially with the office being in another town. I grab any paperwork I need from the car glove box and storm inside the building. The summer was getting on me nerves as well. A black uniform in the summer is a death sentence, especially if I gotta chase after some debt owner. They'll smell me miles away. I throw open the glass double doors, run through the pristine white interior of Her Majesty's

19

courts, make my way up the office door and just start going at it until someone opens it.

"David open the door!" I'm yelling to him so he can let me in or someone else can.
"Open. The. Door!"
"Fuckin' a'ight mate" David yells back at me. "I'll let you in."

I stand back to let the door open. As soon as I heard the door unlock, I threw it open and shut it just the same.
I confronted a man similar to me but more physically fit. He was like me but a worse and younger version.
Then I saw David, looking shocked at me. Why would he? He's like me but taller and younger than me.
"Mike, mate, what the hell are you doing here?"
"Extra shifts David? Fuckin' extra shifts! I'm doing, God knows how many, hours a week with two boys on me hands and you want more from me? I fuckin' can't do it, David!" My hands are going out of control. I can't control myself. I've been in this insanity for months now. I'm burnt out. I've had it. He backed away from me slowly which was good. He was taking me seriously.
"OK Mike, let's calm down."
"Don't you *fuckin'* tell me to calm down!" I'm pointing my finger at him, ready to turn it into a fist and lay into him with it.
"OK, OK."
"What do you want then? I can tell Mark afterward." He was backing up towards his desk.
"I just…" The anger just disappears, and I feel a flood of tears about to come out of me eyes.
"I can't do it no more mate." I grab a chair and put it on one side of his desk. David sat down with me on his side.
"Talk to me, mate." He said. He was finally fully invested in me.
"Fuckin' today I had to deal with someone hanging from the ceiling cuz they couldn't pay their debts. I had to call it in. I had to deal with it all. ME!" The entire time I was pointing towards myself like I was some gorilla trying to be all hard.

20

"I heard about that. Mate I'm—"
"You're fuckin' not so don't bother." We were both silent for a while before he broke it.
"Do you need some time off? It sounds like you've been through it."
"I'm fine, I just need to provide for me boys."
"But are you—"
"I said I'm fine!" I shouted loud enough to wake up the whole building, thankfully everyone went home. I took a deep breath and just gave him an answer.
"I just need tomorrow off, then I'll be sorted".
"Right Mike, I just—" before he could finish, I left the office. I said my peace and I didn't care for much of anything anymore. I was just ready to explain everything to my boss Mark in the morning.

Sidorovich
19:32

The night was humid in this place. I sat on the pews with my thoughts and my memories. I lit the candles with matches, keeping the atmosphere sombre. I perform my tasks to the best of my ability:

- Wax the wood.
- Polish the metal.
- Cleanse the stone.
- Say my prayers.

I walked towards the office and saw the mess that it was. I grabbed my old black bible and opened it to where I kept my secrets. Two photos. Two isolated photos. One of my old squad mates from the war. One of my wife and my son together, before he went to war.

My son was dead, but his memory lives on inside me. I felt his ghost haunt me as I went on in the world, his soul calling me towards whatever afterlife he was in.

21

My pipe was my ward against his call, my preservative to his decay. Soon I couldn't stand the self-inflicted haunting anymore, I made myself a smoke and speed walked towards the front door of the church. I felt anger now. The rage of battle, the screams of men hounding at my ears begging to be released. So, I released it.

I threw a fist into the wood of the door. I felt the shock hit my bandages and the crippled hand they held. I was hunched over against my opponent, with my spent fury leaving me vulnerable to attack. It wasn't long until I smelt the sand, felt the heat, and saw the bodies.

I felt young, younger than I had ever before. I walked into that hell with nine men. Nine of the finest men I had ever known. We were returning from our trial by fire via truck ordered in by another squad and sat in fear, riddled not by bullets but by shock. It was the first taste of combat any of us had seen. We fought and killed but not all of us came back from it unscathed.

I was the radio man carrying the heaviest gear in case we needed to call for help. I was still skinny, but I wasn't scarred by the curse of my bandages or my religion. Instead, they were cursed by shaking that would not end.

Kars was the man who walked in there with me. I knew him before the war, we were so young and so full of hope. His name was not Kars, but it was what we called him, after the city he was born in. He suffered the most due to coming from Turkey and having a similar skin colour to the men we were sent to kill. Other Red Army soldiers would make jokes at his expense, but he got used to it as everyone knew his worth in speaking the local language.

Vasya was the jokester, he was a small man, coming from a poor family near the border of Russia to Ukraine. He was our medic and he never stopped smiling when we started the war, until that day. That day was when his humour turned grim, that day his kind nature turned into something darker.

Dima was always skittish. His paranoia had helped us survive the skirmish. He has a supernatural gift; he knows when things will go wrong every time. Without it, we would have not come out of there at all. He was clutching the side of his head where a shard of shrapnel had grazed his round face.

Lev was our heavy weapons man. He was deceptively strong carrying the RPK on his scrawny back. In another life, he would have been a model in a fashion magazine with how well his features were presented. After the battle, the colour in his face had drained leaving his sapphire blue eyes to stand out from the rest of his pale appearance. He was still in shock and why wouldn't he be? He just watched his brother die.

Alyosha was the second youngest and the charmer of the group. He was a man who could talk for hours but would say nothing to you. He was handsome, sporting tattoos on his arms but never settled down. Always drifting from one woman or one gang to the next. Never to find comfort being in one place or another. He was driving our transport after the original driver was killed and kept us rolling along the sand and dirt roads behind another truck.

Arseny was a boy. He had just turned eighteen. He ran from his parents as soon as he turned. He looked like a boy and only just started developing facial hair. The dirt on his face made him look like a child caught playing in the mud but we were no children, and he was slowly starting to understand that when his blonde hair started turning grey.

Mikhail came from singing in clubs at Vladivostok and was a local favourite until a rival pushed him out of his business, making him join the army as a last resort. He believed it was fate and god's will that he joined, but in reality, he used fate as a way to excuse misery. As the battle raged on with the screams of men and the command of warriors, it took away the grace of his voice and turned it hoarse like an old general's, making his blocky face heavy with sadness.

Ilya was Lev's brother and was the first to go, his body lying flat on the floor of the truck. He never got his dream of owning a boat in the black sea, it had disappeared with the left side of his face.

Slava was the squad leader. He was everything the Red Army wanted in a soldier. Big, tough, the definition of brawn, and prideful of the nation to the last. He sat there, silent, and sombre, never looking up from his feet where the blood and dirt were pooling around his boots.

The noise of the truck and the bumps in the road felt numb to us. Nothing would take us away from the horror we witnessed until someone made it worse.

"I failed him." eked out Slava.
"Shut up" demanded Lev.
"I didn't know those Bastards had set a—"
"Shut the fuck up, Slava!"
"Both of you shut up!" Alyosha Intervened through the driver's window. "What good is talking about it?"
"This piece of shit got Ilya killed!" Lev shouted, pointing his index finger like a weapon against him.
"He was dead when that shrapnel hit his head!" Vasya screamed back.
"He was dead Lev!" Mikhail uttered, barely being heard after his voice had turned into a guttural rumble. "I was next to him; you can't stop fate!"
"No, but I can get rid of the person who led us there." Lev focused his eyes full of hate towards Slava. He stood up from his seat and pointed his sidearm at the squad leader's head.

The truck was in uproar, everyone alive was trying to calm Lev down. All except Slava. He just sat there with his head down and his hand on his rifle. He grabbed the barrel of Lev's pistol and held it against his head, not raising his head at all.

"Do it." Slava said. "I'll be sure to tell your brother in hell who murdered me."

Slava's head finally rises only to show singular hatred in his eyes towards Lev.

"They didn't know we were coming!" cried out Kars.
"Stay out of this!" Demanded Lev. Slava not breaking gaze in the slightest.
"Did you forget? I speak Pashto! They were just as surprised as we were."
Kars stood up and stood against Lev face to face pointing at Slava.
"Kill him and you'll be helping the enemy win!"
The gun was still trained at Slava. The truck was silent apart from the sound of the tires moving across the dirt roads. Lev took a deep breath and finally let his words out.
"So how did you manage to get so close to hear them and not get shot…?"
Kars was stunned and now the attention was on him. He gave a brief scoff and said, "I just did." Lev's anger was uncontrollable now as soon as he heard that.
"So maybe I should kill you instead you Mouja fuck!" Lev wrestled his pistol from Slava's grip and pointed it at Kars.

Whilst distracted I hit him in the back of the head. He was not out cold, but he was stunned long enough for Slava to deliver the finishing strike. Lev was lying down next to his brother, face down in the blood and dirt. Vasya took the gun Lev dropped and safeguarded it.

"Well, that was entertaining." Joked Vasya. He gave a nervous chuckle, but our nerves were too fried by the heat of the moment to give him anything but hostility.
"Shut up," I growled at him. I dragged Lev away from Ilya's remains and struggled to prop him up against the seat of the truck with all his gear.
As I finished my task, I felt a hand on my shoulder and I heard Kars' voice: "Fedor, are you ok?"
I turned around and was not greeted by a ghost but something more real.

I turned around and the sand and blood were gone and replaced by the church I was preaching in.

I turned around and saw a friend who was concerned for me.

"Fedor…" Samara said. "Let's get you home."

Unlikeliest of people

Ava
Twelve in the afternoon

"Bern, what are we doing here?" I asked.
"We're watching an action film in my house." smartass replied.
"I know, but I need more from life." I got out of his arms and got off his sofa in the living room. "I can't keep looking after you! I want to live my life like a queen. Like Queen Victoria!"

He's good and he tries especially when he's got school and work almost every day, but I need something from him.

"I'm working as best I can. I can't help it, Ava." He whinged. Excuses, excuses Bern.

"I know but I need you to be here. You've been so vacant ever since the exams!" I'm starting to raise my voice at him. "You work with fast food and are doing education! I need you to get it together." I leaned forward and put my hand on his cheek. "I need my prince with me here."

"Ok." Bern said. He was as vacant as I saw him in the bathrooms. But something was wrong.

Switch

The pathetic mass on the sofa was embarrassing to look at. How dare he not give me the attention I deserve?
"I want to feel like I'm being loved here. I want to go on ballroom dances and such." I casually demanded.

"You know I'm working hard and doing my best for my education, but I need everyone to work with me." He was still lying down on the horrible sofa. Just completely not moving and watching the film.

"Lisa told me something was wrong with you!"

"When I meet Lisa then I can talk with her and tell her how sorry I am." He finally got up from the sofa and was leading me out of his house. "But until then, I need to meet her, and I need you to leave me be."

Bern was in just a rugged t-shirt and jeans, but he was quickly getting his shoes on. He looked like he was about to go out.

"Where are you going? Are you not going to stay and talk with me?" I hissed.

"I'm just tired and I want to be left alone." He whined.

Switch

I got my stuff together but to say I was annoyed was an understatement.

"How come you're kicking me out?!" I was completely pissed off at him. Screaming, shouting, everything. I just wanted more from him.

"I want to be left alone." He murmured.

"Lisa was right about you!"

Bern led me outside and got me out into the street.

"After six months together, this is how you're going to treat me?" I screamed.

"I've never met her. Let me talk to Lisa in person then I will tell her I'm sorry until then, please leave me alone."

"Fine!" I spat. "I'm going to the town centre lot!"

"Why?" He argued.

Switch

Because they're fun. I like them, and they're more entertaining than this. A hot girl needs her fan base.

"Because I want to feel wanted." I lovingly explained with a smile on my face.
I pressed my hand against his cheek and gave a few taps to it. They got a little harder per hit, but it was ok. I heard no complaints. I turned around shuffling for a cigarette to smoke but then he was gone.

He just left me. He just left me on the street. No word of warning, no nothing. He went back into hiding just like the bathroom, except he vanished from existence.

Switch

Bern
1:52pm
15 days post exam

The last two weeks were a blur. I didn't know who I was or what I was doing. All I could do was work, clean, and take care of my brother. I didn't have any friends and I could barely make time for Ava. I loved her and I should be happy but as I held her in my arms, I felt repulsed. I felt ill. I don't know why I left her like that, but I did. I felt my stomach churn and the world closed in on me. I just needed to escape. I took a bus to nowhere with what little money I had from working at my pointless job and let myself drift off to an unknown destination. After passing by in the heat, the sun-scorched tarmac, and the amber wheat fields that surround my town, I felt that this stop was the correct one. A forty-five-minute journey, counting thirty-two stops to avoid the boredom and I was here. This place was nothing significant, a suburban area with houses, roads, and signs, all of this was… grey to me even though I was not colour blind. I walked up the road which led me to a fork. To the left was towards what small little village marketplace there was and to the right was the road towards the wheat fields. I don't know if I wanted more nature or if I wanted to feel the texture of reeds on my skin, but instinct told me to turn right. Freedom told me to go right. I walked, closer and closer as if I was walking towards the land of the sun where the colour was saturated yellow. And then…

29

I. Had. Seen. It.

One little church, looking so cold in an area so warm. The church was more the size of a chapel than a full-fledged church. It sat on the edge of the joy with golden yellow fields at its rear. Almost crawling towards the little graveyard which didn't get any bigger. Opposite was a row of houses, not very interesting to me. Irrelevant. Although it looked as if their clay-coloured bricks judged the drab grey that was the church's mortar. Grey was the colour of the outside with the stained-glass windows somehow looking like the life from their visage was fading. The bell tower, its only port of call, was cast and sealed inside from its cage. This was a corpse in a ground of joy. And I welcomed it.
I slowly approached this monument, but I wanted more from this place. Some life I could sap for myself. I quickened my pace as I crossed the road, the wind blowing only humidity towards me until at last it was the final push towards the black wooden door and had as much energy as the rest of the building. I was ready to open the door until I heard shouting, some in English and some in different languages that I couldn't understand. The shouting is muffled behind the wood. I try to listen, but I can only hear what sounds like an argument with pitches being raised and some of it being more muffled than the rest. I could smell something aromatic as well, sweet, earthy, almost coffee-like. This couldn't be the field. I looked around to see if I could find myself a vantage point to investigate the building. I run left, of the door, into the courtyard and pave my way towards what lost friends this graveyard held. I follow the rear of the building. Nothing. I circle towards the other side of the church to find myself towards the front of it again. I stopped to catch my breath, wiping sweat off my forehead and that's when I realised, "Bern you idiot! There were holes in the wood." I whispered. Or at least I thought I whispered. One voice quieted down and the other was still going.
"Damn, did they hear me?" I thought to myself.
I crouched down to try and seize the moment. I bent down to try and get my eye into one of the small holes without risking a splinter to the cornea and the smell of tobacco finally appearing

30

itself. This wasn't any tobacco I had smelt before either, this was something fouler yet more aromatic. As I looked inside the hole, I saw the silhouettes of two men in black robes about what I thought was the same height. One was acting frantic, waving his arms in the air, and moving his volume up and down as if he was a music box of angry ravings with no control whilst the other had smoke coming from what looked like his head. I could barely see anything. The cobbled path, inside the church, rows of pews, a regular church. I hovered my ear closer to the hole after I thought I saw it all and I could just make out some of the things being said and I will never forget it to this day.

"I dare you! I *DARE* you to lock my spirit cabinet again! That's like if I hid that horrible shit you smoke."

After hearing this, I snorted and wheezed whilst I was trying not to break out in laughter. Then the fun stopped when I heard a thick Russian accent say.

"If you listen, you will realise we have guests."

I instantly stood up, trying to look innocent but whilst getting up I caught a splinter to the ear and winced in pain.

"Ah, fuck!" I winced.

Holding my ear like a baby.

Still nursing my wound, I didn't realise what had happened until the smell suddenly revived me.

"'Ey child, what are you doing out there?"

"I umm…"

I was caught between pain, embarrassment, and confusion. I didn't realise what was happening even though I felt my face going bright red.

"Nice poker face", the man said.

He was small, about 5'5, fat, short brown hair with it starting to just grey and bald. He had an accent I hadn't heard before and good god did he stink of alcohol.

"Good god! You stink!"

"A hello to you too," he spoke to me sarcastically. "Now do you want to come and have a chat with us or are you just going to be rude?"

He crossed his arms and leaned to the side of the door arch with one of his greying eyebrows raised in obvious annoyance.
I was still feeling the splinter in my ear, but I wanted to get out of this with as much face as I could. I turned whilst holding one hand on my ear and tried to look him directly in the eyes. For one so small and pissed off his eyes sparkled like oceans from a tropical beach.
"I'm sorry, I'm just out exploring… I umm… don't want to interrupt your guys' conversation."

"Then you can speak to me."
Before I knew it, the Russian had walked up to the door. His voice sounded guttural. He was tall, about 6'2, very skinny, and had a face so angular you could almost see the outline of his entire skull if some of it wasn't hidden by wrinkles. short thin grey hair, completely clean-shaven. He held an old, dark, and crooked wooden pipe in his hand which encapsulated the horrible-smelling tobacco. The fat man without breaking gaze returned upright and uncrossed his arms finally revealing a more open form of body language.

Both were wearing black robes.
Both were looking very upset with me.
Only one of them had bandages on their hands.
I was worried.

"I umm… I don't want to go in there." I said practically quivering.
"Because?" I could feel his cold stare whilst uttering those icy words. Even in the heat of the summer, I still felt a shiver down my spine.
"Umm… because you're priests and I'm…"
"Too old." Thankfully, before I could say anything foolish, the Russian finished it for me.

He's getting annoyed. He uttered these words in clear coherence through his thick accent to emphasise the point.
"Look. I am not the forest strip killer, and you are not my type. Get inside or I'll drag you inside." Those words were echoing

inside my head. Intimidation was his goal, and he was succeeding.

The Russian lifts his scrawny bandaged arm holding the pipe, places the stem of it into his mouth, and takes a deep puff. If he didn't radiate gelidity, I would have thought it was an insult when he blew the smoke to my face, but instead, I took it as a threat and I'm going to listen.

The one without the bandages saw the situation for what it was. A possible downward spiral. He tried to attempt to remedy it through his jokes. "Don't worry boy, we're not going to Guantanamo you." He was just as flamboyant with his hands as I saw inside. I knew he wasn't going to but in my mind at that moment, I felt like he was planning on something. I don't know if he saw the fear on my face or just saw how young and curious, I was. He rubbed the bridge of his nose in what looked like his way of processing the situation, I chalked it up to allergy season catching up to him. After he finished, he left a black smudge on his face which looked similar consistency of charcoal, and uttered, "How does my face look? Am I ready for the Milan catwalk?" He made the joke in a way to show that he understood me. He wanted to connect with me. I was still hesitant to go anywhere with them, however.

He took a deep long breath through his nose to the point where you could hear his nostrils squeak like hinges whilst closing his eyes and once again rubbing the bridge of his nose.
"I'm sorry," he said, now with compassion and warmth in his voice.
"We just don't know you and we were in a heated conversation. Please try to understand, we just want to know why you're here." He stepped out of the doorway and away from the tall one. His hands displayed some energy but at a more tempered rate to follow along with the pace of his voice. He waddled his way towards me at the speed of a snail still recognising I was intimidated by them. My focus was purely on him. His arms are partially outstretched as he walks. The little one points one hand at my ear.
"In the meantime, we can have a look at that ear."

I took my eyes off him for a moment to see what the Russian was doing, and he was just… standing there. No emotion, no fear, the most effort that came from him was when he put the pipe to his mouth and smoked. He stood there like an unfeeling overseer.

Before I realised, the fat man placed one of his hands on my shoulder. The smell from him was pungent with the red in his nose becoming all the clearer.
"Please come inside and we'll talk."
I reluctantly looked them both in the eye, and I entered this corpse of a building. I feel both the cool musty air from the church and the icy presence from the Russian envelop me.

Ava
Half five in the evening

"I don't know what's gotten into him. Bern just walked off. I'm calling you because I've nowt to do about it." I'm frantic, I'm panicking. I honestly don't know what's happening. He just walked off from me for no reason. Lisa is on the phone with me to try and figure out a solution as to why this happened.
"Look, love, you gotta tell me more about what's happening with it. I can't help you out here. You gotta be honest with yourself and you gotta be honest with me."
How can she say that? She might sound like she's coming from a place of compassion but how am I not being honest with her?
"What the hell do you mean?! I'm being honest with you! He fucked off and just left me there. No goodbye. No word of warning. Not even a fucking text!
He. Just. Left."
How could he just leave me? ME! On the street by myself. I'm his girlfriend and he couldn't just say something like: "Oh sorry love, I gotta head off quickly" or something like that.
"Maybe he just needed to withdraw, Ava. Maybe he just needed time."
"Time?! What time!? I find him on the floor with his problems in the fucking bathroom and he expects me to give more? How can

I? I'm giving it all I've got in this relationship and not to mention exams are happening".

I'm stuck in the garage of my house, screaming into my phone and this girl wants to give me advice on my own life? The gall on her!

"Ok, I'm sorry. That came out wrong. How about we try again?" She calmed down her voice to try and play counsellor again. I know what'll come out of her mouth now.

So, what do-

"-You want in this relationship?"

Switch

I knew it.

"Just stop right? Just stop. Leave me be."

I hung up the phone and threw it in this shit tip of a garage. It hit a toolbox which led to it being knocked over from the worktop spewing tools everywhere.

"FUCK!" I screamed that to the top of my lungs which was loud enough to have the world hear.

I just slumped against the garage wall and slid down it till I felt my backside hit the cold concrete floor.

I couldn't control myself. I honestly just looked like I was in the foetal position but up against the wall. I just buried my face into my knees till I started crying uncontrollably.

Well, I guess the world heard me since I heard a knock on my door.

"Ava. You alright in there?" Said my dad, of course, it was my dad.

"I'm fine. Just leave me be!" I said whilst trying to control my tears.

"Are you sure love? I heard a commotion." He said, banging against the door as a sign of existence.

His only sign that was loud enough was to break through my tears and my pain.

He lets off one big sigh and says the words I didn't want to hear, "Ok, I'm coming in."

"No!" I screeched. "Don't come in!"
Of course, he ignores me. He always ignores me. He walks
through the door. His balding grey head sticking out through the
door. I buried my face in my knees but with odd glances up. He
was wearing his old mechanic clothes which are permanently
soaked in oil and dirt. These aren't what you'd expect, this is a
white shirt with the Harley Davidson logo on it and a pair of
jeans he's kept around when he first had me. They look too big
for him, like a kid wearing his parents' clothes and you wouldn't
think that this skinny man was a coal miner when meeting him.

When I was catching sneak glimpses, I saw him look around the
garage and I think he was more surprised by the tools
everywhere and how none of them hit his precious motorbikes. I
am almost sure, I'll get a bollocking from him.
"What happened here, Ava?"
"Nothing, Alright?! Shit just happened!" I wrapped myself
tighter, screaming at him through my knees.
"Come on love, that's not nothing. All my tools are everywhere.
What's *really* happened?"
I was still sniffling, trying to hold back the tears as best as I
could. I tried to explain but it felt like my voice was giving up on
me. I felt helpless.
"I was on the phone with Lisa, and I got upset by her and Bern.
He just left me in the middle of the street. How could he?"
I went back to sobbing after that. Before I realised what had
happened, my dad slumped up against the wall, stood upright
and put his hand on my shoulder. Like that was any comfort.
"We'll sort this out, love. We will."

Bern
N/A
15 days post exam

The two-robed men led me inside their church. The description
from the peephole was far more different than the inside. As I
entered, there were pews of dark wood, pristinely polished and

varnished. They were organised in two columns to allow an aisle down the centre.

The floors had been spotless to the point where I felt stepping on the cobbled floors was sacrilege. To the right of the entrance, there was a font that had an elephant carving on the rim with different murals etching into the virtuous white bowl.

"Come on boy, don't be shy." said the little man.

I was so awestruck that I had forgotten that they were there and had to be reminded by a gentle push on my shoulder. We moved towards the front of the pews. Near the preaching stand, there were multiple wreaths and bouquets of opulent and colourful flowers that would make even the best gardener envious. I stepped my way past the first few rows and then I noticed the stained glass. The sun was shining its perfect visage onto the floor to reflect the picture of Jesus in gold and purple. The size was proportionate to how it looked outside. This was still a small church.

"Come on, nearly there." Said the Russian. His pipe smoke clouded the air, giving it a foul aroma but somehow adding to the beauty of the church with the gold from the glass window sparking and making ordinary tobacco smoke look like living fire.

Closer to the front rows, I see a marble statue of Mary holding Jesus, perfectly pristine like the rest. In front of it was the altar being, covered in a double layer of luxurious fabrics. One cloth scarlet, one white, and not all, they acted as servants towards the centre piece. A gold and jewelled cross. It had blue and fiery red stones appointed at each point. The strangest thing was, I had never seen a cross like this before. This cross looked like a typical one but with two more horizontal beams, both smaller than the main horizontal beam, one above it and one below but crooked.

Behind the altar is a pair of doors hinged shut and clasped onto what looked like a fold-up wall. This was the only evidence that this church was potentially used for something else. What it was, did not matter. The wall was painted to such extravagance. Various images of Jesus and Mary with gold lettering of a different language sprawled from edge to edge. Behind it must have been such reverence.

"OK. Sit!" ordered the Russian. I was positioned in front of a pew, hesitating to sit down. I didn't fully take him seriously; I was still stunned by the beauty of the church.
But the most mystery was in how there was a perfectly maintained door to the left of the altar. Deep brown oak, and a black Victorian metal design on the door. I knew the design as I loved learning about past creations and artefacts from obelisks to simple door handles. Seeing this made me wonder; what was in there?

The Russian put his hand on my shoulder and proceeded to gently push me down onto the right-hand pew row. This snapped me back into reality, finally re-engaging my fear of him.
"Now you're going to tell us what you're doing here." The warmth of this church was defeated by his presence and authority. He stood across from me, the eyes on his gaudy face narrowed in what looked like spite which made my posture slump in anxiety.
The short one tried to calm the situation down with what looked like his token humour and gestures.
"Don't worry about grumpy over there, someone pissed in his cereal." He joked. "We just want to introduce ourselves."
He took a seat next to me on the pew, it creaked from his weight.
"My name is Father Angelo Samara and the big teddy bear over there is Father—"
"Batushka" The Russian quickly interrupted before he went back to smoking his pipe.
The father next to me rolled his eyes in what looked like frustration with his head following.
"Of course. Batushka Fedor Sidorovich."
I assumed it was a rank or something along those lines, so I made the mistake of asking.
"Sorry, I've no right to be asking questions but what does Batushka mean?" I tried to be apologetic, but with the Russian

taking a sudden stop from smoking I didn't know if it was to
answer to club me with the pipe.
He blew the smoke to the right side of him, and he answered
solemnly.
"It's Russian for father. My turn." He took another smoke from
his pipe to prepare himself.
He made a low grumble which made his sound even more
scarred.
"How did you know we were priests and not a pair of killers?" I
thought my eyes were deceiving me, but I swear to God I saw a
little smirk on his face.
"I saw the robes and… you were in a church, so I put two and
two together." I said timidly, fidgeting with my hands.
He allowed himself a small chuckle. I thought I was dreaming
when I saw this.
"You see Samara, boy has a brain unlike you."
Samara started rubbing the bridge of his nose again. "You see
boy, this is why I'm starting to go grey." He gestures at the gaunt
man enjoying his pipe with a widening smile on his face.
 "How you just started greying is beyond me." Sidorovich
remarked.
"I'm greying because you have hidden a key of mine. I
am *eagerly* waiting for its sweet return."
Sidorovich was now amused, especially after finishing his pipe.
He set it down on the altar, making sure none of the ashes from it
would spill onto the fabric.
He reached into his bandages which were tightly bound on his
arms and struggled to produce a key and struggled even more so
to make sure the bandages were at their correct place after taking
out the key.
After great effort, he finally pulled it out.
"Happy Hanukkah!" he grinned like a Cheshire cat and dangled
it in front of Samara like it was bait on a string. Samara moved
with more speed than was possible for someone with his
physique and snatched it away from him.
He powerwalked towards the door with great haste whilst
grumbling something about a cabinet.
"Keep an eye on this one. He's crafty." Samara pointed two
fingers at his eyes, gesturing that he was watching him whilst

narrowing his eyes at Sidorovich. He makes his way to the door
that piqued my curiosity, tightly gripping his prize.
"Boy, do you want a drink?"
At this point, I was just simply baffled at what was happening in
front of me. I didn't know people like this could exist.
"I don't drink, I'm not old enough."
"That's ok, I respect that." He turns and points to Sidorovich.
"Now thieving piece of shit, do you want anything?"
"More tobacco please." he replied but not before letting out a
chuckle.
"Don't end up like him boy, he'll be the death of me."
Sidorovich blew him a mocking kiss before his fellow priest left
to get whatever was behind the door.

Sidorovich
14:23

My colleague finally put in his place after a long time of over
stepped freedom and I was revelling in it, however, I had been
given an unexpected visitor from God. I did not know if this was
a blessing or a curse, but time would tell.
I would try to speak to the boy as best as I could, but I fear that
he is intimidated by me.
I put myself on the opposite pew and took my pipe with me.
"So, who are you, I must ask?"
I crossed my legs and leaned against the arm rest of the pew. The
boy was clearly nervous, he had not stopped playing with his
hands since he sat down.
"I'm… Bern." He eked out.
"Nice to meet you boy."

There were a few moments of silence. Neither of us knew how to
start. Until he showed a bit of confidence.
"So, who are you people?" he asked.
"We're priests *Bratan*!" I emphasised. Good god I am bad with
children.
"What like Christians?" He turned to me, coming out of his poor
posture.

"We are Orthodox Christians boy. Look at the altar."

"Oh… What's the difference?"

"Stick around and we'll explain. Although don't let that one start you on it." I pointed at the door. "He'll get you going with his stories in Heraklion instead."

"Hera… what?"

"He's a Greek boy. Have you never heard a Greek before?"

"Not really no."

I nearly jumped out of my chair when I heard that. How has this child been so sheltered?

"Who doesn't know what a Greek is?" As if on cue Samara bursts through the office door carrying his spirits to meet our new guests. I didn't react of course.

"*Ublodok!*"

"Fedor, I'm not an enemy from a foreign land after your women. You don't jump in front of guests," he joked whilst gesturing to the boy.

"Loud noises *debil*! You know this!"

Samara puts his back side on the same pew as the boy and pours himself a glass into one of his crystal glasses.

I look him dead in the eye, raise an eyebrow and ask, "Did you bring tobacco?"

"Oh no, I…!" He starts patting himself down looking dumbfounded. Finally, he pulls my tobacco from his sleeve as if he was a magician and holds it in the air as if it was his white rabbit.

"For the sin of theft, I'd say you're winning." He remarks with a hint of bitterness.

"Catch." He proceeds to throw it at me. "Nice catch!" The boy stated.

"Now child." Samara said before taking a sip of his glass. "Why are you here and how much of that conversation did you hear outside?" Samara leans back into the pew putting strain onto it with its groans. The boy falls back into his slump.

"Why do you ask? Am I in trouble?"

41

"No, of course you're not. It's just we're not allowed to have these". We hold up our own poisons in unison. "We would get in trouble for this, you see. Even priests need to live."

"You don't seem very priest-like." The boy observed. It was clear we were a different type of people than he was used to. "Unfortunately, old habits die hard." I added. I rubbed my bandages to confirm that, hoping no one would see.

"He speaks the truth for once." Samara added, "Sometimes people seek the thrill of life, but rules can hold those people back on their journey, but it always better to never start it."

Samara drank from his glass again. After he finished it, he poured himself another whilst I set myself ready for another smoke.

"Sometimes boy, those types of people can go one of three ways on that journey." He holds his fingers up to keep track of his message and give it emphasis. The boy came back out of his slump and fully paid attention to him.

"1) Something makes him stop in his journey. 2) He finds comfort in the journey and keeps to where he is on that road. 3) His journey ends and he leaves this world, never to find fulfilment."

He may not have realised it, but that old drunk was teaching the boy. "But be warned, child, you can find yourself on that journey more than once."

"So where did your journey take you, father?" The boy asked. He was stunned. I could see the gears slowly moving in his head. Then he turned back into his energetic self with these words.

"Oh, back in my day I was king of my town! Every day I would go drinking and whoring like the best of them."

The boy burst out in laughter and that laughter brought a warmth to my heart.

"Look boy, we have duties to fulfil, we won't force you to be here. Feel free to go when you want if we get too much for you." I said. I didn't want him to leave but I had tasks to complete, and I couldn't bring myself to have more reminders of my past come to present. Samara gave me a look of annoyance from across the room.

"Thank you Batushka. I'm happy not to be in trouble but I will have to hear more about this 'drinking and whoring.'" He exclaimed in a mood, better than the one he started with.

"You were wrong, Fedor. This boy has more brains than both of us." Samara's laughter echoed through the halls, filling them with cheering enough for ten men. It even made me smile.

"Go on!" Samara cheered. "Get out of here before the old man ruins it."

"Thank you, father. Batushka."

The boy gathers himself and goes to leave out through the door, but not before giving us a wave goodbye. I wish it was as simple as that, but he stops and stares at the door for a moment and my heart accelerates. Stroking his hands on the numerous holes and dents in the door. I can only assume he was just wondering as to why it was not only replaced, since he gave us a smile and closed the door behind him. We waved back until the doors shut, still sitting on the pews.

"Did you get the splinter?" I said to Samara. He raised the small wooden curse in his fingers. "Never even noticed it was gone." He gave me a wink and a smirk.

Failure to Stand

Bern
9:32pm
15 days post exam

My mind was going in circles about who those men were. After my tasks went on and I was made to go to work or look after my brother, I lay on my mattress on the floor trying to figure out who they were and what stories they had to tell. They were something else. My mind was wandering. I needed to go see them again, but I needed to wait until I had time off again.

I heard my phone buzz. I slipped it out of my short pockets to see who it was. Ava was on the screen, making my heart race. She was going to be pissed off at me, thinking I just ran away from her for no reason.

"Hello?"
"Where the hell were you?!" Yeah… she was pissed. "How fucking dare, you leave me in the street!?"
"I needed space away Ava, I'm sorry." I sat upright against the wall, now using the mattress as a makeshift stool.
"How much space do you need?!"

The more she spoke, the more my spine sank into the floor, as if my soul was being swallowed up by the ground.

"I just—"
"Just what Bern? I paused, a minute and gave myself a moment to think. Finally, an answer came.
"I'm sorry." I eked out. "I'm sorry I left you there… I just needed to get away."
I could hear her sniffling over the other side of the phone, it was hard not to cry myself.
"Lisa asked me what I want in the relationship, Bern".
"And what do you want?"
"I want you to be honest with me. Where have you been?"

44

I didn't know if I should tell her but if this was what she wanted. I must reply.
"I went to church." I said.
She went quiet for a moment. I think it was due to shock.
"I didn't know you were religious."
"I'm not. I just went to see a pair of priests."

I could feel the gears turning in her head, trying to process the situation. Nobody knew about these priests except for me.

"They didn't—"
"I'm too old." I joked.
She burst out laughing as if in an instant her sorrow turned to joy. But those weren't my words, those were the old Russians'.

A moment of silence passed between us. It was awkward but somehow comforting like we knew each other was somehow safe and it was enough to put a small smile on my face. Finally, Ava spoke to me.

"Please don't do this again otherwise..." She took a minute to pause. "I don't think I can survive it again". She sniffled again as if the tears were ready to come back at any moment.

"I promise."
"You better, dickhead." She made a small chuckle before saying our goodbyes.

I felt wrong. I still felt ill, but I was confused. I still feel joy but somehow, I still feel empty... A living, breathing contradiction. I hate apologising, not because I was stubborn or anything like that. It was because I felt like I had to keep everyone happy.
"Bernard, can you come down here?" My dad yelled at me. I got up out of my bed with barely enough energy to move and moved with more energy than I thought possible... this was my dad and I wanted... no... I needed to impress him. I saw him there on the black leather sofa sipping a beer with one hand and paperwork on his knee, surrounded by boxes and boxes of overdue letters, planned routes, and owed debts.

"Sit down mate."

I did as he instructed and took a seat next to him, trying not to land on his makeshift workspace. He sat back on the sofa with both hands dragging back into his scalp to try and relieve what stress it could by revealing his small collection of grey hairs. He sighed before placing one of his hands on my shoulder and hugging me.

"We're in the shit mate." he said with such sadness in his voice, gripping my body even tighter.

"What's the matter?"

"We might lose the house if we don't get it together financially." I was stunned. I couldn't believe what he was saying. All I could do was hug back. We sat there for what seemed like an eternity, time had no meaning here, only fear. He let go before continuing with his paperwork. That was the first hug I got from him in years, and it wasn't out of love for his son but from fear for his family.

"I've been asked to do more shifts at work, but the problem Bernard, is that I can't support the house by meself, so I need you to help me out more."

"What do you mean?" I asked. I thought I was doing enough.

"I wouldn't be asking if it wasn't true mate. I need you to do more hours at your job. You broke up for the summer holidays, so if you can help me out here, I'll be dead grateful towards you."

"I…" I didn't know what else to do. I was already so tired; I was sacrificing what life I had already to keep the place going with what misery was going around in our lives.

"I don't know dad…"

"I know lad. I just honestly don't know what to do anymore." The air was dead and still. This felt like a post-mortem of my life, and I saw what my future could become through my dad. Overworked and absent from life.

"I need to get back to it mate. Please."

"Do you want another beer, Dad?"

"Please, lad. Feel free to get one yourself. I feel like you earned it."

"I'm too young, Dad."

"Sorry, that's me forgetting." He chuckled nervously.

I walked into the kitchen. Somehow this room was more ruined than the rest, staying more on the side of Victorian with the walls tiled in bright orange and mint green. I grabbed a can of his favourite beer from the fridge and rushed it back to him in all haste.

He moved aside his finished can and immediately cracked open the new one.

"Cheers for that." He spoke.

"How much do you need from me, Dad?"

"I need five hundred pounds a month from you."

My gut sank. I barely made six-hundred and fifty a month and that would leave me with barely anything.

"Are you serious!?" I exclaimed, my voice cracking at the sheer shock of it.

"I wish I wasn't." He didn't even look me in the eye when he asked. He kept his head down into the paperwork.

"I need to focus, mate. Can you leave me be for a bit?"

I didn't know if he was ashamed of asking me for the money or if he was just overworked but I needed to get him that money somehow. I made my way to my room without saying a word with the air feeling foreign to me as if I was thrown into another world. My feet dragged up the stairs and my body fell into my mattress. I was still, not a move or a sound was made. I was a living corpse made hollower through these words.

"Bernard, can you make your brother some dinner?"

12:30pm
17 days post exam

"That'll be six forty-nine, please." I said to the customer.

The smell of grease clouded the air like a thick smog. The stink of food attached to my clothes was like a curse. My time there was miserable. I hated it there in that little local fast-food shop.

"Pay by card, please."

"Thank you very much. Next please."

A place full of fake smiles and grease burns. The place was an average on-street takeaway shop with its staff members all clad in black uniform with the company logo on it. It felt blurred. It felt wrong.

47

"Pay by cash, please."

"Brilliant, thank you. Next please."

I felt my presence there was alien. I had to take the job to support the family and now I was working extra shifts. Even more tired, even more greasy, and even more painful.

"Pay by card please."

"Thank you very much, please."

My sanity was slipping as the day went on and now, I had to do this five times a week to keep everything afloat. I felt like I was getting a lesson in adulthood, but this felt more like a lesson in torment. I felt like I could do so much more, but I had to see what my practice exams said and see how I could go about it from there.

"Pay by cash please."

"Cheers for that, next please."

When I had a free moment to slow down from the chaos, all I could do was think about those strange priests that I saw. What sort of lives they had and why they were here. So many questions raced around my mind.

"Hey, Bern."

"Ava… I was…"

"Head up your arse, I know." she joked. "I thought you only did three days a week!"

"I did, but I've had to do more shifts."

"How come?" She asked. She was holding up the queue for the line and I didn't want to get in trouble.

"I'll tell you after work. I'm a little busy right now."

She was pouting like a child. I think she was expecting me to tell her then and there that I was ready to give all my information to her and drop what I was doing.

"Fine!" She shouted at me. Her tone turned brattier as if was about to have a tantrum. Instead, she decided to storm out. Some customers were confused by the situation whereas some decided to leave with her, thinking I was giving poor customer service.

"What was that about?" a customer asked.

"Just personal stuff…" I took a deep sigh to gather myself before putting on the customer service facade.

"Can I take your order?"

5:04pm

My monotonous shift finished. I was covered head to toe in grease, sweat, and despair as I left the front of my work. This was a little place in the back of the town centre. It was a little run down, but what do you expect from some takeaway shop in a working-class town? I went to wipe my forehead with my arm, accidentally smearing dried ketchup onto my forehead.

"No! Come on!" I yelled in frustration. Then I heard a sharp cackle. Ava...

"Look at you ya twat." She bellowed. She hid in the alleyway which was next to my work. Lord knows how long she waited there for, but I knew that I couldn't get away now.

"God, you'd be helpless without me." She always prods at me as her form of 'love' but this time I couldn't cope with too much of her 'love'.

Ava approached me like a lynx after its prey, moving with a gentle grace that was most likely given to her from her leopard print Def Leppard shirt. She licked her thumb and rubbed the ketchup from my forehead. "Right come on, we're leaving." She demanded.

"Wait what?"

"Yeah. We're talking now. Come on!"

I was not in the mood. I could feel my clothes sticking to my skin and the sweat dripping down my face. I of course followed my orders and made my way down the alleyway with her.

"So, before you so rudely shooed me away. What did you want to say to me?" She gave me the same pout as before with more frustration.

"I was working. You know I can't talk much at work." My posture sank in again and my voice failed me.

"Well, you've still got a job so I don't see why I can't."

"I just—"

She threw me against the alleyway brick wall without me expecting it and held me by the shoulders. I could overpower her obviously, but I just felt so weak at the time. So helpless.

"Tell me!"

"I..." I felt her bony hands dig into the joints of my arms. She was hurting me. "I had to take more shifts at work."

49

"What?!" She was enraged. She let go of me and started kicking any empty cans around the alleyway. "I bet your dad made you do more shifts!"

I nodded my head quickly. I was still scared thinking that she was going to use me as her next target.

"Please." I whimpered. "Let's just—"

"Don't you fucking tell me what to do!" She grabbed my greased shirt and pulled my forehead against hers. "How dare he take you away from me?!"

I couldn't do anything but just feel hopeless. "You need to be with people who are good for you, Bern!"

"Ok." That was all I could say. I felt anything else at that moment would get me killed. She hugged me so tightly that I felt her crushing my back. I was still paralyzed, some of it came from fear but the rest came from her digging her sharp nails into my flesh, ready to pull chunks out.

"I'm just doing my best for you." She said it with such venom, such hate, I was more scared of her than anything. All I could reply with was "Ok".

She leaned in for a kiss, but my body was stiff. I was repulsed when I could feel her lips on mine with my expression crumpling up like paper.

"I love you Bern."

"I love you too."

Sidorovich
13:52

It had been more than a week since the boy had come to the church. We had finished the Sunday sermon and continued to talk to our local churchgoers. They were mostly old men and women who came to church not to learn about God, but to socialise and talk to others.

Samara sat on the pews, gossiping like a schoolgirl with some of the pensioners here, he was making another one of his attempts to get me to talk to some of the widowed women here.

"Maggie looks good." he would say, "go get laid, you'll feel better."

I always got a good laugh from it, and the women would always be ready to slap him for being so crass.

We would start cleaning the place from our guests. Well... I would. Samara would give me 'moral support'. I didn't mind it since Samara struggles to keep himself tidy, let alone a church and it would not hold up to my standards. Spotless, dust-free, and presentable like an armed brigade. When our guests left, I immediately began my tasks, and we could be ourselves. I was cleaning the windows of the church on a ladder with a duster and glass cleaning solution.

"Put your back into it, Fedor. You're missing spots." Samara bellowed.

He could be found by the altar, rehearsing the sermon for next week, but still, he would bother me.

"If you don't shut up, I'll ram this dust stick up your ass."

"Good!" he bellowed. "As long as you don't give me the stick up your ass."

I nearly had the window to the standard it deserved when the door opened with a notable creek.

"Sermon is over I'm afraid." I said, still high off the ground.

"Hello Batushka."

"Oh *churt*!" I yelled out in shock. I lost my balance momentarily on the ladder and quickly recovered.

"Fedor, stop ignoring our guest and behave yourself." Samara yelled out.

"You get your ass up here sometime!"

Samara came back at me as sarcastic as ever. "I would but I'm afraid that I'm no match for a big strong man like you."

"Big strong man will get the little shit soon." I pointed my duster at him like a weapon whilst I was coming down the ladder from the window. When I hit the floor, I heard the boy giggling at us. Samara came from behind the altar and started dusting himself off like he was ready to perform in front of an audience.

"Welcome back boy!" He said with joy. Samara approached him with his arms outstretched and hugged him with almost suffocating amounts of affection which was visible on the boy's face.

"Ok Samara, let him go before you snap him in two." He did let go, but not before almost winding the poor child. He put his

51

hands on the boy's shoulders before saying that was too predictable.

"Not the first time I'll break someone in half." He let out a hearty bellow. "Come boy! Have a drink!" He raced off into the office to get a bottle of spirits.

"Tobacco!" I called out to him.

When he reached the door to the office, he fully outstretched two hands and slapped one of them on the back of another.

"*Moutza zon tovolo!*"

So, he proceeded to storm into the office with the attitude of a baby after his bottle.

"That was interesting," the boy said with confusion.

"He's an… interesting animal." I move myself towards a pew to sit myself down. "Tell me, boy, how can we help you?"

"I came here to learn more about you guys."

I was stunned, I thought we had scared him away or been too intense for him, especially after Samara's little performance. I sat down on the nearest pew from my position and leaned back.

"And what do you want to learn?"

"I wanted to learn about you guys and what brought you here." My mind was racing. What was enough? What was too much? Would he ask about my scars?

The boy finally spoke, "You're not a regular priest, are you?"

"No boy, I came from the army." The boy was confused. He sat down next to me with his posture slumped, like how we first met him. He was nervous, this much I could see.

"Oh… did you fight in the Afghanistan war?"

"Which one?" I replied. My bandages itched; I felt the horror again. The memories would flood back anytime now, and I would be vulnerable to them.

"Umm…" The boy was dumbfounded, he didn't know what to say afterward.

"There was more than one in that godforsaken place boy. I was with the Red Army when it happened."

"Wait what…?" Now he was curious. His spine straightened faster than a bullet and made him open to me now.

"Yes, I fought and killed… and now I'm here."

"What's it like to—"

"Don't ask that question." My bandages burned now. I turned to him and looked at him in his soul. His posture went back to what it was.

"I'm... sorry."

"Don't be. That kind of question is common. To take a life is different from person to person, but there are two ways to look at it. Can you sleep at night, or can't you?"

There was a long pause between us until the boy broke the silence.

"Do you have any good stories?"

"Depends... how old are you?"

He paused for another second, wondering why I asked.

"Seventeen..."

"Good, then I can tell you."

The memories were here now. But this time I did not feel anger or hate but joy.

"Me and my friends Vasya, Kars, and Slava, we wanted to play a joke on..."

I broke out in a chuckle; I had forgotten the brotherhood we had.

"We wanted to play a joke on this boy Arseny. We decided to sneak a prostitute into the army camp. Now this boy had never been with a woman, and we needed to fix that..." My face couldn't contain it anymore. I was smiling like a fool. "By almost giving him the gift of venereal disease."

The boy broke into a chuckle.

"Because Kars could speak the language, he did the talking and got this poor Afghani woman with us. Because Slava was so big and strong nobody would want to mess with us. It was Vasya's idea, but he was guarding the camp and let us smuggle them in. We snuck this woman into the dead of night and Kars told her to 'go in, he's expecting you'. She walked into his tent and then all you could hear from the tent was '*AAAAAH BLYAAAAT*'."

The hall was echoing with laughter from the both of us.

In that moment joy radiated in this place which gave it a fresh life that had been gone for too long.

I quickly sobered up and said, "We nearly got shot for that, but thankfully they needed everyone back then."

"What other stories have you got?" The boy asked.

As if on cue, Samara came back with spirit and tobacco and was confused.
"What did I miss?"
"Story time." I replied cheerfully.
Life was good. Life was peaceful.

Ava
Half eight in the evening

"Yeah Lisa, I do understand. I just want to make sure everything is ok with him." I said to my friend. We were walking down the street to the town centre lot hoping to get some joy into our lives. We did the complementary duo of dark and light. I wore dark makeup, and dark clothes and teased my hair to look like Robert Smith but Lisa was dressed more colourful. She dressed like a normal person with a red shirt and pristine white jeans. Although she wore basic makeup with bright red lipstick and bleach-blonde hair. Think Marilyn Monroe but modern and simplistic.
"I don't understand how throwing him against the wall is 'OK with him' Ava." She said back to me. "That's a bit mental."
"Sorry, but I had to get some sense into him somehow." I joked to her.
"I don't care!" She stopped me round the corner from the town centre lot before we could go meet them.
"You just abused him. You better have a good reason for doing this!"
My head was spinning, I didn't know what else to say except…

Switch

"I hate him."
She paused to get her shock together. The switch was flicked. I couldn't stop hating him. "I loved him to pieces, but I just couldn't control it anymore, so I snapped."
The waterworks came on now and I was ugly crying in the middle of the street. Lisa took me to some back alley that stank of piss and tried to calm me down there.

"It'll be ok, lass."
"No, it won't. I'm a monster! I'm a monster!" I screamed out to her.
"No, you're—"
"Yes. I. Am! I know he works hard but I just wanted some time with him. I'm a selfish bitch."
She was holding me in her arms, and it was the first time I felt like I had the support.
"Don't worry, we'll get it sorted."
I felt the tears washing away my black eyeliner and mascara, I was too scared to get it on her red shirt, but I needed this.
"Do you need to go talk to someone?"
"No!" I screeched out, immediately letting go of her. "I'm fine!"
We were at a standstill. She had been telling me to go see someone for ages.
"Ava, I know you've got problems, but your behaviour is getting crazier."
"What do you know?" I screamed at her.
"It's less like a mood swing, more like a roller coaster." She played around with her hands to show the point. "I remember how you found Bern, you were happy as can be but when it comes to something going wrong, it gets bad with you."
I'm scared to go to the doctor. What if they called me a freak or that I got something that would get me locked up? I didn't want to be put in a padded cell or something.

Switch

But after hearing that, my anger all went away, in an instant.
"I'm fine." I spoke.
Lisa looked horrified. She could only see a bright smile on my face with my ruined makeup smudged all over. "Sorry about your shirt." I said to her.
"It's... OK" she was confused, and it looked like she was trying to treat me like glass. I am glass, but I'm prettier, like stained glass fit for a church.
"Let's just..." She paused. "Go see the town centre lot." She said, with hesitation.
"Ok, let's go."

55

I could smell the stoners from a mile away and hear their trashy drill music. They were hiding in some derelict shop smoking whatever cheap shit they could get.

"Whoa! I love the crying make-up Ava!" one of them said whilst roller skating around the shop.

I was simply happy for the compliment and to be back with one of them. "Thanks, it's a talent." I winked at another one with a poorly bleached bowl cut. Here I could get all that I felt was missing. All that I wanted. Here, I felt like I got more out of life.

Michael
Nine-ish

It was payday today. I was expecting the first payment from Bernard today. I was sitting at home finally having time to sit on the sofa and relax. I put on some popular soap operas and just let myself unwind with me youngest. It was alright for a while, and I could see that Jason was getting into it.

Then Bernard walked in.

"Have you got the money?" was the first thing to come to me head.

"Yeah, Dad I do." He gave me a big huff and puff and handed me the cash. "Cheers for that mate."

"You know I got my exams back today?" he said.

"Oh yeah?" I took a swing of my beer, but I was still watching the show. I think a big twist is coming up.

"Yeah, I got As and Bs." he said.

"That's great. I'll order a takeout from somewhere to celebrate."

"Can we not just ta—"

"I'll order it in a sec, lad. Don't worry."

"Who do you think is gonna get killed next Dad?" Jason chimed in.

"Bloody hell, I missed that!" Now I was dead annoyed. "Just go upstairs or go to your missus. Let me relax please."

As I was rewinding the show, I heard him slinking upstairs. I'll just order the usual for him.

"Right now, where was I?"

Bern

9:49pm

42 days post exams

I spent that time in my dark lightless room crying. I felt like there was nothing I could do. I stuck my greasy fingers into my slowly darkening hair and rocked back and forth on my floor mattress. I tried not to let the gaps of my blinds show the world my vulnerability too much. In a fit of desperation, I tried to call someone about what had happened. I didn't have any friends since I was always working or had to take care of Jason, so I had to call Ava.

I grabbed my oily phone from its charger and sent a text message.

Hey, can we talk?

I waited and waited for what felt like an eternity until I heard a ding from my phone.

Sure! What's up?

I didn't waste any time. I began to dial and waited for her to answer.

"Are you ok?" She sounded harsh, almost bitter.

"Yeah, I'm fine I just—"

"If you're fine then you're fine."

I didn't know what to say after that. I just felt like I wasn't good enough no matter how hard I worked.

"Did I catch you at a bad time?"

I thought I could hear her groan but all I heard was a lot of the noise was drowned out by EDM music blasting through the phone.

"Don't worry about it, you're here now. What's the problem now?"

I was hesitant to say anything since I could tell I upset her. What I was really confused about was that she always wanted attention from me but now it felt like she didn't want me to even come near her.

"Are you with the town centre lot again?"

"Yeah, I am!" She became extremely bratty as if I was accusing her of something. "These guys are doing better at giving me what I want than you are!"

I was hurt. I was in pain and now the knife was being twisted.

"Go get a life if you don't have one!" and then she hung up. I put my phone back on charge then I just laid there in my room, completely empty and alone.

Death Eternal

Sidorovich
16:54

Summer was waning and making way for the rainy season to come in. I was roaming the halls of the church but unfortunately, Samara had fallen sick. That or he was hungover. I scrubbed the pews, washed the stones, and made it look immaculate. At the end of the day, I would retire to the office and open the metal case where I kept my most precious things, hidden away in the desk like a curse. A secret burden for nobody to know. Samara knew what was in it, but he would never dare tell a soul.
What was inside felt like a treasure that should never be found:

- Old medals
- A collection of CDs
- A jar of sand from that hell hole
- My old blood type patch (B-)
- A photo of my family
- My black leather bible with eroding embossed gold and a prayer rope in the spine
- My old service Makarov with twenty-four rounds of 9x18mm
- What was left of Mikhail's old prayer rope

Samara would never tell anyone of my past and let me tell it to them if I chose. But I haven't chosen for nearly twenty years. The last person I told it to, was my son and he is out of the picture.
I took out the photo of my family and there they were. Olega and Grigori were what kept me sane for many years to come but they like many others had left like smoke vapours dissipating from my pipe.
"I'm sorry..." was the only thing I could say to them. I held a lit match close to the photo but something in me just couldn't follow through with it. I couldn't kill anything else, especially not a piece of me.

"My son is dead because of you!" Screamed whatever spectre
was haunting me that I could not exercise. "My precious boy!"
I left the photo in the steel box to curse me at another time. I felt
like I earned the punishment. My son was dead, my friends were
dead and this I must endure until I am finally with them. Until I
have earned my atonement.

"Hello?" I heard a familiar voice cry out. "Batushka?"
The boy was here, and I needed to go meet him. I hid my box in
one of the desk drawers and marched my way to the hall pipe in
hand.
"Hello, boy. How can I help?"
"I just wanted to talk, Batushka." he said. Although I could tell
this boy had sadness in his presence.
"Of course." We sat on one of the pews and began to talk.
"I feel empty Batushka. I don't know where to begin."
I wanted to offer a counselling ear to this boy, but he felt like a
ghost that came back to haunt me. A lost memory of the dead
man in me.
"Do you want Samara for this? I feel like he would be better for
this."
"No…" The boy started to chuckle a bit before saying something
that sounded like it would fall out of Samara's own sewer for a
mouth. "He'd just tell me to get drunk and that I'd feel better
about it."
My eyes rolled after hearing those words and hearing it from this
boy we were teaching showed me how impressionable he was. If
we were teaching him then my fellow priest was teaching how to
party, meaning I needed to teach him to be humble.
To be better than us.
"You know…" I started to take out my pipe and my tobacco
from my pockets, ready to smoke. "What we can do is this. Talk
to me as if I am a friend to you and I will keep everything here. It
will not leave this church at all."
Silence passed between us for a while before he looked at me
with his saddened blue eyes before whispering "OK."
He took a deep breath, and I could see his face choke up as he
was holding back a river of tears. He bowed his head as if he was
praying at the altar and tried to fight the flow with his hands, but

his brave mask was failing as I could see tears seeping through. I did not know what else to do. I was hesitant but I knew I had to do something, so I put my free hand on his shoulder and tried my best to comfort him. "It'll be ok boy." was all I could say to him, and I feel like my response may have been cold to him, but anything was better than nothing.

"Thank you." He said to me as he was wiping away his tears on his dark sweater. It sounded like he knew I was giving him sympathy, but he was too busy pouring his heart out to me. "I just feel like I'm not good enough."
He was emotional and I barely knew this boy, but I wanted to help him as best as I could.
"Tell me and we will figure it out." I responded.
"I just feel like my work and the people who care about me are not there for me."
"Let it out, boy." I said as I tried to give him a comforting pat on the back.

Michael
Quarter past five-ish in the afternoon

It felt like a dream. A blur. It felt like I was waking up in me nightmare of virgin white lights and office desks. "Mike?" The voice called. Was it a ghost? "Mike!" I heard it again and it was louder than ever.
I felt unreal until I felt the hand on me shoulder and then I woke up.
"You alright there mate?"
"Yeah David, I'm fine." I responded.
"Alright. You just went away for a bit." He took his hand off me shoulder and sat back down at his desk. "Are you sure you don't wanna go and speak to someone?"
"I can do me job if that's what you're asking." I got a little annoyed at his question. I was in a dream and then I woke up in hell.
"That's not—" He held his face in his hand and took a deep breath before quickly changing the subject. "How's Bern?"

61

"Bernard's fine." I got suspicious. I don't know what his game was, but I didn't like it. I sat there in that rubbish black office chair, and I glared at him. I could see right through him as if he didn't exist and into his taekwondo trophy case.

"Right…" He held up open hands whilst sitting down, showing the gold signet ring on his left hand. "I'm just trying to make small talk. I know you haven't been yourself since that *incident*."

He was right. I wasn't meself. I used to be the life of the party but now I'm what kills it. "You used to be a happy bloke but now it just sounds like you're…"

"Spit it out, David."

He paused for a minute to get his thoughts together and find an answer to not set another of my moods off.

"Do you need anyone to talk to?" he said, fidgeting with his ring.

"No…"

We sat there for a moment getting our paperwork together for the door calls we had to do.

"I went to his funeral, you know." I said. I felt like I was putting myself in some sort of danger by saying that in the office.

"Who's?"

"The guy who hung himself in front of me."

He gave me a shocked look. "You know you shouldn't have gone there, Mike."

As soon as I heard that, I flew up from the chair and went off on one with him. "And you think I care?!"

"I didn't mean…"

I was practically screaming at this man, "How fucking dare you tell me what I can and can't do!"

David wheeled back from his chair closer to his trophy case, holding his hands up.

Then without me realising, my boss Mark had walked in, and he was giving me such a scowl.

"Office! Now!"

I can't believe this lanky; skinhead was telling me what to do. Boss or no…

But I needed my job and I needed to keep the boys safe…

62

Bern
9:20am

53 days post exam.

I was preparing for my last year at school. I washed my uniform,
got my belongings, and helped my brother get ready for school. I
still felt shakes and pains, but I couldn't get rid of it even when
sitting outside the door of my house. I was waiting on the
doorstep for Ava since she walked past my house every day, but
I couldn't see her.
I reached into my phone to check if she had sent me a message
or anything but there was nothing. Only the lock screen of us
together with our tongues sticking out trying to look cute as can
be... Well, I was trying but when I looked, she had eyes like a
predator stalking its prey.
Staring at that lock screen made me miserable and my face
showed it.
Although as if on cue I felt a push on my shoulder.
"Whatcha doing stranger?" She yelled. Her expression was
happy, but I felt her words sting me a little. "Ready to start
walking?" It felt more like a command than a question since she
pulled me up by my arm and dragged me along by my hand
before I could react.

"Come on, can't be late for the first day back!" She exclaimed in
her giggly attitude.
I felt helpless at that moment, but I couldn't talk at that time. I
had to wait for my opportunity to say how I felt being with her. I
needed to learn to stand up for myself, but not in the middle of
the street with witnesses that she could use against me.

Sidorovich
09:30

I had been alone in the church for more than a week now with
the occasional visit from the boy when he wasn't too busy. The
church was growing colder the longer I was here. I sat down on
the pew that cradled my bible on its wood and readied a smoke

to give myself some warmth from the approaching autumn and the encroaching isolation. The Bible was calling to me like a temptress trying to seduce a stalwart knight and I answered it. I flicked through the pages to find my old photo of my brothers. I wanted this to torture me. I wanted to feel like I deserved to die and why shouldn't I? Only one came back sane.

I hear a loud bang from the front door. The kind of sound you would hear from a bomb going off, the kind of sound that would take more people's lives.

"Shit!" cried out Mikhail. Everyone braced themselves in case we were about to die.
The truck in front of us had exploded from a landmine, turning it into a flaming wreck and killing whoever was in it.
"Stop the fucking truck!" Screamed out Slava.
The squad was in a panic. We just survived a fight for our lives and couldn't afford to get into another one.
"Where are they?" screamed out Arseny. He positioned himself near the personal entrance of the truck.
Everyone readied their weapons but was terrified to get out of the vehicle for fear of landing on another mine or a sniper or whatever god wanted to throw at us.
Dead silence passed over us and the only things we could hear were the wind and the burning truck ahead of us.
"Fedor, get on the radio and tell them we're stuck." Vasya suggested.
"Yeah, that's a good idea," Slava replied. I wasted no time and started the procedure. I got on one knee near the edge of that claustrophobic truck and tried to call for help through my headset.
"Yakov 3-3, Yakov 3-3 calling in for cargo 200."
All I heard was dead noise.
"Anything?" Asked Vasya.
"Yakov 3-3, Yakov 3-3 calling in for cargo 200. We have sustained heavy casualties! Come in!"
I was screaming desperately into the radio… and still nothing.
"Fedor… stop." Said Alyosha. "There's a hole in the radio."

64

Everyone stopped. Everyone stared. All except me who was kneeling with my mouth wide open and my heart on the bed of the truck.

"Get it off…"

"Are you—"

"Get it off Alyosha!" I snapped at him.

"Vasya, get the medicine!" ordered Slava.

I unbuckled the straps holding it on me and let my squad pull the portable radio off me. As soon as they did, I felt weak. I felt my body fail. My vision blurred and the hellish desert I stared into turned darker.

"How bad is it?" I asked hesitantly.

"Fedor… your back is bloodied." Kars said.

As soon as I heard the news, I touched my back and felt my warm blood on my dust-covered hands and all I could gasp out was, "Well fuck…"

My vision went black, and I felt the world pull me outside the truck.

"Catch him!" Someone ordered.

I fell from that world and into the cobbled floor of the church with a familiar face holding my bandaged arm.

"Are you ok Fedor?" Asked Samara.

He sat me upright on the pew with me clutching my head, disoriented, and confused.

"I'm fine…" I lied of course but I didn't want him to know, especially with him finally coming back from his illness. I missed the peace, but peace was lonely without his company.

Ava
Half twelve-ish

I just finished Mr. Manto's class, and it was the most boring thing ever. History… gross.

I was happy to be gone from him as soon as I left the class with my stuff and my spiky, black, and white bag. I rushed to Bern as soon as I could, knowing him. He's probably sat somewhere sulking, so I need to go and dazzle him with stunning makeup skills.

I get all sorts of people looking at me through the school hallways but the only thing that races through my mind is, do I want to go get Bern? I feel like he won't give me what I need.
"Nice makeup!" someone would say to me.
"Nice hair." someone else would say.
God, I missed this.
Eventually, I did find Bern in an empty classroom… reading a book. That's different…
I could see him propped on the teacher's desk next to the whiteboard. I bet he thought he was a teacher or something.
I opened the door and shouted, "Hey Bern!"
He fell off his chair and instantly just snapped out of whatever world he was in and presumably, shat himself. Honestly, I found that really funny.
"Can you not?" He snapped at me, whilst getting up off the floor.

Switch

"Excuse me. 'Not' what?"
"Just don't burst in and make me look like a fool please."

Switch

"Oi!" I snapped at him. "Behave!" I clicked at him with my fingers.
He took a deep breath and then just sat back down to his book.
"Excuse me, I'm right here!"
He took another deep huff and then just threw the red-covered book on the table.
"I know, I just want time to myself."
"Well, I'm here now. So, tell me what you're reading."
"…a Bible…" he responded.
"You what?"
"Yeah, I'm reading a bible."
"It's not those priests that got you to read it?"
"No, I wanted to read it myself."
"When were you religious?" I started snapping at him.
"I don't even know if I am." He did his trademark slump and couldn't even look me in the eye.

66

I got into a huff and sat on the table that he was at. I pick his chin
and make him look at me.
"I wanna go see them. OK?"
"But I don't—"

Switch

Before he could finish his sentence, I slapped him hard enough
to make him see sense. The noise echoed through the class and
hurt my delicate hand doing it. He was sitting there clutching his
face trying to hold back tears.
"...OK. I'll take you right now."
I knew the classroom was empty so there would be nobody to
say otherwise.
But is it wrong to say that it felt good?

Sidorovich
13:54

Samara made me take time off my duties to rest. He's seen me
do this before, but I feel like these attacks are getting worse. He
tried to care for me by passing me food and tobacco and told me
I was god's gift to the world.

"Fedor, it's a miracle that god hasn't kicked your ass into hell at
this point."
"I love you too Samara, now be a good mother and give me
tobacco."

We both settled in well enough and thankfully Samara was well
enough to conduct his *own* duties, albeit with a vintage drink in
hand from his famous spirit cabinet.
I sat on the pew with my pipe in my mouth adjusting my
bandages to make sure they were not scuffed or that they
damaged what was in them. Thankfully, the autumn weather had
not come into full yet, as it would turn this church into a freezer.
However, the climate added a sort of hovering dread and started
to kill the flowers we had in the church.

Suddenly, I don't know why but I felt my heart sink and my face drop like a sandbag was hanging onto it.

"Fedor, did you run out of tobacco?" Samara jokes.

"Somethings coming." I replied.

Out of nowhere the church doors flew open.

"Ah boy, how are you doing?" Samara called out. "And I see you brought a lady friend."

I turned around and saw the boy looking defeated with a red mark on his face, being accompanied by a girl who looked like she was almost emaciated, and her face had makeup that you would only find the band Agatha Christie wearing whilst singing about an opium dream.

"We have food and drink, plenty here." Samara added.

Without a second passing, I heard this girl start making demands.

"Stay away from Bern!"

After hearing it I stood up from my chair and readied myself for a conflict.

"Excuse me?" Samara was stunned by the audacity of her.

"I know you're filling his head full of ideas. He's mine!"

"The boy is his own person." I interrupted.

"He's mine! I love him unlike you creepy old men!" she screeched out.

"How dare—" Samara yelled out but not before I interrupted him.

I stuck my hand out to him to try and call him off whilst holding my pipe with the other.

"I've got this Samara" The boy was looking miserable and recoiled more into himself as the argument went on.

"Boy, how did you get that mark on your face?"

"She…" his face was trying desperately to hold back an ocean's worth of pain and suffering.

That one word was all I needed to hear before I would lose Samara on her like an attack dog. I gave him a look to confirm my order and watched the show unveil.

"Get out of my church girl!" Samara ordered.

"Not a chance!"

"If not then I can put you in one of the graves outside, you already look like a corpse ready to be buried."

She was stunned. She was clearly a person who knew how to give abuse but not take it.

"I'm…" her face was going so red you could see it through her pale makeup. "Not leaving without him."

"Dear girl, you don't have a boyfriend anymore. You have a prisoner. Now release him so I can tell him what to do."

The arguing quickly turned into a screaming match.

"Why, so you can make him your *'prisoner'*?"

"No girl, so I can give him advice."

"Oh yeah and what advice is that?!"

"That he needs to find a woman with an ass. That he needs to stop dating boys."

I admit, I cracked up at that comment and it almost certainly made that girl want to retreat to whatever hell she came from. She was still in shock and was stumbling over her words "What are you laughing at bandage man?"

"You." I gesture to her with my pipe hand. "You're pathetic if you have to hurt your lover."

The boy finally spoke up. "Leave Ava. Don't come near me again."

This girl finally understood the situation and stormed out of the church but not before screaming out, "You'll never find another woman like me!!"

Samara called out to her, "Good, why would he settle for trash?"

She left with a pout and a scoff but not before slamming the church door behind her.

The boy had been held hostage when walking in. After that show with his woman, the boy was lost and hurt from us having to fight his battle. He laid there on the front pew not knowing what to do with himself, crying like a newborn baby and soaking the polished wood beneath him with his tears if the wax didn't roll off the falling salt water.

"Look boy, she wasn't good for you. You must understand that." Samara stammered drunkenly towards him on the pew.

The boy's voice echoed through the hall. "You called her a boy and trash!" He wailed out in anger.

"I hope so. Finally, the trash took itself out!" Samara paused for a second. Even drunk he knew his mouth ran faster than his brain. "I'm sorry boy. I just wanted to protect you."

The boy was still there sobbing onto the pew. All of Samara's drunken efforts would do nothing to ease the pain.

"Samara, go into the office please." I said to him. Even drunk he acknowledged with a simple nod and followed my command and by that time the tears had stopped. I moved up from the cold cobbled floor to the boy's position and sat on his curled body, placing my hand on his head. Silence passed through us for what felt like the death of time until I dared to speak.

"Did I ever tell you about the time I nearly died?"

I heard nothing from him except the occasional sniffle.

"I was a radio man for my squad in the Red Army and I got into a gunfight for the first time. By the time I left, I didn't realise I had shrapnel go through my radio pack which thankfully stopped me from being killed."

He stopped moving suddenly, this time, he was listening to me. "I had my friend Vasya remove shrapnel the size of my thumb from my back." I held my thumb up to show my point. "Vasya said, 'You must have god watching over you to survive that'".

"What happened then?" The boy finally responded.

"We were in an army truck, and it had turned to the dead of night. I got out of the truck feeling these bandages on my back and was given an orange medicine kit box with medicine saying, 'for god's little angel'."

The boy had turned with his head facing up to me now, still lying on the pew. With him doing so I moved my hand to his shoulder.

"I was laid down in a truck and afghani nights were freezing so I was shirtless and hurt until another friend of mine, Dima, walked in to check on me, cigarette in hand, saying 'How's our little miracle doing?"

We both chuckled at Dima's poor attempt to tease me.

"I told him: 'Better looking than your miracle face'."

"Miracle face?" the boy asked.

"His face dropped every time something bad would happen to him or people close to him."

The boy looked confused, and why wouldn't he? If I was god's miracle, then that man was god's prophet.

"Anyway, he came in with an MRE and a cigarette and out of the blue said, 'Ever seen a man's balls in a vice? No? Then your dying face looks worse than my miracle face.'"

We all burst out laughing. Me, the boy, and Dima. I could hear the old ghost's laughter after so long, reverberating through the church as if he were there.

I took a deep breath and leaned back with the boy next to me. I closed my eyes and opened them to find myself in that same truck with Dima sat down next to me and Ilya's body in front of me. The colour drained from it long ago and the pooled blood was stale.

The others were outside and close to the truck opening. They made a small fire with whatever expendable equipment they had to keep warm from the tyrannic Afghani nights. I could hear them make stupid jokes and listened to whatever scraps conversation they held with whoever they hated the least. Empty MRE packets and used utensils littered the sand.

"We should bury him." I gave a dower start at the dead brother in front of me.

"I know..." Dima acknowledged. "But I don't think we'll be able to carry him all the way there. This truck will just have to be his tomb." Dima Stood up and leaned against the side of the truck, trying to light a cigarette with a match.

"Lev won't like this." I winced.

"Doesn't matter." Dima said with a cigarette in his mouth. "We stay here, we die. It's an easy choice."

I knew the cost of war, but I didn't know the tragedy of it. To leave a brother behind so you wouldn't join him in death. What a misery.

"Before I forget." Dima exclaimed.

He dug in his army fatigue pockets and pulled out a dark wooden pipe. Crooked and curved.

"A present from Kars. Catch!"

He sharply threw the pipe to me with a swift gesture of his hand which landed at my chest. I dropped the pipe, as I was unprepared, and heard it clatter on the truck bed.

71

"Good catch." He joked. He gave me a cocky smirk and left to rejoin the others. As soon as he exited the truck, I saw Kars looking at me with a brotherly smile on his face. He didn't show it for long, he didn't want to show his vulnerability around the squad members he was with.

I broke eye contact and gazed at the pipe. I picked it up and closely examined its grooves and curves. It was beautiful. I played with it for a little while, inspecting it like a rifle. I found underneath the bowl a hastily made carving that inscribed, "Sidorovich".

I held the thing in my one hand and gripped it tightly; my other on the shoulder of Ilya, who's been dead for some time now. I rested, leaned back, and blinked.

"I loved those men but after that night, I woke up with cheap vodka in my belly and a sore back." I said to the boy.

Whilst the boy was still looking at me, I pulled the fragments of the prayer rope from my bandages, and he gave me the most confused look.

"These things may be a curse, but I've become really good at hiding things with these." I think I cracked a smile when I pulled out the black velvet pouch containing this old, battered wood. It made me feel at home.

"This thing has been with me since the war and was given to me by a good friend." I opened the pouch and inside was the cross, some knotted beads, and what was left of the rope holding it all together. I pull out one of the beads and place it in his open palms.

"These have kept me alive for so long. I trust you, boy, so do not lose it."

"Are you sure about Batushka?"

I closed his hands and made sure he had a tight grip on it. "I'm sure, boy."

Silence passed through us for a while. We did nothing. But somehow, I felt something I have not had in years. A purpose, a reason to live. Somehow, I felt my son was with me.

Ava
Ten past two in the afternoon

I never heard of anything like it. The audacity! I was in tears and just so full of anger that the only thing I could do was call up Lisa about what happened. I frantically searched for her name on my phone and started speed-walking my way towards the bus stop.

Buzz tone... Buzz tone...

"Hello?"

"Lisa, you have to help me!" I wailed at her. At this point, I was bawling my eyes out and my 'corpse' makeup was smudging and running down my face.

"Woah! What's the matter?" she asked.

I was sniffling and crying like a baby. I held my other hand to my face, trying to cover up my embarrassment, not caring if my makeup got ruined. It was already ruined.

"Bern left me!"

I heard her take a huff and puff on the phone. She's getting sick of my shit at this point.

"What happened Ava?" She sounded like she was bored of me.

"These stupid priests think that I hit Bern."

It felt like a pin had dropped as soon as I said that.

"Wow..." She was *clearly* shocked judging by how she sounded; it was more from disbelief. "And did you?"

I got out the last of my willpower to scream to her, "No! Of course, I didn't!"

"Then you have nothing to worry about." she tried to say calmly.

"I'm going to go with the town centre lot."

"I don't think..." She sounded like she was halfway through giving me advice but then ended up doing a deep sigh and said, "Just go for it and try not to get hurt. I'm doing stuff right now so I gotta go."

I was at the point where the anger had left me, and I just felt drained. "That's fine." I eked out.

I hung up the phone and finally, I got myself to the bus stop, hoping to escape this horrible place.

73

I put my phone in my black trouser pocket but then realised that I had used my makeup-smudged hand.

"Oh fuck!" I yelled out in frustration. Thankfully, the street was quiet, and nobody heard. I tried to wipe it off onto the navy-blue blazer and white dress shirt of my uniform, but it ended up smudging more and made me look like I was an abuse escapee. Finally, I heard the teal bus coming down the road and tried to wave it down so I could get on.

As soon as he stopped, I got out my black purse that had a white spirit board design on it from my bag. As soon as I opened it, I realised that I had no cash on me and that I had left my bus pass somewhere at home. I'm not walking home.

I went towards the bus; he was a bald old man in his 70s with a long scraggly white beard. He wore Oakley sunglasses and a black and teal uniform for the bus company.

As soon as he saw me his mouth just dropped, and his eyebrows went up so high they could touch the roof of the bus.

Switch

Show time.

I pulled my best emotional victim performance. I made sure I was heard by passengers with my voice all high pitched and looking like a damsel in distress, especially with black makeup all over my clothes and a face like a victim.

"I'm so sorry, I've just escaped my abusive boyfriend. I don't have any—"

He pointed his thumb to the back of the bus. "Get on." He interrupted. "Don't worry about it, just make sure next time you have something." he said in a polite but secretive way.

"Thank you!" I gave him a hug making sure to show how desperate I was and then Immediately rushed to the back.

There was barely anyone on the bus, but I didn't care. I still got my way and I'm still heading to the town centre lot.

Michael
Half seven at night

74

Jason was at home with me playing his games in his room whilst I was in the lounge watching TV on the leather sofa, doing paperwork, and surrounded by takeaway cartons and empty beer bottles. I had ordered takeaway from a kebab shop and bought some beer with me for tonight as well, but I was just waiting for me lad to come back home. Eventually, I had him stumble through the door.

"Ah, Bernard!" I tap on the seat next to me. "Sit down please." At that point, I wasn't even looking at him. I still kept me eyes on either the paperwork or the TV and didn't pay him much mind.

"So, the good news is, because you're back at school you can cut your hours down."

I keep talking whilst taking the occasional sip of beer and writing down what routes I took and what calls I made to debt owners. "But I still need you to carry on with paying me the same every month."

I felt like I was speaking to a debtor. Some scum off the street, so it hurt when I asked him for that money. My son was not scum, but I was asking money from him like he was.

He finally sat down, and I passed him my opened beer bottle as some kind of 'well done'.

He refused and told me that he was, "*Too young*". I raised him too well.

The only thing you could hear was the soap opera on the TV playing and smoke billowing off me pen. Neither of us spoke a word to each other but I still felt he was there with me. Eventually, I saw a stray drop falling onto my paperwork. I turned next to me and saw Bernard crying next to me. "Are you ok, mate?" He's facing the TV and sitting upright, eyes burning red from all the emotion he's having to let loose. He doesn't say anything to me. He doesn't even budge. I tap him on the shoulder, but he shifts it off him.

I take another swig of my Polish beer and then move my paperwork to the floor covered in junk and rubbish. "Bernard, I know I'm not here often but I'm here now. Please talk to me." I feel like I came off too strong after I said that. He moved away from me and started walking upstairs, but not before leaving this month's payment on the sofa next to me in a beige envelope.

I was pissed. Not at him, but at meself. If I thought I raised him too well, then he must see me as a bully and a debt collector. I felt my blood boil and threw the envelope at the patchy, crimson-painted walls that chipped even more paint off the walls. It made the envelope full of twenty-pound notes fly all through the room. One of the notes flew towards me and landed on top of where I put the paperwork. I picked up the purple plastic notes that had the queen's head staring at me and crumpled them up in my hand. I felt like I was losing me boy.
"I'm so sorry mate..."

Bern
10:32am
62 days post exam

Each time I would go to school, I would dread the risk of running in Ava. The whole scene in the church caused me to feel uneasy with myself and I felt like I would risk an anxiety attack from even seeing someone who looked slightly like her. Eventually, it came to a short break. I would go to the school library and request the same, red-covered bible to borrow. Then I would retreat to the same classroom that Ava found me in. I would go towards the teacher's desk and find the page I had left a corner on. Where Ava last interrupted me.

Psalm 98:4

Where to carry on and where to leave? I felt like I was slowly starting to understand the priests more through their religion but not their practice. It felt like they were the best kind of friends but the worst kind of priests. I leaned back further on the black office chair behind the desk and dared to put my feet up on the desk. Soon I would go through Psalm, then the Song of Solomon, then Ecclesiastes, and more. I would lose myself in the scripture.

76

Eventually, time passed by so quickly, like I blinked and appeared in another time zone. The school bell made its electronic ring and signalled that it was time for me to leave. I would pack up my things and proceed out the door before the teacher using this room caught me at his office of command. However, my plan did not go off flawlessly, I encountered resistance.

"Are you Bernard?"

I stopped and froze. I had never seen this person in my life before. Even though she was in the navy blazer, she stunned me with her bleach-blonde hair and fifties-style makeup.

"I'm Bern. Not the biggest fan of being called Bernard." I made a small chuckle. I was nervous around her, and I felt like even talking to this person made me feel she was out of my league. "Sorry, Bern." She responded. Although, I don't feel like she wanted to talk about anything happy. "I'm Lisa, Ava's friend."

I suddenly had a deep stabbing pain in my chest and felt like the wind was sucked out of my lungs. I tried my best not to show it, but I still gave off a shocked look.

She held out open palms with partially outstretched elbows like she was surrendering. "Don't worry, I come peacefully." she said. "I just want to understand what happened."

I was still hesitant about her. I didn't know what her plans were, but I was tempted to listen.

"Please, just meet me after school and then I won't bother you again. I'll be waiting by this classroom for you."

After hearing this, I nodded in agreement.

"Ok, I'll see you here." She quickly made her way past the classroom and towards her next lesson. I didn't know what was going on, but I felt like she was a completely different person from who Ava was. I needed to talk to her and say my peace.

3:15pm

School had just finished. I packed my things into my desert camo military bag and rushed through the school building back toward that classroom, not thinking about getting home. As I was making my way through the decrepit hallways, I left my dad a text message to say that I would be home a little later than usual. The classroom I was heading to was on the other side of the school building. I was trying my best not to be held up by the sea of navy blazers and the odd spattering of a person wearing a thick coat that looked like a polluted stain in the dark blue ocean. I felt like a teenage Moses parting the hormonal sea when I pushed past the other students and made my way toward that classroom.

First flight, then the second, then to my first left. Walk about three doors down and...

There she was... As promised. She sat on the teacher's desk with her legs crossed and staring at her phone. Finally, she noticed me and put her phone by her side.

"Hey, Bern." She said, "I saved you your spot."

She left that black office chair for me to sit on. I was still hesitant to even step into the room with her. I felt like Ava was gonna come out of any hiding spot like a horror movie monster.

"Hey..." I said to her weakly.

I approached the presented chair and sat down, throwing my bag behind me but not too far away in case I needed to make a quick escape.

"So, I wanted to talk about Ava." Lisa said, as she shifted herself closer to one of the windows and opened it. She then got out a packet of Marlboro cigarettes and took out a cigarette with her short nails that matched the colour of her lips. She lit it with an old Zippo lighter and smoked it near the open window, whilst leaning by the wall in case a passer-by caught us.

I don't know why but I felt almost entranced by her.

"Is this about the priests?" I asked. I was on the edge of the office chair, anticipating what she was going to say in order to paint me the villain.

"Yeah..." She sighed. Her carmine-red lips opened to unveil smoke as she spoke. I felt like I was speaking to a mythical dragon, something from a storybook or a time long gone by.

"She said that they think she hit you." Her beautiful eyes turned into a fierce flame, I felt like her eyes would shine like stars, but they only sparkled for the truth. "Is that true?"

"She did..." I replied to her. "She—"

"Don't worry…" She took a deep inhale of her cigarette before flicking away the ash outside the window. "… I believe you." Immediately my guard dropped, and I was shocked to hear what she just said.

"Don't worry Bern, she told me that she me threw against a wall or something. It's why I'm trying my best to get away from that mess of a person." Her shining eyes turned dim with heartbreak. "I've been friends with her since nursery and then she got involved with that band of junkies and ravers from the town centre."

I sat there. I didn't know how long they had been friends and suddenly this felt like not only a betrayal but a heartbreak to both me and the person across me.

"I will warn you, she's a spiteful person now so whatever you told her, she will use it against you."

I suddenly realised the purpose of this meet-up. This was a warning.

She finally finished her cigarette, stubbed it out on the window which left an ashy stain, and threw it outside the window. Lisa took out a bright red bottle of perfume from her blazer pocket and started spraying it on herself to hide the smell of smoke. "Oh, and one more thing." She added. "This never happened. The less she knows the better. Trust me." I gave her a brief nod to say I understood. And then…

She left. No word of warning, no exchange of details.

She. Just. Left.

Sidorovich
19:37

Autumn had come into full effect and the church's heaters had barely been working, especially with the holes in the front door and the age of the building. Samara sat in the office with me, wearing his casual clothes. Blue jeans, brown boots, a thick coat, and a white vest top with a thick gold chain. I, however, was in a suit. Pure black with shining and spotless dress shoes and still covered in bandages, though I had decorated them with the odd silver ring.

Every month we would find some way to come as we are and not let our professions get in our way. We would come here as friends, not colleagues.

Our sides of the office would look like a mirror of each other. Samara would pull out a vintage alcohol from somewhere before our time and open it as a celebration. I however would get out cigars that would be imported from Cuba and reveal my old CD player that I kept around for only God knows how long, with Samara bringing a compilation of our favourite songs on one disk. His half of the disk would have old English pop songs from the 1980s, while I would have Russian rock and pop songs. To my luck, the first song that would appear would be 'What is Missing' by t.A.T.u.

"What should I drink this time?" Samara asked. He greedily scanned the contents of the cabinet awaiting his next aged poison.

"I don't know, I don't drink that stuff." I replied.

Eventually, Samara picked out two bottles. One was a grey bottle with a wax seal covering the top of it. The other was a bottle corked, clear bottle, containing a yellow liquid with the label faded to near unreadable.

"So, we have death in a bottle…" Samara held up the grey bottle to me, "Or we have Croft Blend." He said as he showed me the other bottle.

"Drink your death bottle." I joked with him.

"And I thought I meant so much to you, Fedor." Samara said sarcastically. "Just because I love you so, I'm having the Croft Blend." He put the wax-sealed bottle back into the diamond windowed cabinet and sat down on his chair.

"Damn." I cheered out, "My plot has been ruined."

"Yes, yes, mister killer, now smoke your cigar."

I leaned back and bore a grin on my face. "With pleasure." I expressed.

The room was filled with laughter and joy that was not there in months. I smoked, he drank, and we both started sharing our best stories from our past. Samara about his party life and me in my army days.

"Did I tell you about the time I met my wife?" Samara asked. Already three tumblers down.
"You did but enlighten me again. I want to see how much of a good husband you are."
Samara gave off a scoff before shaking his head and giving a small chuckle.
"Me? Good husband? What friend have you been speaking to?"
"Not a good one." I joked.
"No, the best." He jeered.

"Anyway, Story!" Samara exclaimed.
"After I gave up my party life, I met her in a shop she was working at. I remembered her since I met her in a bar but couldn't remember how we met."
I leaned back into my chair and let him carry on with his story whilst he was drinking and speaking.
"I walked up to her to try and pull my..." He leaned in from his chair "...Casanova moves on her." After saying that he started making a poor attempt at the tango with his upper body.
"I got to the counter, and she said, 'I remember you; you piece of shit! You didn't pay for your tab at the bar!'"
I was laughing so hard I felt the smoke choke up my lungs, making me come out in a coughing fit.
"Don't die until the story ends." Samara demanded.
"No promises." I replied to him.

"So, I stood there like a fool, and I essentially said that I'll pay off the tab if I take her to dinner."
"OK, so where did you take your blushing bride-to-be?" I said sarcastically.
With a stone-solid expression, he said "Fast food stand." Before taking another sip of his poison.
I burst out laughing at the sheer boldness of the man.
"It's a wonder you've not been killed yet." I called out to him.
"You laugh, but I'm the married man here."
"And I imagine she regrets every day of it."

81

"Maybe." Samara shrugs, "But I need someone to yell at me." he jokes.

I finally take my time savouring the different flavours of the cigar. I take a deep inhale into my mouth, sit back, let the smoke sit in my lungs for three seconds, and finally exhale through my nose. Finally, peace. As soon as I had exhaled, Samara would get a drunken twinkle in his eye that could be reflected through his crystal tumblers.

"What about your life before the war, Fedor?"
"What about it?" I asked him.
"You told me about a friend you had called Kars. You never said why you two both went into the war together." He took another drink from his tumbler. At this point, one of his songs started to play.
"Kars was in the same neighbourhood as me, growing up in a little city called Kovrov. It's on the Klyazma river."
I took a long smoke to try and make sure only my childhood memories came back.
"I remember, before me and Kars got to the age where women were always on our minds, we wanted to try and escape to The West to go and live the lives of kings. But then again, we were only boys that barely knew what the world was like."

"Come on Fedor, give me details." Samara pleaded.
I took another smoke.
"Ok, ok." I leaned back into my chair and tapped the ash from my cigar into an ashtray. "We played old rock music. We heard rumours of Woodstock and we wanted to act like that." I gave a small chuckle at my foolish youth. How full of hope we were. "We thought we played well but…" I gave an embarrassed scoff. "We weren't Victor Tsoi."
"What made you stop?" Samara asked. He filled up another tumbler and offered it to me and I refused with a simple hand gesture.
"Money." I gave a light shrug in my chair. "After I met my wife, Olega. We tried to get a better life, but we went into the military for that better life. Ironically, after I went into the army, I got

better at music…" I gave a deep sigh and then lifted one of my arms in presentation towards Samara. "Then this happened. Now I can't play anymore."

"Sorry about that Fedor, I didn't mean to drown the mood." Samara spoke like a child who knew they did wrong but didn't realise the consequence of their action until it happened.

"It's fine." I replied. "Pass me a tumbler. I want to see why you drink this poison."

His face lit up like a firework. Samara passed me the tumbler he previously made and made himself a fresh one.

"What do we toast to?" He asked.

I paused for a second, breathing in the last of my cigar before stubbing it out.

"To our younger, stupider days." I cheered. I raised my glass. Samara matched my movement and replied with a jovial smile.

"To our younger days, you old bastard."

Ava
Half five-ish in the evening

At this point, it was close to October. I had been bunking off from school with help from the town centre lot. I always left the house in uniform so my dad would think I was going to school, but that simply wasn't the case. There were a few adults who would call the school for me and pretend to be my dad so I could skip classes. I've lost count of the days I've been away, but I felt free.

Even in the derelict shop, we were hiding in, full of old toys, trash, and tipped over shelves… It was mine.

I would always keep a can of deodorant to keep the smell of weed from getting into my clothes too much, but I always got scared when I heard any motorbikes. I always felt like my dad would be close to finding out what I was doing and then he would ruin me.

I was sat by a fire pit that we made from old trash and petrol and tried to keep myself warm. Unfortunately, school uniforms aren't the warmest. Eventually, I saw Nova trying to slide next to me.

"You want another drag?" He asked. He held out half of a joint as he flicked his poorly bleached bowl cut away from his face.

"Sure." I spoke. I felt tired though, even when mellow or on something I just felt empty.

Nova picked out his name because he wanted to be one of the 'cool guys', even though he was twenty-four and still acted like someone half his age. He wore trashy printed clothes that would make even some modern-day rappers too embarrassed to wear them.

"Listen Ava—" he got even closer to me, "I've managed to get some happy pills."
As soon as he said the word 'happy', my ears pricked up like a bat's. He got out a little cling film bag full of white pills that had different symbols carved into them. The most common symbol was a smiley face.
"What's the cost?" I asked him.
"For my best friend, nothing!" He gave a massive toothy grin. So wide you could see his rotting teeth. Something was up. He never gave me anything for free unless there were strings attached. I didn't care though, after that whole scene with Bern, I just wanted to feel some sort of joy in my life.
"Fine… give me one."
I reached into the bag and took out one which had a cross on it. Nova's bloodshot eyes fixed on me with intent. "Which one did you get?"
I didn't even answer him. I just threw the damn pill back into the bag and wiped the dust on my trousers. His face was confused as to what had just happened.
"Are you—"
"I'm going home, Nova." I said to him. "Push your pills elsewhere."
As soon as I got up, I felt a grab on my arm.
"Are you su—"
"Take your fucking hand off me!" I snapped at him.
He backed away like the coward he is and let go.
I made my way out of the derelict shop with my belongings and went straight for home.
I tried to make my way towards the bus stop, but my dad found me instead, equipped with his motorbike and his leathers.

He saw me and swerved his silver 1986 Kawasaki closer to the pavement until he got to me. As soon as he pulled up, he flicked off the engine and flipped up his visor.

"You doing alright Ava?" he asked.

"Yeah Dad, just fine." I replied. I stood there not looking him in the face with my hands in my pockets.

"Do you want a ride back at least?"

"Sure."

He gave me a spare piss pot helmet from his top box and let me get on the back and he started up the engine. I feel like he could smell the weed on me and decided to ignore it. I wasn't too certain though since I didn't have time to spray myself to get the smell off.

"Hold tight love." Without warning, he kicked the bike into first and then set us off.

Bern
10:32am
76 days post exam

I returned from work with a wight on my chest. I was covered in grease, misery, and downtrodden from managing difficult customers. I would be stuck at my job with my uniform and just try my best to make it through each shift that came up.

Eventually, lo and behold... I felt a cough force its way through my lungs. Thankfully, it was the morning and not too many people wanted their blood pressure to go through the roof by that time.

I excused myself to the back and let out a chesty cough. I leaned myself next to a half-painted wall, thinking the barely hanging wallpaper would stop me from hitting the ground. I could feel my lungs rattle, and my chest hurt. This felt like I was barely breathing but I was trying my best not to let my manager hear me. Unfortunately, my worst fears did appear.

He was a decently sized man, if not obese. He stood there with a food-stained apron from working in the kitchen all day and gave me a scowling look.

85

"If you got something, then I need you to go home." he crossed his arms, allowing his sagging meat to show from the weight he put on.

"I'll be fi—" Before I could finish the sentence, I had my lungs give me another attack.

That was it, the cover was blown.

The manager backed away slowly to avoid getting caught by my illness.

I could read his face, and I was not impressed. His poorly groomed moustache was poised to slap me home, but instead, his words did it for him.

"Go home, don't come back till you're better." He said in a thick Eastern accent.

Those were all the words I needed to hear to know I wouldn't make this month's payment. I would have to get money from previous months to help me make up for this month.

I knew this wasn't the life of a seventeen-year-old, but one of a burnt-out adult.

I left that place, out through the front door, and coughed my way past the customers. I couldn't control myself and with each cough, I could feel the manager's moustache twitching more.

As soon as I got outside, I let the full force of my cough come loose. Even though it was autumn and starting to get colder, I felt like I was burning up.

"Fuck!" I coughed to myself, trying to make sure pieces of my lungs weren't coming out.

Something finally hit me, and I couldn't work anymore in that place until it left me.

I knew I wouldn't be in the state to walk home, so I had to try and catch a bus home and hope that I wouldn't cough the place down.

Back home towards that half-complete house, back home to a dad who I let down.

11:43am

I finally did get home, through no small effort.

The bus ride caused me to cough even more with its rancid air, making any passengers who were on the bus cower away from

86

my violent coughing fits. I stumbled out of the bus, still coughing up the disease in my lungs, and made my way down the street and to my home.

The place was far from quiet, I could hear my brothers screaming and shouting at his games, which felt nonstop. I dragged myself towards my room. My mattress. And I collapsed onto that slab of springs and hardcovers, not bothering to shower first.

I started throwing my coughing fit, making me feel vulnerable and ill.

'I could do more.' I thought to myself. 'I could do better'. Instead, I couldn't do better. I just let myself become sicker and more ill whilst on a bare mattress, like some lazy bum.

I picked up my phone which was covered more in grease and began to text my dad:

Came home.
Caught something.

I laid there for hours, just coughing up my lungs and feeling more worthless by the moment.

I laid there for hours, to see how badly I would be ridiculed for missing work from getting ill.

3:32pm

I was left weak and dying on my mattress. I would be left there in peace thankfully, although in isolation. No friends to talk to, only those priests. Eventually, I heard the front door creak open. "How are you doing Jason?" I heard the visitor say. This was a voice I had not heard before.

Eventually, I crawled out of bed, still in my greasy work clothes, and made my way towards my bedroom door. As soon as I got closer, I felt a cough forcing its way through my lungs.

"Bernard, are you home?" My dad's voice echoed.

"Yeah..." my breathing sounded like I was with an oxygen tank. I couldn't take deep breaths, only short gasps like a fish out of water. Except this fish would look like he was straight from a deep fryer.

The door opened to expose me clinging to the side of the wall, trying to prop myself straight but unfortunately being brought low each time to cough.

"Are you alright mate?" The voice revealed itself to be someone from my dad's work.
"Yeah, I'm fine." I replied to him.
He was a built man, almost like my dad except with a better physique and better groomed.
"Sounds like a nasty cough you got there. Not caught the flu going around, have you?"
As if in an instant, my dad's voice came through.
"I hope not! Can't afford to get sick."
"Dad can—" I began to cough more into my hands before I could finish the sentence.
"We'll talk later mate when you're better. Come on David." He dismissed me with such ease and took his work friend with him into the lounge.
I pulled my way back towards my bed, but not before shutting my door. I throw my grease-ridden body onto the bed, feeling too weak to move myself to get a shower.
"Please…" I said to myself, staring at my own reflection in the mirror doors to my wardrobe. "No more."
A final greasy tear rolled down my face before breaking into another coughing fit.

Sidorovich
12:32

My colleague and I were preparing for the next sermon. The church was nearly spotless, however, it felt empty. More empty than usual.
"Fedor!" My little friend would call out. "Could I have your bible?"
"Why? What reason?"
"Just for something important." He held a mischievous smile on his face.
"Fine but break anything on it and I *WILL* kill you." I said sternly.

I left the pew I was located on and made my way into the office.
I retrieved the metal lockbox I kept on my side, unlocked it, and
pulled the black leather book out.

As soon as I locked up the box, I saw my colleague appear from
out of nowhere.

"AH BLYAT! Sneaky little shit!"

"I know, but not as sneaky as you." He replied smugly.

Samara revealed a small parcel from his robe pockets. It was a
sparkling silver packet with a little bow tie on top.

"Sophia wrapped that up with love."

I was stunned, I felt my heart melt with this small little parcel.

"Tell your wife, I appreciate it."

"She loves you too. Now! Open!" He forced the parcel into my
bandaged hand.

I placed the bible on the desk and opened the small parcel. I tore
the paper like a small child on Christmas day and inside almost
made me feel like a child.

"What do you think?" Samara asked.

I dug my hand out and pulled out a silver prayer rope and a
packet of Laika cigarettes.

"The necklace is solid silver. The cigarettes are from the wife.
But don't smoke them, they're out of date by… a lot."

I cradled these treasures and pushed them into my chest for a
small while before putting them into the metal case.

"Happy birthday, you miserable shit!" Samara bellowed out.

I was embarrassed to say that I had forgotten my own birthday. I
would be sixty-two now. Good lord… I am old.

"Thank you, Angelo… I mean it." I couldn't look him in the eye.
I just kept staring at my box.

"You wanted my bible?"

"Yes, and a pen." I dug through my organised desk to find a
black pen for him to use. Samara opened the first page which
was held together with old tape.

"Write in it." He held out the brandished pen and held it out to
me.

"What do you want me to write?"

"Make it yours Fedor."

It felt wrong. Desecrating a bible and making it my own but I felt
like I was duty-bound, and I did what I was ordered. I picked up

the pen but touching it felt foreign. Holding it was painful and messy but eventually, I printed my name in English first but as soon as I finished, I looked up and saw Samara's disapproving look. I proceeded to sign my name again, this time in Russian. Observing the page, it looked like a child's handwriting, but I wanted to finish my task.

Fedor Sidorovich
Федор Сидорович
1957 - Смерть Вечная

"Finished." I exclaimed.
"Good to hear!" He exclaimed. He walked over to see what I had written.
"What does that mean? Next to your year of birth?" Samara asked.
"Death Eternal."

Imprisonment

Bern
2:43am
80 days post exam

My body feels sluggish, slow. I wake up to find myself in my bedroom, still feeling the effects of my illness. I felt like I wanted to get back to sleep but something important was keeping me from sleeping, but I didn't know what. There is no light peeking through the broken blind, almost like the sunlight had been murdered and I was witnessing the darkened aftermath of a dead sun. I collect my splayed limbs from the side of my body and pull myself up off the mattress. As I stand up, a sharp yet slow pain flows down my back, not so much a stabbing but the kind you would get from a sunburn. It was followed by another coughing fit which I tried to smother into my shoulder. Fighting through the pain, the only sounds that could be heard were the creaking of the wooden floor and my occasional wince and cough. Then silence…

A thick visage of onyx permeates the air, hovering over this land like a soulless, suffocating void. Using what energy I had, I shifted myself to find my phone in the dark and fumbled around aimlessly to find my one light source. Eventually, I kicked my phone by accident with my foot and discovered its location. I pick it up and start playing with it until I find something to put me to sleep.

3:12am

Too early… But I notice something in the reflection of the screen, almost as if there was something on my face. On the same stand with a quiet wince, I reach to turn on my room light and try to pull away this void around me. I looked in the mirror of my sliding wardrobe doors and realised I had been mistaken but I didn't go back to my mattress. Instead, I cradle my face with one hand. The place where Ava had hit me. I rubbed it as it

91

was still fresh but the feel of it never faded. I don't know what overcame me next, but I lifted my greasy work shirt to reveal my skinny body. I saw the bones protruding from my skin. The diet of nothing but one or two meals a day was finally starting to catch up. I was kept weak and starved; I couldn't even afford my own food without giving it to my dad.

"Is this how people live?" I gasped to myself before collapsing onto my mattress from a coughing fit.

Eventually, my body did fail me, and I was left to smother another coughing fit into my pillows to not draw attention to myself. I couldn't sleep that night. My mind was racing with all sorts of ideas. Instead, I decided to do something a bit more productive. I did research.
I grabbed my phone and started to search:
'Wars in Afghanistan'
There was a lengthy list of information about 9/11, Taliban, Bin Laden, etcetera.
This wasn't what I was looking for. I was stumped. There was almost too much to look through for the wrong kind of war.
'Russia vs Afghanistan'
I next typed in.
This time, better results.
1979 - 1989.
It was known as the USSR's Vietnam.
The more I looked, the more I wanted to find out. Different images and pictures cropped up on the screen making me want to look at it more. I was morbidly intrigued.
Dates, times, locations, battles.
It was all there to see.
All this information sparked even more questions towards that old Russian.

Ava
Half nine-ish in the morning

The town centre lot have been especially quiet. I knew this as I wasn't able to go see them. I had to keep quiet from them since my dad came to pick me up.

Instead, I was walking in the town centre with Lisa, but she looked worse than her usual self. Her makeup was minimal where she wore nude lipstick instead of her signature bright red, her clothes were wrinkled and looked trashy, and she kept going back to her cigarettes. Opening them and smoking them like they were candy sticks.

"What the matter?" I asked as we passed by a jewellery shop.

"I'm fine." She replied. She took a long drag of her rolled Amber Leaf cigarette. She gave me a look. Something different was with her.

"I'm just going through a tough time."

"What do you mean?" I asked her. We stopped by a high-street clothing brand that was too bland for my tastes. 'Too normal'.

"I'm fine." She repeated. This time half finishing the roll-up cigarette before tossing it on the floor and stamping it out.

Switch

I felt the anger come out and this time I couldn't control it.

"What the Fuck is your problem!?" I lashed out. She didn't even flinch when I raised my voice. She just stood there and stared at me.

"Am I not your—" Before I could finish my sentence, Lisa put her hand on my shoulder.

"Just… stop…" she said. She stared at me with puppy dog eyes, and I couldn't do anything to resist that, so I just stopped and listened to her.

"I spoke to Bern." She had said.

At that moment, time felt like it had stopped. My head was split into all sorts of different directions. What was the next switch to flick? What would be the best reaction?

"You properly fucked him up." Those words felt like she was trying to cudgel me to death.

Switch

93

I thought of no other reaction except to have my own puppy dog eyes come out. I made my voice break a little and made it look like tears were about to fall out.

"What did Bern say about me?"

Without a moment's hesitation, she brought up her nude lipstick from her wrinkled jacket and applied another layer on her lips. She bowed her head and puckered her lips together, then gave me my answer as she pulled her head up in defiance.

"He told me enough."

Switch

"What does that fucking mean?" I snapped back.

In a sudden, she turned from a little puppy, into a mean terrier.

"It means I don't want to be near you anymore, you crazy bitch!" She barked out. "You abused him, and I can't be anywhere near you for that!"

This sent me into a fury. I started screaming every hurtful thing I could at her in the middle of the town centre street.

I would throw every bit of anger at her, screaming:

"You cheap, bleach blonde slag."

"Trashy bitch who's can't get a man!"

"You can't get anyone with makeup that belongs on an animal testing subject."

She tried to be strong and stoic. But eventually, my words got through to her and broke her.

"How fucking dare you?" She snapped back at me.

"I've been there for you since nursery!" She threw her hand into her chest, as if it would protect her like a shield, then pointed a finger at me like a sword.

"And you, have started treating me like shit ever since you fell in with the town centre lot."

She was wrong about me. I've done my best for everyone I knew.

"Maybe you're just upset that I've found some actually good friends!" I shouted back at her.

And with that scowl on her face, she snapped. She threw a slap at me and smacked me across my face, right in the view of the people on the street. It caused people to stop and stare or quickly walk past us to avoid getting caught in the drama.

"Hey! Leave her alone!" Some old man came up and intervened. He looked like your average elderly man with old clothes and poor-taste shoes. He hobbled as fast as he could across the street with his walking stick and was yelling out.

"Leave that poor girl alone!"

"She's the abusive one!" Lisa exclaimed. She tried to explain herself, but the old man would wave around his wooden cane like it was a glow stick and keep yelling at Lisa.

"I saw that slap young lady. Now get away from her."

As if on cue, Nova from the town centre lot passed us by on the street, and even off his face on whatever mad concoction he was on, he would still come to me. It was a surprise even to me, as I thought they were trying to be a little smarter than coming out in the open, but we were here now.

"What's going on?" He would scream out. Nova charged in with his tracksuit covered in anime faces with his poorly bleached hair trailing behind him and stinking of piss.

"Who are you?" Lisa screamed out.

"I'm Nova, Ava's boyfriend."

He really wasn't but I didn't know what else to do. I was just so shocked and let my face show it. How dare he say something like that so bluntly. I did the only thing I thought to do in that situation.

Switch

I linked his arm with mine and wrapped my hand around his. He turned from angry to proud.

"When did this happen?" Lisa asked.

"It just did." I snapped back at her. I slowly dug my nails into Nova's hand further and further, as the seconds passed. He gave out a small wince and looked at where I was causing the damage. He got the message.

Lisa tried to speak but stopped herself with the first syllable and said these last words in a cracking voice before walking in the opposite direction.

"Fuck you Ava and your junkie boyfriend." She left sobbing away in the middle of the street. I just got rid of this person and now I had a situation to salvage.

As soon as she left, the old man came up to me and tried to reassure me.

"If you see anything like that happen, please don't be afraid to call for help."

"Thank you." I replied to him.

As soon as the old man left, I dug my nails even further into Nova's hand where it drew blood. He winced and struggled to pull his hand away.

"Ow Ava! That hurts!"

I turned to Nova; nails still attached to his junkie skin with a furious look on my face.

"Don't you ever say you're my boyfriend, ever again!" I let go of his hand and let the damage be shown. Blood was trickling from my nails and his hand.

"Let's go." I barked.

My lackey didn't say anything. He knew his place and did as I asked without question.

Lisa
I don't know what time it is!

I ran. I ran as fast as I could away from those horrible people. My tears ran down my face and smudged my makeup. I didn't know what to expect from it, except that I had to deal with losing my best friend to a bunch of junkies. I ran around the corner, closer to a bus station, waiting to go home. I grabbed a pre-rolled cigarette from my pocket and tried to light it up, but my hands were shaking from what just happened when I struggled to meet the flame of the cigarette. I don't know why but the first thing I thought of was Bern. I wanted to tell him what happened and that he needed to stay away from her, but I couldn't contact him in any way.

I decided to get out my phone and scrolled through my pictures folder to find all the photos of me and Ava together. One of us in primary school, where I had her dad take a picture of us with the school building as the background. We both looked like kids. We wore jeans and hoodies with canvas trainers and loved it. We didn't care how we looked. Of course, my hair wasn't bleach blonde, it was light brown.

One of us was at a theme park, whilst we were cuddling a giant tiger teddy bear. It was the middle of the night, and we stood in front of a roller coaster. That was during the winter when we were in big puffy coats. Ava loved teddy bears back then, she was still skinny, but she was deceptively strong like her dad.

The memories flooded back to me, and they hurt me more than I expected. I took the occasional puff of my cigarette to help me cope with the pain of it all.

Then came the photos of when we got into secondary school. When she got into her darker side.

One photo of us in year eight where I still looked like a kid in normal clothes, but she started wearing a lot of black. Her makeup wasn't as extreme back then, just the odd bit of eye shadow.

Then came year ten. She started hanging around the town centre lot and she got worse. She started wearing harsher clothes with big spikes, fishnets, and short skirts and I started wearing more fifties-style clothes with floral patterned dresses and high heels. Her body started getting skinnier and more emaciated. She held a cigarette in her hand in the photo, but she posed like she was proud of it. Like she wanted to get in trouble.

Then came the year eleven prom photos. We came into prom in a hearse and posed in front of it. She came fully in a long partially see-through dress and styled it like a Victorian. You could see almost her entire skeleton. Her hair was teased, and she came with corpse makeup, looking like she was straight out of a metal album. She posed with a smile on her face, but I felt like her eyes were like a shark. Cold and dead, looking for its next prey. I however came in a copy of Marilyn Monroe's famous white dress and had my hair bleach blonde. I started wearing my red lipstick from that day and posed exactly like her famous photo in 1954. We were a power couple! We were loved!

But something made us fall apart.

I hovered over the delete button for the prom photo, but this felt like I was about to kill what friendship we had. Before I could, I heard the bus coming towards me. I put my phone away into my pocket and I held my arm out to stop the black and teal.

I had an old man with a scraggly beard on his face and Oakley sunglasses stopped to pick me up.

"Coming on love?" He asked.

"Yeah," I said to him. "Get me away from here please."

As soon as the bus door closed behind me, I felt a part of me die. I felt that my other half had just left.

Sidorovich
13:32

The end of October was near. The bitter months took away the glaring light of the sun that would shine through the spotless artistic windows of the church. The church was an old building that did not keep the warmth effectively. It was even more handicapped by the damage on the door, which would let the heat escape through its holes and splinters.

I would pace the church and clean the altar whilst wrapped up in a thick grey wool coat I would wear over my robes. I wore Samara's gift around my neck and made it visibly present. I would use brass polish and a rag to clean the massive cross. However, the polish would stain my bandages and cause me great discomfort. Although old habits compelled me to finish until I could see my reflection in the cross.

Eventually, my task was complete. The cross would be spotless and the time for selfcare would arrive. I would position myself in the office and sit down on one of the chairs, hunched over my desk.

I took the small first aid kit that I kept in my wool coat and revealed its contents. More black bandages and antiseptic wipes. I started to unravel the bandages that covered my hands and showed my shame.

Burn scars. My own little reminder of that desert hell.

The scars stretched from my hands to my elbows. The feeling of the frigid air on what was left of my skin felt like reliving it all over again. I grabbed the antiseptic wipes and began to clean myself of any polish that seeped through the bandages. As soon as it contacted my flesh, I felt it sting and sear my hands. I would curse and moan with each second the wipe was on me. I finished one arm and moved on to the second. However, I heard the office door creak open. Without hesitation, I would find the metal case which held my belongings and grab my pistol. The sting of touching anything was too great, but I felt I was in danger and pain could wait.

I grabbed the old Makarov and loaded it. The touch of the metal ached my still-exposed hands.

I stacked up against the wall next to the door and readied myself for whoever came by.

"Samara!" I called out.

No reply.

I aimed the end of the pistol at the door waiting for the intruder to come in.

Soon the smell of sand came in. The heat. The fear.

Time was blurred between the past and the present.

"Come get me fucker!" I blustered.

There was no response.

I pulled open the office door and breached the church hall.

Nothing. The hall was empty.

It was the wind gusting through the church. I retreated to the office to avoid causing any further embarrassment and immediately unloaded the pistol magazine and pulled back the slide to remove the round in the chamber, but the bullet fell on the floor of the office. The freezing air burned my skin and caused it to sting harsher the longer it was uncovered. I could only ignore the pain for so long, but I pushed through to the metal case. I threw in my pistol and magazine but left it open. I tried searching the floor for that bullet but found it had rolled over to Samara's side of the office and hidden itself underneath his spirit cabinet. I moved over and laid on the floor to retrieve the bullet, trying carefully not to damage the silver necklace I had been given by dragging it on the floor. Touching the brass with my exposed fingers

Eventually, I felt a presence on my shoulder.

"Fedor, get your gear!" Slava ordered. I woke up on my face lying in the truck. The wound on my back was still throbbing. The squad had slept upright on the seats; however, Ilya's body was still on the floor of the truck. The colour on his face was completely gone and flies were circling around his corpse.

"I'm not leaving my brother in this truck!" Lev whimpered out.

"We need to get out of this desert!" Slava barked. "Alyosha! Get his gear!"

"No." With that simple response, the squad was broken.

"I'm not doing anything you tell me." Alyosha glared at Slava from the seat of the truck.

"I'm finding my own way back!"

"You're deserting?" Slava replied.

"What are you going to do? Get blown up by yourself?" Arseny cried out.

"I'm not dying for a cause I didn't sign up for."

"Then you'll die from your own stupidity!" Lev called out.

"What do you think you'll do when you leave?" Mikhail gasped out. His voice barely recovered from the last engagement.

"I'll get away from the idiot who volunteered us to that death trap." Alyosha screamed back.

His eyes glazed over with hate and directed them towards Slava.

"Don't you put their deaths on me!" Slava spoke through his gritted teeth. "We either stick together or we—"

"Do what? Die for the Soviet Union like true patriots?"

"If it comes down to that…" Slava stood up from his seat, he towered over Alyosha in both mass and stature, having to bow down to avoid hitting his head on the roof of the truck. "And you will do as I say, you fucking conscript!"

"Let him go." I said, with bitterness in my voice. I pulled myself off the floor of the truck and felt the wound on my back sting as I stood up.

"I should—" Slava tried to blurt out. I held my hand up to stop him from speaking further.

I rummaged through my equipment to find my pistol and looked at Alyosha.

"Thank you, Fedor." He said with relief.

But I didn't spare a second. I pulled my pistol out and pointed it at him.

"Get out!"

His face dropped.

"What do you mean?" Alyosha wailed.

"You're a deserter now." I pulled the pistol slide back to load the bullet into the chamber. "Now get out."

The bluff was set. Arguments were made over small petty things, but this would kill us if not managed. I locked my arms and stared at my target. I took it upon myself to trick him into staying by pressuring him to go. Like a parent pretending to leave their child so they would scamper to their side.

"And go where?" Alyosha asked.
"I don't care." I said with a dry tone.

I looked at the rest of the men but kept my weapon trained. "Anyone else who wants to go, go! But If I see you again, I will shoot you." I focus back on Alyosha. "That includes you. You can take your chances and leave, or you can stay with us and survive."

I lowered my gun, freeing him to make the decision that would make or break the team.
He paused. His tattooed hands wrapped around his scalp. His emotions battled, his risks weighed, and his time in this world depended on what he did next.

"No. I won't stay."

The bluff had failed. I failed and now he would leave, potentially taking how many people with him.

"Those who want to stay can stay but I'm leaving."

He didn't say another word. He just grabbed his gear and left the truck. He walked into the desert and around to the front of the truck.
"I don't think that was a good idea." Dima moaned. As soon as he said it, his miracle face came on. I had realised my mistake by that point. My eyes widened and my wounds ached further. I prayed to myself that I didn't just kill a man or worse, damn the rest of us to a terrible fate.

"He won't survive long Fedor! He'll be killed on the spot." Kars chastised.

"Maybe he'll be blown up by a landmine or something." Vasya grimly jested.

Seconds passed as everyone contemplated leaving in search of a way out, but all ideas and hopes were destroyed. Vasya's joke was a grim prophecy. We heard an explosion first but then the metal sides of the truck vibrated and warped. Nobody saw what happened, but we saw what was left of the aftermath. A single severed finger had landed just outside the truck opening. We knew what happened. But we didn't want to believe it.

In my misbegotten attempts to save life, I sent a man to the embrace of death.

Whoever was left alive in the truck. They stared, stunned, and shocked at the display which occurred. I walked outside of the truck and passed by the people I called brothers whilst clutching my wounded back.

My boots hit the shifting sand and dirt which felt alien to me. So soft but riddled with danger.

I crouched down to pick up what was left of Alyosha. Then I turned around to face those men. They were horrified. Even Slava who just argued with the newly deceased couldn't believe it.

I observed the finger in my hand and blinked. The splintered bone and minced meat vanished. I no longer felt the bloody warmth of flesh but the cold shell casing of a bullet.

I took a deep sigh and returned to my desk. I loaded the free bullet back into its magazine. I grabbed the old service pistol and its partnered magazine and locked the weapon back in the metal case.

Finally, I would restart the procedure. This time I would look at my own hands and see the dust from the church, clinging onto my burnt hands.

"I'm sorry." I whispered to whatever ghost haunted me, hoping in some vain effort that they would hear me. I clutched the necklace Samara gave me in some hope that it would protect me. It did not work.

I opened another pack of wipes and began to clean my arms to make myself suffer again.

These wounds would not heal, and neither would these scars.

Bern
8:42am

87 days post exam

The illness was getting better. Although I missed the half-term holidays. I was sick through the whole week we would have that break. I spent that week in bed, looking at random things on the internet, and generally had no purpose. I would help to look after my brother when I could, but it would result in him covering his face each time I would cough.

I would walk around the house trying to clean up the takeaway cartons and empty beer containers that were scattered around the house when I had my strength. It made me feel like I was still doing something whilst ill.

That I was still being a good son.

Today, however, school had finished, and I was forced to go back to studying. I was well enough that the occasional cough was not alarming but not so violent that it caused people to fear me like I came straight from a leper colony.

I grabbed my desert camo bag that was placed on my mattress and threw on my school uniform. However, it was wrinkled from not being ironed for weeks. I hoped the blazer would hide the wrinkles, but they would be exposed to an occasional gust of wind that would show my lack of presentation.

I left outside and then paced towards the bus station. Got picked up and waited to arrive.

10:15am

The bus dropped me outside the school building. Close to the entrance, where all the students flooded in and out like an ocean. I blended in with the crowd seamlessly, like nothing had ever happened, and got to the main hallway where students were sitting on scattered benches and fuzzy chairs. Some stood near

103

the walls in their own circle of friends, trying to keep their conversations private. Back to the routine of education and work. Although, that routine was interrupted before it could start. The mythical girl was in front of me.

"Hey, Bern.

"Hey, Lisa." I was shocked. After our last meet-up, I thought she would never want to talk to me again.

"Do you want to walk with me?" She asked. There was something wrong. It felt like she was going to admit to something, but I didn't know what.

I gave a light shrug. "Sure." I replied.

We walked back out of the entrance of the school building, pushing past the flow of students.

She led me out of view of other students to a more secluded area. The local park was around the corner of the school.

There was nobody there. The climbing apparatus and the children's swings were rusted with only scraps of paint clinging on for dear life.

The autumn had drenched the grass into a muddy mess. Lisa dragged me to a blue and yellow metal gazebo that was covered in graffiti and overlapping gang logos.

We sat down on the metal bench that was attached to the side of it. She took a packet of cigarettes out from her light brown handbag and lit it up.

She enveloped her bright red lips and took a deep smoke.

"Do you want some?" she asked. Her lipstick marked the end of the cigarette. "They're my favourite."

"No, I don't smoke."

She gave a small chuckle and crossed her legs.

"Probably better not to get into this habit." She spoke.

There was a still silence between us. Neither of us said a word.

All you could hear was the occasional police siren, the wind, and her occasional puff of smoke. She eventually broke the silence with the worst thing possible.

"I spoke to Ava."

My gut sank and my chest hurt.

I worried with anticipation that she would reveal some dreadful news.

"We're not friends anymore."

"Oh…" I paused, trying to pick my words carefully. "What happened?"

"She happened." Lisa responded. Her smoking hand started shaking.

Her voice began to crack. She bowed forward to her knees and held her forehead whilst still sitting on the bench.

"I've lost her to those junkies." I didn't know how to help her. I was panicking about what to do. I put my hand on her shoulder, and she gripped my hand with hers.

"I loved her like a sister." She howled. Lisa tried to take another puff of her cigarette whilst still bent over her knees, but her cigarette had gone out by itself.

"Fuck." She eked out.

She lifted her torso and tried to rummage around for her lighter. After much frustrated cursing she found it. She put the half-smoked cigarette in her mouth and tried to flick the lighter.

"Come on! Come on!" She snapped. Her words were muffled by the cigarette in her mouth.

The wind kept blowing it out even though she tried to block it from blowing out the gentle flame.

After her agitated attempts, Lisa growled threw the lighter out of the gazebo, and slumped back against the wall. The lighter landed in the mud but was held upright.

I didn't say a word. I just got up and got the lighter which was protruding from the thick sludge it landed in.

I wiped away the dirt from its silver case and saw a little heart scratched into the side with the initials 'A + L', carved inside.

I turned around and she was slumped against the vandalised wall of the gazebo, her now extinguished cigarette hanging lazily from her lips.

I walked up to her, but her eyes were almost glued to graffiti and wouldn't distract me in any way.

I grabbed the cigarette hanging in her mouth and hovered it near mine. Her eyes were now on me. Slowly she came out of her slump and became more attentive to me.

I clutched onto the cigarette with my own maw, holding it in position with my lips and teeth. It tasted horrendous.

I flipped open the lighter and clumsily tried to ignite the poison that was in my mouth. After a few failed attempts, I finally did it.

I took a small inhale but that was my mistake. It burned the back of my throat and felt like my lungs were going to explode, especially after just recovering from my illness. I gave a furious cough trying desperately not to let go of the death stick or its fiery partner.

"Rookie." Lisa snickered.

She left her seat and grabbed the cigarette out of my hand.

I handed her the lighter and looked into her eyes.

There was the fire I was looking for.

"Give me your hand." She politely demanded. She put the lighter in her breast pocket where the logo of our school was. A yellow quartered shield with two red arrows crossed.

I did as she ordered and held out my palm for inspection. Lisa held the cigarette in her mouth and pulled out a black ink pen from her blazer.

She started writing numbers on my hand.

Her voice was again muffled from the cigarette in her mouth.

"This is so we can stick together."

She pulled the pen away and took another puff. Out of nowhere, she hugged me. I was statuesque still.

I was just trying to process what was happening. I closed in my arms to return the hug but not with the same strength she was giving.

She let me go and gave me a coy smile. "Don't be a stranger." She went back to the gazebo to grab her bag and headed in the direction of the school building but not before giving me a sly wink.

I swear to God I blushed when I saw that.

I looked at my hand to see what she wrote. She wrote her phone number with a little message.

thx 4 coming xxx

Sidorovich
17:23

November started with the crack of fireworks and explosions of colours in the neighbourhood. The bright flashes shone through the stained-glass windows, creating a myriad of colours and a cacophony of loud bangs and whistles. Along the street, you could see some houses holding a ritual burning for an age-old terrorist in a Puritan hat. It would get darker at this time of month, so we had to turn on the lights, as dull and lifeless as they were. They hung lazily with each electric candle giving some solace against the void.

I was sat on the front pew, closest to the altar with a lit pipe in hand, my wool coat on my shoulders, and the silver necklace around my neck.

"I'm going home Fedor." Samara said. "Try not to ruin the place."

I held my pipe in my hand and took a deep puff of my Turkish tobacco.

"Yes Mother, now go." I replied sarcastically.

The crackles of colour and thrashing explosions kept erupting, I didn't even notice the door open.

"We're clo—" Samara called out, but he interrupted himself. "Hello, boy!"

I instantly turned around to check if my ears were deceiving me but there he was.

"Welcome, boy!" I called out.

"Hello, Father. Batushka."

Samara at once rushed into the office. "I'll be back boy!" He called out with a smile on his face.

"Come, come." I took a puff and tapped the seat next to me on the pew where I was residing. "Sit."

He moved up the aisle with a smile on his face.

"What's got you so happy?" I asked.

"I met a girl!" He exclaimed with joy.

"And this one isn't a walking corpse?" I joked.

"Nope!" he moved up to where I sat and leaned back into the pew. "Although I did have my first smoke."

As soon as I heard that my heart sank, and my back straightened off the pew.

"Oh, no boy! Don't turn into me."

"Why not? You guys are awesome!" The boy cheered.

Samara charged through the office door with bottles and tumblers in hand.

"Yes, we are awesome!" He bellowed. He balanced his bottles and tumblers like a waiter carrying dishes around a restaurant, but rudely leaving the office door open.

"Now, tell us what brings you here?" Samara asked.

"I just wanted to check you two didn't die of old age yet." The boy joked.

My eyes widened, and my lips puckered further on the wood of my pipe when he heard what he said.

Samara continued to walk with his alcohol towards the pew. But as doing so he declared, "You little shit!"

I chuckled and then choked on the smoke. I coughed out the contents of my presumably tarred lungs and gave him a pat on the shoulder.

"You're one of us now boy, welcome to the club!" I said, my voice now grizzled even further from the tobacco being inhaled wrong.

"Now tell us about this girl you found."

"What girl?" Samara set down his crystal and glassware on the pew but held a crystal glass towards the boy. "Did you take my advice?"

The boy grabbed the tumbler.

"Well, I don't even know if I like her." He responded.

"What do you mean?" Samara blurted out.

"She might be better than the last one." I inputted.

"Well…" The boy fidgeted with the empty tumbler in his hand, presumably from our interrogation. His head was hanging over his knee with a small smile on his face. I stood up to close the office door Samara charged through whilst the boy gave us the latest gossip.

"She—" Before he could finish, I heard an explosion from something too close to me. I blinked and I felt my blood boil as it would set fire.

I was still standing up, but felt I was breaching an open building. I felt my throat drowned from grains of sandstorm that had hit us. My skin felt raw and flayed. I turned around and I saw the inside of the little shithole I stormed and there he was…

Vasya!

With his gun!

And his evil look!

Bern

A firework that was alarmingly close to us had made me and
Samara jump. It had shone through the glass windows, painting a
colourful picture, and almost blinding us with its light. Although
I just saw Sidorovich standing there. He didn't react. He was just
standing there silently.
"Fedor, the smoke didn't affect your brain. Did it?" Samara
joked.
He started pouring a tumbler for himself and leaned back into the
pew, causing the wood the creak under his weight. I put my glass
on the floor next to my foot. There was no sound. Not even from
the fireworks outside, just the dull echo of wood hitting stone. I
looked at the floor beside him and his pipe scattered hot ash and
still burning tobacco on the cobbled floor, exposing the fresh
aromas.
The old Russian turned around, but he was different. His eyes
were vacant, and his teeth were bearing like a trained attack dog.
His bandaged hands flexed and tightened with the strength to
crack a wall nut. This was something terrifying. He got into a
stance, placing one foot behind the other at a forty-five-degree
angle.
"Fedor… are you ok?" Samara asked. He placed his drink beside
him and leaned forward with a dumbfounded look. He was
concerned. He was scared like me.
"Shto tu skazal?" He hissed through his teeth.
"Get behind me, boy! Now!" Samara's voice quivered. This was
not my priest. He looked like him, but his mannerisms and
movement were different. It seemed like he was possessed by a
demon that somehow got onto consecrated ground.
Me and Samara both bolted up from our seats. Samara grabbed
my shoulder and positioned me behind him. The fireworks had
continued their bombardment and flared up the church through
the windows.
"Nye obegry ot menya!" The demon screamed in his fearsome
tongue that was too alien to understand. The lights of the church
dimmed. One died as he pointed at us with his dominant hand,
giving power to the fear we had. The slowly extinguishing ash of
his pipe illuminated and outlined him contrasted with the light of

the church behind us and the cursed hellfire that exploded behind him.

Samara held out a bottle by the neck and pointed it at Sidorovich as if it was a sword to slay the beast.

"Fedor we're friends! Friends!" Samara cried out desperately.

Sidorovich

"How can I be friends with a child killer?!" I screamed at Vasya. The ferocity of the sandstorm raged. My throat was agitated from breathing in the grains. I smelt whatever herbs these poor murdered afghanis were burning and it made me sick.

My muscles tensed, my hate unstoppable and a monster was in front of me. Almost goading me to make him face retribution. One handheld his rifle by the handguard and the other was warding back our youngest member, Arseny.

Vasya's uniform was bloodied by our previous engagement, trying to keep Slava alive. Our uniforms were dirty and tattered. Like our faces. Like our spirits.

"What the hell is going on?" Arseny called out.

"Go get Slava!" I ordered. I pointed at where the door should have been for this brick building.

"What?" Arseny replied in confusion.

My voice was raised as loud as I could make it with my weakened voice, but I needed to be heard over the storm. "The man you left, with his legs blown off! Go! Get him!"

Arseny's childish face turned pale white whilst caked with the filth of the land.

"Where do you think you are?" Vasya called out. He pushed Arseny further behind him and stepped closer to me.

"I'm in Afghanistan, with people who want murder and leave comrades behind!" I approached closer with my fists close to my chest. I clutched Mikhail's wooden prayer rope that hung from my neck and gripped it tightly.

Soon I noticed a small painted vase by my foot. I picked it up and held it by my side, ready to weaponize it.

"Don't you dare!" Vasya cried out. He shouldered his rifle and was ready to fire but I was faster this time.

I threw the vase at him. Vasya dodged out of the way, and it smashed harmlessly against the shoddy brick wall. I got my opportunity to charge Vasya with my fists. First, I struggled with him to get the rifle out of his hands. I overpowered him with a swift knee to the stomach. He bowed over like a servant. One hand cradled where he had been struck, the other held out like he was surrendering.

"We're friends. Please." Vasya begged. I saw a tear stream down his filthy face and create a clear watermark that washed away the dirt.

I grabbed him by his uniform collar and pulled him up.

"I'm friends with no monster." I hissed.

I raised my fist to strike him for his sins, but Arseny tackled me to the ground.

I felt his body weight move me from my target and I saw where I was headed. I hit my head on a chair positioned to the side of me and I was pulled out of that world.

Then I smelt tobacco and alcohol.

Bern

I heard a loud thud when I tackled that demon to the ground. I gripped his rigid body tighter and tighter but there were occasional bouts of movement and struggle.

"Let him go, boy." Samara cried out. I looked over to him and saw him clutching his stomach where Sidorovich had driven his knee.

I let go of the monster, got up, and realised what I had done. He hit his head on the edge of the pew. There was the occasional groan and in between clutching his injured skull.

I ran quickly to Samara to check if he was ok. I wrapped my arm around his shoulder and tried to move him towards a seat.

"I'm a fine boy. Don't worry about me. Check on him." He wrapped his arm around me to give himself some stability from the pain.

Soon I heard the shifting of broken glass and crystal scratching across the stone floor. The demon was waking. They slowly rose with a groan, hoisting themselves up with the pew it just hit.

"Samara…" He groaned. "What happened? Why was I on the floor?"

Was this Sidorovich back or another trick?

"Fedor? Are you ok?" Samara gasped out.

"Yes, I'm fine. Just hit my head." He rubbed the back of his head. "Did I have an attack?"

'At last!' I thought. My priest is back.

He stood up, cradling his head, and gave me a squint.

"When did Grigori arrive?" He asked.

Samara raised his head and was noticeably shocked at what he heard.

"Fedor…" Samara paused to catch his breath. He clutched his abdomen in pain. He must have been hit hard. "Grigori's dead."

"No, he's not!" Sidorovich points towards me with his other hand, still cradling his skull. "He's there."

I was even more confused. This was a life I had never heard of from these two. I still held onto Samara, but I noticed his forehead wrinkled and his lip quivered. Soon he sighed.

"What year is it?" Samara asked shakenly.

"What kind of a question is that?" He replied.

"I'm a drunk, remember?" Samara gave a small chuckle before wincing in pain.

"1996" My jaw was on the shard-ridden floor as soon as I heard that. "Come Grigori, I want to speak to you about something."

Without a moment's hesitation, Samara inputted still holding onto his guts.

"Me and Grigori have a school project to finish for tomorrow."

"What project?" the Russian replied.

"Don't worry about it, we'll get it done." Samara turned his head to me and raised his eyebrows, signalling me to be his accomplice in the lie.

"Umm… yeah… we will." I stumbled with my words. I felt wrong. Dirty almost.

"Ok, fine." He shrugged. "I'll wait for you at home. I'll get a taxi back."

"Good, good."

"I'll see you tomorrow," Sidorovich replied. He left out the door still clutching his head and didn't dare to move until we heard the wood slam shut to confirm our safety. Me and Samara were still in shock.

"What the fuck was that?" I asked.

Samara turned to me instantly, his eyes locking with mine.

"He is not a bad man!" Samara wailed. "He is not a bad man; he is just haunted by his past."

"His past?! He attacked you!"

"I know!" Samara screamed out. "I have known that man for twenty-five years and trust me…"

Samara groaned in pain and clutched his stomach.

"He is a good man!"

Samara bowed over his knees.

"I'll be fine, go home boy. I'll clean this."

"But…"

In between grunts, he gave his voice a sort of weak authority.

"Go home!"

In a flash, he gripped my shoulder with his meaty hands and locked his wounded eyes with me.

"Please." He begged, his eyes welling up with tears.

I sat him down on one of the pews and then I got my phone out.

"Give me your number so I can check on you later."

"Fine." He gasped out.

He clumsily typed away each digit onto the screen and then gave a cursed groan as he finished.

"I'll call you tomorrow."

"Thank you."

I walked out of the church, trudging over shards of broken glass. As I walked halfway down the aisle, I heard Samara call out to me.

"Boy!" He grunted out. He was still facing the front of the church, where all I could see was the back of his balding head.

"You would have been an amazing son to him."

I didn't respond. I walked away and closed the splintered door behind me.

Michael
Six-ish at night

Bonfire night was in full swing. Me and my boy Jason were away with David and his younger brother in some distant field. It had the golden wheat collected from it ages ago when it was time, so it's just got people running around instead of crops. We heard the sparks and bangs of fireworks. Jason held a sparkler and waved it around, making different patterns and making drawings from the bright crackles he held in his hand.

David and I sat in deck chairs whilst David's wife played with Jason.

We had a long row of houses behind us and a small little church that felt like it was casting a bit of a shadow on us.

You had kids with parents and little stands giving out food, glowing toys, and sparkler sticks.

Some mad people even set up bonfires with a little straw doll of Guy Fawkes on top.

"How come your oldest isn't with us?" David asked. He sipped his beer can from his hand.

"He just does his own thing," I replied. "I can't look after him forever."

I took a bite out of me burger that cost more than it was worth. I started chewing the poor-quality meat and spoke with my mouth full.

"He's nearly a man."

I swallowed.

"He's got to learn to be there for himself."

Then I had Jason come up to me, running like he was excited for something.

"Dad, can I have some money to get more sparklers?" He yelped out.

I put me burger on my lap and sifted through me blue jeans pocket for me brown wallet.

I opened it and inside was the envelope that Bern gave me for last month's payment.

It was nearly empty with only two banknotes inside.

I grabbed a twenty-pound note and handed it to Jason.

114

"Here you are, just don't spend it all in one go." Eager thing that he was, he snatched it out of my hand and ran off.

"Thanks, Dad!" He called out with joy.

David turned to me as I was stuffing the wallet back into me blue baggy jeans, trying carefully not to have my food fall to the muddy ground.

"How do you keep being able to afford everything?" He asked.

"I work hard, that's how." I gave him a stern reply.

Whilst leaning back on the deck chair I saw Jason run towards the sparkler stand and spend everything he had on the sticks. I couldn't help but feel a little warm, even when I was stuffing food in my face.

Jason turned to me with his newly lit-up stick and was completely entranced until he saw something.

"Look! Its Bern." He called out. He was pointing behind me whilst holding the sparkler in his hands. His fascination with it was gone now.

I turned around and I saw him, just walking in his school uniform towards a bus station that was further down the street. I reached into my pocket, clutching my food with the other, and tried to call him.

I saw that lad dig into his pocket and pick up.

"Hello?"

"Look to your right lad."

He turned right and I waved him over with my burger in hand. He flicked off the phone and came towards us.

He slowly trudged to us with a slump.

"What's he doing here?" David asked. "I thought he wasn't coming."

"Doesn't matter. He's here now."

Bernard walked closer to us, but he looked scruffier than usual like the colour was drained from his face.

"What are you doing here mate?" I asked him.

"I just went to go see friends." He said meekly.

I saw dust and scuffs on his knees and one side of his clothes. It looked like he fell somewhere. So, these were either rough friends or he's lying to me.

"Alright." I took a bite into me burger and then turned to him with my mouth full. "Where you off to now then?"

115

"I'm going home."

"So, you're not staying?" David butted in.

"If the lad wants to go home, he'll go home." I dismissed.

I took the last bite of my food and then wiped my greasy hands on my jeans.

"I'll message you in a bit. Let me know when you get home." I said to him.

"Ok." He walked off in a slump and put his hands in his trouser pockets.

"Did you see the scuffs on him?" David inputted.

"Yeah, I did, and something is going on with him."

Bern
7:59pm

I took the long bus journey home and finally got into the ramshackle house. After seeing my dad, I was worried that he had found out what was happening. Who I was seeing, and if he was gonna stop me from seeing them. I sent him a couple of texts saying:

Got home ok.
Hope you guys have fun.

But now, I wasn't concerned with my family, I was just terrified of what had happened with everything. It felt like Sidorovich was about to kill his friend and Samara was trying to excuse his behaviour. Something wasn't adding up. It felt like Samara knew this was happening, so why did he stay there for so long with that potential killer?

I headed up to my room, but the house was freezing. The incomplete housework left it vulnerable to the elements.

I headed to my mattress and wrapped myself up in my blanket to try and keep warm.

I had nobody else to talk to about what happened. Until I saw my hand. Half covered in dust and dirt, covering the digits to my lifeline.

I patted away the dust, trying not to wipe away the number or the message on my hand.

116

I dial the digits, some of which have faded away from wear and sweat and time but are still recognizable enough to read.

Buzz tone... Buzz tone...

Nothing. Just a generic robotic voicemail.

I try again.

Buzz tone... Buzz tone...

"Hello?"

There she was. Although this felt too familiar. I heard EDM music which would belong in a nightclub blast through the phone.

"Hiya, It's Bern. Is this a good time?"

"Yeah, it's fine. Just give me one second." She called out, trying to speak over the music.

The music got quieter and quieter, but it was replaced by a creaking door and the occasional noise of traffic.

"Sorry about that, how have you been?"

"I've been alright." I courteously lied.

"That's good to hear!" She replied with joy.

"How are you?"

"I'm ok, I'm just out with people."

"Oh nice, anyone I know?" I was curious. I knew almost nobody, but I just wanted to find out more about this girl.

"Yeah, you could say that..." Her cheerful voice was gone in an instant.

This suddenly put me on high alert. Anyone I knew, I was not on good terms with, or I was terrified of them.

I heard the creak of a door and then the soft clinking of metal.

"Umm, excuse me, I'm on the phone." Lisa said with sass.

Then my evening got even worse.

"Sup nerd!"

"Hi Ava..."

There was silence for a moment. It was hostile, where either of us could rip into each other. She was faster on the draw, but she wasn't speaking to me.

"Why the fuck are you speaking to Bern?!" She screamed out.

Her voice was distant, but the phone was still on.

"I can speak to whoever I like!" She retorted.

The screaming match dragged on and on and all I could do was listen to them try to kill each other.

117

However, this time, I couldn't intervene in the slightest.
"You'd have a record on you if it wasn't for me," Ava screamed out. This perked up my ears like never before.
"I slapped you because you deserved it for all the horrible shit you were saying."
"Oi! Behave! I've got witnesses and I can still get you in trouble."
"Is that before or after you've got them drugged out of their minds?"
At this point, I was even more confused and wondering what the hell was going on.
"The phone's on by the way," Lisa said snarkily.
"Fuck!" Ava called out before disconnecting the life.
As soon as I heard the tone, I pulled it from the side of my face and saw the text from Father Dearest.

Glad to hear mate! If you got this month's payment, leave it by my paperwork for me.

After that disaster, I gave out a deep huff and puff, threw my phone to the side of my mattress wrapped myself up tighter in my blanket, and uttered out some final words in my cocoon before trying my best to get to sleep.
"What a fuckin' life huh?"

Sidorovich
09:30

I walked into the church but there was no sign of Samara. There was not even the faint smell of alcohol. The air was still and morbid, it felt like I was seeing the post-mortem of a corpse. I approached the altar and towards the office feeling a small headache. As I opened the door to the office, I heard the scratching of glass being dragged from underneath the door, leaving a noticeable mark across the cobbled stones.
I crouched down and tried freeing the shard from its captor but when I saw the design, it shocked me. It was one of Samara's crystal glasses, with the diamond cut pattern being too distinct miss and no bigger than my finger.

This would never happen. Samara loved that crystal ware as if it was his children that he never had.

I carried the piece in my broken hands and sought to set it down on his messy side of the office...

Although the spirit cabinet was still open. Something was awry. I rushed towards my metal box to see if all my belongings were there. One latch, then the lock... it was all there.

I heard the creak of the front door and quickly moved toward the main hall with the crystal shard in hand.

There he was. However, he was out of uniform. My fellow priest came in his casual clothes, but he was hunched over and clutching at his belly.

"Samara, are you ok?"

He gave me a horrified look. He stared at me like I was a stranger, a thing.

"Is everything okay?" I asked.

"Fedor, what year is it?" He asked, still grunting in pain.

"What-?"

"Answer the question!" He barked.

I was taken aback. I had never seen him like this.

"2019."

Samara gave a relieved sigh and grunted in pain as he walked closer to the front of the church.

"Fedor... we need to talk."

"What happened here, Samara?"

"You did." He grunted. He reached the front of the church and slammed down onto the pew. "You attacked me and the boy."

"What?"

How could I do this? I saw what pain and suffering I caused, and I felt vile.

"What happened?" I asked. I didn't dare to sit down. Not especially with the man I presumably injured.

"You had an attack... and then you attacked us."

I held the crystal shard and gripped it hard until I could feel its sting in my crippled hands and walked over to a glass window. I felt the deep purple wash over me and stared at the deity of my church. Even whilst on the cross, I felt his sunken head judge me for what I had done.

119

"There's one other thing…" Samara said. I pushed my skull against the artistic glass and clutched harder on the crystal. "I had to go the hospital last night… and they think that I have cancer."

Cancer… that word echoed around my head for eternity with only one conclusion. One more friend added to the pile of corpses I built.

I heard the creak of the old pew and tried to look for my pipe… but it was nowhere to be found. I frantically patted myself down and checked every pocket and hidden sleeve I had but it had left me.

I felt a meaty grip on my hand.

"You forgot this." Samara forced the pipe into my hand but outstretched his opposing hand.

"Give me the shard Fedor. I can see you hold it."

Caught in the act I turned to him and handed him the broken object of his obsession which showed the blood pooling in my palm and past the bandages.

Samara gave me this pained glare as soon as he took the shard out of my hands but didn't want to say anything.

"How did they find out?" I asked. I turned back to the window and readied my pipe; it tasted bitter and foul as soon as it encountered my lips.

"When you struck me, they found out the pain I was having was from tumours in my liver." He moved up towards me and stood by the window by my side as if we were on parade.

"They said, the strike might have caused it to rupture… they tried to help me as best they could but…"

I heard what he said but I didn't want to listen. I just ignited the pipe with this foul taste in my mouth and took a bitter smoke.

"I murdered you," I said to him.

"No Fedor, you didn't murder me…" He looked at the broken and bloodied shard in his hand.

"Your ghosts did."

I couldn't look him in the eye. I couldn't face my crime or my victim.

"How much time?"

"A year…"

"The treatment?"

"There is none…"

"What do you mean?"

Samara turned to me and pulled up his shirt to reveal a large and freshly stitched cut on his belly. Dear god… How could I do this?

"I mean there is none that would help." He said.

"What do you mean? I will pay for any—"

"Fedor stop!" Samara threw away the shard to some distant part of the church and forced me to turn. He bowed his head and placed both hands on my shoulders.

"I am going to die. There is no denying it. Priests aren't the richest people so I will not see you go into debt to give me a few extra painful months. But I do want to spend my last days with my friends and loved ones."

He pulled his head up to make eye contact with me. I couldn't look him in the eye, so he placed his unblooded hand on my cheek to force the action.

"This changes nothing. So do nothing."

"But we—"

His voice turned stern, like a mother chastising their child. "I don't want to hear it! So, help me God Fedor…" He moved the hand from my face and pointed his forefinger into my chest like a dagger. "I will make you sit on your hands until you find your balls again."

I understood the message if I didn't fully accept it.

But this is my friend and will obey his last wishes.

Soon a vibration echoed through the church. Hearing the small buzz caused Samara to back away and reach into his pockets. He pulled out an old silver flip phone from his pocket, so old you could barely see the original company logo from all the scratches and fading.

"Hello?"

Bern
88 days post exam

"How are you doing Samara?" I asked from my little prison of a room.

"I'm doing fine boy." He sounded better. Much better since last night. "I have someone here to talk to you here."
"Hello boy…" Sidorovich eked out.
"Hello Batushka."
"Samara told me everything that happened." I felt like an apology was coming but I just wasn't ready to hear it. Even if he did mean it. To me, I was still speaking to something else.
"I can't begin to tell you how sorry I am. I pray to God you can understand." He was desperately trying to repent for his actions, but it felt more and more sick as I spoke to him.
There was no speech between us, not a single word for an eternity until one thing came to me from last night. One thing he confused me for.

"Who's Grigori?"

I could feel the air being sucked into a vacuum. I may never speak to these people again, but I needed to know.
I heard a deep sigh from Sidorovich and then, something I didn't expect.
"He's my son… He's dead."
"What?"
I couldn't speak. I couldn't even move. Forming words was lost to me.
I stammered like a child learning to speak for the first time.
"What… What happened to him?"
"He's dead. He died in a war."
The more he spoke, the more I understood. My heartstrings weren't just tugged at, they stretched until they were on the brink of snapping.
"I'm so sorry boy. If you don't want to come back to the church, then I will not hold it against you."
I covered my face in disbelief, clutching the phone as if my grip was failing from the revelation. I sank further and further into Sidorovich's life, and I felt like this was too much for me.
I heard a puff from his pipe and then a great sigh.
"God bless you, boy. Take care of yourself."

It sounded almost too final for my liking. As if he was trying to protect me from getting hurt any further. The phone disconnected and clicked away.

I felt sick. I needed help, but I was terrified of coming anywhere near him.

"Bernard?" I heard a bear shout.

"Can you come down here?"

After hearing this request, I had to leave. I moved through the trashed house and towards the requestee but there was something off. The lounge my dad was in was messier and more destroyed than usual as if someone tore through it without relief or respite. The black leather couches that would usually accommodate my dad, were piled with junk and rubbish and papers were scattered around the wooden floor. I saw him there, in his black court uniform.

"Where's the money, Bernard?" In broad daylight, I saw the horrible side of my dad.

"Where's the money you're meant to pay?"

I shuddered and shook, and he raised his voice further and further, even being louder than my brother when screaming at his games.

"I asked you, where's the money?"

"It's not payday yet..." I quivered.

"Yes, it is!" He marched forward to me, with his black combat boots stomping on the surface they crashed over in his approach. He pressed his forehead against mine and I felt a heavy push. His eyes locked with mine as he tried to bully me over my finances.

"Where is it?!" He demanded.

"I don't have enough yet. I need to get to work."

"That's not good enough!" He screamed.

In an instant, I felt a push against my shoulders that threw me into the emerald and crimson tiled hallway and made the mosaic tiles the unfortunate victims to catch me.

"Give me what you have, then pay me back for the rest next month."

I was still on the floor when he barked his order.

I looked up from it and saw him hovering over me with malicious intent.

"You pushed me."

"I didn't push you; you fell." He blustered out.

He moved away from my broken state and moved back towards the lounge to dig out his paperwork. I could hear the shifting of papers and crashing of clutter hit the wood floor riddled with the occasional curse and grumble about my incompetence.

I picked myself up off the floor but not before I could hear the marching again. He stood in front of me like a drill instructor, ready to chastise me for the slightest infraction.

"I'm going to work. When I come back, I want that money, on that couch." He points behind him whilst locking his gaze with me.

He pushed past me and aggressively threw open the front door, he gave me a filthy look of disappointment before slamming the door with the same force.

After that, I slumped down on the cold tile floor and sat there until the cold would kill me and take me away from what just happened.

Then I heard it.

"Bernard, could you make me breakfast?"

That was the breaking point. I began violently sobbing on the dual-coloured floor tiles, but nobody could hear me. Nobody cared, they just cared about what I could be used for.

Ava
Eight in the morning

Today is my birthday, I turn eighteen and I feel like my own adult. If still a little like a teenager. I honestly didn't think I'd make it this far. I felt like I would die before I became an adult. I got up extra early today, I wanted to feel something. I wanted to get Bernard back... Even after those priests. He'd be easy to get. I still wanted more out of life. I wanted more and I will get it today. I wanted to feel like I was in a ballroom dancing to my prince, even if he was a little bit of a pauper. My makeup was stunning. My hair, spectacular! My sex appeal, perfect!

If I can't get him, then the boy is blind. I checked my black and white spiked bag to make sure I had everything.

- Books
- Phone
- Purse
- Vodka

We're ready to go! I hope on the bus and the same driver with the Oakley glasses and long white beard took me aboard.
He stared at me for a while, probably to admire my beauty.
"You look... Umm... Better." He stammered. Oh my god, I look perfect! If I'm stunning the driver who saw me in a state, then I must be. Here we go world!
"Thanks." I gleefully said to him. I gave him the exact change and skipped towards the back of the bus to let my new audience of kids from my school gawk at my beauty. Each thud of my platformed boots crashed onto the floor to draw further attention to me. I slammed my joy-filled body onto the seat of the bus and gave off a cheery smile with my perfect teeth. I did a small dance with my arms and torso as soon as the driver took us away. I'm going to get that boy and he will be mine forever!

Bern
8:34am
91 days post exam

I finally arrived back at school with a feeling of inferiority that was unshakeable and absolute. The people I thought I could rely on had all turned on me except for my routine.
A thing.
Not warm like flesh and blood, but a cold social construct.
I walked closer to the front of the school and wanted to get out of the cold as fast as I could. Hordes of students conglomerated and dissipated like tides to an ocean, allowing me to be swallowed by the torrent.
Currents of adolescent teens carried me up the stairs and towards the library.
Same bible and, the same red cover I would order to borrow.
Up the stairs and take the first left. Closer to my one place of solace, the classroom with the black office chair.
Further down the hallway turn right into the room.

125

Nobody was there. Finally, peace.

I sat down and leaned back on the chair. I heard the creak of the cheap plastic and the feeling of heavy wear which gave me some small comfort. I let myself drift away. No more money issues, no more crazy girlfriends, no more problems. Finally, tranquillity and a smile on my face.

I'd realise that I would be eating my words very quickly.
I was suddenly roused by the sounds of clinking and clanking which would reverberate through the halls as if the sounds of chains were being dragged along, almost like an army of slaves was approaching in shackles.
Instead, it was something far more horrific.
Clink, clank went its platform boots. Covered in studs and chains. Its makeup and hair are even more extreme to the point where I don't know how the school allowed this creature to walk through the doors. Their eye-wing makeup looked so large that they looked like they would fly away. The skin on its face was painted to a bone white. Its brown hair was teased to mirror famous post-punk singers from the eighties. All clashing together with the uniform they wore.
"Watcha doing stranger?" Said the witch.
My heart rate accelerated and my will to live evaporated.
"Leave me be Ava." I said with disgust.
"That's no way to treat your girlfriend." She pouted.
What on God's earth was she talking about? I thought it was crystal clear that we were broken up.
"You're not my girlfriend."
"Oh yes, I am!" She marched to me with her out-of-school regulation boots. She looked out of proportion like she had balloons for feet but everything else was equivalent to a grapevine.
"And you're gonna—"
"Fuck off." I hissed out. I had enough, I was tired and angry, and this creature dared to violate my peaceful sanctum.
It, however, was stunned and confused. She sat on a random desk, bowed down, and did her best to smudge her gothic makeup.
"I thought that you loved me though."

126

"I don't." That was a lie, I still did but I was too hurt to admit it. At this point, I wanted to hurt her as much as she hurt me.

As soon as I said that the clicking of heels hitting the floor could be heard echoing through the hallway.

"I want you to leave me alone."

"But… I missed having you stay round my house. I wanted to have you there again." She said, with her crocodile tears streaming down.

"Find a prostitute if you're lonely."

I opened the red bible and carried on with where I left it.

Hebrews 13:16.

"But I love you Bern and I want something more with you!"

I continued down the page and carried on reading.

"So go get laid, you might become a better person."

As soon as I said that I heard what sounded like Lisa cackle the door frame but didn't walk into the classroom.

"Come out girl," I said sternly. These words however were not my own. This was something else possessing me to say such things.

She stepped forward and exposed herself, wearing her typical red lipstick, but this time she curled her porcelain white hair.

"You betrayed me," I said whilst turning the page.

"What do you mean?" Lisa retorted.

"It means what it means. You lied to me. You said you fell out with Ava and yet here you are with them.

"I was walking past." She petulantly bellowed.

"It doesn't matter if you was or wasn't, you were there with her the other night and I just feel I can't be around you..." I pointed at Ava. "If you're with that."

Ava threw herself up from the table and howled out like a banshee "What do you mean by 'that'?"

No response was worth it. My peace was broken. I slammed the bible shut, stood up from my little sanctuary, and with a bible in hand, I walked past Ava without batting an eye. I approached her accomplice and imparted some wise words to her. Wise words that she needed to hear before it was too late.

127

"If you're going to keep hanging around with that then she will drag you down with her." I gave her one final look in her eyes which looked more like an ashy char than a blazing fire. "Leave her. Kick the habit." She didn't react. She stood there like a deer in the headlights trying to process what I was saying.

I walked past her and left them to their troubles. I will not accept more pain than was needed.

I strolled down the hallway and left those two at it. It took five seconds to go by before their arguing restarted. Five seconds for this so-called 'friendship' to crumble again, and this poor girl was imprisoned by it.

Life is Cheap

Bern
9:32am
125 days post exam

The freezing chill of winter bit hard on our vulnerable bodies. It felt like nothing could protect us from the icy winds or the fast-escaping heat of the half-finished house. Most of the residents had wrapped up in thick coats or blankets to protect themselves against the creeping cold. My old bright red coat had lost its vibrancy over the years of abuse it suffered. I had it since I was fourteen, I grew out of it, but I still had a use for it, even though it was too tight on me, I needed something to protect me from the cold.

"Bernard! Payday!" Called my lord.

I moved towards the lounge, moving past my brother's unknown cursing and towards where he sat on his throne and saw him there with his feast, surrounded by his loyal subjects composed of peasantry takeaway cartons and lordly glass bottles.

I offered him his damn money when I was still covered in grease from the night before. I walked through the lounge with my bare feet, feeling what heat there was to escape through the gaps of the wood floor. His servants surrounded him in preparation for their consumptive master to receive tribute.

"Is this everything?" Dad asked.

He reached out his right arm and still sat down on the black leather sofa. He was clothed in early 2000s mainstream fashion that left him looking like a trend chaser who was almost twenty years behind. The lime green zip hoodie barely hid a printed shirt. This was crowned by boot cut jeans which were showing their age from the by gone time he bought them.

"Yeah, it is." I could still feel the sweat on my brow and hear the cursive insults given by my co-workers behind the back of customers that slowly irritated them.

"Even what you owe me from last month?" Dad raised his eyebrows to confirm the payment. Even out of uniform, it felt like he was still on the job as a debt collector.

129

"Especially what I owe from last month." It took everything I had and even did some overtime to get it all in.

"Where's the interest?" My stomach sank, brow sweated.

"Interest?" I hesitantly asked.

He cracked out a smile and patted me on the back from the comfort of his black leather throne.

"Don't worry, I'm joking."

I slumped my head to the floor and let my posture follow.

"...ok." I eked out.

I walked away and disappeared. I had nothing again. I was penniless and devoid of any pleasures of life except what Dad had deemed fun.

No money to go out, nothing to do, only work.

It meant I was trapped in never never-ending tide of exhaustion and work.

"Bernard could you—"

"No!" I screeched out towards my brother from across the house.

I had enough! I was tired, I was coming home every day in grease and missing school just to keep up with the bills.

Just to keep up with this brick wall I was slamming my head into.

"Oi!" His lordship called out. "Don't talk to your brother that way."

Never had I seen him move faster from the seat than just now.

"How can you speak to him like that?" He bellowed at me with ferocity to match his indentured victims.

"I've been working for a month straight!" My voice echoed through the hallways, giving light to my issues. "Other people my age don't have to do this!"

"You're not other people!"

"You're right I'm not, I'm better for all the shit I've had to endure!"

"Don't you fucking swear in front of your brother!"

"You just did it."

His face lit up red. He was furious.

"Fuck off to your room! NOW!" He directed me upstairs, through the disintegrating wooden steps of the house.

"What room? All I have is a mattress and a wardrobe!"

"Oh god! You're worse than your mum!"

"At least she treated me better when she was around!"
The house was silent. Not even the howls of my brother could be heard.
Dad's face was racked with shock and fury.
"To your room now!"
For the first time I disobeyed. For the first time, instead of going to my room, I left the front door with my phone in my pocket.
"You get back here now!" He screamed at me as I left the door.
I didn't respond, I just kept walking and marched my way toward the bus stop, even though I was headed to the lair of the man who threatened my life… he was still someone I could talk to.

Ava
Half ten-ish in the morning

How does time fly? How do moments shift? What does the world mean?
These are questions I asked when laid down on the concrete floors of that derelict shop. I was wrapped up more in my thick Victorian-themed coat which by now had the back of it covered in dust and leftover ash of whatever the hell we smoked.
"Your turn." I had Nova pass me the poorly wrapped-up joint he was smoking, and I could see it practically leaking the product inside the flimsy burning paper.
I rose from my weed-induced contemplation like a corpse from a grave. Like I was his Queen Victoria to Prince Albert.
"Give me it!" I snatched the shoddily made blunt out of his hand and put it to my lips. I took a deep puff of the homemade death stick, but something felt off about it and I didn't realise it till it was too late.
"Did you pay for that?" Another member of the lot said, rolling around on his roller skates and poorly maintained mall goth outfit.
Oh no…
Nova *NEVER* gives anything out for free.
When my rotted brain had put the pieces together, I coughed out the smoke and saw it had turned thick grey with a tinge of amber reflecting from the firepit light.
"What's in this?" I coughed out to him.

"Weed." He gave a simple shrug and a short chuckle that left his trashy fringe covering half his face, only exposing his corrosive smile.

"What did you do?!" I stood up from my little slab on the floor with bits of ash and dirt clinging desperately to my coat and loomed over this idiot.

"Nothing... I..."

There was a short pause, this poisoner hung his head over his black Adidas tracksuit hid and his face from me.

"I might have put half a pill in it..."

My heart stopped. I wanted to bawl out crying but I felt like a deer in the drug-fuelled headlights.

"What did you say?" called out Partridge.

Partridge or party as we called them, wore nothing but Lolita clothes in pastel colours and badly done stick-and-poke tattoos that showed through her neon pink tight that belonged in a K-pop music video.

"That's not good!" She called out. The twenty-seven-year-old marched over in her white platform boots that had silvered cat skulls on them.

"Thank you!" I called out to my friend.

"You gotta pay for that shit Ava!"

"What...?"

"You gotta pay for that stuff, honey!"

"But—"

"But nothing babes. If he's given you a pill, you gotta pay him for it."

"Who didn't pay?" The roller-skating mall goth intervened.

"He spiked me, Greg!" I screamed uselessly at him.

Greg was the only other person my age, but he looked forty from his poor skin and his awful appearance. He dragged around his leather trench coat that was riddled with holes, chipping leather, and fraying threads.

He rolled his barely functioning roller skates towards us whilst the other five or six members did their own thing in their section of the shop.

"What the fuck happened?" Greg petulantly screamed out.

"She asked for a pill, and I gave her one." Nova said. He didn't bother lifting his head, he just kept his face buried in the floor whilst sitting upright.

"Well..." The stoner paused. "You've got to pay for that then."

Greg shrugged.

"Right?" Party affirmed.

"I didn't—"

"Doesn't matter!" Party hissed. "Make it up in some way!"

"But!"

They didn't stop to listen to me, Party re-joined the bigger group whilst Greg went back to skating around clumsily."

I stood there dumbfounded and paralyzed. I grabbed my scalp to try and process it further.

"I can think of a few ways you can pay me back." He didn't even look me in the eye, that filthy scum! He just drugged me and expected me to pay him back. Instead, I looked at the firepit and what I saw was something else.

Switch

I just saw my vision blur and colours shift. The flames danced like licking tongues, perpetually changing their hue and dancing to a melody that I couldn't hear. The more I stared, the more I wanted to become its partner and listen to its silent bird song. It was the most beautiful thing I had seen ever. Finally... some colour.

I took my hand away and looked at the clump of dark brunette hair that was left in my hand and then I realized the true cost. It felt like the price for this beauty was my life.

My voice was shaken and my understanding of what was happening in my world burned away like the firepit.

"What do you have in mind?"

Sidorovich
11:21

"Fedor! Fedor!" The voice called out.

I heard the words, but they felt like whispers in the night, I was too absorbed in my ritual to respond. The flesh ached, the

133

cleaning wipes stung, and the cursing from my tar-blackened mouth never stopped. Even after many decades of dealing with the maintenance of my past mistakes, it still hurt endlessly.

I was caught in my hidden shame; the door blew open and my dead friend walked in on me. "Fedor, we have a guest!" He blustered in when I was finishing wrapping my second arm.

"Oh... I'm sorry." Samara's excitement relented when he saw what I was doing.

"Don't! It's OK." I continued to sit on my chair and finally pin-tied the bandages to my elbows to cover myself for the guest. "Are you ok?"

"I'm fine, who is here?" I grabbed my pipe from the desk and filled it with tobacco.

"Batushka?"

Hearing that word wrenched the whispers into loud screaming forcing my ears to awaken, my mind to race and my mouth to shut.

Oh, my lord... was this the boy? Did he come back?

"Are you here?"

I wasted no time, neither did I hesitate. I sprinted as fast as my old legs could allow and blew past Samara like a northern wind with a pipe in hand and entered the main hall.

"Boy!" I called out to him in rejoice.

I ran to him and hugged him without a second thought in my mind.

"I'm sorry my boy! I'm sorry for everything I've done." I felt like I was giving him a death grip and was about to break his spine, but I didn't care. I was just happy to see him. Soon I felt his arms wrap weakly around me and... Soon I felt a lone tear crawl across my face.

"Are you ok?" He asked still wrapped in my arms.

As soon as I heard that I let him go out of my trap and placed one of my broken hands on his shoulders.

"I'm ok boy, I'm just glad to see you return."

He was hesitant. I could tell he still harboured some fear of me.

"Can I talk to you?" The boy asked meekly.

"Of course."

He led me towards one of the middle pews that was closest to us and sat us down on the well-maintained mahogany. As I looked

to light my pipe, I saw that most of the pre-set tobacco had
spilled out, forcing me to expend more for my excitement. I
pulled out more of my Turkish tobacco and began to set it in the
pipe.

"I…" The boy gasped out. He was as shy as we first met him as
he slumped his posture over his knees.

"I want to talk about Grigori."

Grigori… my boy. My precious child. My guard was up when I
heard this, and my hands trembled from my failure in their newly
cradled bandages.

"What about him?"

"You got me confused with him when you…"

"When I attacked you… I know." I bowed my head in shame and
silence. This was unacceptable for a man of my power to be
assaulting friends and young men.

I took a deep inhale from the accursed wood that was in my
hands and temporarily calmed my nerves.

"He died in a war."

"Which one?"

"The second Chechen war."

"I never heard of it."

"Good, it means my son did his job…"

That sounded bitter, almost patriotic… But that was not the
person I was. I couldn't forgive the Union for its crimes, or the
old men who sent my son to their death.

There was a moment of peace in the church. An uncanny calm
before the storm.

"What did he do?"

"What?"

"In the war I mean, what did he do in it?"

My bandages itched; my face vacant. I felt the spectre of what
was left of a man long before coming back to life through my
ghostly visage when I ran through all the memories in my head.

"He was a tank operator in a T-80."

"I bet you must have been proud of him." The boy said meekly.

I should have been, but I was scared for him. What father
wouldn't be? I saw the effects of war on my own damn arms,
and I couldn't see him come back to me in a box.

"I was..." I took another puff from my pipe but there was something that yearned at me a long time. A burning question that lingered in my mind since I met him.

"What are your mother and father like?" I passed a small glance at him and saw something that looked like shame. He played with his hands until he interlocked his fingers.

"My mum left years ago when I was little..." His head bowed "And my dad, he's ok. He's just trying his best."

Hearing this, I tried my best to ignore the comment about the mother. That was none of my business. The father on the other hand piqued my interest. This boy was living a hard life and I wanted to know there was at least someone looking out for him.

"Trying his best?" I said inquisitively. "That doesn't sound like he's doing good."

"He's just..."

"Do you want to talk to Samara?"

"I'm ok. I can talk." He stopped gripping his hands and started to relax back into the pew. Then he asked me a question that would forever haunt me.

"Can I have some of your pipe?"

"Why?"

"Because I feel I want to know why you smoke that stuff."

That question span around my head for too long. It took me getting into hell to start smoking, so I can only imagine whatever this boy is feeling.

"Do you know how to? You inhale into your mouth, not your lungs."

"Yeah, I watched you do it enough."

I hesitantly handed him the pipe and watched him press the decrepit wood against his lips. He took a small puff and exhaled as if I would. Then leaned back into the pew and presented a smile on his face.

"Way better than that cigarette." He spoke.

What have I done Olega? Have I raised another misguided son?

The boy passed the pipe back to me and I felt like I had just poisoned him.

Soon Samara made his presence known in the hall through a bone-chilling creak from the office door with a tumbler in hand.

I tried to give him a stern look, but I was too distracted by what the boy had just done.

He took a small sip of his ancient alcohol and clutched his stomach whilst doing so. He did it so dramatically that he keeled over like an injured horse waiting to be shot. Even the boy saw.

"What's wrong Samara?"

"Don't worry about me boy, I'll be ok." He waved his hand in front of his face as if he was dismissing any anguish or worries that would come to him.

"You don't look ok." The boy said. He leapt up off his seat and came closer to Samara to check on the old drunk.

As the boy walked closer toward him, I followed, and Samara limped closer towards the front pew.

Soon, the creak of the mahogany would make itself heard, accompanied by a guttural moan from the Greek's mouth.

"What's wrong?" The boy said.

"I'm dying."

The boy was distraught, but I was terrified. I was scared that Samara would drive the boy away with what he was about to say. The boy, however, didn't say a thing. He just stood there like a soldier on a battlefield. Waiting. Observing. Calculating his next move.

"How come?" There was no emotion left. He spoke like me. He spoke like someone who lived through hell.

"I got cancer." Now the emotions finally revealed themselves. Samara keeled over to the side of the pew and exposed the underside of his belly like a turtle in a robe.

The boy despaired quietly, strongly, and proudly. I, however, stood there like a coward. I couldn't meet the boy I was influencing or the friend I helped to kill.

The boy sat down next to Samara's balding scalp and held his right shoulder.

"How did they find out?"

Samara let off a light chuckle before erupting in a painful groan.

"I got mugged and the idiots who struck me hit a tumour."

Samara gave me a look and winked at me. I was paralyzed and I felt sick to my stomach. He knows I did and even then, he helped me.

"Mhm," The boy acknowledged.

137

He knew. He stared at me with his blue eyes that pierced my tainted soul. His eyes narrowed like a predator waiting to pounce and held his gaze.
There he was, even for a small second.

Grigori…
Like his image flashed before me.
The boy finally broke his gaze and focused on his patient.
"Is there anything I can do to help?" The boy said.
"You can grab a dying man a bottle from his cabinet."
"Cabinet?"
Samara without any response, forced the key to his cabinet into the boy's hands.
"Spirit cabinet boy! Bring me the bright green bottle. From the office."
Samara gave his instructions and pointed towards the aged door with the twisted iron ring for a handle. The boy stormed off towards the door and I took my chance to sit beside my friend.
"You didn't need to do that." I said to him.
"Don't worry. I'm not throwing you under the bus."

Michael
Twelve-ish

I finally gave myself the chance to get back to work. Bern threw that money in me face and why should he? He's paying to live here as well. I sat in me company car gripping me steering wheel and it still roamed around me head.
Was I the bad guy?
I kept staring forward into the street and I saw people living their lives without a care. Kids playing in the frozen streets. People walk around in thick coats and wool accessories to try and keep themselves warm.
Then I saw something that caught me eye. A dad with his little girl. He wore standard stuff: blue jeans, boots, and a brown coat. His little girl though was dressed all in pink with a fuzzy hat and earmuffs. She was playing with him and kept tugging against his coat. The snow fell and covered them up like a blizzard which made them too hard to see. They just faded away.

138

I heard a knock on me car door and leaned over to the opposite
side of the car to let someone in.

"Got your coffee, Mike."

"Cheers for that David."

He bent down to fit into the car and brought our hot drinks to
help keep us warm during the winter.

"You alright?" David asked.

"Yeah mate, I'm fine." I took my hands off the steering wheel
and leaned back into me car seat. "It's just Bern gave me a bit of
grief this morning."

David handed me the coffee and took a sip of his.

"What happened?"

"Just a falling out is all."

"Oh…" That was all he could say for the time being. He sat there
just figuring out what to say next but all he came out with was,
"Do you want to talk about it?"

"No mate, I don't think I do. Let's just get back to work alright?"

"Alright mate, Let's wrap up soon." He said eagerly. "I've got a
taekwondo tournament to go to tonight."

I sat up, put me drink in the cup holder, and switched on the car.

"Going to try to get another one in the trophy cabinet?"

"Oh yeah!" He exclaimed.

"It'll look great in the office. Might make the boss jealous."

He gave me a cheeky smile and gave me a tap on the shoulder to
signal me to go back to work.

Ava
Seven-ish at night

Switch

"Where are you taking me?" I said to Nova.

"You'll like it. Don't worry."

He took me into the frosted-over street. The frost glistened the
dying streetlights and illuminated the falling snow around us that
covered the remnants of leafless bushes and weathered brick
plant pots.

I didn't like this. I was on my own with him. We walked in the high street but because nobody dared to get in the way of Mother Nature, we were by ourselves, freezing in the bitter winter.

The snow fell but it wasn't as colourful as the flames, but it left a vacancy, a void in the world.

The controlled euphoria was gone. The beautiful had visions left and all that was remaining was the miserable come down. The snow turned umbral; it looked as if it was seeing inverted colours with small halos reflecting off each falling flake.

"Where are you taking me?" I said to Nova.

"Somewhere." He grinned. He paraded around in his fleece which looked too thin to keep him comfortable. "You'll like it."

"But what's happening?"

"Don't worry, just trust me. Do you want another pill?"

I couldn't think, I couldn't even remember where the last few hours of my life went. I was trapped in this hell where I could barely tell what was going on; the only way to get rid of the pain was through more.

"Please…" I begged him. "Show me the colours again!"

He pulled out a little plastic clingfilm bag and retrieved another pill. Another one with a cross on it.

"You're getting in a bit of debt with me." With a smirk on his face.

"I don't care. Give me the pill!"

I took the pill and swallowed it dry.

I looked back at him and his filthy smile.

What have I done?

"What do I owe you?"

"A game." He said coyly.

"What kind?" We hunkered down in an alleyway that was covered by an arch which stank of the last person sleeping there and the souvenir they left to mark their spot.

"Truth or dare." He stuck his hand out to reveal three digits, each of those capped with a different colour of chipping nail varnish. "We'll get three turns each."

This was some strange behaviour; I've never seen him play these games before.

I nodded my hood-covered head in compliance.

"You go first." He spoke.

140

I took my time to think, desperately trying to understand this person better but I felt the drugs hit me. The colours came back, and the joy returned.

"Truth." My balance was starting to fail me, and I felt like I was almost drunk on emotions. "Who are you?" I asked clumsily.

"Nova! My turn." He growled.

"But—"

"My turn!" He snapped at me. "Truth. Do you know how much you owe me?"

He hovered over me menacingly. I could smell the stink radiating from his clothes like it was the one thing grounding me to reality, but I was too far gone to recognise what was going on and what he was trying to do.

"I don't know." I drooled out. I was too far gone to even respond coherently.

"Too much."

"My turn." I giggled.

"What is…" I pointed my finger to my chin and looked up at the arch thinking I was cute.

"Your favourite colour?"

"Black." He chided. "Truth. How are you going to pay me back?"

He sparkled. He glistened even. I felt the drug take hold which drove for control of my thoughts and actions.

"I don't know." I leaned back on the wall and felt the thin ice behind me crunch. I was still thinking I was the gorgeous manic pixie dream girl, but I was in my own euphoric world.

"Truth!" I exclaimed. "Why did you bring me here?" I straightened my elbows, interlocked my fingers, and flirtatiously pouted up to his face whilst rotating my upper body left and right.

"For you to pay me back."

He leaned forward and pressed his hands on the wall, his elbows trapping me in a makeshift cage of flesh and odour.

I smiled and looked at one of his hands. I saw the damage I caused, forcing my grin into a sudden wave of terror.

"Dare."

Switch

141

The marks I left in his hands seeped open and poured out smoke and white flames as if I revealed something that hid in the skin of a questionable man. The drugs allowed me a moment of clarity or at least a moment of horror. The phosphoric white fire spread from the little crescent-shaped nail marks and enveloped his hand as I blinked. My eyes followed the monochrome flames as spread across his body. They took his hand, then his arm, then finally surrounding his face and body with his bowl cut turning into nothing but erupting smoke that was as black as pitch and suffocated the whole alleyway with its viscosity.

"Kiss me."

"NO!" I screamed out. "Get off me!"

I felt his burning hand grip onto my thigh as he tried to force his lips onto me.

"Help! He's burning me!" I called out uselessly.

The smoke smelt like burning ammonia and his clasped fingers felt like they belonged to another world. Each touch of the phosphor felt like it left singe marks or burn scars.

"Somebody!"

My voice was drowned out by the winds and the arctic environment. I couldn't hear anything but this thing's cursed hands on my legs and my hips. Its scorched lips ran down my neck and closer towards my collarbone.

The flames enveloping me whispered through the smoke and told me, "You don't expect to give me grief and get away with it."

It unzipped my coat and left my uniform exposed to the elements. I heard crunching the sound of footsteps in between the nausea-inducing grunts and groans.

One last attempt.

"Help me!" My voice quivered and my body went limp. I died there. I died there and there was nothing I could do to fight it off.

"Oi! Get off them!"

I heard someone shout out in the dark.

The burning man released his grip on me, rising from his dominant position to face his opponent. I looked to my left and cradled myself in my arms to protect myself from what occurred.

A blazing myriad of colours blazed bigger and brighter than the monochromatic spark in front of me. The interloper only showed the dark silhouette of a man bigger and stronger than whatever assaulted me.

Surrender

I slid back onto snow that was freshly trampled by my dance with the devil and let my consciousness slip from me. Colours, darkness, heat, or cold, all escaped me as I fell from that world and left my body to the whims of the victor.

Bern
8:03pm

My room was solitary and freezing from the lack of heating in the house. I stayed in my thickest clothes and cowered under my blanket to provide some comfort against the cold.
Death closed in on the world to take its warm-blooded victims.
"Bernard!" I heard a call from across the house. "Bernard!"
I rose from my shelter and moved towards the lightless unknown. The silent hallways exhaled their glacial breath.
"Bernard!" The voice reverberated through this dying building. Each creak of my footstep felt like I was walking on dead arboreous flesh, haunting the place with frightening death moans through its occasional creeks. Soon I saw it's still beating heart. The light coming from the lounge room. I stepped forward and saw its occupier.
"There you are!" Dad was spasming and frantic. His eyes widened and his voice petrified. "We're going hospital now!"
"What?" I was confused, cold, and not in the mood.
"Get Jason, we're leaving in a minute."
He stormed out of the room, car keys in hand and left out the front door. I was given my task to follow, and I had to do it begrudgingly. I didn't know why he was acting so frantic; he bolted and left me there to go get his son.
I roamed the halls of this decrepit patchwork house and looked for my brother. I could hear him screaming and shouting at his games once again. I approached the door which only emitted a

143

slight glow underneath the door. I opened it and suddenly the noise and the smell of sweat and despair smothered the last remaining clean oxygen. I entered and saw him playing on his brand-new black frame desk cradling the most modern and advanced computer of the time. The room was lush with electric-guzzling lights which shone like moonbeams from a 1970s disco ball. His bed occupied red satin and thick furs which looked like it offered more warmth than even my old red coat. The walls, even though being illuminated with a culdoscope of hues and flashes, you could see the freshly painted walls which looked almost like they were store-bought.

My little brother sat there with thick headphones, shooting virtual enemies, and screaming at his pretend squad mates for their ineptitude.

Was I funding all this?

Why am I living in poverty whilst he lives in luxury?

"We're leaving," I said to him, he continued to hurl abuse and insults towards these distant people.

I repeat myself and still no reply. I move closer to him and tap him on the shoulder to get his attention. Finally! A response.

He turns his head towards me and rests his headphones on his neck. His bloodshot eyes opened wide like a goldfish with his mouth following in suit.

"We're going hospital."

"Why?"

"Dad says we have to."

He wasted no time and turned off his computer, if in some measure of dissatisfaction. He raced downstairs, showing his idleness had not affected his ability to move. However, he left all the lights and gizmos running.

"Oh my god, am I paying for all this?"

I looked around in pure awe to find that my money looked to be going up in smoke to fund this child and his opulence.

I started to turn off all the lights and anything that was connected to a wall socket as fast as I could before moving downstairs and outside. I locked the door behind me and walked towards my dad's parked work car with my brother already in the backseat.

"Took your time." My dad chastised.

"I had to turn everything off." I replied, still walking to the car.

Jason kicked up a fuss when he heard this. His arms crossed whilst his legs were actively kicking the chair in front of him. "Stop it!" Dad yelled at him. He turned his attention to me now, "Get in!"

I struggled to open the car door which had been glazed over with frost and entered the car.

The engine flicked on and set us on our way to whatever was so urgent.

8:39pm

The drive was uncomfortable, to say the least. Nothing was worth talking about. Each question as to why we were going there was deflected or shot down.

Eventually, we arrived in the hospital parking lot and left that box on wheels.

"Come on! Come on!" Dad hurried us through to the entrance of the hospital with utmost haste. The sterile nature of it was a welcome start. Almost as clean as the church.

Dad rushed us to the receptionist who was ready to go home and pressed the badge of Her Majesty's courts against the glass window.

"Where is Ward Nine?" He demanded.

Her gaping middle-aged expression was so focused on the badge, she forgot how to form words.

"I...I..." This poor woman stammered.

"Where?!" He raised his voice and snapped this woman out of her trance.

"Take the left, then follow the signs." She whimpered.

"Come on boys!"

The family broke into a run with the receptionist gawking at us as we sped away.

The grey and white corridors blended as we followed the only guide we had in that maze.

"Keep up!"

We found the deep ocean blue signs and finally found ward nine. We passed under the metallic archway and under the eight-by-eight sign showing we were in the right location.

The ward was a straight and narrow corridor with most of the cubicles being covered by yellow and blue patterned curtains to protect the patient's dignity.

"David!" He bellowed out. "David, where are you?"

The roaming night staff were both appalled and taken aback by this display. Even though some were wearing surgical masks, you could sense the emotions they hid. Soon a singular hand emerged from one of the curtains, over by the far-left side.

There was no time wasted, we ran and moved closer toward the singular exposed limb, pushing past the over-exhausted staff that worked tirelessly for their patients.

"In here mate!" The limb hollered at us. It retracted as we drew closer to lure us into its den.

Dad wasted no time in ripping the polyester curtain from side to side and exposing this pitiful scene.

Ava…

She was barely recognizable. I just made out who it was by her black and white spiked bag that sat next to her bed frame.

She looked like she belonged in a morgue. Her hair was patchy, her skin was pale and covered in pimples, and dark circles surrounded her eyes. She was hooked up to a ventilator. Her body was covered in a white and sky-blue patient gown but even the smallest gown they offered looked like a tarp over her almost skeletal corpse. It looked like this life support was barely keeping her alive.

David sat on a green plastic chair with a bruise on his left cheek and craned his spine in brooding. His hands interlocked and his forearms rested on his blue jeans.

"Fucking hell mate, you, ok?" Dad blurted out.

"Yeah, mate…" David responded, he leaned back into the uncomfortable chair and gave a wince. "No thanks to the fucker who attacked this poor girl."

"Is that a—" David waved off the sentence before it could be finished.

"Nah mate, from the tournament." He pulled out a silver medal from his front jeans pocket. "Got second." He proudly stated.

I approached the side of the bed, the beeping of the heart monitor acting as my only way to tell that this girl wasn't lifeless.

"I know her." I said solemnly. "She was my girlfriend."

The room went silent for a while where only the heart monitor could be heard with each beep lasting an eternity.

"I didn't know you had a girlfriend." Dad responded. He showed his shock at the news when his forehead retreated into his hairline.

I didn't move, I just kept looking at what was left of the girl I loved. "We dated for six or seven months before…"

"Before this happened." David chimed in. "Did you know she took drugs?"

I swivelled my head like a spinner and thought my ears were deceiving me.

"By that look, that's a no." David identified. His gimlet eyes saw through me and recognised the situation. "I won't lie to you lad, they found ecstasy and weed in her system."

Is this what happened after I left? Did she turn into a junkie after our breakup?

I tried to place my trembling hand on her weak and dying brown hair. The horror of seeing her like this was too much. When my palm caressed her hair, it felt like straw. Rough and course. I stroked what was left of her hair and as soon as my hand left her scalp, it captured a few strands along with it.

I tried to balance myself against the bed rail to avoid collapsing in shock. "Where did you find her?" I asked desperately.

"Some fucking yob was trying to have his way with her. He ran as soon as he saw me, but I couldn't get a good look at him." David stood up and placed his hand on my shoulder. "We'll get through this mate."

I looked towards my dad, and I saw him just standing there with my brother, looking less than amused. He crossed his arms and scowled at me whilst Jason was tugging at his trousers for them to go home.

"We'll be heading home if you don't need us." Dad scolded. David took his hand off my shoulder and held to palm of his hand to make him stop.

"Hang on Mike," David said.

"He's got this mate; I've got a little lad who's got school tomorrow." Dad gave an eye roll and a frustrated sigh. "Just call us when you know what's going on."

He walked out of the cubical with Jason and sped off with his youngest making demands about what new stuff he wanted at that time.

David was shocked at this display. He stood there trying to understand what just happened, but I think he gave up in the end. He walked up to the curtain and closed it to protect us from nosy patients.

"Do you know if her parents are coming?" David asked me.

"Her parents work at the coast most of the time," I responded.

He collapsed back onto the chair, thudding his body directly into the plastic as if he were trying to crush his disbelief.

"So, she just lives by herself?" He despaired.

"Sometimes… when her dad is here, he does try to stick to her like glue."

148

"He just isn't here that much…" He paused and sighed. "What a way to live mate. I don't blame her for going down this route if that's the home life."

I turned my gaze back to her and stared at her for a while. This still didn't feel real.

"Look mate, I need to head off as well." David exhaled in defeat. "But I'm not leaving you with nothing."

He reached into his back pocket and pulled out his desert camo wallet. He pulled out two twenty-pound notes and handed them to me.

"Get some good scran. I know how hospital food can be."

I hesitated and just stared at him for a while, completely dumbfounded. He got up and decided to grab my wrist and force the money into my hand.

"You don't have to pay me back or anything mate. I just don't want you to suffer whilst watching over this girl."

He was compassionate. He was kind. Even then, I felt like there were strings attached to the money he was giving me.

I clenched my hand into a fist and gripped the money and put it into my red coat pocket.

This felt wrong.

"Take care of her, alright?" He said solemnly.

He gave me a friendly tap on the shoulder before heading away.

He did his part, now it was my turn to look after this…

Whatever was left of this.

149

I want more… and I will never get it…

Lisa
Half eight-ish in the morning

It had been a while since I heard from Ava or Bern. More than a month to be precise.
I was on my own there. I walked out of the school building trying to figure out what to do with myself. I only had Ava as a friend and her 'town centre lot'. I knew she was skipping school but from what I barely know about Bern, it felt out of character for him.
I walked out to the park where I went to smoke. The mud was frozen over with small crystal flakes caking the glacial sludge. I paced towards the metal gazebo which now looked like it had been completely taken over by gang tags of wannabe thugs. I once again looked at my phone to look through the photos. In my heart of hearts, I didn't think I would see her again. I selected the folder where I had all her photos saved and then…

I erased her. I got rid of our memories together. They were behind me. All the years we had, were now suddenly gone. She was dead to me.
I took out my lighter and lit up the cigarette, trying to cover the flame against the wind. I sat there and thought about what I was doing. Why was I here?
I had no company except the fizzling tobacco and the fading smoke.
I took out my phone and searched through the memories I had with Ava, and I felt…
Nothing. Not a single feeling. I was just too tired from it.
I was happy, content even.
So…
Why did I decide to call her?
Why did I decide to speed-dial her number on my phone?
Why did I wait for that damn buzz tone?

Someone picked up but to my surprise, I could hear a faint beeping. What sounded like a heart monitor.
The voice was male and not what I was at all expecting.
"Hello?"
"Umm… Hi Bern, is Ava there?" I was surprised but not too enthusiastic.
"She's dead."
The call went silent. I tried to say something… anything but I just stammered and gulped like an idiot. I was still in shock. Was she dead or was Bern just angry at her or something? Please, anything else but dead…
"What do you mean she's dead?"

Ava
N/A

Where am I?
Am I still real?
Oh god, have I died in that fire?
"Yea," said a guttural voice in its pride, surrounding the hollow void.
I floated in the dark and cold. Not aware of my surroundings. The air was still, and the light was gone. Gravity felt heavy and breathless. The contradiction of my thoughts and emotions surrounding me and chaining me down through the human condition.
Where has my life gone?
Why do I feel empty?
I look down at what I thought were my hands. They were covered in a black satin. I looked up and I could see myself in an outdoor ball. Classical music played with concubines and lords roaming around their circular estate garden. The hedges were trimmed to perfection; and the rose bushes plucked to purity. Each dancer pirouetted and galavanted themselves to otherworldly grace, alongside the beat of the orchestra. Gothic Victorian music played with the gentle pull of the cello and violin strings, comforting me with elegance and harmonious romance. A place in me felt fulfilled. The cobbled paths carved their stage into the healthy grass, each section giving way to its

own troupe. Offering them their own performance. Their own admirers. All intersecting to the centre.

The dancers paraded around in opulent colours and the finest materials of the time. Powdered wigs dressed the scalps of the guests. The females were adorned in seventeenth-century rococo dresses, whilst the men were wearing Victorian mourning suits. Was this heaven?

I moved around the lavish garden. The gibbet moon reflected to illuminate the flora, which shone and sparkled across the bushes, revealing the health and full green of the leaves. They complimented the warm summer breeze, wafting freshly cut grass through the garden. They glowed. They saw life. The nineteenth-century gas lamps surrounded the garden and offered crude light to where they were needed.

In the centre of the courtyard, there stood a white wooden gazebo surrounded by fireflies.

Something drew me closer. Some presence wanted me there.

I felt the click-clack of my heels crash against the cobbled paths. I could feel the weight of my own black rococo dress. Each forward step moved me closer towards my goal. I felt joy. My polished gold jewellery jingled as I sped up my pace and broke into a run. The faster I ran, the more the participants stared at me. Their handsome faces followed my movements. Further down the cobbled path. Further down to what I wanted.

More.

The sky glistened and sparkled as if it supported my decision to run. Although, as I looked up at the night sky... it bled. The moon turned into a midnight eclipse. Suffocating the sky in a carmine red. I made my way through another layer of the garden and what came next felt unreal.

A clump of ash landed on my satin glove.

I stopped for a second and looked at what it was. How did this happen? I stopped, looked at the sky, and saw more thick clumps rain down. The moon drained its hue from red to crystal white. These beautiful colours I saw now disappeared. The orchestra band turned sinister. Each note sounded perfect but sorrowful. Each guest stood patent and stared. The colour pooled away from their beautiful clothes and jewellery, leaving a thick syrupy mass at the bottom of their feet.

I gazed carefully at my transformed company and saw the guest's faces disappear into thick smoke. All that could be seen was black shifting smog with the buzzing fireflies acting as their eyes.

"I'm sorry." They mumbled.

Each of them repeated the same words over and over in unison. Their once beautiful clothes became filthy and stained with grey-white dust.

As I turned my attention towards the centre of the garden, I found I had already made it there,

The steps were inviting. As I gripped the wooden handrail, the texture felt wrong. Each touch didn't feel like wood but instead cotton. I looked at my hand and saw it covered in ash. I looked outside and saw this once beautiful world being drowned by this falling dust, almost as if a monsoon had cried its last tears and wept cinders.

This however didn't stop the orchestra from playing its symphony for the damned. I moved up the steps, with each treat making the orchestra speed up into and then...

The music stopped for a surreal moment, and I saw the silhouette of a man. He was dark and emitted shadowy vapours. The flies surrounded him and took away the darkness around him. First, they revealed his finely tailored clothes, his handsome dress sense, and his impeccable jewellery. That didn't matter much when I saw who it was. When I saw his rotting teeth and filthy hair.

"Come!" It hissed. It's English and speech far more advanced than possible. "Die with me beloved."

The band broke into a violent crescendo. The music sounded terrifying and impactful but hauntingly beautiful, the quartet followed the movements of the demon before me. Nova faced me with his arm outstretched, while the other was behind his back as if preparing to bow. His deathly visage and his atrocious hair cut staring at me.

My face dropped, each backward step of my heels shook dust off my dress and created a trail around me.

"Get away from me!" I screamed.

He gave a smirk. The Fireflies surrounded him and moved with blinding speed to race around him. They sparked and fizzled, flying faster and faster to where I couldn't keep up with their speed. They only left a white trail to show their existence.

Each step Nova took made me move back faster.

Both his arms were now outstretched, and he exposed his hands to the world. They both lazily erupted into sparks and flames.

"You're mine now." He jeered. A sadistic grin cracked on his face, except there were no teeth left, instead more fireflies poured out of his gaping mouth like he was a makeshift hive. Faster and faster the flies flew. Nova slowly raised his dominant hand and set the flies on me.

They swarmed me and surrounded me. I felt the heat of their wings, the ceaseless buzzing, and eventually... I smelt burning ammonia.

I looked at my gloves and saw them emit viscous black smoke. I looked at my dress and saw flies bite into the dress and setting fire to the pristine fabric.

"No!" I screamed to them. "Stop!"

He said nothing, he stood there and grinned as more flies flew out of his maw. I kept moving back closer to the edge of the gazebo and made a mistake.

My feet missed a step.

I tumbled and hurled myself out into the ash wastes. Out into this pitiful nightmare.

I felt the softness of the ash on my back, and I struggled to fight off the flies.

"Help!" I screamed as ash rained into my mouth. My voice drowned out by the buzz of flies and the crackles of erupting sparks.

I looked at my hands one last time before seeing them combust. The pain, The searing pain of it. I couldn't take it. I rolled around on the ash trying to put out the flames, but it was to no effect.

I screamed out pained cries and the occasional cough. Eventually letting out a final pained screech before closing my eyes and awaiting death.

Instead, the sky fell. The ground tumbled and the ash faded. I opened my eyes, and I woke up in a hospital bed. I saw Bern over the side of my bed, and I needed to tell him what I felt. But I felt a tube in my mouth and decided to pull it free so I could talk.

Bern
7:37 am
126 days post exam

The plastic chair wasn't too uncomfortable to sleep on. I managed to buy a charger from the hospital shop at an extortionate amount and ordered some takeaway food. I hovered around this pile of skin and bones, barely leaving her side. The room felt cold and vacant. Nothing to be found here except the look of pain and misery on her face, only showing the withering skull making its last gasps of air and its fleeting pulses of a drug-withdrawn heart.
I looked to check on her condition but all I found was her still lying on her back. Until she opened her eyes for a short time.

She sharply inhaled through her ventilator and weakly ripped the thing out of her throat.
As soon as I saw this, I was shocked in place and didn't know how to respond to something that looked displaced between life and death.
"Am I dead?" she gasped out. Each syllable was a choke and a splutter. With the ventilator gone, her teeth were revealed to be a deteriorating mess of yellow and black. Her gums receding and plaque hardening around her mouth.
Her eyes darted fearfully; she looked like she was suffocating. She must have taken it off wrong.
"Nurse!" I cried out. "Nurse!"
No response.
I grabbed Ava's hand and gripped it as hard as I could. Her heart rate monitor is racing, each beat reflecting this girl's frantic panics and desperation to stay alive. She wasn't the only one terrified. I didn't want to see any more suffering, even to a person who wronged me. Especially to a person I still care about.

155

"Nurse! Anyone?!"
She continued suffocating, each breath she took sounded thick and crackled. Almost like a wet snore.
She couldn't even cough, she just laid there gasping like a fish out of water.
"Ava, please!" I called out to her. I turned behind me and my voice broke from screaming to the top of my lungs. "Get me a fucking nurse!"
I turned back to Ava and grabbed her other hand to try and calm her. I had tears running down my face from fear of losing her. She looked at me with her dying eyes and gasped out these final words. Three final words that made me understand her. Three final words that even though the wet snarls she took to breathe, I understood. Three final words that will haunt me forever.

"I'm so sorry..."

She placed her frail, struggling hand on my heart. I could feel her touch even through my thick red coat. She clenched her hand with mine as hard as she could, her grip was weak and fleeting. She raised the hand on my chest and moved it to my tear-stained face. Her touch was cold and distant.
I clasped the hand on my face and turned to face the curtain. "Nurse!" I finally screamed out. As soon as I uttered those desperate words, I heard a monotone drone. I recognised what this noise was, and I hesitated to turn back around, but I knew it was necessary.
Flatline.
I turned back to Ava, and she was gone. Her once frantic eyes turned cold. Her movement is still. Her weak grip was now limp. Her face was expressionless. She finally passed away.
She died there. In that hospital, in that bed. With me as her last comfort. She died there, having her young life getting cut short.
Soon a nurse ripped open the curtain and examined the scene. She saw me cradling this poor girl and immediately turned apologetic.
"Oh god, I'm so sorry! It was a shift change and..." She covered her surgical mask with her gloves and stood there unsure what to

say. She was young, maybe early twenties and she walked in on a situation that didn't need to happen.

I didn't say a word to her. I just stared at what was left of Ava and let go of her hands.

"I'm sorry." That was all I could say to her. That was all I could do at this point... Ask for forgiveness.

I made my offering by placing a single kiss on her frail forehead which was drenched in sweat and littered by stray hairs.

"Leave me alone." I chided the nurse. "Let me be with my girlfriend."

"I'll get a doctor." She said miserably. Her posture was slumped and low, even when standing.

She quietly followed my request and left out the cubical. The curtain around a metallic screech across the rail and gave us privacy from the outside world.

"I'm so sorry Ava." I waited. I waited to think the body would resurrect itself and come back to life. But unfortunately, it didn't happen. This was life and sometimes, life is cruel.

Soon I heard a buzzing from somewhere close by. I searched around me and found the buzzing was coming from the recent deceased's bag.

I searched the bag for the phone and saw who it was.

"Hello?" I said to the caller.

Sidorovich
12:32

Samara cradled himself over the altar. His stomach pain grew more and more intolerable. He groaned and wheezed consistently as he drank more and more. His new set of diamond-cut crystal glasses were resting on the fine fabrics of the altar, each filled with their respective poisons.

"Samara, are you ok?" I asked him. I cleaned the glass windows and made sure that the place was up to the standardised perfection I set.

He looked up at me, still hunched over from the pain I caused him.

"No Fedor..." He took a deep breath and moved around the altar closer to me. "I don't think I am."

157

He made weak stumbles in his short stride towards his seat. He did his best not to spill the drink in his hand. Seeing this display, I stopped my duties and attended to the wounded.

I made careful steps off the ladder that held me up to cleanse and bless the artistic windows.

"What's the matter?" I charitably spoke. I moved closer to my friend and sat next to him. He hunched over like he was trying to hold his guts in place.

"I could have done more Fedor!" He sat up and placed his sweaty hand on my shoulder. He looked up at me. His forehead was drenched in sweat and despair.

"I could have done so much more!" he painfully cried out. "I wanted to live more." His voice reverberated through the church. The light of the winter sun which shone so brightly dimmed and dulled when his anguish was borne to the holy site.

There was no way I could comfort him. No way I could support it. I caused this and I still felt the guilt itch into my bandages. I clenched my fist in self-frustration, but Samara saw me do this. He gave me a disappointed and pained look, accompanied by a scoff to cement his anguish.

"God will help you." I said softly.

Samara gave a short bellow before collapsing into pain.

"I had too much of a life for that man." He showed his warm smile and spoke like he was healthy again. "I think he likes them inexperienced." He winked and chuckled painfully.

His smile faded sharply as he bowed over in agony.

"Do you not feel like he will protect you?" I questioned.

"No, I don't think he will. He'll most likely kick me into hell." He said painfully. He gave a deep sigh before swirling his swill and taking a sip. "At least I know it won't be boring." He nervously chuckled.

He might be right. We've lived too much. Done too much. How does a priest seek forgiveness, especially with his past life?

"I want to be left alone Fedor." He said remorsefully. "Let me die in peace."

"Are you sure?"

"Yes. I am. Now leave me alone." Samara attempted to stand up, but his body weight was proving too much for him to lift. I sat up and tried to lift him gently by his elbows. He made it halfway up before he noticed the notion and shrugged me off before finally collapsing back onto the pew with a violent creak.

He leans back onto the pew a deathly moan and then a frustrated groan. His head rested back and faced the ceiling of the church. He shut his eyes, unable to look up due to the pain.

"I'm not useless yet!" He said through gritted teeth.

"I'm not saying you're useless. I just—"

"I don't need help! I need a drink!" Samara demanded.

He tried to lift himself up again but this time with greater effort. Sweat dripped from his brow and each tensing muscle tried desperately to accommodate for the years of alcohol abuse. I couldn't watch anymore, I needed to help him up. I placed my arms around his torso and felt his weight through the pits of his arms.

I did manage to help him up, but he turned frenzied and shook off my arms with a fury I hadn't seen in a while.

"Get your hands off me!" He roared. "I don't need a babysitter!"

"I just—" Samara interrupted me. He pointed his hand at me like a knife, his fully extended fingers just inches away from my face.

"Fuck your help! I'm leaving." Samara hastily waddled to the altar where his remaining drinks were left in his new crystal glasses. He circled the altar and kept himself balanced against it with one hand.

"You're getting worse with your drinking." I chided.

He reached the altar and picked up a tumbler.

"Oh, and what are you? My wife?" He bellowed scornfully and sarcastically. "Sorry, the bed is a little crowded."

I was quickly getting infuriated by this display; this was not how a priest should act no matter the condition.

"How dare you speak to me like this?" I spoke coldly, almost hostile.

"Me?" He raised his voice in anger and hate. His free hand pointed to him and then was redirected to me. "How dare you?!" He threw his arm at me whilst his forefinger was still hanging away from its siblings. He repeated the motion, walking around the altar and closer to me. The excessive movement caused the drink in his hand to spill on the stone floors.

"*YOU* who judges others for things you have done yourself!"

"*YOU* who wallows in misery and pain!"

His words cut deep like daggers. Samara was many things, but his greatest gift was speech and now he was using it for ill. Samara took a few hasty breaths before lowering the volume of his voice. He took a quick sip of his tumbler, of which half of its contents spilled on the floor.

"Listen to me…" Samara's speech quivered as if he was begging. Pleading to something or someone. His hand clenched into a fist and was brought towards his chest which shook for each point he made. His head raised to the ceiling. "I've had a life; I've had many women…"

I crossed my arms and spoke to him coldly. "So, you keep saying."

Hearing this Samara threw me a fiery stare and pointed his arm back at me.

"Fuck you Fedor, you listen to me!" He erupted.

Samara's bombastic gestures followed his words, and his volume was to a contained low, slowly rising to the point of explosion. "I've been around the world. I've been to the biggest cities. I went to all the best parties and drank with oligarchs." He closed his distance to me slowly. "I watch all the beauties of the world through the bottom of a *GLASS*! I've been with the finest women on the earth! I did drugs with hookers and didn't pay a damn thing!"

His voice was raised so high as if he wanted God himself to hear him. He raised both arms into the air before throwing them down again.

"I fucked the world! And the world called me back in the morning!" He hatefully boasted. Although this seemed like Samara felt slighted by the world and begged God for a punishment. What is happening to us? What are we becoming? I could think of no appropriate words. I was paralyzed by fear of what to do. Instead, I tried to tell him a story.

"When I was in—"

"Oh, save your war stories for the boy!" He waved off my words in frustration. "He'll care more than I will. I'm leaving." Samara scolded.

160

He placed his tumbler on the altar and limped out the door. "Samara!" I called out to him. My cold exterior was gone, I tried to show him how much I cared but it was clear my best wasn't good enough. He ignored my summons and left the church in frustration.

Samara slammed the door behind him which chipped some of the splinters in the door and cracked the wood further.

The sound... The sound was awful.

I blinked and saw them there. My squad brothers. I looked down at the floor and saw only the sand and the lone finger left there. Whatever was left of the man I sent to die.

"You bastard!" Cried out, Lev.

Lev tried to charge at me whilst inside the truck. Kars and Slava held him back from taking his well-deserved retribution out on me.

"Get off me!" He screamed at the men guarding me. "You're just as bad as this thick slab!"

Slava grabbed Lev by the collar and threw him outside. Kars was powerless to stop him. The rest were too scared to go outside for fear of hitting another mine.

The force of the throw sent Lev flying into the sand which left him partially sunk into the earth.

Lev stood up with ferocity and determination, revealing a man-sized imprint in the sand. Slava started undressing from his gear inside the truck to reveal just his stripped undershirt and bear-like physique.

"Leave him alone!" Slava demanded. He sounded tired. Cold. Even in the heat of the sand.

"I'll fight two murderers if I have to!" Lev called.

"We're all murderers here." Slava said grimly. He stepped outside the truck and closer to Lev. The claustrophobic nature of the metal box on wheels hid Slava's true height. He towered over Lev. He stood at least a foot above him. A mountain of muscle against a deceptively strong reed.

We knew who was going to win. All we could do was watch until someone spotted our saving grace.

"There! Look!" Mikhail called out, his voice still partially guttural.

161

The men looked at Mikhail's observation. There were two horses with men on them. They were dressed in the typical garb of the local populace. Patterned turbans and rags adorned them to protect the strangers from the dust.

We straightened up and grabbed our guns.

Kars was the first to speak.

He pushed to the front of the truck and called out in the local language.

No response.

Again, he called out, this time he shouldered his rifle and called out more aggressively.

Finally, a response, a single hand raised to the sky by one of the riders.

They approached us closer to the truck. Both covered their bodies and visages, only their eyes could be seen.

The men were hesitant and fearful. Each held their weapons in protection in case this was a cruel trick.

"Ask them what they're doing here." Slava ordered.

Kars relayed his message.

"They say that they heard the explosion and came to check on what happened."

He paused to listen to their responses.

"He says that we need to leave soon as a storm is predicted to hit soon."

"A storm?" Lev asked.

"A sandstorm."

The men's morale dropped. We didn't know what to do or what to expect.

I turned to Slava. "What do we do here?"

Slava gave a profound sigh and dropped his guard.

"Kars asked them where they came from. We might be able to follow them back to safety."

"Are you sure?" he asked hesitantly.

He didn't say anything, he just gave a brief nod.

The conversation was long and heart-pounding. We placed our lives in this man and hoped that he would be able to get us out of here. Each foreign syllable spoken felt intimidating. Some were looking for an excuse to shoot these people from the slightest feign of hostility.

"They said that there is a town four kilometres north. The road should be clear from the way they came."

"How do you know we can trust them?" Vasya asked.

"They came, didn't they?"

"They could be scavengers for all we know." Mikhail called out.

"It's the only way we've got to get out." Slava said. "Kars tell—"

"NO!" Lev called out! "I'm not following some dushman into my death!"

"You have a better idea?" Slava cried out. "Get your equipment boys! We're leaving!"

"Slava!" I rushed towards him. My footsteps crunched on the sand. "They'll shoot us on sight. We can't go in there in our uniform."

"Fuck!" He pinched the bridge of his nose in frustration. "Kars, do they have any rags we can use?"

Kars relayed his message.

"They've got some, but not enough."

"How many do they have?"

"Enough for three."

There was a long pause. Slava needed time to think. He paced back and forth in the sands for a few seconds before looking at his discarded uniform.

"Tear your uniforms." he said grimly. "Make rags out of them and cover as much skin as you can."

Before long, the tearing of fabric could be heard. The ripping of pride rippled through Slava. He held his uniform jacket in his hands and looked at the hammer and sickle buttons sewn into his khaki jacket sleeve.

"Are you ok?" I asked him.

"No, I don't think I am." He took a moment for his decision to fully wash over him. "But I need to get you boys back home and out alive." He tore the patch and discarded it on the ground and threw it into the truck. "Leave the heavy stuff behind. Take only your essentials!"

"What about my brother?" Lev moaned.

"Burn the truck." Vasya said.

"But—" Lev was interrupted by Slava placing his hand on his shoulder.

"I'm so sorry this has happened, but we need to leave. Don't let your brother's dream die here, take it with you." Slava gently placed the knuckles of his fist into Lev's chest. "Carry it in here."

Only the wind and the tear of fabrics could be heard. No one said a word.

The hellish world focused on Slava and Lev.

"Burn it." Lev finally spoke.

Slava nodded and turned to his men.

"Does anyone have any spare vodka?"

Mikhail raised his hand and passed his flask to Lev.

"I'll let you take care of it." Slava said.

Most of the men were finished disguising themselves for the trek ahead.

In some sick way, this was some appropriate send-off for the fallen.

"Does anyone have any matches?" Lev asked.

Kars ran up to him only half disguised as he could pass as an afghani from his skin tone.

He passed a matchbox to Lev.

"I'm sorry about this." He said before running back to finally help the others with their disguises.

"Take your time." Slava said. He gave him one final pat on the back before going back to tearing his pride.

Lev walked up to the truck and climbed inside to see the cold visage of his brother. Half of his face started to host uninvited flies which clung onto his rotting flesh.

I couldn't make out his whispers. Lev threw me a side-eyed stare and we held an uncomfortable gaze with each other before he broke off and tended to the dead. He stroked his brother's scalp before pouring the flask onto his kin's body. He scattered scraps of uniform and discarded patches to help feed the flame.

And finally, he ignited the match and dropped it into the alcohol. The men watched it ignite into flames and slowly engulf the truck.

"We need to leave." Kars said. "Before they find the smoke."

164

"Get your guns" he ordered. "Travel light, we're leaving!" Slava ordered.

Dima approached me with his new disguise. His whole body was covered by a mix of rags and ripped uniform. His face was shrouded, and his eyes were covered by the military goggles issued to us.

"You've been quiet." I said to him.
"I don't like this, Fedor. Something reeks about this. Why is he helping us?"
"I don't know but we have no other choice. We need to go."

I turned around to face my direction of march and found myself in the office.
The smell of smoke lingering in the air and dim lights were my only company.
Samara was right... I do wallow in pain. But how can I forget them?

Bern
12:26 pm
132 days post exam

Misery.
Misery was all I could see here.
The sub-zero environment turned the soil to stone which made digging the earth much more difficult. The ebony coffin was slim and tiny with gold emboss and carry handles surrounding the edges. The few faces that were there to pay respects looked like they couldn't care less. Well... they still put on a show but inside you could tell they couldn't care less. I think out of the ten people there, only two cared. Me and the priest. Not mine of course, but you could even see his interest waver from doing this sermon repeatedly. The only difference this time was the age and the cause of death but still the same cold funeral.
The family members there who turned up to pay respects looked to have some sort of relief but there was a looming spite. A dark cloud circled the father. The middle-aged man who was too

165

skinny for the suit he wore paced back and forth. A plan was forming, but what was it?

Somehow, they felt it appropriate to engrave her cause of death on her tombstone. I don't know if that was her idea or if it was theirs.
The tombstone was an anchor with a broken chain, which had *"death rattle"* engraved into the curve.
I stood there in my darkest and most wrinkled clothes. It was a combination of my school uniform and work clothes. Nothing I had was funeral-appropriate, but I tried my best. I looked around the frozen fields and I couldn't see Lisa anywhere. I chalked it up to it being too painful for her to attend. That, or she couldn't bear to see my face after being the bearer of bad news.
I was the last one to see her alive, but I didn't know how to process it.
Even after the funeral, after the hallow biblical words, there was no getting through what just happened. The moment they lowered the coffin into the ground, a part of me died with her. She may have treated me like shit, but I still felt that connection.
I had no other choice, I needed to talk to someone. I needed to confess.
So, I did. I went to those priests and confessed. I took the first bus I could get there, not caring about anyone else but myself, my own feelings.
I left the bus with the Oakley-wearing bus driver and made my slow approach to the church.

There it was… it stood in front of me like a monument to all the sin that happened in its walls. There were no lights inside and there was a sign on the door saying closed.
I walked up to the door. It looked more splintered than usual, showing its fresh cracks in the wood, revealing the original colour of the wood before age took it away.
I ignored the sign and opened the door with a retched squeal. The air smelt musty and unkempt from its usual clarity. I could hear the faint thumping of music. The church was dim and lacked the smell of alcohol or tobacco. Aggressive guitars strummed and

166

drums banged in the small office with a man singing rock music in a language I couldn't understand. Was that where they were? I approached slowly with my school shoes echoing around the prayer hall. I walked up the aisle and I saw more and more imperfections around this place. The closer I walked the more the smell of smoke and alcohol could be recognised. This must be where they are. The music got louder the closer I got to them. I put my hand on the door ring and pulled it open... but what I saw was unexpected.

It was just Sidorovich. He sat there in a black suit with the top two buttons undone, revealing a small silver cross on his chest. He wore a thick grey coat which mirrored the style of Russian great coats.

"Batushka?" I said to him.

He paid me no mind. He sat there smoking a cigar and held a crystal tumbler in hand.

I looked around the small office and I saw a little CD player, blasting music.

I walked closer to the player and finally, he spoke.

"Touch that and I'll kill you."

I froze in place. I didn't dare to turn around and face him.

"Can I turn it down?" I asked.

He took a small puff from his cigar and gave me an acknowledging grunt. I lowered the volume and finally turned around to speak to him. He stood up from his chair and his sudden appearance startled me, forcing me to stumble backward slightly.

"What do you want?" He frustratedly asked.

"I just wanted to talk."

"Talk to Samara, I'll just make it worse."

This was new, I had never seen Sidorovich in this state. He was hollow like the will to live had been taken away from him.

"What are you doing here?" I asked.

"What does it look like? Smoking and drinking." He spoke. His mood was foul. He quickly sobered up and collected himself to

167

be more presentable. "I'm sorry boy, me and the Greek had a falling out."
He quickly put down the vices and sunk his face into his bandages.
"I killed him, you know?"
"Who?"
"Samara."
"No, you didn't."

Sidorovich raised his head and put his cigar in his mouth.
"Yes, I did boy. I killed him." He said sombrely. He took a long puff of his cigar and let out a cloud of smoke. "I should have died there."
"What do you mean?" I asked.
"Afghanistan boy. I should have died there with my friends; I shouldn't even be here. Then I wouldn't have murdered my friend."
Sidorovich reclined in his chair to let the guilt be over him. Was he confessing to me?
I stood there unsure of what to say to him. I thought long and hard for my response to try and show some kind of empathy towards him. To give him that reason to live.

"If you didn't survive then you wouldn't have been friends with him in the first place. Then you wouldn't have become a priest and tried to help people."

"You've seen how we act; we are the worst priests you will ever see." He gave a small chuckle. "Although I like to think we're at least entertaining."
I sat down on the other chair in the room and fidgeted with my hands for a few moments.
"What happened in the war?" I asked.
"Too much…" He took another puff. "I walked in with nine other men and only one came back somewhat unscathed."
"Do you want to talk about it?" I asked.
"Why do you want to know?" He asked, he poured himself another glass. He revealed the bottle, it was not some age-passed

liquor but some cheap spirits from likely the nearest off-license he could find.

"This swill is awful." He stated grimly. He poured more cheap vodka into the tumbler which Samara assumedly kept in the church.

"I thought you're more of a smoker." I blurted out.

"I am…" He sighed. "I only drink when Samara is here."

Sidorovich leaned back into his chair and took another puff of his cigar. He let out smoke through the sides of his mouth which made the smoke pattern out.

"I missed this…" He uttered. "I miss him."

I stood up and took the spare tumbler for myself. I turned to the priest still standing.

"Why is he not here?"

"We had an argument." Sidorovich took slurp. "We try to make plans outside of our jobs but always end up here. Playing music and indulging in our vices."

I sat down and fidgeted with the tumbler in my hand. I could smell the foul aroma pouring from the glass.

"What if I indulged with you?" I spoke.

Sidorovich straightened his spine from the chair.

"I thought you're not old enough." He hastily questioned.

"I am now."

I lied to him of course. I wasn't old enough; I wouldn't be for at least another two months. But I wanted to see why they lived like this. Why they were the way they were.

"Ok…" He weakly spoke.

I don't know if I was dreaming or if the light tricked me, but I thought I could see something in him. Something I had never seen before…

A small twinkle in his ancient eyes that slowly rolled down his cheek.

2:43pm

How that place echoed with laughter. How this place felt like a home. I had a cigar in hand and a tumbler of cheap vodka in the other. Both made me feel a bit sick, but I still did it anyway. The

169

cigars made me feel like I could fly but the alcohol sent me crashing back down into a murky earth. Each puff made me want to cough up a lung, but the alcohol burnt off my taste buds. "Samara would—" Sidorovich continued. "He would try to chase me around the church with a broomstick shouting, 'How about I chase you away like you chase away my women.'"

We burst into a thunderous roar that echoed through the church. It took a moment or two before I could recover myself. I took another sip of my third tumbler which tasted not as bad as the other two.

Still, I could start to feel the room spinning and my speech turned sloppy.

Sidorovich sat there with a smile on his face.

"We loved this you know." He spoke.

"What?"

"Me and him, we sat here and smoked and drank before going back to normal..." Sidorovich paused. "Or before they went away." He took another puff from his freshly cut cigar.

"You mean Samara?" I asked.

Sidorovich paused and thought about his response. He drank almost as much as me, but he had more experience drinking, and somewhat retained his constitution.

"My boy..." He quivered. "My poor boy. We did this before he left for war."

The mood turned grim. The room felt suffocating.

Sidorovich

There sat a spectre before me. There sat something that felt wrong. Even with these poisons flowing through me, I felt some semblance of understanding. Like God in all his wisdom gave me a cruel second chance.

I lifted my tumbler to try and block out the memories, but I couldn't drink their contents. The Cuckoo by Kino played its haunting song, emitting its ethereal presence from the old music player which left me powerless.

"My Grigori..."

The boy sat there confused and half drunk. He had never seen me this vulnerable. I didn't even know why I was welling up with

170

tears or why I was telling him this. He just sat there like my son. Talked like my son. He was my son...

"I'm so sorry that you have to see this, boy." I wailed. I cast aside the crystal and put my palm to my face. The other still holding my cigar. I could feel the small glistens roll down my face, with Victor Tsoi's majestic voice exacerbating my sorrow.

"Are you ok?" He asked, half slurring his speech.

I didn't respond. I was enthralled by the lyrics. Before I realised, I was mouthing along the words; palm still covering my face. I felt my memories call back out to me. My time with my child. Each time I held him, the times I played with him.

Soon, I felt a warm embrace around me. Thin arms, the same size as my boy's. They gripped my battered body and squeezed. I responded and held his arms with my free bandaged hand. His spirit was there. I gripped tighter and tighter to keep him here but eventually, I had to release the vessel and let him go.

"I sang this to him, you know." I spoke. I wiped my face and steeled myself.

"Sang this to who?"

"My boy... It was the one thing I have left of him."

"What happened to him?"

"He joined the army, he wanted to run away from his mother in Russia."

There was a moment of pause.

"After you attacked—"

"After I killed my friend, you mean."

"He's still alive, don't forget that."

I took a sip of the alcohol.

"Samara said I would have been a good son. What did he mean?" He spoke.

I felt embarrassed. I didn't know how to respond, so I caged myself.

"I saw something in you." I murmured.

"What do you mean?"

"I saw something that would have made you as such."

"But you barely know me."

171

"I know enough to see a person when they are going through hell, and you are tougher than you think. You're just a boy who is trying his best at something I can see is troubling you."

I was speaking out of turn. But I felt these words would heal him.

The boy glanced down and finished his tumbler.
"Thank you…" He half slurred. "I mean it." He reclined in his chair and sat there for a moment. "What do I do now?" He asked.
"What do you mean?"
"I lost someone I loved, Batushka." His head sank and his posture slumped.
"Who did you lose boy?"
He placed his palm on his forehead and leaned forward.
"I feel like I've lost everyone."
"Who's everyone?" I questioned.
"My family, my girlfriend. I don't know what to do." He allowed a stressed chuckle. "I can't even cry about it anymore."

Now I understand, now I see the pain this boy is going through.
"What do you want to do?" I asked.
"I don't know." He shrugged. "I just want peace."
"Peace?"
"Peace as in…" He paused and gave a frustrated sigh. "I want to fucking leave it all behind. I don't want my dad to keep bothering me for money, I don't want to work full-time and go to school, and I didn't want Ava to die."
My god… he *has* gone through hell.

"I'm so sorry this had happened."
"Thank you." He weakly responded. "Funny thing is, I can't even cry anymore about it. I guess I'm just that used to it. "
"Listen, boy…" I pulled my chair closer to his and placed my broken hand on his shoulder. "I will never understand what you're going through, but I will do my best for you."
He gave me a lightning-fast hug that could have snapped my spine in half.
"Thank you." His voice trembled.

I wrapped my arms around him. My son is dead... but I feel like his spirit lives on.

Michael
Half Seven-ish in the afternoon

Where the hell is Bern? He should have been here hours ago!
I've got Jason upstairs thankfully safe and sound, but I don't hear a damn thing from the eldest.
Soon after being surrounded by paperwork and having some soap operas on, I heard the door open.
"What time do you call this?" I said furiously.
"Oh... Shut up!" He blurted out.
My blood boiled and I was immediately in a frenzy.
"What the hell did you say to me!?"
I threw meself up off the sofa and threw open the lounge door. I could smell the booze and cigarette smoke on him.
"Where the fuck have you been?!"
He collapsed on the floor with his hair in a mess and ash down his clothes.
"Having a life." He slurred out. He was drunk.
He tried desperately to pull himself up off the floor, but it was clear that he couldn't handle his drink. The lad only flailed around his arms uselessly like a little kid.
I picked him up by his arm to help him to his feet.
"Get off me!" He struggled and screamed as much as a drunk could. "I hate you!" I tried to drag him up the wooden stairs and to his room.
Jason was still in his room playing whatever games could be heard. Bernard still struggled against me, screaming at me whatever he thought could hurt me. I was losing me temper with him, but nothing got to me too much.
We finally got to the landing where barely any lights lit our way. I dragged him to his room; his energy had finally gone. I slammed open the door and took him to his room and threw him on the mattress.
He was lying there, still, and silent.
I thought that was my cue to leave. I was halfway out of the door before I heard the lad speak.

173

"Why are you working me so hard?" He whimpered out.
I turned around and saw him splayed across the bed. Even though his face was in a pillow, I could tell he was crying.
I just stood over him and took a second to respond.
"Because we need the money."
"Is this what happened to mum?"
I was frozen in place for a second, not knowing what to say.
"I…"
"This is, isn't it?" He turned around to face me, still lying on the led. "She was barely around in the house, but this is exactly what's happening, isn't it?!"
I lost me temper then and there.
"Do you know what I have to go through?" I yelled. "I have to walk into work and be the bad guy and sometimes are so scared of me that they hang themselves."
"So, find another job!" He screamed.
"Find another house then!" I screamed back.
"Or what? You'll make me run away like mum?"
Hearing this, I was pushed over the edge… I kicked him. He let off a horrific shriek.
I stood back and saw what I had done. I struck him in the face with me work boot and he was there holding his face.
I don't know why but I just kept kicking, and kicking, and kicking. This time I was hitting his stomach. Held back each time, trying to restrain myself but whatever was controlling me, kept winning. I kept at it, with each thump being a battle in myself.
Thump.
Thump.
Thump…

Life or death

Sidorovich
14:21

The depressing month of January was here. December had died and everyone had spent their money. Everyone outside of my church that is. It was the sixth, meaning it was Orthodox Christmas Eve. I was singing the liturgies along with whatever elderly choir singers we had. The hall had no more than five singers, including myself and Samara who sang the liturgies. We didn't dare have any helpers in the church as we felt we didn't need it but with Samara's condition, it was evident that we would soon need extra bodies. He tried to keep a cheery face, but I could make out the occasional pained expression and hushed wince. I wafted the censors towards our guests and sang from the divine liturgy. We had to sing in Slavonic as we spoke the liturgy with guests bowing and making the sign of the cross each time we said "*Hospodi*". Usually, another church of our order would have no pews and make the practitioners stand for the sermon. However, we decided against that since most of our flock were too old to stand for long periods of time. It was also more comfortable.

Samara gave his speeches and offered communion to the pensioners whilst I helped with confession. This was our Christmas, and it meant the world to us. Soon the men and women would leave and go off to enjoy their holiday. When the church was left empty, I lit up my pipe and began to smoke.

Samara's fist flexed and tightened whilst his other hand clutched his belly. He fumbled toward the closest seat and slammed himself down. I tried to comfort him by placing a hand on his shoulder, but he shrugged it off.
"How are you feeling?" I asked.
"Fine, I feel like I'm twenty again." He jibbed sarcastically.
"Can I get you anything?"
"A drink please."

I stood with a pipe in my mouth and paced towards the office. The door opened with a notable squeal, likely from me not tending to it for a while.

"Which bottle?" I asked, halfway out the door frame.

"Napoleon Natur. The green bottle." He groaned. "Key should be on my desk."

I walked towards his desk picked up the key, unlocked the cabinet, and pulled out his bottle. It fits the décor of antique poisons as the label was fading and the chipping.

I kept my pipe in my mouth, brought a tumbler with me, and balanced it all towards my friend.

Samara saw me enter back into the hall. He was bowled over but still tried to put on a smile. "Did you get one for yourself?" he asked.

I was confused. It must have shown on my face since he gave me a coy shake of his head with a smile still on his face.

"What's the occasion?"

"An apology, now go get one for yourself!"

I froze in place for a second before feeling my heart swell with joy. I gave him the bottle and tumbler before I went back into the office and got myself a tumbler. I sat down next to him and tried my best to act natural.

We sat there for a moment in silence. Only liquid poring and tobacco burning could be heard until Samara broke the melancholy.

"I shouldn't have shouted at you." Samara said. "It wasn't fair of me."

I leaned forward and rubbed the bridge of my nose.

"You were right." I said miserably.

"No, I wasn't. I was being an idiot and I didn't mean to hurt you." He retorted. He turned to face me and placed his hand on my back.

One question persisted in my mind. Why does he want to speak to his killer?

"I want to say, that I still think of you as a friend. You were always there when I needed you and I don't want to drive you away." He spoke.

"What did I do to deserve this?" I said.

"What do you mean?"

"I mean you ki—" Samara interrupted me. He gave a theatrical gesture to waft away my words.

"I wouldn't be here without you, you fool!" He took a hearty gulp of his drink. "Without you, I would have died years and years ago."

"So… are you in debt with me?" I questioned. I was a little offended, but I wanted to hear his words.

"Without you, I would have gone out like a fart in the wind."

"It was nothing." I dismissed.

"Nothing?!" He scoffed. "Nice to know what I'm worth." He joked.

"Just don't go on that path again." I counselled.

"Yes, mother!" He dismissed dramatically. "I'll do my best to make you proud."

I gave a small chuckle. I'm thankful to hear that he didn't hate me, but I was still far away from accepting the situation.

"I can see you're still a little upset…" Samara pointed his thumb toward the church door. "I can get you a date with one of the ladies in the church if you feel like it." He whispered like a schoolboy planning mischief.

I laughed and waved off his idea.

"No thank you. I know what you like." I chuckled.

"I'll have you know; my women are the fruit of the earth. I only pick the best." He exclaimed bombastically.

Immediately the church doors creaked open. Hearing this, Samara and I hid our vices and tried to act like priests for once. Samara put out my pipe in his own way… by spitting into it and quickly drank the remained of his tumbler. I quickly straightened up and stood up from the seat to face the guest.

"Hello again, did you—"

I was stunned to see our guest.

"Hello, boy!" I bellowed out.

Samara turned. His eyebrows were raised in surprise, and he slowly lifted himself off the pew.

"Merry Christmas!" Samara yelled out jovially. "Fedor, get a tumbler for our guest!"

Samara forced my sullied pipe into my hands.

177

"Did you spit in this?" I asked. I saw a wet mark in the bowl filled with half-burned tobacco.

"I had to think quickly!" Samara opened his arms dramatically and then shrugged.

I rolled my eyes.

"Piece of shit!" I said to him. I childishly bonked him on the head with the bowl of my pipe before going into the office and getting more crystal glasses.

By the time I re-entered the room, they were in conversation already.

"How was your regular Christmas, boy?"

He looked confused. I think he never heard of another kind of Christmas.

"What?" He mouthed.

"Oh, we have Christmas tomorrow but not like regular people in December." Samara explained.

"Oh!" He exclaimed. "It was ok, got to eat some food and got some decent bits for myself." The boy sat by Samara with a small wince. "How about you?"

I saw this and I called him out on it immediately.

"Are you ok?"

"Yeah..." He paused. "I'm just a little sore."

"See Fedor, he's tougher than both of us." Samara joked. He gave a hearty pat on the boy's back, causing him to fall into a groan. Samara was surprised at what had happened. His face was gaping open with shock, but he quickly steeled himself and tried to make amends.

"Oh my god, I'm so sorry!" Samara blustered.

I rushed over to him and put the boy's glass on the floor beside him. "My god boy, what happened?"

"Nothing." He tried to assure us.

"I don't believe you." I said to him sternly. "Something happened."

"Come on boy, we won't judge you." Samara chimed in. My colleague leaned in, placed his hand on the boy's shoulder and gestured towards me with his drink. "Don't worry, that miserable stick is pretty good at patching himself up, I think he should be able to help you out."

A few seconds passed, and the boy let out a sigh and got up. He kept his back up but revealed a horror. He lifted his shirt and revealed his bruised back to us. Samara and I were in shock. His back was almost covered in black and blue.

"My dad did this." The boy whimpered. "Can you fix this?"

The shock soon turned to rage for both of us after hearing it. We looked at each other and gave a confirming look.

"Fedor, get your gun!" He turned to me, his brow was wrinkled in spite. "I'm killing this piece of shit!"

"What?" The boy yelped aloud.

"You're not getting a damn thing from me!" I said sternly. "Let's think about this before—"

Samara interrupted me.

"Think about what?" Samara's voice was on the brink of cracking. "Have you seen him?" He gestured to the boy.

"I'm not helping you kill anyone; those days are over!" I escalated my volume.

"So, I'll do it. I'm dying anyway, I might as well take someone with me."

"And what's your plan? Turn up to his doorstep and blast him in the face?"

"Yes!" Samara roared. "How hard can it be? It's a gun, you point and shoot."

"Look! Be serious and stop being a clown!" I pointed at him.

"I am being serious, it's not that hard!"

"Look, you're still being a clown! If I squeeze your belly hard enough, will you honk?"

"If I kick you in the balls hard enough, will you fall to the floor?"

"Enough!" A voice echoed through the hall. The boy came between the two of us and shoved us aside. I was shocked by the level of force used, I think any harder and my colleague would have fallen on the floor instead of a small stumble.

"No killing!" He commanded.

Samara quickly recovered from his stumble. "I'm not letting someone beat you to a pulp boy!"

The boy turned to Samara. "What does it matter to you?" He cried out with a slight petulance.

179

Samara was frozen for a second, before taking the time to form a response that wouldn't be clouded by his drinks.

"Because you're our boy." He said charitably. "Because you've proven to be there for us, even when we didn't deserve you to be there, and I will sooner go to hell myself than let some poor excuse for a human being beat on you!"

The boy stood there for a while as if his muscles were paralyzed. He turned to me with a feeling I didn't think he had ever experienced before.

Love from a father.

He came in a hugged the both of us. One arm around each priest. In return, we held him in ours.

"Thank you so much." He whimpered.

I briefly looked at Samara and I saw him smiling. I looked back at this child and felt my son with me. We let go and I sat down on a pew. The other two stood up and Samara kept a hand on his shoulder.

"What do we do?" The boy said.

"Come back here tomorrow." Samara said. "Me and this idiot will figure something out by then." He gestured his thumb towards me.

"I can't I have work tomorrow." The boy said.

"We'll stay extra open, don't worry." Samara replied.

I grew curious and took a swig of my drink.

"Where do you work?" I asked coldly.

"Takeaway shop on Waterloo Street."

Oh lord… Why did he have to be there?

Samara and I gave each other a worried glance but tried to keep it hidden enough from the boy.

"Leave it with me." I said before taking a drink from my crystal.

"Get here for elven tomorrow."

The boy looked confused, like he unearthed unheard history. He did, and he just stepped in the middle of it.

"I know the owner. I'll take care of it, and I'll make sure you get paid for it."

"But…"

"No buts boy, I want you here for service and then we'll talk, OK?"

The boy accepted defeat and bowed his head.

"OK." He spoke.

"Go home for now and we'll figure something OK, OK?" Samara said.

The boy walked out but not before saying goodbye and a few comforting words.

The door closed and sealed us off from the world.

"You're not going to speak to him, are you?"

"I must."

"Is this a good idea Fedor?"

"No, but he owes me."

"Old debts have a habit of being forgotten." He said glumly.

Lisa
Half six at night

The snow was starting to turn into thick brown sludge from the cars and human traffic coming around the town. I walked past the high street and slowly made my way toward the more isolated areas of the town where less than savoury characters hang about. I marched closer and I could hear the faint sound of blasting music. Far enough away from the major area where normal people hung about. I pulled my bright red coat closer to myself to keep the cold away. The music got louder, and I came closer to the derelict shopping sector of the town. I was smoking my last cigarette to try to give myself a little courage before confronting these people.

I wanted to talk to these people. I needed the closure, and I was begging to hear them admit it!

Soon, there it stood in front of me. The derelict toy shop where these junkies hung out.

"Found you." I said to myself before stubbing out my cigarette with my high-heeled boots.

The shop had most of its windows boarded up, but faint stands of amber light escaped from their prison. This looked like a squatter and or a drug den but not many people dared to enter.

I walked up to this disaster of a building and held to rusted door bars. I wanted to open the doors, but something was stopping me. Was it the music, was I not strong enough, or was it the fact that weed could be smelt wafting through the door cracks? "Come on honey, you can do this." I tried to pump myself up. I gripped the rusted door bars firmly with my black leather gloves. "One... Two..."

Suddenly, I felt the door fly open with all the music and smells escaping it. It was like an herbal mortuary, where plants and songs went to die.

A lady wearing white platform boots with cat skulls and a neon-coloured dress opened the door for me. She eyed me up and down whilst holding a can of beer in her hand.

"Can I help you?" She scowled.

"I want to talk about Ava! They're saying her death was—"

"We heard." The woman sounded annoyed. "I know who you are as well so again, can I help you?"

"Why did she have drugs in her system!?" I demanded.

"I dunno, maybe she took some?" She said sarcastically.

"I know it was you guys, she hung around you guys the most!"

"Strong accusation. Got proof?"

"I don't need proof to get police here."

She took a sip of her beer and disinterested frown.

"Try it bitch." She said dismissively.

That made my blood boil. Who does she think she is?

"What did you say?" I yelled at her.

"You heard me." She leaned on the door frame and crossed her arms.

"Party!" Someone called out. "You good?"

"Yeah, I just got this bitch saying she's going to call the cops on us."

Uh oh... I think I'm screwed.

"What?" The voice called out in shock.

I heard the clatter of trash and shifts of movement.

"Who said what now?" The man with the bowl cut said. "I'll—"

He stopped himself when he looked at me.

"Oh..." He paused. "Hello." He gave me a disgusting toothy smile, that is if he had any left. His rotting teeth made me feel sick to my stomach. That or his smell. I backed away slowly as soon as he came to the door.

"You strike me as a lady of class, I myself consider myself a man of taste." He perversely said.

"I might be classy but I'm not going anywhere near you. You're wearing a tracksuit, and you probably have trashy tattoos and such."

The woman looked less than amused but the man was a little too interested. She gave an eye roll and went back inside.

"Whatever. Have fun with her Nova." She said disinterestedly. He gave her a brief look before refocusing on me.

"Well love, unfortunately, my Gucci suit is in the wash, and my tattoos are stunning I'll have you know!"

I kept backing away slowly, but he matched my pace and kept following.

He pushed up his sleeves and pulled back his bowl cut. There were no tattoos I could see. Until he started to pull down the waist of his tracksuit bottoms, still covering the parts I didn't want to see.

"I can show you the rest, but you'd have to come inside with me."

I didn't give a second thought. I turned and ran as fast as my heels could take me.

"You'll come back!" I could hear him calling.

I ran with my heels, trying my best to not slip on the ice. I kept going until I got to a bus station surrounded by the odd scatterings of people. I cried on a small metal bench, letting my makeup drain down my face. A few people walked and gawked at me, but their views didn't matter to me. Not as much as the group I just saw again. I expected a little compassion, some sort of sadness for her death. But no...

This was the gang in full swing... Uncaring junkies and addicts.

Sidorovich
20:36

Even in the working town atmosphere, this place looked bleaker than usual. It was the stuff you would find lowlife trying to spend any money they had to be drenched in grease and artery cement. I approached the doors and saw the inside of it. It was a little messy but that was to be expected of a fast-food shop. It looked a little run down, but it expected better. I could smell the thick grease wafting through the air clinging to my smoke-ridden robes. Deep fryers and the whirring and girding of machinery could be heard over the few smatters of customers sitting on poorly maintained furniture. I approached the counter, garbed in my robes, where some teenager who looked too young to have been here greeted me. Behind her was a maze of kitchen appliances and foodstuff with a workforce that was not much older than her but not much younger than the boy.

"Hiya, can I take your order?" She said disinterestedly.

Her dark hair was pulled back to expose her caramel skin and umbral eyes which were surrounded by smoky makeup.

"Owner." I said frigidly.

Her disinterest evaporated in an instant and she mustered her best customer service voice. Still, however, it sounded a little condescending.

"I'm sorry, but he's away at the moment."

"I'll wait." I pulled out a pipe and readied a smoke. "He knows me."

Her expression turned to shock as I readied to light up a smoke.

"Umm… I'm sorry but you can't do that here!"

I looked to some patrons to my side. They gave us shocked faces. I was finally getting some attention. The girl frantically looked around her surroundings, perhaps to look for help, perhaps to look for an escape. It does not matter. I glared at this poor young girl which made her back down. Like a puppy who was disowned by their master. Behind her, the adolescent mass stood helplessly, unsure of what to do. Some tried to ignore me, some couldn't help but watch.

"Fine!" She said in frustration. "I'll get him!"

She walked away from the grease-stained counter, chiding me under her breath as she went.

I waited there for a few moments, but I heard the aggravated bellows of an old brother.

"Just throw this idiot out!" He screamed at the poor teenager.

"I tried but he—"

I could hear the volume rise as they came closer. The spectators could only watch in horror. To them, it sounded like a fight was going to happen.

"No excuses!" He bellowed. "I'll show you how it's done."

"He said he knows you."

"He'll know the feeling of my fist in a second."

They turned the corner and revealed themselves to the counter.

"What do—"

The man stared at me dumbfounded. His mouth was gaping open, making his thick moustache curve into a horseshoe. A ghost was in front of him now.

"Hello, Lev." I smirked at him taking the pipe from my mouth and holding it in my hand. "I've come to talk."

"Get out." He backed away for a few steps. The girl next to him had never seen him in the state. I could only assume that he led his workforce by force.

"Sorry boss." She whispered to him. "I've got to get back to work."

He waved her away, still holding that dumb expression on his face. She went back to the counter taking her orders, pretending that nothing had happened.

"What do you want?" He gasped out in Russian.

I responded in our language. "Like I said..." I lit my pipe. "To talk."

20:57

He led me to somewhere we could talk. Past all his workers and the disgustingly grime-caked machinery. The work surfaces were less to standard and there was little pride in their work. Although I couldn't blame them. He was a stubborn bastard back then, but now I feel like not much has changed.

We conversed in Russian.

"Why are you here?" I said as I smoked my pipe.

"I came here like you. Away from a country that hated me." It was clear he disdained me. Even though we fought together, we weren't brothers.

"I meant why are you here in this dump?"

185

He stopped us in our stride. He turned to me and was ready to let his new facial hair do the talking. His upper lip twitched, and his eyes narrowed.

"You haven't been here for thirty seconds, and you insult my business, offend my workers, and break the rules?" He pointed his fat forefinger to my face. "You've got some balls on you, you know."

"I know… and I've come to you for help."

He turned away from me and continued his march.

"That's rich." He scoffed. "Why should I help you?"

He turned the corner and unlocked his office.

It was a mess of old posters with half-naked women and the occasional trophy he scattered around. The room was dark and barely lit with a dim yellow bulb being its only illumination. It was a mess. The man forgot his training and his discipline.

"There's a boy under your employment." I said to him. The smell of the room finally hit me. It stank of sweat and despair.

"I have a few people under my employment. Has someone offended?" He walked behind his desk and slammed his full weight onto a barely maintained leather chair, half of which was peeling off and exposing the lime green sponge underneath. Whereas I sat down on a cheap plastic chair.

"No, it's someone that means dearly to me."

Lev opened a drawer that had a bottle of cheap vodka.

"Why should I care?" He questioned whilst unscrewing the cap into two paper cups.

"The boy was attacked by his father." I sat down on a wooden chair in front of him.

"Again, why should I care?"

"You should care because it's the right thing to do."

"And why should I care about the right thing? He comes into work, and leaves. Anything else is not my concern." Lev pushed a paper cup towards me and took a sip from the other.

"What happened to you? Where has that purposeful anger gone?"

"It was left with those Mouja or Taliban or whatever you call them now." He reclined and swirled his drink. "It was left with those people who killed Ilya."

"What happened to the boat he wanted?" I asked him.

186

"The dream died with him when Slava… he got him killed."
"You still blame him, don't you?"
"Of course, I blame him!" Lev erupted into a fury. "He led us into that ambush! He deserved to die there!"
"God would… say otherwise." I tried to console him.
"Of course he would, but then again we don't know his plan." He responded sarcastically.
"He would also say you need to let go of that hate."
"When you take that advice, I will." He said solemnly.
"What?" I mouthed the word before I said it with shock; I was caught off guard.
"You heard me." Spoke coldly like he was throwing shards of ice toward me. He threw me a menacing glare. That dormant hate was starting to emerge.
"You preach to me this wisdom, but I know you still hate Vasya for what he did to that child. For what he did to Kars." Lev stood up. "Look at your own hands, you never left that place! So how dare you speak to me like I am without sin or flaws?" He pointed to the door. "Get out of my building!" He demanded.
"I'm not leaving, you still owe me!" I stood up and matched his energy.
"Get out! It won't take Dima and his magic to realise what I'm going to do to you if you don't." He hissed through his teeth.
"Is that what Ilya would want?"
"Don't you bring his name into this!" He screamed.
"He was the kinder of you two, he would want you to help me."
"And what do you think Grigori would want?"
I stopped talking and felt sadness in my heart. I took a second to collect myself before slowly becoming enraged.
"Don't you bring my son into this." I hissed.
"Then don't you bring my brother into this!" He yelled. "Last chance! What do you want?!"
I took a breath and glared at him.
"Pay the boy his wages, give him the day off tomorrow, and get me a photo of his father." I said coldly.
He gave me a bombastic chuckle before scoffing in my face.
"You ask for a lot." He leaned closer over the desk. "And where is this money coming from?"

"I'll pay for it." I reached into my pocket and pulled out one hundred pounds. "Give this to him."

Lev sat down and reclined in his chair. He stroked his moustache for a moment before finally answering.

"No."

I was shocked at his reply.

"What did you say?"

"I said no, I'll give him the day off work, but I won't give him any money and I won't stalk a customer for you. Do that yourself."

"But—"

"Get out of my office Fedor." He said gesturing at the door. He was angry with me as if he were angry at a helpless insect. It simply wasn't worth it.

I turned towards the door in defeat, ready to tell the boy I failed him.

"I'll say I gave the money to you." Lev said. "I can't let my work staff know I give out free money." He screwed the cap on his vodka before putting it back into his desk. "No promises on the father though."

I walked out the door and back out into the freezing cold. I didn't fail, not completely.

Bern
10:53am

I did as I was commanded. I got a call from my boss about not coming to work today and that he would pay me for the day. I hardly believed it, but the old Russian managed to get it done. Although the boss didn't sound like himself... He sounded sadder. I took the bus to church and turned up in my makeshift funeral clothes. I tried to dress to impress as best as I could, even though I didn't know what to expect. I walked through the church doors, and I saw... people.

Other people besides me and the priests. It felt alien and suffocating. This was our space and others invaded it, but I also understood that this place was their home as well, so I kept my mouth shut and respected it. People sat on the pews and awaited instructions as they chatted amongst themselves. Mostly older people, but they stared at the new member that they didn't recognise before. The women had their heads covered in thin scarves, most of which had some kind of pattern on them. All there were dressed smartly. Finally, I saw the priests. Both wore gold vestments. Samara wore white robes underneath, whereas Sidorovich wore black. The shine of the glass through the windows gave the church a beautiful purple aura and I swear the plants there glowed. It was beautiful.

I saw the altar there. It had a picture of Mary and Jesus, but it was guarded by their two protectors there. A pair of golden candle pedestals, the top of them covered in sand where yellow burning candles darted their individual pedestals.
I walked up to the priests, and they were warmer than ever. They smiled.
"Take a candle and bow to the altar." Samara whispered to me and gave me a yellow candle. I was half attentive to the sick man, but I was interested in what was behind the fold up wall. The doors were finally open and behind it I saw another altar, this time with various pieces of gold and silver, surrounded by lazily burning candles. Another piece of reverence. Another piece I must learn of.

"Put it in the sand after you light it." I looked back at him, and the colour of the candle in my hand almost matched his skin. He was dying and these were the later stages of his death sentence. But even dying, that warm glow was still there with him.
I did as I was commanded, I took the candle and lit it with the others by pressing my candle wick with the burning ones. I left it in the sand and then took my seat at the front.

"And now, we begin." Samara said to the church.

"*Hospodi po mo insa.*" Sidorovich echoed in return.

Samara started chanting in a strange language, closer to what Sidorovich spoke. This was strange and peaceful. Some might

189

say reverential. The elderly stood up and made a sign of a cross. Sidorovich walked by the edge of the church and wafted a censer to the crowd, blessing us with its smoke.

The church and its small community blazed with a rapturous symphony. This place felt peaceful and perfect.

Michael
Twelve-ish

It was lunchtime at me work. I thought about giving a visit to the shop where Bernard worked to get some cheap deals on food and to check that he was working still. I drove up to his work and parked outside the takeaway shop.

The place had a small queue. I join the other people and keep a lookout for me lad. From the back of the queue, he was nowhere to be seen. I shrugged it off, but I was getting worried. People thankfully got out of the way quickly, meaning I could get a full view of the people inside.

I got to the front to place me order and… there was no Bernard. Just some young girl was there.

"Can I take your order?" She said in her customer service voice.

"Yeah… triple cheeseburger with fries and a large coke."

I was quickly scanning the room whilst she put my order into the till.

"Where's Bernard?" I asked her.

"I don't know." She casually shrugged away.

"What do you mean?" I pushed.

"I mean he's not around sir, I'm sorry."

I wanted to flip over the counter. How could he not be here? He was meant to be working!

"Right, but I'm his dad and I need to speak to him!" I pushed further, really trying to press this girl.

Suddenly, this big guy with a moustache came to the counter.

"It's ok Grace, I've got this." He said calmly. "Take the other people's orders."

He turned to me.

"I'm sorry but Bern is doing an errand for me right now. He'll be back soon."

"When's soon?"

"Soon enough." He dismissed me. The nerve on him. "But he has nominated you for customer of the year."
Nominated me for what now?

"It means that you get a free meal and a picture hanging on the wall." He pointed to a section of the restaurant wall. The photos looked old, but I never noticed them until now... weird. "Does that sound good?"
I was blown away. I never thought I'd get free food and a picture from the lad.
"Yeah, it sounds good." I cheered.
"Excellent!"
This Russian guy pulled out a mini print camera and told me to get ready.
"Say cheese."
"Cheese." I roared with a giant grin on me face.
"Perfect!" He called out as the camera printed out me face. "I'll get this on the wall before you know it and your meal today will be free of charge!"
"That's amazing, thank you!"
He wafted the photo in the air.
"Don't mention it."
He walked up to the girl that served me and whispered something in her ear. I can imagine that it was about my prize but when he pointed at me, her face sank a little. I don't know what was going on, but I got a bad feeling. So, I waited, got me food, and then went back to work as fast as I could.
Food got cold when I reached the office building as well.

Sidorovich
13:13

The sermon ended as it began, in harmony. We all wished each other a merry Christmas whilst talking about their personal lives and struggles. Samara meanwhile did not care for such things and proceeded to try flirting with some of the older women. Summarily, they grew tired of him and walked away thinking it was a joke. He took it in his stride and said, "Maybe it'll be my present for next year."

His skin was turning yellow, and his hair was starting to grey more than usual. The boy was there, shy as ever, and was hesitant to talk to any of the older churchgoers. Soon, our elderly patrons walked out of the church and into the bitter cold. The church was finally ours again and we could be ourselves once more.

The door slammed shut and the world was gone.

"I think Maggie is getting the hots for me you know." Samara joked.

"You wish." I responded. "Where's these famous moves I've been hearing about?"

"I'm saving them for the really good-looking ones?" He smiled and winked.

Samara walked into the office, presumably to grab a drink for himself.

"Boy, do you want a drink?" He bellowed from inside the office. "Please!"

"OK, I've got a treat for you!"

I could hear him rummaging around the office and the creaks of his cabinet doors opening.

"Piece of shit, do you want anything?" He said jokingly to me.

"Tobacco." I called back.

He rushed back into the hall. I in the meantime was taking off my vestments to reveal more of the black underneath.

"How was the service?" Samara asked the boy.

"I loved it."

"You're a natural you know." Samara jovially praised. He handed one of the tumblers to the boy and opened a dusty dark green bottle. "You know, I thought communion would have caught you out but no, you did well. I hope we can see more of you in the sermons." Samara threw me my tobacco and leaned next to whisper to the boy. "I can get you hooked up with some of the ladies here."

The boy jumped back with a mixture of shock and joy.

"Umm… I'm ok thanks."

I gave a small chuckle whilst readying my pipe.

"I think they're a bit old for him."

"What's wrong with a cougar?!" he said to me.

I rolled my eyes and shook my head at hearing this.

"Anyway, me and this stick thought about getting you some Christmas presents."

The boy was shocked and delighted. His face lit up like a star and he stood to attention.

"What did you get me?"

"Step into my office." Samara got up and clutched his belly, leaving the crystal and bottle in the hall. Me and the boy followed him there. The office was cramped with the three of us there but that did not matter. The boy stepped in, and his Christmas was made.

There were two presents, one from each of us. One was large and shoddily wrapped in silver wrapping paper whereas the other was small and packed neatly in golden foil.

The boy stood there paralyzed.

"Well go on!" Samara roared.

"Don't leave us in anticipation." I chimed in.

He turned and looked at us with that twinkle in his eye. He wrapped his arms around us and nearly broke us with the strength in his arms. We returned the favour and gently hugged him.

"Thank you." He hugged tighter before letting go.

He went at the paper like a ravenous dog. He opened the bigger one first and it revealed a suit. It was a three-piece and black and white. The lapels of the blazer were silk, and it glistened in the dim light. Underneath the suit was a pair of patent leather pointed shoes which shone like polished marble.

Samara grinned. "I thought you might need some good clothes for when you next bring a lady friend. Just remember, find a good one this time."

The boy's lip quivered. He looked like he was about to burst into tears.

"Go on, open the other." Samara blustered.

The boy wiped his eyes and moved to the other present. He slowly unfolded it and revealed an ebony wood box. He slid the top of the box off and exposed my present to the church.

"A pipe!" He exclaimed.

He turned and showed it to us. It was a small thing. The bowl was red with a wooden pattern on it whilst the stem was solid, polished black. Both were connected by a thin silver band. Inside the box were all the accessories a new smoker needed. Tobacco, a tamper, a packet of cleaning sticks, and a jet lighter. As well as the one hundred pounds that I tried to get Lev to give him.

"I saw that you liked smoking mine so I thought you should have one of your own." I said to him.

He collapsed on the floor, still holding the box in his hands. Then he started sobbing.

"Oh God boy!" I gasped out. "Did I get you something you don't like?"

I got on the floor and tried to pick him up.

"No…" He sniffled. "It's perfect."

15:32

"Do you think he'll like it?" Samara asked.

"I think he'll love it!" I said back to him.

We waited on the pews in anticipation for what seemed to be an eternity. Soon eternity ended and out he stepped from the office door.

He looked like a true gentleman. Our boy stepped out in his suit, and he looked like he could dazzle women walking past him. The suit was a slim fit, but it looked like Samara thankfully guessed his size correctly.

We sat there like proud fathers and gave him bright smiles.

"How does it feel?" I asked with my pipe in hand.

"It feels amazing, if a little tight on the stomach."

"You look amazing!" Samara exclaimed. He patted me on the back. "Don't you think Fedor?"

"He does." I proudly remarked.

The boy walked up to us and pulled out his new pipe. He readied it like I showed him and lit it. I couldn't stop smiling.

His tobacco smelt sweet like whiskey and gave of fruity, almost cake-like notes on the nose.

"You look like a true gentleman." I said joyfully.

The boy smirked and bowed his head.

194

"Drink?" Samara asked.

"Please."

The new gentleman sat with us and was given a tumbler of whiskey. He looked like an old man in a young man's body. He looked like he was meant to belong here, and I thank God that he brought this boy here for me to raise.

"So, what happens now?" The boy asked.

"Now boy." I said. "We celebrate Christmas."

Lev
20:32

I left my business in the hands of a capable person. Someone who was at the very least competent to lead. I drove to the church where my old squad mate was and what I saw baffled me. I assumed this would be a quick post and go but it wouldn't be since there were still lights functioning inside. It looked like they were beams straight from the sun which were painting the frigid night with religious colours. I walked up to the door, and I saw small dots of light that tried to escape the consecrated ground and into the darkened void partially illuminated by streetlights. I knocked on the door with a force hard enough to get the occupants' attention but not hard enough to break this fragile door. I pounded my fist three times at first and I could hear the sound reverberate inside. No answer…

I pounded again and then finally I could hear someone.

"Good God!" I heard someone yell. "I'm coming!"

The door creaked open, and I saw a slightly small yellow man there in a white robe.

"Is Fedor here?" I spoke bluntly to the man.

"Yeah, he's here." He sputtered. He made a small hiccup and then turned around to face the church. "Fedor, your lover is here!" He yelled out.

It made my face twitch and my stomach turn hearing those words. I rolled my eyes and waited for him to come to me. I folded my arms and felt the squeak of the polyester coat on my arms. Soon that hypocrite came to the door. I could smell the cigar smoke get stronger and stronger as he walked closer and

195

closer. Then he stood there in his black robes looking unimpressed like I ruined his wedding or something similar.

"Here's the photo." I said to him. I quickly pulled the picture out of my pocket and placed it in his scarred hands. He was dumbstruck that I had managed to get it done.
"How…?" He mouthed to me.
"Don't ask and I won't tell."
"So…" he took a quick puff of his cigar before putting the photo away and up his sleeve. "I guess we're even."
"No, we're not."

Fedor's face twisted into a hideous shape at me uttering those words.
"Think of it as my Christmas present to you." I said to him.
"I didn't think you were a believer."
"I'm not, but I know you are." I sighed and stroked my forehead. "I'm too old and too tired to keep track of petty things. All I know is that whoever that man is, he offended my staff and if he does that to the little people, then God help your boy for how he treats him…"

The priest gave a slow huff and glimpsed inside. He shut the door and took the light away from us. He placed his hand on the door and leaned against it whilst bowing his head away from me.
"He beats him." Fedor meekly said to me in our language.
The news shocked me and made my forehead visibly wrinkle.
"What do you mean?" I responded to him in the same tongue. My mind still couldn't process this.
"I mean…" He sighed and rubbed the bridge of his nose. "My boy walked into the church one day and he showed us the marks on his back from his father beating him." Fedor straightened up and looked me in the eye. "This is why I need to find out who he is, so I can protect him."
My mind was racing with solutions. I tried to figure out what to do.
"What if we get him away?" I spoke.
"And put him where? I can't keep him at the church, and we can't take him home with us."

"What if we get police involved?" I rubbed my moustache. "They'll do nothing since I've been told he works for the courts. So, who's side will they take?"

"Fuck..."

I was trying to think of something on the spot, but nothing was coming to mind.

"Do you know how much he must pay a month Lev?"

I stood to attention. I did not know he had to pay for anything at all.

"No. How much?"

"He must pay five hundred a month."

The old anger in me was being awakened. I felt hate I haven't felt in years.

"What?!" I yelled out. "That's extortion!"

"Exactly!" Fedor said. "So, he can't lose his job and he can't run because he needs to finish school. So, what can we do?"

I paced back and forth.

"But he can't keep working since his grades will suffer." I pointed out.

Suddenly an idea came into my head.

"I can promote him!"

One of Fedor's eyebrows raised.

"Why so he can get extorted more?" He said harshly.

"No, I side-promote him."

"What?" He yelped in confusion.

"As in he still works for the same pay, but I have him work in my office. Easier work and he can study in the office with me." I exclaimed.

Fedor was quick to point out holes in my plan.

"Won't you need to replace him?"

"Not if he works hard enough."

"What about your other workers?"

"What about them?" I responded whilst flapping my hands about like a madman.

"Won't they suspect something?"

"I'll tell them anything I need them to believe." I threw my arm in the approximate direction of my business. "I told them today the man was a retired stripper, so they stop giving him the time of day as much." I chuckled. "Now I can add he beats his own son. Whatever I tell them, they'll believe it. I'll tell your boy in a couple of days. I'll let him enjoy his hangover."

Fedor gave me a pat on the shoulder before opening the door. It opened with a violent creak, but he stopped in his tracks.
"How did you trick him?" He asked.
His back was turned to me and his face was almost faded out by the light.
"With these." I pulled out the souls of old ghosts and showed him it.
Fedor turned back into the dark his angular jaw was practically on the floor.
"Our old war photos." He whispered to me.
"Even dead they still help us." I stuff the photos back into my pocket. "Like I said, don't ask and I won't answer."
Fedor bowed his head and gave small nods. We didn't say another word to each other. He walked back into the light and the warmth of the church whereas I stood outside and waited for the door to close with the horrid squeak.
The light had vanished, and I walked back to my car.

Lisa
Half nine-ish at night.

I can't take it anymore. I feel lost in this place. This school in the night is a haunting place. I come here to think about what to do and to collect my thoughts, especially when mourning. I like to break in here through some of the bushes and slip into the building where one window was always left open. I knew where to avoid the cameras and I would usually go and smoke in one of the science labs since they would think that it was just a burner going off again. I sit by the teacher's desk, in a dark lab with only my cigarettes being the brightest thing around. I kick my bright trainers up onto the desk and lean back. I couldn't even crack a smile. I just felt empty inside. She died; she treated me like shit under her platform boots but the fact that she was taken by those junkies only made me feel hatred towards them. At the end of the day, she was my friend… But could I still say that after this? I guess I felt partially guilty as well. Like the universe knew to kill her off as soon as I deleted the photos of us together.

But I felt hatred particularly for one of them, that one with the bowl cut. It felt like he was a predator trying to chase after his next victim. I don't know why he tried to pursue me; he never did before when I last went there with Ava. Maybe her death changed it, maybe not. It doesn't matter.

I finish my smoke and then throw the cigarette butt into one of the lab basins, flushing it down with water to hide the evidence. I walk through the hallways and roam like a phantom in a graveyard. The empty classrooms felt strange and somewhat inviting. I walked past some of the displays and stalked the teachers' lounge to see if there was anything I could scavenge from the fridge that they left behind.
I was lucky this time, I managed to find a can of cola, some fruit, and a chocolate bar in the fridge. The bar was solid enough to break teeth, so I started snacking on the fruit instead.
I walked closer to the art block and saw the various levels of artistic skill and creativity. All the different mediums took form into something completely different thing in the dark. The statues and the paintings looked like creatures of the night.

I cracked open my can of cola in the hall, the pop of the can reverberated through the corridors, and the vulnerable carbonated sugar water fizzed into silence.
I slurped from the can occasionally and then I walked past… oh god…

It was *her* section.

She was an amazing artist. She focused on an ink medium, where she used ink on canvases and paper. She took a tattooist-style approach using hatching and cross-hatching in her works. She focused on people and mainly some sort of macabre looks. Skeletal figures darted around the board. I swear the ink and the shapes shifted and changed around the board. Like her world was alive, even after her passing. They kept it up there with a big yellow sign saying:

"We miss our best, Ava Vincent."

A pitiful excuse at a memorial. She wasn't even in school that much. She would have even hated that piss yellow colour. They just did it to look good after the death of a student. In short, a publicity stunt to save face. I couldn't bear to look at it for another moment. I grabbed my phone and did the unthinkable. I tried to call Bern. I ran away from the display so fast that the chocolate brick in my pocket fell onto the floor and echoed through the ghostly halls but not so fast to spill my drink. I ran into the nearest classroom without cameras, hid under the teacher's desk, put the drink to my side, and started dialling on my phone.

Buzz tone… Buzz tone…

"Hello?" I whispered.
I could hear music being played in some foreign language, the odd bits of laughter, and some Russian accent over the phone.

"Hello, good wife. How can I help you?" He slurred.

At least someone is enjoying themselves. It felt like I was speaking to the town centre lot, but this was different.

"Good wife?" I whisper yelled. I calmed down and vented all my rage from that immediate comment out of my nostrils. "Are you ok?" I whispered through gritted teeth.

"Never better!" He cheered. He sounded half drunk and struggled to form the syllables.

"Boy!" Another voice called out. "Stop calling your hooker and come join us."
What the fuck did he just call me?

200

"Sit your arse down Samara." He retaliated. "Go grab us another bottle!"

"And some tobacco!" The Russian voice called out.

Already I had heard enough. This was far too raucous for the person I knew, and I felt that he had lost himself to another similar group. Fucking addicts… But who am I to talk to? I still smoke my cigarettes.

I hung up on him and sobbed into my knees. I felt the tears stream down my face, where the grief and anger exposed themselves. I kicked my arms and legs like a toddler having a tantrum before burying my finger into my hair.

"What the fuck do I do now?" I whimpered into the empty classroom.

Bern
8:57am

167 days post exam.

That was perhaps the best Christmas of my life. We drank, we sang, we ate, and we partied as if we were going to die. The only thing I didn't like was the hangover the next morning. That hurt like no tomorrow, the interesting part was hiding it from my dad and brother. I took a page from Lisa's book and started spraying myself down with deodorant to hide the smell in my clothes. Worst of all, I had to pretend that I was ok. I guess I could take that statement in many forms. Today I had to work. Even though I was starting to hate my flesh and blood, I needed to make sure we had a roof over our heads.

I walked to work, cured of the world's second-worst hangover, and pretended like nothing had happened. I had a feeling of a dream hangover me though. I wondered what the priest had said. I know he wasn't the gentlest person in the world, which was Samara's job when he was in the right state of drunk. I walked through the door in my work uniform and tried my best to act natural even though there was a bruise on my face from my patriarch's latest outburst.

My 'natural' act didn't last long when I walked through the door and my manager was there. Nobody was in the shop. No customers, no other workers. Just him...

Oh god... what's going on?

"You're late." He spoke with crossed arms. "I want to see you in the office."
He pointed towards the back of the restaurant and waited for me to start walking getting angrier and angrier the longer time passed to follow my command. I walked in that direction and then my boss followed me. I walked into the room full of mess and the occasional pornographic poster. I sat down on this rickety plastic chair and waited to get my sentence. Soon my boss followed and landed on his deteriorating leather chair. He took a deep sigh and finally spoke.

"I'm promoting you."
The words felt like some kind of sick joke. I felt like I was about to be ambushed by cameras on put onto the trendiest social media page for my reaction.
"What?" I gasped out in shock.
"You heard me." He reclined back into his chair and rested his hands on his stomach. "You've been a good worker."
For some reason, my first reaction was to pull out my pipe from my jacket pocket. I was still in shock, but I had the craving to smoke for some reason.
"You can smoke in here."
I was doubly shocked. He gave me a confirming gesture. Allowing me to proceed to ready my pipe for a smoke.

Lev
09:32

I sat there in my office with Fedor's boy opposite me. I grabbed a bottle of spirits and poured vodka for myself and him into paper cups. He sat there with his new pipe, cradling it like a puppy. He didn't look too much older than some people I knew

202

or the others that he worked with. He finally became a man and Fedor made him that way. I passed a packet of matches to the boy, and then I passed a cup to him and took a swig from mine. "I imagine you got into some heated argument with that man." I said protectively. As protectively as I could for someone else's boy.

"You could say that." He pressed the bag of meat harder and harder onto his face as if it would make the bruise disappear faster.

"Arguments like that..." I pointed to the mark on his face.

"Don't happen for nothing." I responded.

The boy puffed on his new toy.

"He thinks I'm not doing my part for the family." He said glumly.

"What part is that?"

"The part where I have to pay him five hundred a month."

I was broken when I heard this from Fedor, but it broke me once more when I heard it from the boy's mouth. That is the price of some people's mortgage.

"Why do you have to pay him that much?" My moustache was twitching.

"Help the family I guess." The boy shrugged. He put down the ice pack and drank from the spirit cup without flinching. This caught me off guard, as most people his age would have retched at drinking the stuff.

"I'm guessing Fedor's friend taught you to drink." I stated.

"I know, what a good son I'm turning out to be." He remarked sarcastically.

I reclined in my chair, trying to think of something to say but the boy beat me to it.

"Sidorovich told me about you."

Now this had my attention.

"And what did he say?" I leaned forward on my desk.

"He thought you were the only one to get out of the war intact."

I released a scoff and a smile. I shook my head at hearing the words.

"None of us did. We're all still there in one way or another." I emptied my cup into my mouth and swallowed. "Anything else he tell you?"

"That you killed someone… someone called Slava."
Of all the things to tell a young man, he calls me a killer. Typical Fedor.
"I did…" I said calmly. "But I got back at him for killing my brother."
"How did it happen?" The boy said with his mouth full of pipe.

To live in that hell again. To tell that story once again. All I could do was tell the truth and try to show him how we were all monsters.
I breathed in, the tobacco and exhaled.
I closed my eyes. And breathed in the sand and then opened my eyes.

"What the fuck are we doing here Slava?" I roared with a rage long gone.
"Shut your mouth! We're near a town and that…" Slava pointed towards the storm in the distance. "Is about to hit us. We need to get inside."
I looked around for any Mouja traps whilst we were being led by two afghanis. Dima, Kars, and Fedor all clambered together while Mikhail, Vasya, and Arseny walked in timid silence.

I moved closer to Fedor's group.
"Kars, where are we going?" I said through my shroud. My mouth being partially muffled.
"We're going where they tell us."
"And what if that's a trap?"
Fedor stopped the group and intervened.
"Back off Lev!" Fedor scolded. "He's our only lifeline and he's the only one who speaks the language."
"So what?" I hissed.
"So what?" Dima yelled, partially baffled. "It means he's our only guide you fucking idiot!"
"What's the problem?" Slava called out.
"Nothing!" Fedor responded out loud. "We just have an idiot here!"
"Idiot?" I got more frustrated.

"Stop!" Vasya demanded. He sounded fed up with the constant bickering and the hold-ups. "Are you coming with us or not?" "We're coming, don't worry." Kars responded. They moved forward giving me filthy looks which could be noticed even through their goggles. Fedor's shoulder barged into me as he went past making me lose my step for a second."
I huffed at what happened and I pressed forward. I joined Vasya's group, and we kept walking.
Suddenly, Arseny, our youngest spoke to me.
"Why do you keep poking the bear?" He curiously asked. He looked at me like a child, his eyes barely showing through the dust of the goggles, but they were visible enough to expose the innocence to the world.
"Because I don't want to die." I bashed sand out of my gun and quickly patted down my disguise. "Because I made a promise to my brother."
Arseny mirrored my actions whilst trying to think of a response. "You mean the boat?" He said casually.
"Something like that." I held my hand out and I could see something in the distance. Across from the flat dune, there was a pack of men numbering about twenty. It was hard to make sure of the distance. We barely had any cover and were exposed with a rocky hillside next to us. The nearest cover was to some wrecked soviet vehicles which were about four-hundred kilometres away. We were boxed in and if there were any snipers we were fucked.
"You sell out!" I screamed at the two afghanis. "You killed us!" I pulled back the bolt of my machine gun ready to shoot them. The Afghanis were now terrified. One of them gripped their horse's reins and looked like they were about to fly away.
"Lev, what are you doing?" Arsney panicked. The rest of the men saw what was happening and rushed to the scene. Vasya and Kars pointed their weapons at me.
"Put your gun down!" Kars yelled.
Slava wrenched the gun up by the barrel and pointed it away from the two men.
"What is your problem this time?" He bellowed in frustration.
"There are men over there."
Slava paused and let go of the gun.

"What do you mean?"

"I mean…" I pointed to the figures in the distance. "That there are about twenty men near those wreaks."

Slava wiped the sweat from his goggles and saw the same thing. "Does anyone have any binoculars?"

Mikhail gave his to Slava. He stared into them for a moment and confirmed our worst fears.

"They're not just afghanis. I think they're rebels!" Lev gave the binoculars back to Mikhail. "You can kill them, Lev!"

"Wait!" Arseny desperately called out. "Maybe they didn't know."

Slava frustratedly sighed.

"Kars can you ask them who those people are over there?"

Kars spoke to them. The tension was high, the men were demoralised and tired. The only thing a lot of us were thinking is when are we going to die.

Kars finally gave us the answer.

"They say they're refugees."

Slava turned to me and gave me the executing nod.

I felt the shock of the weapon hit my arms as I killed these two men. The bullets cracked throughout the dune and echoed with a ferocious whip whilst pained gasps and groans could be heard from the people I killed.

The men stood there, some of them were horrified at what just happened. Some of them grew used to it.

I killed these two men, but their horses ran free from the terror. One of them dragged away a body, heading towards the figures, whilst the other body was left for food by the local animals.

"Let's go." Slava ordered.

"Wait, how do we get through to that town now?" Vasya asked.

"We can't go over the hills, it'll take too long, and we'll be caught in the storm."

"What if we go back?" Mikhail suggested.

"Back to the minefield?" Kars ridiculed. "Do you want to end up like Alyosha?"

"I don't want to die, is what I am saying." Mikhail gritted through his grimy shroud.

"Relax." Vasya jeered. "You'll have God to look forward to if you die."

"Shut up Vasya!" Slava barked. He placed the palm of his hand on his forehead, then swiped it to the back of his skull. The pressure was clearly getting to him, and it was showing.

"We have to go through." He dourly said. "We won't make it in time otherwise."

"You want us to get into another fight with the dushmen?" Fedor exclaimed with shock and fear. "We barely survived the last fight and that was with a full convoy of men getting attacked."

"We can take them!" Slava said. "If not, then Kars will have to do some pretending for us."

"But what about that horse?" Arseny pointed out.

"And the gunshots from your little execution." Vasya chided. Slava threw his hands and head up in the air in frustration and turned to Vasya and Arseny. His body tensed and his fingers were like claws. "I have no other answer!" He screamed in frustration. "Either you think of one or we're going to fight some more afghanis."

We all looked at each other, looking for someone to give us an alternative but no one could say anything. We couldn't think of solutions because there were none, all we could see was our leader losing himself, and when your leader is a mountain of man then it becomes even more worrisome. It was the unfortunate case of which death sentence we want, and I think we can agree that a bullet is the quickest and cleanest.

"Then we're moving." Slava ordered. "Get your weapons ready!"

"Wow…" The boy said with shock. "I had no—"

"No Bern, I imagine Fedor didn't tell you because it was too horrible."

"I guess…" The boy took another sip from the paper cup. "What happened next?"

I gave a nervous chuckle.

"I think I made myself look like enough of a monster." I sighed and stroked my moustache. "You know you look like someone I know…"

"Who?" He sounded confused.

I thought I was experiencing some form of déjà vu.

207

"Nothing, forget I said anything." I dismissed. I opened the bottle of vodka and poured another drink. "Do you want another?"

Lisa
Half eleven in the morning

The school building looked grimmer than before. I walked around the school waiting to look for a futile escape to my prison. The aged metal bell cracked and rang throughout the dilapidated hallways signalling it was time for tutor gathering. Hordes of younger and older students rushed around with some stragglers trying to avoid the hive of navy-blazered bees. Some of the lazier or more delinquent slobs hung around the lesser-known nooks and crannies around the school, trying to have a smoke near less watched areas, although the rookies forgot about the smell of smoke or the vapes around their trashy disposable vapes. No class.

I followed the workforce and walked into my section. Not more than twenty were there with a few looking out of place or unable to function. Solely seeking to leave the room.

I sat down at my desk and slumped on my chair.

"I have an announcement." Said the middle-aged and over-stressed teacher. "Someone broke into the school a couple of days ago."

This pricked up my ears. Did they find out?

"We caught the perpetrator on our cameras, and we found out that they broke into the teachers' lounge."

The room was silent for a few seconds... that is until one of the boys spoke up.

"Ah, Sir!" He belched out. "How do you know they went in the staff room?"

"Because—" The teacher straightened up and wiped his face. "Mrs Lovell's Parisian chocolate was found on the floor and there was evidence of someone smoking in the science room from the left-over cigarette butts." The teacher then looked at me and stared.

Oh shit, I've been caught...

Half three in the afternoon

My makeup was smudged and leaked all down my face. I
begged. I pleaded. Nothing was working. I told them it wasn't
me even though that was a blatant lie. I just didn't know what
else to do. My parents drove off in their dull car and left me to
find my own way home. I begged and pleaded more to have
them take me back with them, but they were on the brink of
disowning me. They drove off in their black Ford car and left me
by the school gates.

"I hate you!" I screamed at them as they turned the corner. I
collapsed to my knees and showed my back to the world. My
hands pressed against the patchwork concrete pavement,
stopping me from ruining my clothes even further.
I was there on all fours for a good minute until I mustered up the
courage to get up and walk to the park. I shambled there,
sniffling, and sobbing into my navy blazer of the school I was
just expelled from. I reached into my handbag trying to rummage
around for my cigarettes and lighter. I was furiously trying to
spark a light, but my tear-stained hands kept fumbling with the
spark.
"Come on!" I demanded as if the lighter was alive.
I fought with the case in my hands and tried to press the flame
against my cigarette.
I finally got the tobacco to light and felt the nicotine take effect
on my tastebuds. I ended up walking through the muddy park
and landed at my destination. The blue and yellow metal gazebo
and then…
And then I sobbed uncontrollably.
I was wailing and howling with uncontrollable anguish. I was
bent over my knees whilst sitting down on the metal bench
attached to the gazebo. I hated this life. How could I go through
this world now, especially with my exams so close?
Did I just fail?
Did I just ruin my life?

"Rough day?" Someone said in a snarky tone.

209

I saw a filthy claw creep around a gazebo support pole, followed by a tacky weed print sleeve, and then finally a poorly bleached bowl cut. He leaned against the gazebo finally making his whole body visible, from his unkempt hair to his filthy white trainers. I didn't even look at him. I didn't want to acknowledge his existence, but I had to respond to him.

"How did you find me?" I whimpered whilst crying into my lap. I could hear the mud squelch from his odorous footsteps. He slowly approached like a weed-spotted hyena stalking a deer. I felt his disgusting hand on my back, more specifically around the area of my bra strap.

I jumped up out of my seat and turned to face him.

"You look stunning." He said with a half-rotten smirk on his spotted face.

"You look like shit." I yelled back at him. "And I'm leaving." This creature stood up and tried to block my escape with his arms outstretched.

"Woah, woah, woah." He bellowed. "I think we got off to a bad start." He outstretched his hand to me. "I'm Nova."

"I'm not interested." I responded as I took another drag from my cigarette.

He retracted his hand and crossed his arms. "I haven't even given you anything to be interested in."

"Get the fuck out of my way!" I screamed at him. I sobbed further into my hands and dropped to my knees into the mud. "Oh God!"

I felt a small embrace and the smell of weed.

I struggled and tried to fight him off, but his grip got tighter.

"Get off! Get off!"

Eventually, I just stopped, and I let my body go limp.

"I'm here for you." The thing said.

I was just there in his arms uncontrollably sobbing.

"You people killed Ava."

"We didn't kill no one."

He continued to hold me as I kept crying. I felt defeated and I felt alone.

"We didn't kill no one, but I can at least make you feel better." He gripped me by the shoulder and the smell became nauseating.

"Look at me." He said softly. "I can help take the pain away, but you'll have to come with me. Then I can show you what happened to her."

A Storm of a Thousand Chords

Bern
3:23pm
220 days post exam

I felt a lukewarm breeze cross my face and saw a meagre patch
of bluebells situated in the clay classroom pot. I had heard the
rumours of Lisa getting kicked out by keeping my ear to the
ground. News in a school spreads like wildfire, even among the
other teachers who haven't fully grown up from the mindset of
gossiping schoolgirls. I brought my work clothes with me to
school so I could get changed just before work started. Lev was
decent enough to help me out with my education, even though it
took a while to even get him to say his name. I walked out the
school gates with my now scruffy-looking uniform. I quickly
speed-walked to the bus station, and I saw a familiar white
silhouette sitting on a moss-green bench.

Lisa was smoking a cigarette and pressed their back against the
metal frame, which was the same colour as the bench, except it
had actual moss growing on it. She wore a snow-white shirt and
jeans with red canvas shoes.

I stopped in my tracks trying to think of a way to get around this
situation, but it was too late. She spotted me. Her eyes narrowed
like a predator and stared at me whilst enveloping the cigarette
with her freshly painted lips.

"Sit with me please." She kindly demanded. She moved up the
bench in a ridged fashion, pushing her body away with her arms.
I sat down next to her and brought out my pipe that I hid in my
blazer pocket.

I figured I could use the smoke if I had to talk to her. She looked
surprised. Not in the fact that I had started smoking, more so that
I was smoking from a pipe.

"When did you start smoking weed?" She blustered out in
disgust.

"It's not weed. It's tobacco." I spoke sternly.

"From a pipe?"

"Yes."

212

"Alright, Sherlock." She sarcastically jibed, as she fluttered her hands theatrically.

I started to make myself a smoke and tampered it down.

"Look, did you wait for me here to insult me, or did you want me for an actual reason?" I had little patience for her since I had to go to work, and she was interrupting my smoke.

"I did." She pulled out a small cling film bag from her jeans pocket, holding inside a few white pills. I pushed Lisa's hand down against her thigh to hide the pills from any onlookers. I leaned in closer to her. "Where did you get those from?" I whispered, my voice holding both surprise and embarrassment. I looked up and down the street to make sure no one saw.

"Where do you think?"

"How did you get dragged in with them?"

"It doesn't matter." She ripped her hand away from mine, causing her elbow to contract away, and put the pills back inside her jeans. "What matters is that I'm going to get some answers out of them."

"You won't." I sternly whispered.

"Says who?" Her brow wrinkled at hearing the words. She threw her cigarette away and folded her arms.

"They're smarter than you and me. Don't let them lure you in."

"But they're not!" She cried out. "I know what I'm doing!"

"I'm sure Ava did as well." I coldly said. I finally lit my pipe and took in the first few puffs.

Lisa's face was crumpled. She shook her head slowly and clenched a fist.

"I should slap you for saying that!" She scolded.

"Like how she slapped around the both of us?" I coldly said as I glared at her with the side of my eyes.

"Why can't you let her family or her dad handle this?"

"He's disappeared somewhere, nobody knows. He's just gone!"

I could see her face turn red through her pale white makeup. Each word added fuel to the vocal fire like her saliva was made of petrol. "Where's your support for her?! You were meant to be there for her!"

I took a deep puff of my pipe and then emptied the small ash bundle onto the floor. Any embers still burning faded out quickly on the concrete.

"Come to my church." I said calmly.

"What?" She scoffed. She momentarily splayed her arms open, and her head cocked up like a meerkat.

"Come to my church and you'll see why." I pulled out a pen from my blazer. "Give me your hand." I scribbled on the address and the details of the correct bus to take on her hand. "All will be understood after that."

The bus turned to corner from and street and drove towards our stop. I outstretched my arms to signal the driver to stop.

The folding doors hissed open and the bus driver wearing Oakley sunglasses sat there impatiently.

"For what it's worth, I'm sorry about what happened." I spoke as compassionately as I could whilst being in a rush, before finally stepping onto the bus.

The doors hissed behind me, and I was locked in.

"Didn't you want to say goodbye to your girlfriend? She's a very pretty girl."

"Yeah... She was."

Michael
Twenty past twelvish

I was driving home from the office to pick up some papers. I had David in the car with me and we grabbed some food along the way. I went back to Bern's workplace and grabbed some food from there. I once again didn't see him there, what's more, the picture wall for the customer of the month thing was gone. So, I guess nobody could see me accomplishments.

I opened the car door, hopped inside, and gave David his takeaway bag.

I ripped open mine and started devouring it like I hadn't eaten in months.

I could feel his eyes on me, so I glanced up and just saw him giving me a disgusting look.

"What?" I said with my mouth full.

"Mate, I'm saying this as your friend and all but—"

214

"But what?"

"Mike you're getting massive. You haven't been the same since that guy offed himself."

"What? You think I'm getting too big?"

"Well…" David sank his head. "Yeah mate. And it's worrying me."

I just ignored him and carried on eating. I wipe me mouth with a napkin and just pushed the car into first gear.

David was getting his drink. As he put the straw through the plastic cap, I jolted the car which caused him to spill his Diet Coke all over him.

He gave me an annoyed face. I just simply replied with "Sorry, the car hasn't been the same since it's been in the accident."

I drove us towards me house and left David to clean himself up in the car. I grabbed the papers, but I went into both Jason's and Bern's rooms. Jason was the same as it was. Full of toys and gizmos but Bern's room felt off to me. I decided to search his room for anything he might be hiding from me, and I found nothing at first. I searched his wardrobe and then found a suit protector bag at the bottom of it. I knew he was hiding something from me!

I had to go back to work, but I will come back for this and see what it's about.

Sidorovich

12:32

I could see my friend getting weaker. He sat there on a pew, bathing in the light of the sun coming through the opulent glass windows.

"Are you ok?" I asked him from the height of the ladder.

I was cleaning the windows to make sure that he was given as much light and comfort as he could.

"Yes, piece of shit, I'm fine." He bellowed with a smile on his face.

I quit my task and joined him on the pew. He barely had the strength to hold a glass, let alone pour one. I opened the bottle and began to pour for him until he would weakly wave his hand to stop.

215

"Thank you." He spoke weakly.

"It's ok." I replied as I closed the bottle.

We sat there in awkward silence until Samara broke it.

"I want to go home Fedor." He took a sip. "I want to go back to Heraklion."

"So, why don't you?"

"Nice to know I'm appreciated." He spoke sarcastically before the smile on his face reappeared. "If I went, how would you get laid without me." He nudged me on the shoulder, and I gave a brief smile accompanied with an eye roll.

"So, tell me about home." I said after I took a swig of the bottle myself.

"Do you want me to go that badly?"

"I mean it." I said softly. "Tell me about Heraklion."

"Well, the women are as beautiful as –"

"Stop." I interrupted. "Without the jokes."

"What are you my –"

"Please."

Samara sat there silently and contemplated for a minute. He fidgeted with his glass for a moment before answering.

"I miss the pier." He took a swig of his drink. "I miss the warm summer breeze. I would walk on the docks and wander like a stranger with a small bag of olives. I would say that the women there were wonderful but, truth be told, I went there because I could see the sunset where the boats on the horizon looked like tiny, jagged specs." He gestured his hand out to emphasise how small they were. "I miss that pier." He spun his crystal tumbler in his hand before finally answering. "What about you?"

It took me a moment to process the question, as I had not thought about my life too much before the war. I pulled a cigarillo from the monthly get-togethers we had. I thought it appropriate and lit it as I thought about my answer.

"I miss Kovrov." I sucked on the cigarillo. "It was a military city but that's where I met my wife and old friend from. I had Grigori when I was young, just before I went off to fight."

Samara cocked his head.

"You didn't answer my question. What do you miss?"

I took a deep puff and then exhaled.

"I miss the music I made there. I miss the marching and the sounds of disciplined men. I met Olega at the recruitment centre." I smiled and then raised an eyebrow at Samara.

"Ah, so you like them in uniform." Samara cackled as he patted me on the back.

"I guess you could say that." I laughed.

We both burst out with laughter but as it died out, we both lost the joy in us both.

We leaned back into the pew and then Samara spoke.

"We can't let our boy become like us."

The statement caught me off guard.

"What do you mean?"

"I mean, that he's becoming too much like us. He picked up your smoking and my drinking. He has his whole life ahead of him. I don't want him to turn out like us two miserable pieces of shit."

"He won't." I responded. I finished off the cigarillo and flicked the but into the corner somewhere out of sight so it would give me a task to do later. I needed to keep busy somehow.

"Promise me." Samara said as he places his yellowed hand on my shoulder.

"I promise." I responded as I placed my black bandaged hand on his.

The church doors flung open. Samara was too slow and in too much pain, so I slid the bottle between his legs and did the same with the glass he had.

"Hello!" I blustered with forced kindness. A girl with white hair and red makeup comes into the church. I folded my hands around my waist and Samara turned on the pew as best he could, but he looked like he was over-twisting his neck to the point of breaking.

"Is this where Bern comes to?" She spoke. The girl walked around the place like a deer grazing. Light-footed and ready to run at a moment's notice.

After hearing this we were on guard, the last girl that our boy brought in did not leave us on good terms.

I dropped the act and spoke to her plainly.

"What do you want with our boy?"

"Your boy?" She reacted harshly. "What do you mean your boy?"

I could hear Samara grunting up and focusing all his efforts on getting up.

"I've got this Fedor." I rushed over to help him up, but he waved me away. "We know him, but you'll forgive us if we don't trust the people the boy brings in. His last guest left in tears."

Her face dropped as if a sudden realisation had hit her.

"You mean Ava." His shocks turned to rage. "You're the priests that upset her!"

Her accusations did little to offend me, but they instead enraged me. I hid enough of it to not seem like a raging lunatic but expressed my anger to show who was in charge.

I scratched the bandages to alleviate the pain, but this only proved to worsen them.

"I don't care about your little friend." I hissed through gritted teeth. "I wouldn't allow her to hurt him!"

"Hurt him?" She screeched with shock. "What do you mean?"

"She hit him." Samara intervened. He pushed me behind by placing a weak grip on my arm, signalling me to calm down. "She hit our boy, and to my mind, she got off easy." He moved his hand up to my shoulder. "My friend here was ready to kill her for such a thing." He exaggerated. He was trying to make me look intimidating, but this worked. She backed away like a scarred cub. Samara put a flat palm on his chest. "I, however, am more compassionate."

"And why should I listen to you?" The girl said as made slow backward steps towards the door.

"Fedor." Samara squeezed my shoulder to attention. "Get us some drinks."

"What bottle?" I said, not breaking my gaze from the intruder.

"Booz's Old Cabin. The blue house bottle please, from the cabinet"

I felt his grip leave my shoulder and left for the office. I ratted about the unlocked cabinet for the bottle he asked for. It was ancient, which was typical of his tastes in spirits. There was no label, just the shape of a house on the bottle with markings of the year embossed on the side. A vintage from 1840. Older than both of us combined.

I looked around for anything suitable to bring. And the grey wax-sealed bottle caught my eye. It looked the oldest. And sat in the cabinet the longest. That bottle always intrigued me, but Samara kept the thing under lock and key.

I shut the cabinet and grabbed a pair of crystal tumblers.

When I returned to the hall, I saw them talking in peace, sitting on the same front pew.

"Ah, right on time!" Samara weakly cheered.

We divided the items and poured everyone a drink. Samara took a small swig and then smiled. She looked uneasy but of course, that was to be expected.

"I still don't trust you guys." The girl eked out.

"That's fine." Samara spoke softly. "I don't need you to trust me to listen."

Lisa
Half five-ish at night.

I left that church after I had one stranger sit beside me and the other stood ready to throw me out of the church.

They were different from what I expected from priests. I never expected to be given an alcoholic drink in a fancy cup. I had the occasional threat from the gaunt Russian, but that would be dispelled by the happy yellow Greek. I walked out of there with a revelation. I closed the church door behind me with a warmth in my body from the alcohol which I felt like spitting out. The door with holes creaked shut behind me but someone was waiting outside for me. I approached the road by I could smell smoke. I turned around to see the source but only saw their precious boy loitering by the door.

"How did you find them?" Said Bern.

"They were ok." I said back to him. I folded my arms and left it at that.

"So, what are you going to do now?"

"I'm going to get my answers from that town centre lot." I was more focused than ever. I heard all I needed to from those priests about Ava. I didn't see her in the same light although I guess it was staring me in the face the whole time. All the abuse and all the hate from her.
I got out my phone and started texting Nova.

I want to meet up! Tell me how Ava died!

I felt Bern's hand on my shoulder. I looked up from my phone and saw him hovering over me with a red pipe in his mouth.
"Are you sure you want to go back to them?" He said, his voice stern but gentle.
"Yes. I need the closure, even if she was a horrible person."
I looked back at my phone and saw the message.

Sounds good I'll let you know when and where to go, then I'll show you what happened.

"You're your own person, just be careful with them." Bern said.
"I will."
I walked away from the church was walking towards the street. I suddenly stopped in my tracks and turned to face Bern.
"By the way, let the big one know he was my favourite out of the two." I said with a smile.
"Mind if I tell him that?" He tipped the ash out of his pipe onto the ground. "You won't regret it."
"Sure." I said and shrugged my shoulders.

Bern opened the church door and bellowed into it.
"Samara!"
"What?!" The priest bellowed back.
"She says you're her favourite!"
I will never forget what he screamed out afterward. The volume reached outside, and it made me fall over laughing from the sheer energy he radiated even when he looked ill.

"WOOOOOOOO! I'VE STILL GOT IT YOU PIECE OF SHIT!!!"

220

I could hear angry Russian things being said afterward but I obviously couldn't understand them.

After I composed myself, I gave one last smile to Bern and left it at "I'll see you later hopefully." We said our goodbyes, and then I walked to the street and got the bus home.

Bern
9:01am
228 days post exam

I was awoken by a thunderous roar.

"Bernard!" I could hear the bellows of the beast below.

"Bernard!" I dug myself out of my bed covers with all my sapped might. Working and studying full-time was taking a toll on my body. I dug through my sliding wardrobe mirror doors and pulled out the first set of shirts and jeans. I quickly checked the suit, which was left in the protective bags, left at the bottom of the clothes. It was still there, and it was still safe. I rarely brought that out for fear of my dad finding it and asking for more money.

"BERNARD!" He violently roared from downstairs.

He was losing his patience, and I couldn't risk another beating. I flew down the stairs clutching my left side from the last time he struck me. He learned his lesson and avoided striking the face, only focusing on the body. I turned the corner of the doorway and saw him sitting there with a breakfast burger in hand.

"Ah!" He spoke with a mouth full of food. He made an audible gulp and smiled. "Sit down." He gestured to the other black sofa in the room.

I let my body collapse onto the sofa. I was so tired and felt limp like a corpse.

"When do you think I can get the customer of the month thing again?" He asked before biting into his burger.

I couldn't register what he said. I just weakly said, "What?"

"The customer of the month award thing that you registered me for."

221

What the hell was he talking about? I never registered him for anything.

"When I went in to check on you, some Russian guy gave me free food and took my picture for the customer of the month thing!" He exclaimed. His voice was becoming aggravated and petulant. "I thought you were doing me a favour after I'm working so hard at work. I thought that's why you found me the suit."

My body shot up after hearing this.

"What suit…?" I whimpered with horror.

"The suit in your wardrobe. I thought that was for me. You've gotta get my size right since it was too small for me."

I couldn't hear anymore. I ran upstairs, busted through my bedroom door, and dug through my wardrobe.

"No, no, no…" I was repeating desperately.

I threw the protective bag onto the mattress and saw the damage. It was ruined. The velvet lapels and chest were covered in grease marks. Patches of thick red and white condiments coated some areas, and the stitching was tarnished and ripped due to embracing a man who was four times their size. Even the shoes were ruined. The shining patent leather was dulled and coming off in areas while the soles were starting to separate from the shoe.

I let out a blood-curdling scream to the heavens who have abandoned me. He took it from me. He took the thing I held most precious and bastardised it.

I clutched it against my chest, fell to my knees, and silently wept. I heard the stomps, raised my head, and saw him standing there in my room.

"I hate you!" I hissed.

"It's what you get for not getting my size right." He shrugged.

I fell onto my bed and felt hate. I laid with my back against him and then felt a nudge. I tried to shake it off but then I felt a strike to my back.

"Pick yourself up!" He growled. "It's just a suit."

I didn't respond. I just laid there still gripping the remains of what was precious to me.

"Fine. Stay here then." He marched out and left me to my suffering.

After what seemed like hours had passed, I looked at my phone and saw an advert for military recruitment and then I searched. I searched even though I knew it would hurt my true father if he found out.

Sidorovich
14:49

My soul was tarnished. My friends' bones have long been turned into dust and their blood has been spilled in the grains of the sand. The wind started to pick up and made it so much harder to hear, especially through the rags around my body. Kars suffered the worst due to having less fabric from his disguise to protect his skin from the grains, even though we wanted to fool the enemy, his skin was starting to cook and burn from the heat of the sun and soon it would be shredded by the storm. Most of the men sweltered in their disguises and they could feel the storm approach with its gusts of wind, even though their thicker disguises.

I walked beside Slava, and I could see that our stoic leader was feeling the pressure. He compulsively was checking his weapons and trying to see if they had ammo or if they were clean. We didn't have too much ammunition between us. Maybe only a few magazines but each round was heavy and added to the strain on our backs. I still felt the ache in my back where the shrapnel was. I was the only one wounded now, but this fight might strain me more. We were within eyesight of the town, which couldn't have been more than forty kilometres away from us.

Slava gave his last commands to the group.
"If we get separated, head for the mosque!"
"What?" Dima bellowed.
"The building with the big fucking dome on top!" Kars harshly clarified.

We slowly marched to the enemy, and all were silent, waiting in anticipation for the fight of our lives and possibly coming the realisation of our coming deaths.

223

"How do I do this Fedor?" Slava asked me. His voice was muffed by his cloth mask.
"How do you mean?" I replied.

Slava reloaded his rifle.
"I mean how do I keep going? How do I live up to my name and keep the squad going?"
It took a moment for me to think of a response, but I tried to dismiss it as shock, but I still tried to give him some sort of sympathy.
"You'll think of something. We'll get through this."
Slava shouldered his gun and then dropped his guard.
"No Fedor... I don't think I will." He allows a nervous chuckle. "I don't know how my family would see me."
This threw me off guard a little and made me nervous.
"What do you mean?" I asked.
"I mean..." He responded. He shallowly huffed and pulled back the bolt of his rifle. "What would my own father say about me being here?"
This threw me for a moment. I even started compulsively checking my equipment out of some way to get me away from this conversation. I tried to respond as minimally as I could to try and break the silent tension but not too much as I couldn't say much to distract us from our situation.
"What about your father?" I said.
Slava shook his head and wiped sand from his goggles.
"He fought in Stalingrad." He paused for a second. "How do you live up to that?" He said in humility.
"What?" I yelped in surprise.
"Yes... He fought in Stalingrad now... I don't even know what I'm doing here." Slava sighed and slumped his posture. "I just wanted to make my father proud."

I could hear the others jibbing at each other like bickering schoolchildren. I looked and stared at them whilst walking with our leader.
"We're not going to make it, are we?" I spoke solemnly.

Slava grabbed me by my shoulder with one hand and snapped my attention to him.

"We will!" He sternly exclaimed. "We must! We all have something to live for."

"What do I have to live for?" I dismissed.

"Your boy. Your wife!" Slava took his hand off my shoulder and pointed to the bickering men. "Your best fucking friend over there guiding us out." He grabbed me by my shoulder again and stopped us. "What's your boy's name?"

"Grigori."

"And your wife?"

"Olega."

"So, when you get back to Kovrov, you tell your boy to not become like us..." He took his hand and pointed at my chest. "Become like you..." Then he pointed to his chest. "Become like me... because I didn't listen; doesn't mean others won't."

I stopped in place and saw the wisdom in his words.

"Fedor!"

Slava turned his back to me and walked away into the approaching storm, fading away like a mirage in the heat.

"Fedor!"

I fell into the sand and felt my legs go weak. My arms began burning and the smell of charring flesh was overpowering. I screamed but no sound could be heard over the crackling sparks dancing on what was then, my skin. The pain was overwhelming and numbing. The smoke entered my lungs and choked me... and then I tasted the herbal tobacco.

"Fedor you Idiot! Did smoke finally rot your brain?" He yelled ferociously.

I opened my eyes, and I breathed out the smoke. I closed my old black bible and closed the two photos of my family and squad mates, shutting them back into shame.

"What you old pervert?" I called back at the voice. I stood up from the pew and left God's word on the seat. Flashing beams from the sun brought life and warmth back into the church, making the plants finally start to bloom.

"Boy is here!" Samara answered. He hobbled over, his skin was now a thick and sickly yellow. His hair was greyed but his habits were ever present.

"Ah yes!" I patted down my robes. "How can I help you, boy?" The boy stood with a small beard starting to appear and a pipe in hand. His words haunted me, and I felt an old memory resurface as soon as he plainly uttered these cursed words.

"I want to go into the army."

Bern
229 days post exam

The old Russian's face turned pale, and his mouth gapped open. His hands gripped tightly around the black book he was holding like it was about to slip from his grasp at any second. His other hand flexed and tightened even through the bandages he wore. The church turned silent and the heat from the spring turned icy once again like winter had never left. I fidgeted with my hands out of nervousness and then the Russian spoke.

"Don't." His words were barely recognisable and almost inaudible. He stared at me like the light from his eyes had been sucked out. "Please don't." He now whispered.

"What?" I asked.

"Don't go... I can't lose another one." His grip slipped and his willpower ebbed. The book landed on the cobbled floor with a resounding thud that bounced around the walls of the church. I felt Samara's hand push me behind him. This time he was sickly, and I don't think he could take another beating if Sidorovich had another episode.

"I can't..." His voice cracked and creaked. His fingers twitched and his posture was slumped.

"Fedor... are you ok?" Samara said compassionately. Sidorovich frantically waved his hands in the air like he was surrendering before throwing them down in frustration. He stormed into the office and closed the door behind him, leaving me and the Greek alone.

"Is he ok?" I asked.
"No boy, I told you this would happen."
Samara scolded. "He'll tell you about the good stories from the war like how he snuck in prostitutes into a camp but nothing that stuck with him."
The door creaked open only for Sidorovich to place a couple of crystal glasses and a bottle outside of it.
"Shit…" Samara said.
He rubbed the bridge of his nose before collapsing onto the nearest pew.
"Grab those would you?" He spoke.
I did as I was instructed and grabbed the glasses and bottle. I dropped them off at my objective and returned for the bible that the Russian dropped.
I could hear drinks being poured and the creak of pressured wood. Samara saw the book in my hand and almost shot out of his seat.
"No!" He exclaimed. "Put that down!" Samara commanded sternly.
This was the first time I had seen him act this way which meant that I must disobey him for the first time. I opened the bible and saw inside two photos, both were old.
Both were of Sidorovich but at younger times in his life. In one photo, he was behind the back of an open troop transporter with nine other men. The other was of a woman and someone who looked eerily like… me. Just a little bit younger.

Samara wrenched himself out of his seat and snatched the book from my hands.
"When I tell you to do something, you do it!" He angrily bellowed at me.
I took a step back and I was mortified at the discovery.
"What's going on here?" I asked fearfully, my voice quivering.
"You weren't supposed to see that." He scolded. "There are some secrets even *we* keep."
"What is going on?" I asked again.

Samara sat back down on the pew, left the book next to him, and took a drink from his crystal. He stared at the office door, sighed, then bowed his head.

"He gets confused sometimes." He said plainly. "Sometimes…" He raises his voice and turns to me with a pointed finger. "Very rarely!" His tone softened. "He thinks you're his dead son."

And suddenly it made sense. In those words, I felt like I had a man who was broken in not just body but in mind as well. As if sensing the words we spoke, the office door flung open with its operator holding something in their hand. I knew it wasn't their pipe because I had never heard a pipe click before. Sidorovich stood there in the doorway like the ancient demon was there once again. Sidorovich marched up to where we were, keeping his hand hidden from us. I backed away a few steps, sensing this was different. Samara once again bolted up from his seat and got in between us.

"Fedor…" He compassionately said. "Are you ok?"

Sidorovich finally unveils what he is hiding. His old pistol with a loaded magazine on top. He held it in plain view to us, where even Samara and his short stature could see.

"Fedor…" Samara's voice quivered. "What are you doing?"
"My job as a father." He uttered coldly.

Sidorovich pulled back the top of the pistol and showed the bottom to us, signifying that it was unloaded. He gently pushed Samara out of the way. Samara was powerless against the Russian's in his condition. Samara fell to the side but not before grabbing his arm.
"Don't do this." He begged.
Sidorovich shook him off and pressed forward. He forced the gun into my hands and said one word. One glacial word that shivered down my bruised spine.
"Load."
I was panicking, I was terrified. I wanted to throw the weapon back at him, but some force kept me paralyzed.
"I said load!" He barked.

I was taken aback. I felt the old demon come out of him but this time, he knew what he was doing.

"What kind of soldier are you if you can't follow a basic instruction?" He continued. "Load!"

"No!" I screamed back.

"No?"

"Yeah!" I dropped the weapon on the ground. "I'm not doing it!"

His eyes tracked the weapon on the floor and focused back on me.

"What good are you as a soldier if you can't follow orders?" He walked slowly to me and inches away from my face. "Why do you even want to go into the army?!" He spoke sternly.

I stepped back and stared him down. I turned and lifted my shirt to reveal the fresh black and purple mark on my skin.

"This is why! I can't take it anymore!"

Sidorovich took a quick glance at the marks and stood defiant. After he observed the bruises, I let go of my shirt, turned again, and let it slide down my raw vertebrae.

"There are better ways to escape than going into a meat grinder."

"What ways are there?"

"Something, but you don't have to go back to Kovrov!"

This took me back a bit. I looked at Samara and even in his yellow-dyed face, you could see the worry.

"Fedor..." Samara dragged himself up and placed his hand on the Russian's shoulder. "Are you ok?"

"No!" He raised his voice and shook the hand off. "Tell Olega to stop filling my son's head full of these glorious war stories."

"I am not your son!" I screamed out.

Both priests turned their attention to me. Samara was fearful but Sidorovich was spiteful. His words were as fridged as ice.

"If you are not my son, if you truly want to fight and die for something that thinks you are expendable then I will wait for you here." He picked up his gun and magazine. "I will wait for you here and I will wait for you to come back in a zinc box, and I will stand over your grave when I lay you to rest."

He rushed back into the office and left me and Samara there to wonder and slammed the door to disappear from this world and into his.

I went over to Samara to check if he was ok and there. I grabbed his hand and pulled him up from his seat. He let out pained groans and he stood up. He was hunched over and leaning on me, perhaps due to his balance failing him now.

"I'll take care of this boy." He said softly. "I'm so sorry this has happened."

He groaned in pain with each step. We walked down the aisle as the Greek kept himself propped up on the pews and awkwardly clutching me in tow. Heavy metal music started playing from the office.

"He's just confused, boy." He gasped out.

I dropped him at one of the front pews closest to the office. Samara landed like a beached jellyfish and splayed his limbs around the pew until lying down on the pew.

"Why do you keep hanging around him if he does this stuff?" I asked.

"Because he saved my life boy!" He groaned.

"But he caused this. He killed you!"

"He caused nothing." Samara spat. "I knew this was coming, just not so soon."

This took me back a bit.

"I was ill months ago and going to doctors' appointments before. I knew this was coming, just not so soon and not so violently. You say he saved my life, then I'd call us even." He chuckled a little before letting out a pained groan. He clutched his stomach and slowly relaxed into a rested position. "He saved me, and he will do right by you, he just does it in his own strange ways."

I gave myself a moment to take in what he said before I petulantly asked, "So why am I this guy called Grigori now?"

"Because that was almost the exact same talk, he gave to him." He leaned up from the pew. "Because that was the last day, he saw him before Grigori ran away to Russia and joined the army there. He wanted to be like his dad, but unfortunately, he barely got the horror stories of the war. The difference is…" He pointed at me. "You got all of it."

Lisa
Half one in the afternoon.

I got put into homeschooling ever since I got kicked out. It meant I got some one-to-one support for my A-levels, but it meant I didn't get too much help especially since the tutor was only around for two or three hours a day. That gave me more free time to go and do my own thing. Today I was meant to meet Nova at a pub. He said that he would be there to help me out but still, I felt like he had an ulterior motive. Still, if he can get me free booze then I'm happy. I had to meet him by this old man pub called The Dog by three, but I wanted to get out early to pick up more cigarettes. My parents kept me on tight watch, and I had to listen out for their constant threat to kick me out of the house. I put on my whitest dress, curled my hair, and threw on my carmine red lipstick. It took me a solid hour to get ready, but I looked amazing. I walked out with a faux mink coat and embraced the new spring feeling.
Strange though, it felt like it was dangerous. The only reason I'm doing this is to get an answer from the town centre lot. She only hung around either Bern or them, and I doubt he's going to be helpful in any shape or form.

I snuck out the door and slowly closed it to avoid making too much noise. I got myself onto the next bus and took it to the town centre. Some driver wearing Oakley sunglasses gave me my ticket and then I got going. I would have preferred driving, but my parents stopped my lessons after the school incident, so I had to bus it everywhere as punishment. I walked past my onlookers and got a few good compliments from some of the passengers. Finally, the driver got us going and we drove over to the town centre.

Three O'clock

I got my cigarettes, hung around a few places, and spritzed away any lingering tobacco smells. I know I am going into a dangerous environment but hopefully, I'll have onlookers to help me here if I get into trouble. It's a pub after all, it's got to have people.

I waited outside this horrible-looking mock Tudor place where the beams were freshly coloured in black, and the white walls were starting to peel apart. I waited and waited and waited… and he's late…

I must have waited for something like twenty minutes before he finally turned up, striding along with his hand in his trashy tracksuit trousers, like he was some thug straight from the east end of London or a hip-hop king. Jesus Christ this looked embarrassing. He waved at me with a vape in hand and blew away the vapours.

"Oi Oi!" He called at me from halfway across the street in an exaggerated cockney accent.

I stood there with my arms crossed looking unimpressed.

"You're late." I chastised him.

"I'm sorry…" He nonchalantly spoke. "Can't rush perfection."

We walked into the pub, and it was a depressing sight. The walls of it were a bleached white. The carpet had a bottle and lime green Victorian floral design imprinted onto a burgundy background. The tables were wooden and ridged by design, Bolted together by hoar iron studs. Even the beige wallpaper was peeling off. We passed by the gambling machines where a drunk was betting away his benefits. And the smell was horrid. It stank of stale alcohol and lingering cigarette smoke.

"Grab us a table, would you?" Nova asked with a cocky grin on his face.

I looked around this place and tried my best to find something that resembled some semblance of cleanliness… which was none of it. So, I looked for a bench place with the least stains and sat down. I folded my mink coat and rested it on my lap whilst fully expecting the backside of my dress to come out less than pure white. I saw him come over with two pints of dark fruity cider with ice in them both.

"Hope this gets you excited." He said, showing his disgusting toothy grin.

"Thanks." I nervously respond.

I took the drink and carefully shifted across the sticky bench. I felt some of my dress cling to the wood which Nova took to opportunity to sit on, trapping me underneath filthy buttocks.

"Sorry that I'm on your dress." He spoke.

"It's fine. I didn't like it anyway."

"At least I didn't sit on you. At least, not yet." He gave me an extremely forced wink before taking a slurp of his cider.

He wrapped his arm around my shoulder which caused me to tighten up my posture. I was ready to break the glass in my hand over his head and bolt out the door if he tried to grab anything that wasn't his. Dress be damned.

I worked up the courage to finally speak.

"So, what happened to Ava? You promised to tell me."

"I didn't."

"Excuse me?"

"You're excused." He took another sip. "I promised to show you what happened to her."

"And what happened to her?" I made a slight nudge away to make a quick escape.

"Have a drink and then you'll know."

I paused for a second and stared at the fruity drink in my hand. I felt his grip get stronger and stronger until his arm felt more than skin-tight.

I stared at the drink. The ice sank to the bottom and the drink looked a little cloudy. Surely this is from the dirt and filth of the place, but this felt wrong. Even still, I ignored my gut and drank. I looked back at him, and he grinned a sinister grin.

"Ok… now what?"

"Now we wait." He said plainly.

My face dropped. Oh god, tell me he didn't.

"What do you mean?" I fearfully asked.

"I just showed you what happened to her."

I felt sick. Shivers went up my spine. My stomach churned and my willpower left me. The room started to blur, and dim lights had radial halos around them.

Then I fell…

Right into tightened waiting arms…

Lev
19:03

I roamed around the unusually empty restaurant. I paced around the sizzling grills, hounding workers to sanitise any poor states of cleanliness or puddles of spilled oil. It was the least I could do since the small business I built was a ghost of what it could be. The night would usually have at least a handful of customers in. Not even the old drunks or the professional beggars would come in here to harass us for food or drink. I felt my purpose at the front of this place was concluded so I felt the need to retreat to my office and check on the employee that had special treatment. I left the front to be manned by one of the older workers.
"Look after the place." I would say to the middle-aged.
He gave me a meek thumbs up before turning around and returning to his duties.
I turned the corner and saw the boy hunched over the desk and bound to the peeling leather chair. He was scribbling away at a small notebook and had surrounded himself with textbooks of various subjects and degrees. I could understand none of it, but that was probably for the best.
"How are you doing?" I said calmly.
The boy reclined into the desiccated chair, intertwined his fingers between his short blonde hair released a relaxed groan. His head was stretched over the backseat to the point of snapping, but it looked to release a long-buried pain in him.
"I'm doing fine." He groaned.
I reached into my pocket for the cigarette packet and offered one to him. He slowly leaned forward and lit the cigarette with his lighter. He was hunched over the desk once again and repeatedly squeezed his forehead with his cigarette hand.
I could sense something was wrong, but I tried not to outwardly ask it.
"Are the smart people's books getting to you?" I tried to joke.
"Yeah, a little." He nervously chuckled before taking a stressful puff on his cigarette. "Maybe I'm not smart enough."

234

"Nonsense!" I dismissed. "You're smarter than me, you can understand those books a lot better than I can."
"I guess." The boy sighed.

He flicked away the ash from his cigarette and reclined back into the chair. It looked like he was trying to hide his pain, but his face betrayed him when his lip began to quiver.
"I just wish I had more time."

I was now very intrigued. I leaned against the door frame and folded my arms with a cigarette in hand.
"Time for what?" I questioned.
"I don't know…" He took another puff. The boy paused for a moment to find the words and then let the weight off his shoulder finally. "It's just Sidorovich did something that I'm still trying to figure out."

I should have known that Fedor was behind this.

"What did he do?" I asked sternly, passing the point of subtlety.
"I get why he did it!" He would express with the energy of a broken lion. "So, before you freak out don't be mad at him."
"I'll try my best."
"Good enough I guess." He sighed and scratched his scalp in what I could see and nervousness. "He pulled a gun on me."
I fell to the floor which was accompanied by my cigarette. I felt the ancient fury try to claw itself out which was barely being contained by my twitching moustache. It felt like it was a single guard was on duty for a prison and the guard was drunk.
"I'm going to kill him!" I would grit through my teeth.
"What?!" The boy bellowed in shock. "You're not killing anyone! He's not a bad guy!"
"You didn't fight *and* kill with him!" I argued back.
"No, I didn't, but he's trying his best!"
"Is he trying his best, or are you making excuses?"

I tried to vent the anger by exhaling the vile emotion through my nose like a dragon preparing to breathe flames. It resulted in sparking ignition as I threw my fist into the door. The solid thud caused the boy's soul to jump out of his body and fall back into the chair.

"I'm going tomorrow…" I paused and tightened my raw fist. "You can come with me, or you can stay here."

Sidorovich
12:02

I paced around the church anxiously with my pipe in my hand. I was alone. I had sent Samara home to try and rest as best as he could. I could manage without his presence, but it had been days since the boy last visited. And with both gone, I felt isolated. I brought in my old CD player into the church and let it play. I sat on the bench smoking my tobacco pipe, trying to feel some semblance of peace, but it did not come. I picked up my bible that was positioned next to me and opened it to the photos. I could hear the pipe fizzle and flutter as I shamefully took a deep puff. I saw them, there and they haunted me. I gently caressed the old photo of my son and felt empty without him. My son is dead, and soon will be my friend.

I suddenly heard the doors of the church fling open with the force of ten men, accompanied by the heavy marching of boots. I turned and faced the and faced guest, without time to shut the black book.

Lev marched towards me with forgotten anger and grabbed me by the collar with both of his freshly greased hands.

"I should shoot you for what you did!" He would yell. "The boy told me what you did."

I peered over Lev's shoulder and saw my boy there, my child… standing fearful. Fearful for whom I could not say.

Lev slapped me to attention and drew my focus back to him. "Don't look at him. Look at me!"

I kicked my captor in the groin the escape his grasp and tossed my pipe to the side in preparation for a fight. Lev collapsed on all fours with a high-pitched squeal. I realised what my actions caused, and felt the hate come out of me. I tried to help my old comrade up by extending a gentle hand, but he weakly slapped it away.

I left my old squad mate to recover and approached the boy.
He surprised me by locking me in a death grip, tightening his
arms around my spine as if it were a loving stranglehold. This
caught me off-guard. The only thing I could think to do was hold
him back.
"I'm sorry you had to see that." I softly spoke to him. "I did not
know what else to do."
The boy let go. I turned around to see Lev and his face held a
dumbfound expression. His eyes widened like gibbet moons to
release the shock of seeing what just happened.

He lost. He failed to turn my boy against me as he tried to do so
in the past.

Lev stood up and dusted off his grease-encrusted clothes. He
threw me a look of disgust mostly pronounced by the wrinkling
of his brow and the crumpling of his fuzzy upper lip.
"What is this?" He spat. "Have I just been conned into
something that you two concocted?"
"No!" The boy retaliated.
"Then what is happening?" Lev screamed. "Why am I carrying
dead weight—" He pointed to the boy. "In my business for a
man who has not changed in over thirty years?!"
"I have changed." I said with composure in my voice. "I lost
more than you know and fought in more ways than you think."
"So, give me one reason!" His voice raised louder. "What did
you learn from the death of *our* friends, of *your* son,
of *my* bother? Where is your change?!"
I felt the itch of my bandages call for their release. The feeling of
shredding sand and dying screams wanted to finally see the
captured church light. I unpinned my bandages and started to
unwrap them.
What was left was not the covering shame of black cloth but the
charred peach and stretched pink scars. I was wearing skin that
was not my own, it replaced that which I had lost and still left
the occasional black patches left from the fuel stains. Ingenious
Soviet medical science they called it. I rolled up my robe sleeves
and showed how much the fire took from me. It swallowed my
flesh and left only scars that extended to my elbows. Exposing

my arms felt like living it all over again. Even though I was considered healed, I could still feel the roaring fires and licking flames. I could hear the screaming men and the storm of sand which suffocated me.

"This is one reason." I defiantly uttered. "I don't want people to end up like me and do the things I have done… The things *we* have done." I pointed to the boy. "He will be better than the both of us, and it is my responsibility to make sure he becomes the one thing I wanted our friends to be, the one thing I wanted my son to be."

"And what is that priest?" Lev spat.

"Alive…"

Lisa
N/A

My eyelids felt heavy. The world was lost to me, and I felt frigid air brush against my skin. I felt cold concrete against my buttocks and jagged plasterwork on my back. I clutched my stomach and felt its stomach churn. I focused my remaining energy on opening my eyes and I could see I was in a shop with destroyed toys and shadowy figures. I was propped up against the wall and saw small makeshift fires in metal barrels and groups of people. One of them circled around the place on roller skates like a goldfish in a glass bowl. I looked at my body and saw my once pristine white dress covered in filth and stains that I was too scared to put a label on. I looked at my torn white dress and saw different handprints. My gaze drifted to my tights, and I saw bruising. I tried moving one of my legs to see the extent of the damage but found them covered in more marks which almost looked like handprints.

I felt panic set in which tried to escape in a scream. However, the sound was halted by a repugnant claw which suffocated my voice and assaulted my senses.

"I wouldn't do that if I was you." Whispered the hands' owner. I rolled my eyes to the side and saw him there. The bowl cut menace.

"They're in their own world. Wouldn't be the best idea to interrupt them." He said with a hushed voice. "They're not the friendliest."

My mouth was held still by both force and fear. My eyes welled up with small tears which escaped my eyelids and ran down what was left of my contoured face. I couldn't move I was too weak and too bruised. The only thing that was racing in my mind was what did he want from me?

The disgusting thing that held me down brushed his hand against my chest. It reached down into my cleavage and rummaged around for something. I thought he was doing it to grope me, so I struggled and tried to scream but I felt its hand press my head against the wall. This was nothing compared to the shock when he pulled out a cling film bag full of pills. My eyes widened to show their full whiteness with my willpower escaping me. I felt helpless and more surprised that I had that hidden in my bra.

"I think you're stuck with us at the moment especially since you've been caught with my product." The thing said. "I have a rule here." He reached down and pushed the bag back into my bra. "I never give anything out for free."

He let go of my face and then stood up.

I felt the words seep out of my mouth like my tears trickling down onto my dress.
"What do you want?" I said weakly.

It said one word that made me know I would never leave here. At least not willingly.
"You."

Sidorovich

The two were gathered around me. My CD player still churning out old rock music from a forgotten and foreign era. My scars were still uncovered at the request of the boy. I felt hideous and full of shame. Lev sat there moping and smoking in the church with his cigarettes whilst the boy and I would smoke from our pipes. Thankfully, the fire and smoke alarms did not blare like a chorus of whines otherwise we would have a worse situation on our hands. The boy brought us paper cups from the local shop and poured us some cheap spirit. Likely vodka, although I do miss Samara's taste in liquor.

Some sat, whilst some stood. All were paralyzed in awkward silence, unsure of how to continue forward.

The boy broke the peace first.

"Why do you two hate each other so much?" The boy bluntly demanded from the both of us.

We looked at each other and glared. Hiding back our spiteful expressions through the smoke we emitted. We were like two burning fires ready to clash. It was hard to think we fought together once, but even then, we were uneasy with each other.

"There are too many reasons." Lev hissed.

"You act like you are a saint." I challenged back.

"Compared to you I am!"

"Stop!" The boy commanded. "Talk to each other instead of fighting with each other!"

"You forget." Lev said. "It's all we know how to do with each other!"

"The friends we had were killed." Sidorovich spoke gutturally. "Now all we have is whatever is still standing. The one we could barely tolerate."

Sidorovich took a sip of vodka and then sipped again until you could hear a gulp.

"What broke it for you?" The boy asked us innocently.

"Where to start?" Lev spoke with a grumble in his voice.

He flicked away the cigarette to the side of the church showing the disrespect he held for not only me but for this place I cared for. This place saved me.

"Pick it up!" I demanded coldly.

"No." Lev defied in a similar tone. He narrowed his eyes like a wolf stalking prey.

"I'll get it." The boy declared.

"No!" Both me and Lev sternly commanded in unison.

This was not a matter of cleanliness but a matter of respect and who would bow to the other first.

I felt my bandages itch further and further.

Once again, the boy tried to keep the peace between us.

"What broke between you two?" he would innocently ask.

"He killed someone." Lev petulantly barked.

"We all killed someone." I chided. "Be more specific."

"This monster…" Lev bellowed. "Got my brother and poor Arseny killed!"

"Just like you tried to kill Slava?" I returned.

Lev shot up out of his chair with a clenched fist.

"How about I finish the job by killing you?" Lev screamed.

I didn't get up or even raise my head.

The boy got between us, extending his arms to block Lev getting to me.

"I won't let you!" The boy yelled defiantly. "Not until you tell me what happened!"

"Fine!" He screamed. He fluttered his arms like a pouting child and returned to his seat. "You tell him! But so, help me—" Lev leaned forward with his index finger threatening me. "If you tell me any lies, I will hit you."

The threat was clear, the stage was set, and I let my memories take me.

"What do we do?" called a distorted voice in the wind.

"What do we do?" It repeats.

I feel my hands shake and my back ache. A tug on my side pulled the strips of ragged cloth of our disguises toward them.

"Fedor!" Mikhail whispered harshly. "What do we do?"

I looked across and saw that we were wrong. It was not twenty men we faced but more or less thirty. We stumbled into a scavenging run for the local militia and Kars was not convincing enough for them.

Slava began to panic. Our leader was broken. Lev stood by his side, his hands twitching to cover us with an opening volley. The remaining survivors were broken and thought we wouldn't get out alive.

"We'll have to split the squad into two." I whispered to Mikhail.
"They'll pick us off." The singer responded with fear.
"Not if we're smart." I pointed to two main wreckage points that were the closest to us, composed of broken tanks and wreaked APCs. "If we surround ourselves in the wreckage, we can wait until the storm comes."
"Who will lead the other group?"
"You'll have to." I said, placing a hand on his shoulder.
"What about Slava?"
"I'll look after him. Get your group together but don't make it obvious."

Mikhail nodded but as soon as he tried to walk one of the mujahedeen pointed their attention at him. They were ordering in a language unknown to us. Kars was in the most danger due to being inches away from the rebels. We needed this to go well.

Dima rushed towards me but was detected himself. We didn't need to know what they were saying, we knew an order to halt when we heard it. Kars placed a hand on his shoulder and leaned into his ear. He whispered something to him. Something which both saddened and enlightened him through the patterned clothes on his face.

The storm was a few minutes away, but it felt like days, and we could not survive days.
Kars gestured forward to Mikhail to get Dima out of the spotlight. Mikhail approached the large group but did so slowly to stall for time.
Dima rushed to me and whispered to me. His back was turned to the Mouja, and his face was revealed from the rags.
"We stumbled into an ammo dump."

This was the last thing I needed to hear.

242

"Where?" I blustered in a hushed tone. "Here?"
"No." He pointed to the town in the distance. "There."

Dima wiped the sweat from his brow and lowered the cloth head
wrap to expose his mouth small enough to make him easier to
understand.
"If this is an arms hideout then they have a working radio like
the one you had."

This was now good news, but it was risky. Now our mission was
not only to survive but to get that radio.

"Do you think we can get it?" I asked Dima in a hushed tone.
"We can try." He responded in the same manner.

Suddenly Dima's miracle face appeared. His eyes were held
open as if pulled open by hooks and his mouth dropped to the
floor like it was holding a death bell.
"Kars!" I heard Vasya scream. "Get out of there!"
I then knew what this meant when I heard the shots ring across
the desert.
My attention snapped back to Kars, and I could see him spraying
a volley at the men. He took out three, maybe four. But the rest
of the rebels gunned him down as if he was sent to a firing
squad. Spraying visceral chunks of blood and bone into the
charred earth.
That is when my hatred of Vasya began. He got my friend killed
because of his stupidity.

"Kars!" I desperately tried to scream but the shots drowned out
the sound of my voice.

"Get to cover!" Mikhail screamed. He ran from the Mouja but
was isolated. He hid under a wreaked truck hoping the Mouja
had lost him and focused attention on us. The rest of us ran into
the nearest cover we could find. Only three of us managed to get
to the position we wanted but the squad was scattered in the
ruins.

Lev held down covering fire for the rest of the men to get to a better position, but his big machine gun was no match for twenty rifles pinning him down. The rebels shot like amateurs, but they were trained amateurs who were fighting for their homes. We fought to go home.

Arseny threw a grenade to disorganise them, but the loud pop did little more than kick up sand and dirt. Some charged forward with preternatural ferocity, trying to skewer us with their rusted bayonets and we were powerless to halt them from what seemed like an endless volley of mismatched weapons.

Slava rocked in the corner covering his ears and praying that it would be over soon. He whimpered like a puppy and cried like a child.

Each man was trying to fend for themselves. Our squad was broken, and we were being picked off one by one. Two men charged at me and Dima from our flank. We heard them screaming through the gusts of wind and the whistling of bullets.

Two scarved men with their bayonets charged at us. I tried to shoot them, but my gun jammed. Dima tried but he missed. We engaged in hand-to-hand fighting.

The Mouja who charged me was trying to stab me with his bayonet. I tried to fight him off by grabbing the barrel and magazine of the rifle he held. Not the best positions as they were awkward to grab but it was this or let it stab me.

I was pushed against a jagged metal and felt a sharp spear press into my back. My life ebbed down my spine as the stitches tore and I lost my strength to fight. My arms felt weak, and my bones began to liquefy. The rusted spear drew closer and closer to my face. I could see the whites of his eyes emit vitriol.

With a crack and a sudden spark of gunpowder. The burning white turned into a bloodied red as his skull and brains were splattered on me.

The now-dead man who collapsed into the sand was left to be forgotten about. I collapsed the same, but only to catch my breath.

Dima approached. His head scarf was gone showing the full extent of his old and new wounds. His old facial cut was now exposed to the battle, but it was accompanied by a fresh laceration on his left eye, gushing blood from his own fight, and desperately screamed these words to me.

"Get up!" He extended his hand. "I can't fight them off without you!"

My body felt spirit once more. Even if that spirit was quickly draining from my opened wounds. I felt the pull of the prophet guide me up and lift me off the ground.

His battered and stern face then dropped once more for the last time, as a stray round flew into his side and made the prophet a victim of his own fortunes.

I couldn't say anything. I just pulled a stupid face and then looked to the side. There stood three of the rebels. As soon as they saw me, they turned their weapons to me.

And like a coward... I ran...

I grabbed my rifle and ran as fast as I could. I scurried through the wreckage with a trail of bullets kicking up the sand behind me. I had dived into another ruin this time protected by desert stone and broken trucks. Running through here felt like running through a graveyard.

I hid between two abandoned vehicles and could hear the three men chasing me.

I knew my rifle was useless jammed, so I tried desperately to restore it. Nothing. I pulled out my pistol and prepared myself to die.

I held the piece of steel in my hands. Hoping I could at least take one or two of them with me. I clutched the prayer rope Mikhail gave me in some form of relief and said a silent prayer to myself.

I closed my eyes, inhaled, and then opened them preparing myself to kill these fuckers.

I heard gunshots and screaming men. I was too scared to walk out of my hiding spot. I just held out my pistol and three saw men in rags in the clearing. I started to squeeze to trigger until I heard them speak Russian.

"Hey!" I bellowed.

The men pointed their guns at me.

One of them fired a shot that whistled past me.

"I'm Russian you fucking idiots!" I screamed. I lowered my disguise and revealed myself to them.

"Oh God!" One yelped. "I'm so sorry Fedor!"

The men lowered their cloth headdresses. Arseny, Vasya, and Slava were there.

Slava was paralyzed by the battle; he couldn't even hold his rifle properly. He was in too much shock to pull down his mask, so Vasya yanked it off for him.

"It doesn't matter!" I dismissed. I took a relieved breath to calm myself. "Where are Lev and Mikhail?"

"We don't know! And we don't care!" Vasya said with haste. "We have ten men after us!"

"Wait!" I halted them. I held Vasya by the arm to get his attention before he sprinted off. "They have a radio; we can get help!"

"Ten men Fedor!" Vasya bellowed.

Shots could be heard chasing us, some ricocheted from the metal corpses signalling us to leave.

"Go!" Vasya commanded.

We sprinted forward away from the charging men firing wildly. I grabbed Slava by the arm and forced him to live.

We hid behind a group of broken trucks and collapsed by the gargantuan wheels. Our makeshift barricade was littered with rusted parts and broken mechanical pieces.

"How long before the storm is here?" Arseny called out with exhaustion in his voice.

"Any minute now." Vasya replied. "Be ready to run as soon as it hits us!"

"We need to leave now!" Slava pleaded.

"No!" I yelled. "They can't follow us!"

"I command this squad! And we are leaving!" Slava ordered.

Slava got up and began to sprint away. Arseny tried to catch him, but Slava escaped him.

Slava timed his departure poorly however, as soon as he left the cover, a grenade had buried itself into the sand.

Slava saw this and tried to run from it, but a hail of bullets prevented him from doing so.

Just like that…

Pop

Slava flew backwards towards us with grains of sand and earth
crashing around us.
His legs were in pieces with shards of shrapnel lodged in the
churned meat and bone that were his legs.
"Get him!" I called out.

Me and Arseny grabbed him by the shoulders and pulled him
closer to us. Blood leaked from Slava's stumps, and he was still
in shock from what happened.
I grabbed Vasya by the collar.
"Fix him!" I ordered.
"I'm not a miracle worker." Vasya spat. "He won't survive!"
"Please!" Arseny begged.

The storm was almost on top of us. The storm's winds made
speaking almost impossible, forcing out battered vocals to
perform more under strain.
"Fine!" Vasya relented. "But you're carrying him!"
Vasya looked around desperately to look for something to drag
him with. He ran out and reached for a truck door that had been
previously blown off.
"Rags!" Vasya demanded.
Me and our youngest took any rags we could spare from our
uniform to try and strap our leader and possibly get him home.
We stripped any bloodied cloth from Slava, our hands would
sometimes touch his wounds which felt like bloodied
mincemeat. Vasya put tourniquets onto what was left of his legs
and injected them with medicine.
I looked to the horizon and saw the sands about to impact our
less protected bodies.
"Get ready!" I screamed.

Three…

I turned around.

247

Two…

I saw a rebel.

One…

They raised their gun.

Impact…

The winds blew them off their feet.

We were more prepared than the man there. We carted Slava along with a rope of cloth and expendable fabric. Then we disappeared. Shots whistled after us but were blown off course by the howling storm.

I blink and I see the church.

"That did not matter…" I spoke grimly.

I inhale and taste sand.

"Our efforts were in vain." I said in defeat.

I exhale and smell tobacco.

"For two reasons." I held two fingers up. "The wild bullets carried by the wind got a couple of hits on the man we carried…" I paused for a moment and directed my forefinger to Lev." and him…"

"What do you mean?" The boy asked. Fascinated by the tale.

"I shot those bullets." Lev proudly boasted. "I killed that bastard. The Mouja just helped with the grenade." Lev took a swig of vodka and bitterly grimaced. "I kept my promise to my brother, and I killed him."

248

Smoke and Mortals

Michael
Half nine-ish

Work was as frustrating as it could be. I was sat in the lounge finally able to relax after all me hard work and toil for these lot. I stopped going to work and booked some time off. I needed a holiday. I decided to start shopping on my phone for different places to try and get a cheap hotel in a different country and I wanted to take the little one with me. The other was causing too much trouble so he hasn't earned it yet.

Finally, we found a place in Tenerife going for cheap.

Click

Card details in, and then booked a decent spot for two weeks. Sorted.

As if on cue he walked into my little kingdom smelling of grease.

"Ah sit down for me, would you?" I theatrically gestured me hand toward the other sofa in the room.

He gave me a childish groan and an eye roll before he sat down. I was right to leave him out if this is the attitude, he's giving me.

"What?" He said in frustration.

"Don't '*what*' me." I said back to him.

He gave me another eye roll and shook his head.

I tried to push past his disobedience and told him me plan.

"I'm going on holiday."

"To where?"

"Tenerife."

"Good for you." He jibbed. "Can I go?"

"Yeah, get out." I sneered.

"With pleasure." He replied.

He proceeded to walk out the door and the smell followed him.

"Bills are still paid just the same." I yelled after him.

249

As he left, I realised he didn't care. Why didn't he care? That should have been a punishment, but it was insignificant to him. Something strange was going on. I just needed to figure out what.

Bern
12:32pm
278 days post exam

The exams were close. Closer than I'd like. I barely spoke to anyone about them. The most interaction I would have about them was to ask when they were happening, and which exam came first.

My routine would operate like a strict timetable.

Monday: School, work, look after family.
Tuesday: Work, church, family.
Wednesday: School, work, look after the family.
Thursday: Work, church, look after family, potentially get a beating if Dad was in a bad mood or on the piss.

Etcetera... Etcetera...

I felt tired. My ribs became pronounced through my skin and my face started to lose colour and fullness, making it gaunter and skinnier like Sidorovich's.

Sidorovich...

He would help when he could but the best, he could do was let me fight my battle and plot an escape for me. He and Samara were closer than I had seen them.

In the church, I helped lift Samara from the pew. He was getting so much weaker. Samara needed the use of a cane to walk now. "Get me my stick boy." Samara asked of me.

I walked into the office whilst Sidorovich kept him propped up and partially standing.

I gave him the ash wood cane and prepared myself to catch Samara if he fell.

Samara walked around but now on a hobble. He reached for a tumbler and gulped the thing in one.

"Go home. Please." Sidorovich begged.

"Why?" Samara would exclaim. "Who would keep your life entertaining?"

"The boy can keep me company." Sidorovich replied.

Samara in his perpetually drunk state would say, "Maybe…" He glorified the cane like it was a holy artifact. "But I'm the one who helped pull this stick out of your ass."

Samara nearly fell over making the joke.

We rushed to help him, but he caught himself just in time.

"Please sit down." I pleaded.

"Fine!" Samara pouted, "You win."

Samara creaked back onto the pew struggling to move. He released a pained grunt and then relaxed his spine into the polished wood.

"Dear god…" Samara moaned. "I'm getting old."

"You're younger than me." Sidorovich responded. Moving in front of the altar to light incense.

"Yes, but I feel it." Samara moaned.

And here comes the loving bickering once again.

"I blame you!" Samara pointed at his fellow priest.

Sidorovich froze in place taking it in. "What?" He blurted out in confusion.

"Not you piece of shit!" Samara wafted away the notion like it was a fly and returned his finger to the same position. "That piece of shit!"

Sidorovich moved from the altar and exposed the tripled beamed cross of the Orthodox church.

251

"Why did you make alcohol so good?!" Samara petulantly yelled.

"What did the cross do?" I questioned.

"Not the cross boy, God!" Samara bellowed. "I've been fighting that man since I became a priest.

"If you don't like him, why did you become one?" I replied.

Sidorovich shied away unnaturally.

"Because..." Samara paused. "It's the first thing that came to mind. No call, no billboard, not even a free model on my doorstep with painted crosses on her body. Although..." He pointed to the sky. "Take notes."

I expected nothing less of him. He lived his life as he did, and I could not chastise him for his behaviour. Not now when he is on his deathbed. Sidorovich on the other hand...

"You always did live like a fool." He said sarcastically.

"And you lived like a miserable man." Samara remarked.

"I always hated you." Sidorovich jibbed.

"I love you too, piece of shit." Samara joked.

Sidorovich's lips allowed a small crack in his usual outward posture. He allowed a tiny but noticeable smirk.

"And that's why we are perfect for each other." Sidorovich said.

And this was the loving show I needed in my life. They knew each other, and through all their hardships, they still came together not as priests but as brothers.

Sidorovich sat next to his friend and placed his hand over his shoulder, squeezing it comfortably. They directed their attention to me. I must have looked like a lost sheep or a deer in the headlights.

"Listen, boy, I know I'm pretty..." Samara joked. "But stop staring."

I woke up and felt embarrassed at my actions.

"Sorry!" I exclaimed with shame.
"It's ok." Samara calmly dismissed.

Sidorovich chuckled for less than a second and shook his head.
"Did you know we hated each other when we first met?" He said
cheerily.
This was news to me. I never knew them to be anything other
than what they are. Even when they do wrong, they try to make
it up to each other.
Samara gestured to his colleague.
"Don't become like us." Sidorovich said to me.
Samara followed the word with his free hand like he was about
to catch them mid-flight.
"No." Samara said. "Be better".

1:23pm

I said my goodbyes to the two and left to go to work. I wanted to
get in some more study time, and it made for an excuse to not
going home. I let the door creak to a close and made my way to
the street. I took the bus there and prepared myself for Lev.

As soon as I stepped off the bus and walked away from some
driver wearing Oakley glasses. I saw a black estate car parked
outside the little takeaway shop.
I thought nothing of it at first until I saw its driver get out.

David walked in front and calmly paced up to me, clad in his
black court uniform and stab-proof vest.
"Can I have a word?" He asked.
I paused. I hesitated.
"I have to work." I finally said after forcing the words from my
lungs.
"It's just two minutes. Please." He started walking towards his
car and opened the front passenger door for me. "I'll explain
everything to your boss if it gets you in trouble."

I sat down in the car with him. I trusted him but as far as I knew,
he was still friends with my dad, so I was still hesitant.

I fell into the seat and closed the driver door behind him.

"What's this about?" I asked with a small tremble in my voice.
"You're not in trouble." The bailiff reassured.

I obeyed and walked to his black Skoda car. I heard the car beep
and the locks jut open. I land with a leathery creak on his freshly
upholstered seats and close the door behind me.
I stare at him and wait for him to speak.

"Is everything alright with your dad?" He asked.
"Yeah..." I paused. "He is."
I reared my body closer towards the door for a quick escape.
Although I don't know what good it would do since the closest
place I could bolt to was the takeaway shop. And I don't think
Lev would be kind enough to defend me.
"It's just..." David gripped his steering wheel tightly. "There's
some stuff I've caught him doing and I don't like it."
I leaned in closer.
"Stuff like what?" I knew what he meant but I didn't know the
extent of cruelty David was shown. I leaned in closer and made a
small shift away from the door.
"Oh, just small stuff." He dismissed me with a wave of his hand.
David pushed his head against the car seat and made an audible
creak which spoke more frustration than the bailiff cared to
express. "Just be careful, yeah?" He spoke softly, hiding his true
emotions.

I slumped against a chair and folded my arms.
"Why did you bring me here?" I sternly demanded.
"Because I need to warn you about what's going on with your
dad." The bailiff said.

He reached under his seat and pulled out a stack of paperwork.
He forced the documents into my lap.
"These will tell you everything." He grimly stated. "I'm just
sorry you're going through this. I'll be avoiding the place for the
moment. I hope you understand but essentially, I'd suggest
finding a way to get out of here."

Thoughts were racing around my head. Too much to process and I haven't even looked at the papers in front of me or what evidence they held.

"My number is at the back." David said. "If you need help or anything, let me know and I'll come flying down."

"Thanks, I guess." I spoke. I took a quick glance at the documents and saw they were in a spreadsheet format with number splayed across the tables. I already got a feeling what they were, and my heart sank. "What do you want me to do with these?"

"Read them." The bailiff said. "Just don't let him know you have these. This way I can build a case without him knowing, so if you can, keep these in a safe place."

I nodded. I understood.

"Thank you for bringing these." I said with gratitude in my voice.

He gave a soft smile.

"It's ok mate. Just make a plan and get yourself safe."

I opened the door and left the car to go to work.

I took a slow pace to glance over the documents. They confirmed my fears with the scattered pound sterling symbols. Financial figures with the odd scattering of five-hundred sterling pounds dotted around the pages which exited their bank account in habitual fast-food purchases.

The extortionate monster. Starving me to feed himself and my brother who he spoils rotten.

I walked into work and tucked the papers into the office. I couldn't risk Lev finding them and mistaking them for useless papers. I needed to take them somewhere I knew would be safe. I quickly grabbed some sheets of food wrapping paper and shoddily coated the documents in them.

I then stuffed them into an opaque blue plastic bag with a takeaway carton hidden on top. You could make out the shape of rough A4 paper from the bottom of the bag which protruded from the corners of the blue plastic as it transfigured the light navy into turquoise, but this would have to do for now. Now to wait for the end of shift.

Lisa
N/A

I may have died but not really. The smoke that passes from my lips is acrid. The taste of this pungent tobacco was extinguished with the flavour of a foreign day.
I had no family remaining, except those that sand around a hazardous fire. Their cackling tones and deathly intoxicated rattles echoing the halls.

What am I doing here?

Where even am I?

Why has nobody come looking for me?

My mind rushed with a surging pain. A lingering memory of a past life. I look at the small cigarette packet in my hand. I gaze at the image on the packet and see the tumours hiding in the throat. Some government initiative to scare people from smoking. I never paid it any mind. Not until I caressed my own throat. These fingers which were once like porcelain were now trickling down a vocal river which only streamed smoke. Tears from the valleys fell down my cheeks. They followed the downward flow of my digits, pathetically washing away the impurities from the mountain range and leaving onto the ocean of trash.
The mouth of that river swallowed another trickle of poison, polluting the supply.

This poison was different. This poison held contempt. This poison was accepted by me.

Switch

Anger flowed through me. Feelings that were never so abundant, but they felt different from the numbing herbal vapours wafting in the air. I stand up from my trash pile and face outwards. My vision is a haze.

How long have I been here?

This garden of broken dreams and crushed joy guided me to the door. As is the scattered toys and half-torn teddy bears pointed towards the doorway.

The doorway...

The arches of light flashed with dancing halos.

My legs... My legs felt weak. My time here felt short.

The sticks of marrow attached to my hips which once held flesh and meat were emaciated.

Each step is a crunch on broken glass. I looked down at the shard I stepped on and saw a reflection.

A ghost.

A slave.

A monster...

So, forth the monster lumbers. Towards the light. Towards the end. My head was ablaze. I pulled up my sleeves and the damage.
I saw scratches and shallow cuts scattered across my once milk-white arms.

Switch

Another step. I tug at my stomach and feel each tender bruise radiate across my face as a contorted wince. I moved my hands towards my breasts and felt them be equally sore. This was hell.

I push forward. I'm so close. I reach my arm out to grasp the light. I feel its warmth. I hear the noise and traffic outside.

And then I notice a small prick on my back. I turn around and see my culprit. I see this thing with a bowl-cut dress on its scalp. I collapse back.

My eyes still drifting towards the light that escaped me.

Then shadows.

Shadows which whispered like phantoms and stood like statues. The instruments of pain in their hands.

I felt my body be caressed by the ones that held me.

The shadows charged. Their faces were blurred by dark fabrics and rich wools.

The was an end to my suffering. When I witnessed the dark army march forward like a mob of savages.

Shouting but no noise.

The chanting of brotherhood but no cooperation.

Surrender

A sudden swing of spiteful iron contacted my head but there was no pain.

I let the light embrace me with its warmth. But it was deception.

There was no warmth, only the splash of an abyssal ocean.

Bern
9:32pm

The keys felt heavy in my hand. The blue plastic bag holding my proof of corruption held an unbearable weight in both soul and mind. Bearing the proof of betrayal and having to hide it under the nose of the accused.

258

My hand and heart felt heavy.

The door lock unlatched, and the hinges squealed. My lungs felt empty, and my nerves were on the brink of being shot. I felt my heart beg to be released from its skeletal prison which pounded harder and harder against its ossein bars.

In my head I was praying. In my very being, I was begging for whatever presence that laid in my red bible that my lethargic father would not be sat on that black sofa.

The door fully opens, and I rush through the door and spin around to lock it as equally fast.

"Ah." My captor said. "I was wondering when you'd come home."

I pressed my head against the door and gripped the bag tightly.

"And I see you've brought me something as well."

How kind of him to think that I live for him and only him.

"What thing?" I asked innocently. I knew what he meant but I tried to play it off as if I knew nothing. Ignorance is bliss and such...

"That thing in the blue bag." He raised his now fat ridden finger. "I want it."

Oh god... There is where I'm in for it now.

I walked up to him with my head hanging as if from a noose.

His vigilant eyes tracking my movement as I slowly paced towards him.

I opened the bag, and he peered his head in.

I looked away and clenched my eyelids until my cornea reversed into my sockets, waiting for the end.

"Ah Brilliant."

I slowly opened my eyes and saw him holding up an opened carton of a greasy monstrosity between two burger buns.

"You can go now." He blurted in between mouthfuls of half chewed protein. "I'll eat the other thing in the bag when it comes to the morning."

He won't be getting it. It's not meant for him to have. Not until the time is right.

I didn't say a word. I scurried up to my room and hid the documents still concealed in their hospitality wrappings under my mattress and set my alarm to five AM to catch the earliest bus.
I collapsed onto my mattress and let out a sigh of relief.
"I can't believe that worked." I whispered to myself.
I got my phone and flicked through the speed dial contact, then pressed send.

Buzz tone... Buzz tone...

"Hello?"

"Hey, I need to speak to you guys in the morning."

Sidorovich
06:11

The morning light glimmered through the stained-glass windows. Beams of light shone into the cobbled ground and illuminated the dust specs in the air. The flowers scattered around the church were starting to come to life now. Free from the chilly air and embraced by the warm. I felt the comforting creak of polished wood press against my back and the comforting glow from my pipe, ebbing through my bandaged hands.

I wish I could say the same about my friend. He limped around with a crooked wooden cane, barely holding himself upright. He tried his best in the church to help with the menial tasks that he never did but he could not do much. Perhaps he knew his time was near. Perhaps he wanted to try and do more. Whatever it is. The effort was not unnoticed.

However, we were not alone. Lev paced around the place compulsively. He was tired, trying to keep himself awake with the taste of cigarettes in his mouth.

A dysfunctional band of brothers waiting for the person that binds us together.

"How much longer must we wait?" Lev asked.
"Long enough." Samara replied.
"And how long is that."
"Long enough." Samara repeated with a harshened tone.

"Both of you stop!" I intervene. "He wanted to show us something urgent and so we shall wait for him."

Lev paced further from the basin in the corner to the end of the pew.

"Your new boy had better be worth it for dragging us out here." Lev spat.
"I have faith in him." I responded.
"Whatever you say, priest."

The doors creaked open, gliding along the sunlight behind the child.

We stood to attention. Samara who struggled to do such, raised his spine upright on the nearest pew he could sit on, clutching on his cane as he leaned forward.

"At last!" Lev bellowed. "Your prodigal son arrives."
"Shut up!" I barked.

The boy, holding a blue plastic bag stepped forward but was hesitant to move deeper.

261

"Why is Lev here?" The child asked.
"Because I am." He snapped. Lev flicked the cigarette ash from the end of his burning cigarette onto the church floors.
I threw him a scowl to show I disproved his behaviour. He threw me a narrow-eyed stare in return and held his gaze as he stubbed the cigarette on the church walls.
"You will clean that up when we are finished." I hissed.

Lev continued to hold his gaze without blinking as he flicked the butt of his cigarette into a distant corner of the church.
I marched up to him and prepared to strike him for the insolence, but the boy got between us.

"Just stop trying to kill each other for a minute! Please!" The boy pleaded.

"Then talk." Lev demanded. "And speak quickly."

"It's these!"

The boy pulled out an amalgamation of wrapping paper which looked like the life expectancy of it was coming to a quick end. He pulled off the shell and revealed a stack of spreadsheets and numbers.

"Am I meant to be impressed?" Lev said.
"Look at what's on them." The boy pleaded.

He gave me the documents first.
It was financial figures but the one constant from flicking through the papers was five hundred pounds which dotted from month to month.

Lev sneaked up next to me and snatched the thing from my hands. He scanned them in an instant and appeared more unimpressed.
"What is this meant to mean?" He spoke.
"This is proof."
"Proof of what?"

262

"That I'm being extorted. That five hundred is coming from me."

Lev and I both glanced at each other with worried looks.
I broke contact and gave the papers to Samara so he could examine them.
"Fedor told me about this." Lev said. "What are you going to do with this?"
The boy paused to think and then rubbed his hands together.
"I don't know." He exclaimed, waving his hands around in a distressed motion. "But it's proof. I can do something with it at least."
"Fine." Lev said. "More importantly, how did you get these? I don't think you would have had free access to his finances if you had to go through all this trouble."
"Not important!" The boy shirked.
"It is now." I inputted. "It is important because this could start a war that we can't finish."
"And you would know all about that." Lev sneered.
"We both went there." I said to Lev "But neither of us is smart enough for this kind of fight."

I could hear the creak of wood and the groan of an old friend.
"The boy—" Samara gasped, leaving the papers on the pew, and desperately clutching his cane to avoid falling to the floor. "Said it wasn't important. So, respect that."

I rushed to help my friend, but he wafted me with a swift gesture of the hand.

I let out a sigh and left my now extinguished pipe on a pew.

"I'll keep those papers here in my office but what do you want us to do?" I spoke.
"Us?" Lev barked. "What do you mean us?"
"He meant what he meant." Samara said with a croak in his voice. "You're part of this now."
"I agreed to help with his study, not fight in a court case." Lev childishly remarked.

"And you can keep helping by doing that." I spoke. "Just make sure he has a safe place to go to."
"Please." The boy spoke with despair.

Lev's fury softened. Even if it was only for a second, it was all we needed.
"Fine." He said with annoyance in his voice. He turned away from us for a moment and proceeded to wipe the soot on the wall which he created from the stubbed-out cigarette. "What is the plan?"

"Well..." The boy pondered. "I thought about it for a while, and I need to escape from there."
"And how do you plan to do that?" I asked.
"Well... I need to learn to drive." He responded. "But I don't have the time or the money to learn.
"How much stuff do you have?" Lev asked.
"Not much." The boy said."
"Then you get a motorbike." Samara pitched. "We can at least help with that."

12:21

I waited, clutching my bible outside of the church. I closed it early and changed into more casual clothes. Although most people would call a black suit funeral attire.
Samara joined me and kept himself propped up with his cane, fearing he may not come back up. He joined me in the casual attire but presented himself differently, wearing a denim outfit with thick gold jewellery which captured the sparkling yellow of the fields behind the ancient building.

We could see the boy approach us in the distance. He looked as scruffy as usual. However, this was different. He came back to us clutching his side.
Me and Samara looked at each other and knew what happened. We tried to be ourselves, but we couldn't help but worry for the child.

264

"I'm here." The boy cried.

"Good to see you made it." Samara said.

"What's happened to you?" I asked.

"Getting those documents to you guys came at a bit of a cost." The boy said between winces.

"And those costs…" I gestured to the area he was holding. "Is that the result of it?"

The boy did not say anything. I took his silence as confirmation.

I let a small sigh escape me knowing what had happened and turned to my colleague. Anger guided my emotions, the frustration and hate of my knowing that this boy was being struck by his father still raged in my mind. Although, tempered thoughts must be used now for fear of making a dire situation worse.

"We can't do this now." I said to Samara.

"Then when will we?" He responded.

"When he's better but not in this state."

"This isn't going to change." The boy expressed. "Let's just get whatever this is out of the way."

Me and Samara gave each other affirming nods. We didn't like it, but this was the fact.

"Ok then, if, you are sure." I spoke.

I disappeared into the church for a moment and brought out an old mountain bike.

The mechanical apparatus was freshly oiled, and I quickly checked the machine's working condition. It worked, but more superficial areas like the odd scattering of the original paint that previous owners failed to remove was less than appealing. Parts that were not working were replaced from spare parts I could scavenge. I carried it outside and dropped it near the boy's feet. I could see his face blowing up with embarrassment.

"What is it?"

The boy's head sank towards his chest. "I don't even know how to ride a regular bike."

Oh, this poor boy. This poor child hasn't even been shown what other children learn so early. I was starting to understand the extent of his upbringing.

"Don't worry about it." Samara said gently with a small croak in his voice. "We'll help you."

The boy mounted the black leather seat. The material was starting to crack and warp, but nobody could see it and if it was comfortable, then that was all that mattered.

He tried pushing forward but he immediately lost balance upon taking his feet off the ground.
He quickly steadied himself and set off again, repeating his blunder once again. However, on this occasion, he landed face-first onto the concrete.
Samara tried to rush up and help him, but he was too weak and caused himself great pain from standing, causing him to grip his stomach. Wanted to rush over to the boy but I was closer to my friend and tried to comfort him.
The boy picked himself up from the ground and dusted himself off. He bore a fresh new graze on his cheek and elbows which would be hard to explain to his captor.

Am I making the right decision? Am I truly helping him or am causing more pain in his life?

"Uh!" The boy groaned in frustration. "This isn't working!" He wailed.

"It's ok." I spoke. "These things happen."

"Things?" The boy retorted. "What things? All the things I have ended up falling apart in one way or another." He pressed his hands against his chest. "My life, my relationships, my family…"

"And do you want to know one thing that will be there for you?" Samara said, directing his cane to us like a director.
"What?" The boy replied.
"Us." I said with a smile cracking across my face.

"Let's try again, shall we?" I gestured with open palms to the apparatus on the floor. "I'll help you."

The boy picked up the newly scratched bike and mounted it once more. I placed one hand behind his back and one on his shoulder to steady him.

"Pick your feet up and move with the motion." I instructed.

I glided him along and saw him wobble. He was not used to having balance in any form. He lifted his feet and rested them on the peddles, letting him feel the movement and how to work it. This I felt a flash, a spark of joy. I saw my son and he smiled at me.
I saw his child-like eyes flutter with amazement and the wonders he was committing, that the rest took us for granted.
I felt like his mother was watching, sitting by us, and waiting for the day her flesh and blood could start to become a man.
I glanced over my shoulder and saw her there. Where Samara sat and I felt at peace for a moment. It felt well and right.
This moment would not last. A gang of wastrels in sleeveless puffer jackets and bandanas walked past us and caught the scene unfold.
"Ha!" One of them cried. "Need a push?" They mocked as they walked past cackling like hyenas. I saw the results of their words on the boy from the bowing of his dead and the slumping of his spine. He lost the initial wonder and felt shame for taking so long to learn this skill. A flaw that was not his fault.

I made no hesitation. I released the boy, and I picked up a small rock, hurling it with sharp velocity toward the pack of vagrants.

The stone hit one of them in the face causing him to cover his face from the damage. It would have worked; had I not noticed the small wet pool hovering around the outlines of his mouth. They gathered around their wounded. The boy lost balance but made a sudden stop with his feet close to the group and dismounted the bike, leaving the metal carcass on the street.

"You hurt him you crazy fuck!" One of the trespassers cried. They sounded young. But they had the physique of grown men.

I felt my blood rage with fire. I took another rock and prepared myself to throw it.
The flash of the sun burned away any sense of compassion like a mist of spring water. The heat of the star illuminated me, but it did little to light the darkness that surrounded my gut and strength my talons dug into the natural stone.

I close my eyes, take in a deep breath, and then expose my vision to the surroundings.

The structures fell behind them, crumbling to small wreckages and huts. The locals cornered us. They encircled us and began to move like lightning.
They surrounded a dead man. Lying there close to where Arseny had to make a rash decision and stab the temple imam.

We were out in the open.

A group of them were there. The boy soldier sprinted to the mosque doors and tried to find a way into the building. In that moment we were defiling both priest and temple. Desecrating the sanctity of this place from what we were doing. We were killing this place to live.
I could hear Arseny banging his rifle desperately against the door, trying to break it down with his feeble might.
He was nowhere in immediate sight, but he was our only way to get into the mosque while the rest of us dealt with the greater problem.

They spoke incandescently. Through their foreign tongue, I could hear the desperation in their voice. I saw the weapons they carried, and I felt my grip on my rifle tighten. I could taste the vapour of freshly fired gunpowder. My power was failing.
The few spatters of men transformed into a mob. They wanted our blood. They wanted our heads for the beliefs we held, for the murder of their people, for the invasion of their homeland. They wanted us dead.
"Fedor." Vasya cried.
He was crouched a meter from the mosque entrance, pressing on his wounded stomach, trying flutily to staunch the flood of crimson escaping his body.
"Fedor." Vasya repeated with urgency.
I stood there stagnant. Almost like I could be mistaken for a bloodied effigy if not for the tossing darkened rags covering me and the pulsing veins in my neck. I knew I could not take them on. I knew any wrong move could mean my death. But I must keep fighting, I have come so far, and I will not die here.
They stalked my perimeter like Eurasian wolves hunting their prey. They encircled me armed with their knives and makeshift weapons. One of which was coated with the blood of a squad mate. His time was limited his skin carved open by the rust and filth of the weapon that bled him. They screamed out things and speeches that were alien to me, but familiar to them. It sounded like orders or commands, but I did not care what they said, they were in no position to do so. Not anymore…
Their wraps and masks stole their faces for me to remember. All but there was one who was standing in the back covering his face.
I dropped my gun. I knew it would not do good. It jammed on me multiple times getting here and I was out of ammunition to feed it.
I was defenceless against the numbers in front of me. I paced backward towards the mosque and saw Vasya's face tremble. The medic was worried.
I turned back to face the attackers and heard the crack of wood and breaking splinters behind me.

Arseny broke in and like that, we gained access to the holy site.

I picked up Vasya and moved to the mosque, still facing our aggressors. He held his weapon pointed towards them. The boy soldier returned to me and gave me a scavenged pistol.
I held it to the pack, and this made their ferocity waver.

They held their hands up and dropped their knives, leaving a dull clatter in the cobbled town paths. I shot Vasya a hasty glance and saw genuine fear in his eyes. Not malice, not hate, but terror.
I turned back to our opponents and felt my trigger finger squeeze.

It stopped halfway before the hammer sparked the gunpowder and fired a killing shot.

I did enough killing. So, I turned the weapon's wrath to the door of the mosque and shot the bullet into the door.
The loud bang awoke me and took the taste of blood away from me.
Like I was ripped out of hell and placed back into reality with a blink and a shudder.
This group of troublemakers ran for their lives, but in their escape, I saw the one I injured was a child. No more than fourteen or fifteen and he was running for his life.

"What have I done?" I said with a tremble. I felt the black pit in my guts sink deeper fully realising the regret of my actions. I was not a safe man to be around.

I looked at the freshly fired pistol and spied a frightful vapour, exiting the barrel of the ancient weapon. I stared at it for a moment that felt like an eternity. My name, the name etched shoddily into the side of the barrel called to me. It spoke to me with a frightful whisper, like a vicious predator luring an unsuspecting calf to the slaughter. The carved polished silver spoke, and they wanted their old soldier back to war. A final call to arms. It pulsed and made my broken hands ache with a terrible wounding thump.

I gave the gun to Samara who was clinging onto my shoulder, He was holding his cane forward with the rubber tip pointed towards the running children. He dropped his cane and took the weapon by the grip with his forefinger and thumb. I looked to the street and saw there were no bodies but instead the bike we used to train the boy.

I felt shocked. But this was not the shock of a man who pushed a boundary by accident but of a father who knew their time with their loved ones was coming to an end.
I turned and saw the boy there and he inspected the door. The child must have given me the gun as he was the only one who could reach it promptly. I saw the door and I fully realised the damage, when I saw the collection of cavities riddled into the timber. He poked his finger in through the freshly made bullet hole to check if it was real, and then he faced its creator.
The boy spoke with a new fear. A fear and a revelation that was spread across his brow. That quivered his voice when he knew the man whom he cared for deeply was just as likely to kill him, not because he wished it but because he was possessed. "How many times has this happened?"

Lev
12:43

I patrolled my station for those who came to fill their faces. The army of young workers I employed with the odd spattering of aged personnel work continued their labours with full efficiency to accommodate the crowd of hungry customers. The queue stretched out the door forcing everyone to perform at their peak. The word was carried out. The sizzling of friers and barking of orders were that could be heard.

I spoke to customers and the locals about nonchalant topics like the weather and personal events whilst inspecting the quality of the services provided. The day flowed like water but was interrupted by the sight of a vile man.

271

The father of Fedor's boy was here. He stood in the queue licking his lips and deciding what gluttonous pile of meat he wanted to swallow.

I was caught in conversation with a small group of people in the corner of the restaurant paying half attention to them and focusing the other half on the father.

When he reached the counter to order, I made an excuse to leave the group giving comforting taps and friendly smiles to my regulars before moving. I needed to listen to what this man wanted, to what gossip I could spread to Fedor and the boy.

I hid in the kitchen but stayed close to the counter to not deafen myself with the grilling of meat and fries.

"How are we doing?" He asked my youngest worker.

"Good." She said, exhausted and unamused.

"Can I get the triple cheeseburger?"

"Sure."

"And can you make sure Bern is back home where he belongs?" He said with command.

I had to bite my lip in the case so as to not reveal myself and cause commotion as I knew I would cause a scene.

Payments were taken. Orders were made and the food was being made.

The young girl who was barely sixteen at the time turned around to speak to the fry cooks and left her back exposed.

I peeked my head from the corner to see what he was doing. I saw his eyes track to the sweatpants that this girl was wearing which left her underpants poking through the elastic fabric.

His eyes stared uncomfortably long, scanning her barely matured physique with a savage hunger.

She turned to ask for further questions from her customer, but the father was almost drooling at the site of her as if he hasn't seen a woman in years. The girl turned around, but this time tried to hide her body as much as possible.

Her face sank from the disgust of ever-present eyes. I saw her pause for a moment as she got up with the box. Shame sprawled across her expression but was hidden through a thin customer-friendly veneer.

272

That was it. I will not have my workers violated. I marched from my cover and stood to his face. He was shocked and stunned to see a man his size, to the point where he made a small stumble backward from appearing in his face.

I scanned the room quickly and saw the indifferent looks from some customers but the shared disgust from the ones who knew the staff well enough.

"Get out." I demanded, pointing towards the exit of the restaurant.
"What?" He cried out petulantly. "I did nothing wrong."
"You did everything wrong. Now get out of my shop!"
"Fuck off." The father responded.

"No mate." One of my elderly workers contributed. "You fuck off."
My employees dropped tools to defend me and this young girl. They caught wind of what was happening, and all stood at the counter. She was hiding behind the group feeling still a hint of shame.
"Do you know how old she is?" I asked with vitriol in my voice.
"Doesn't matter." He barked.
"It does!" I sneered, smacking the counter with the flat of my palm. "She's sixteen."
"And?"
The crowd now siding with us felt horrified.
"I think you better leave." One of my regulars said.

He now spun around the room and saw the tide turning against him. He rotated back to me and locked eyes with me for a second.
"Don't come back here again." I coldly ordered with my arms crossed.

The father stormed out of the place infuriated by his humiliation. Slamming the door behind him.

The staff got back to their posts like nothing happened. I asked someone to take over the counter for a moment whilst I pulled the girl to the side.

"Are you ok?" I asked politely.
"Yeah, I'll be ok."
"OK. Just don't be afraid to ask for help from one of us and we'll have your back."
"I could have handled it." She said meekly.
"I don't doubt it." I smiled. "But there is nothing wrong with asking for help. Stay here and take a few minutes to yourself but don't rush yourself."
The girl nodded and made a faint smirk.
"Thank you." She spoke.
"It's OK." I replied. "Just remember, we're here to look out for each other."

Bern
1:32pm
280 days post exam.

The church fell silent. I tried learning to use the bike whilst I was here but there was little to break up the days between the odd bouts of smoking and drinking. There was nothing there except the slow discomfort that was forming between us. No one said a word to each other, Samara sat in the church hall whilst Sidorovich hid in the office and locked the door shut. I left the bike at the church door and approached Samara.
The joy on his face had gone. There was a shadow of a man left there and he felt alone in this world.
"Where did it go wrong?" He grimaced. "Was I not good enough?"
I was shocked at the question. He knew more than I did and kept a friend for this long.
"Of course, you are." I said, putting my hand gently on his shoulder. "You knew how bad he could get but you were always there for him."
"Not this bad." Samara whispered before taking a sip from his tumbler. "Never this bad. I never knew about those." He pointed

274

to the door. "I just thought they were termites or something. But I didn't realise he was trying to murder a door."

"I…" I was caught speechless. What do you say to this? When you discover that your oldest friend could kill you at any moment. Before I could think of something to say, there was a knock on the door. This forced Samara to get up and hobble towards the door.
The knock repeated but it was more forceful as to try and get the inhabitant's attention.

"I'm coming!" Samara called.

The door opened with a creak and a newfound shudder. Cracks splintered across the wood, making it known that this piece of the church was ready to die.
I followed Samara and saw a police officer there.

He was tall, early to mid-thirties, slim but was muscular enough to be a threat. He was accompanied by a young blonde-headed woman who held her hair in a ponytail, likely to be his partner.
"Evening gents." The officer spoke with a deep voice. "Can we have a chat?"
"I'm ok here if that's alright." Samara said warily.

The officer's niceties were ignored. He made a sharp exhale and then slipped both hands inside his black stab-proof vest. The female officer took out a dark leather notepad and started scribbling. The notepad was new, almost pristine, holding the constabulary logo on the front cover.
"Alright, I'll get to the point." He said, dispelling the pleasant attitude with an authoritative tone. "We got a complaint about noise and people nearby said it sounded like a gunshot—" The officer pointed towards the holes in the door. "And seeing these worries me."

"We had some rough kids come over." Samara explained. "They started throwing some firecrackers at us which I think is what caused the loud bang.

"And these?" The officer nodded towards the door.
"Termites." Samara said.
"Termites…" The officers' eyes narrowed trying to spot any gaps in Samara's story.

Samara kept his composure as if he didn't just watch his friend's sanity break.

"These kids." The officer spoke. "One of them had a busted lip and said it came from a tall old Russian guy."
"You know how those kinds of kids are." Samara dismissed.
"We're old men who want to get through our day."

"Hmm…" The officer grumbled.
"Guv." The lady officer chimed in. "If it's who I think it is, those kids have been on our radar for a while, since they have been causing trouble for other elderly people and harassing town folk."

The male officer grunted. "In that case then we'll be keeping an eye on you guys to make sure your story adds up. Have a good evening gents."
"You too." Samara closes the door which causes a further splinter. "Fuckers." He muttered under his breath.

I fidgeted with my hands and paced the length of the hall whilst the Greek propped himself up by his elbow on the font.

"What are we going to do?" I queried.
"I don't know." Samara grimaced. He rubbed his scalp over and over as if he was polishing the yellowed hue to a marble gloss "I don't know how to deal with this. I've never seen him act this way. I've seen the old soldier come out in him at times but never as bad as what he did to those kids." He scooped his hand towards his chest. "Not even when he attacked me."

The priest pulled his hand up to his face and rubbed the bridge of his nose with his index finger and thumb.

"I just want my friend back." He said with sorrow.

There was another knock on the door. This time more forceful than the last. This old piece of architecture was falling apart. The wood bowed and warped, extending like elastic but ready to snap at a moment's notice.

Samara shook his head and started muttering incandescently to himself. There was a sign the old man was ready to fall apart. His will was fading, along with his cheery smiles and crass humour.

This man is broken and on his deathbed. Left with the onerous task of taking care of a friend.

Another knock on the door came. This time splinter flew, and arboreous flesh was flayed. The door was heavy with a disgusting crunch, snapping the priest's attention to the door.

He clenched the twisted iron handle and wrenched it open.

He stood unsurprised or unamused, it was hard to tell with his brow so deeply furrowed.

Lev stood in front of him picking splinters out of his knuckle.

"You need a new door." Lev said, making pathetic small displays of anguish whilst extracting splinters out of the skin with his oversized fingers.

Samara narrowed his eyes and shot daggers at him. "Stop trying to break it down then." Samara spitefully remarked.

Samara left the front of the church and sat on the closest seat.

"What's wrong with him?" Lev asked me. Closing the door behind him. "Did he not have his second bottle of the day?"

"Fuck off!" Samara spat, pushing the flat of his hand in Lev's direction as if the veteran was right next to him.

The hostility was taken personally. The old men bickered with each other like lifelong foes. The occasion threat and personal insult were hurled at each other to break the other but neither won their battle.

The fight ended in a stalemate when the church office door creaked open.

The remorseful killer emerged.

277

Their face was pale. Their hands were exposed from their black cloth coating.

Lev was the first one to turn to him. He lost interest in Sidorovich's colleague and marched to him as if he were still an old comrade.

"What the fuck are you doing?" Lev demanded. Stomping his thick greasy boots closer and closer to the old priest.

"*Ya Bolshi ne znayo.*" The Russian priest said with pain in his voice. "Tebya tak dolgo nye belo. Prosto shtobly naiti ztoo bezdelooshkoo." His eyes widened and his breathing quickened. He placed a scarred hand on his chest and put a death grip on his breast as if he were about to wrench it off and expose the bone.

Me and Samara looked at each other. We knew what this meant. We tried to protect Lev from what was about to happen. Samara bolted out of his seat as best he could in the broken state, he was in. I ran towards Lev, but he warded me off, undeterred by his approach.

I ran to Samara to get him out of what was potentially going to lead to his death, but he was more focused on his friend.

I saw where his gaze was and directed my attention towards it.

Lev marched up to the old priest, grabbed him by the neck, and threw a single headbutt straight into his nose. Sidorovich was sent flying backward, dancing with a failed pirouette and unable to stop himself from falling onto the ground.

"Leave him alone you shit!" Samara desperately wailed. He tried his hardest to stand. I had to help Samara to his feet but after great effort he was mobile. "Get away from him!"

Samara started waving his cane whilst putting all his weight on me. Sidorovich was flat on the floor, his face closely hugging the cobbles and showing his back to the ceiling. He left there broken and bleeding. He did not respond to the blood flooding. There was little sign of him moving at all. There was the occasional gasp and groan which thankfully indicated that he wasn't dead, just unconscious.

Samara rushed over as best as he could using me as a support. We were mortified at the scene. I could feel this man start to bend a quake. The last efforts of his legs which had the strength of snapping twigs. But his voice. Even though he was wounded he roared like a lion.
"You sick fuck!" He bellowed with ferocity, pointing at the attacker, and then moving his finger to the man on the floor.
"That's your friend you just knocked out!"
"And?" Lev said with little care. He wiped the small spatter of blood off his cheekbone and flicked his hand to the ground.
"I should—" Samara raised his cane as if to strike Lev but without the support of it, he tumbled on the floor with a small shriek of defiant agony.
I rushed over to help him up but there was little I could do. He embraced the floor. His chest spasmed with coughing fits. He tucked his legs into his chest and laid there like a corpse. Permitting any sign of life, only to have another coughing fit. I sat there on the floor with him, my hand on his back to try and provide some small comfort.

"Why?" I asked Lev. Not knowing if my question would be given any thought.

"Because…" Lev sighed as fell onto a pew as if he had come back from a hard day's labour. His eyes dulled and his brow softened. Was this his form of compassion or something else? He stroked the cheekbone which had been bloodied and then looked me in the eye. But not with bright, shining fury or hatred, but the small dark blue gems in his skull begged for forgiveness.
"I knew what he was living in. And it was not a pretty sight."

Lev

279

How do you trust your life with those you cannot even look in the eye?

You learn very quickly when the threat of death looms over you, just not in the ways you would expect. Mikhail and I learned to overcome our differences very quickly. Though we were almost unarmed with about a magazine of ammunition to go between us and whatever was left in our side arms, we pressed forward to the town.

The people hid inside, and the streets held nothing except the final fragmented winds chasing the storm. We were broken and bloodied, our will to survive was fading in the hopelessness of the situation. No friends, no translator, not even enough water to wet our lips.

We shuffled like ragged spectres in the field of shoddy huts and flapping wooden shutters. We ran towards the first sign of cover. Into any open hut that looked empty. It was hard to figure out when the blinding white light of the sun bore down on us.

Mikhail stopped in his tracks by the mile of huts. I thought he froze in place.

I grabbed him by the shoulder and shook him to try and wake him from his petrified trance.

"What are doing?" I demanded in a hushed and desperate tone. "We'll be spotted."

"Look!" He said, pointing towards a hut with carved-out holes. It was impossible to determine what it was he was fascinated by. Trying to find something in the buildings before us was like trying to find coal in the blackened night. Shapes and figures blended unless you could reach into the carved rock and grab them.

"What?" I respond.

"I thought I saw something in there?"

"If they're afghanis then let's go! We can't survive another fight."

"Not someone!" Mikhail spoke through cracking lips and a choked voice. "Something."

Mikhail dashed into the carved-out hut. He disappeared into the black and left me by myself.

I had no choice but to either follow or die by myself. I ran in after him and when I entered the building my eyes stung. I felt blinded by the sudden change like I walked from one world to the next.

I moved forward rubbing my eyes to try and adjust them to their new environment but when I opened them, I saw the worst thing imaginable and realised why we got ambushed.

Guns, explosives, stacks, and crates of ammunition of all shapes and sizes, lazily clattered around their clay home. Desiccated tables and knocked-over stools held and shrouded chemicals and knives. Dark shimmers of brass, gunpowder, and death littered the room in tattered wooden crates. To the walls, their rifles and pistols were scattered around which likely would have been knocked out of place by the wind. Some were weapons that came from us, scavenged by our forces whereas there were weapons that belonged elsewhere. Some ancient and some foreign as if they were kidnapped from Father Time. On my right, there was a patchy stockade made from wood planks and scraps, resembling that which was found in the remaining doors of the town. Behind them, they hid bombs, explosives, and enough missiles to combat a battalion of helicopters and tanks. This small hut… This small room could kill thousands and it would, we just had to make sure we weren't one of them.

We stumbled into a weapon cache, hidden inside a town. We could only assume the worst, that the people were involved. To the back of the room, there was a doorway. I paced forward trying to regain my senses of the horror and wonder of the room. I scavenged myself and stowed away some spare magazines which would not be missed. I entered the door and saw Mikhail. My face lit up when I saw what he was hunched over.
"Do you like it?" He said with a smile on his face.
He turned around a radio pack. Like the one Fedor had and it was perhaps the most beautiful thing I had seen.
"I love it!" I said with joyous disbelief, tamed by caution.
Mikhail patted it down and made a speedy inspection to see if it was in working order. He deemed it fit and slung it on his back.

281

"Let's find them." I said with haste. "They can't be far from the most now."

I turned to make a hasty exit, but I sensed Lev was not coming with me. I saw him hunched over an explosives crate and fiddling with wires.
"Mikhail…" I walked slowly with unease to him. "What are you doing?"
"Getting rid of all this." He said whilst continuing to work.
"And then what?"
"What do you mean?" The question stopped his arduous labour for a moment.
"I mean what will we do when *that* goes off?"

Mikhail continued to hide his blocky face from me. He continues his plan and finally utters, "We will find out."

I yank him up by the collar and throw him to the nearest wall away from any potential explosives. In the process, a crate of bullets was knocked over. It fell onto the dusty floor with a deafening crash, rattling brass, and shell casings across reverberating clay. This clatter was nothing compared to what Mikhail wanted. I held one hand over his neck and firmly squeezed the sides. I wanted to intimidate him but also avoid suffocating him.

"What do you mean, *find out*?" I hissed through gritted teeth.
"I mean…" He hisses, staring into my eyes. "They cannot have this."

I feel my side for the pistol just in case we have any trouble and feel it in my grip. I quickly scanned my surroundings pinning Mikhail to the wall.

"And if we do that, every Mouja from here to Kabul with come running here."
"They'll kill more if they have this." Mikhail spat. "You'd let them do this?"
"Hopefully I won't be around to find out."

"I'm destroying this place."
"I'm not letting you kill us."
"Then how are you going to stop me?" He said, leaning his head closer as if he was a dog ready to bite.

It took me a moment to think. But the only thing that whirled around in my mind was the feeling of the weapon in my hands and how easy it would be to solve this problem... To shut him up.

"I see where your hand is Lev." Mikhail said.

This made me stop for a second. I was caught in the act of planning to kill another of my squad mates.

"I am not afraid to die." He said calmly, with a hint of resentment. "Are you?"

I contemplated the question in my mind over and over again. I finally came up with the answer when I pressed the pistol end into his side.

I leaned in and covered his mouth. I hovered my lips over his ear and let only a few words escape me. Words that meant the world to me but not to anyone else.
"My brother was."

I squeezed the trigger and felt the loud pop jolt back against my arm.
His silenced mouth gasped out muffled groans of pain. I squeezed again and again until he finally fell silent and slid down the wall.

I stood back from the scene I had created and saw my works in their full. A good man was killed by me, by my selfish intent. I holstered the pistol and felt the weight of my sin on my brow. I shook my head and stole the radio pack from the dead man. I could hear the commotion, likely caused by actions.

I ran from the building, once again being blinded by the change of environment, and sprinted fast towards the mosque. Groups and crowds of men and women clambered to get to the building where shots were fired. I ran faster and faster; I could hear gunfire crack through the air.
I felt my worst fears come to bear, circling in my mind.

"Please no!" I pleaded with myself, hoping whoever from our band of idiots was not cornered and killed. I turned the corner and saw a crowd of civilians.
"Get back!" Fedor cried. Firing shots in the air to disperse the crowd.
They seemed unfazed. They were seemingly in their hundreds whilst the men remaining were only a handful.

More potshots flew into the sky and the mob closed in. I raised my assault rifle into the air and fired scattered bursts.
The crowd finally took us seriously and left us alone. As they dispersed like a school of fish, I saw them lying on the sand. They killed someone, and now they knew we were here.
The men fell onto their backside. They collapsed in exhaustion, except for Vasya who fell in pain and agony.
They leaned against something that could hold their weight. A door, a wall, whatever could give them some form or respite.
I marched up the steps of this temple which was far too opulent to be in a town like this.

"I found us a way out of here." I decreed to the men.
"Yeah?" Fedor said glibly. "Is it that thing on your back?" He pointed.
"Yes!" I bellowed sternly. "Do you remember how to use it?"
Fedor fell flat on the floor, exposing his belly to the sun.
"I don't know anymore." He said glumly. He wiped his face, his filth-ridden skin with the sweat that came from it. "You were gone for so long…" Fedor paused. Shock and disbelief found their way into his words as it was a mystery unsolvable to him. He made a small scoff and finally let the flood of emotions cloud him. "Just to find that trinket. And where is Mikhail?"

284

I sank my head and slumped my posture. "Mujaheddin killed him."

"Is that so?" He asked, narrowing his eyes. He raised his spine from the ground but remained seated. He held Vasya's wounds and applied pressure to staunch the bleeding. The pains and winces indicated he was alive but the look on Fedor's face showed me he would die soon.

He sighed and then slowly rose, weighed down by the multiple engagements we suffered through.

"Give me the radio and then I'll try to call for help." Fedor stood, leaning his exhausted body onto the mosque wall. "Hopefully someone will come get us."

"And that's it?" The boy asked. Snapping me from that world I was telling, to the one I lived in.

"That's it." I responded to the boy.

"So, you didn't just kill one of your friends, but two of them?"

"*Friends* is a harsh way of putting it." I said puffing on a freshly lit cigarette. "They were more like…" I pause, circling my free hand trying to find the words. "People I was stuck with."

"You monster." Samara whimpered from the floor. The old man was still curled up, clutching his belly, and showing his back to me. He only let out heavy breaths from his eroding carcass but gave himself enough willpower to speak. "You overcame your difference?" He grimaced with a small, pained chuckle. "You overcame it by killing that man. I should never have let Fedor go and speak to you."

I felt my ire spark for a moment, then I realised I would be wasting the effort. I knew that if not for me, none of us would have made it out, so I took a morbid pride in that fact. "Whatever you say." I dismissed.

I stood from the pew and dusted my trousers for any cigarette ash that might have fallen on them. "People don't change." I spoke with indifference. "People don't change their ways only their interests. Just like you boy, who will always be a coward, and you Greek, who will always be a drunk." The boy's head

285

sank, and the old man tried to get up. But even through the grunts of forced labour of aching bones, he was disabled and unable to get up. I strode to the exit and said my peace in sneering disinterest. "Drink some more priest, you might feel better. So much better you might not wake up in the morning."

I closed the fractured door and left them to lick their wounds.

My Son... My Brothers in Arms...

Sidorovich
11:23

Stitch... Stitch... Stitch...
I felt the small wire sutures scrawl across my face. My body sat and relaxed back into the chipped wooden pews which have not seen care since their creation. I gripped my pipe ready for another calming inhale of flavoured smoke. Ready to follow it with a gulp of strong anaesthetising rakija. The candle flames flickered, and the incense burned. I felt the itch of my bandages regain their bitter sting. They felt suffocating this time, like whatever was below wanted to be released. I felt sorrow in my heart as the delicate hands held steady, doing their best to fix my face. Where is the joy in this? What comfort was I given in this world? None is the answer. Even my closest could not take it away from me. I saw a small hand. A virtuous hand reaches over to a red box with white accents. It grabbed a fresh alcohol wipe and shut it. Revealing the small *'Boots'* logo in its plastic case.

The inner duality struggled inside me. Where both the mind and body battled themselves. Phantoms and specters haunted me. I could still hear their cackles and screams. Their joy and hate. Their life and death.
Most figure the makings of a man are but two parts. The mind and body, in my time I saw it as a tripartite. There was a rot in my soul. A rot which took my virtue and rendered it cruel. I gave myself thought while the healer continued to work. I looked at one of my hands and saw my bandages were coming loose. Small shimmers of grease and ointment showed where the topical cream was spread. It still hurt but this was nothing new. I had grown used to it by now. The ring on my right hand felt heavy over the bandages. It ached but it was a good ache. An ache that was worth the consequences.

287

"You need to stop getting into fights with him." The healer said with disappointment.

This made me chuckle. I drew another breath from my pipe and felt my heartbeat slowly.

"And what would you suggest I do?" I callously responded.
"You know he hates me."
"That's not the point, you have to learn to work with him."
"He's an idiot!"
"But you need that idiot!"

I looked away. I couldn't bear to face my judge. They saw this and sighed, but this did little to stop their duties.

"This is not the example I want us to set." They said sternly before mellowing to compassion. "I didn't marry an idiot." They raise my chin to face them. "So don't act like one."

I saw the face of my wife. She looked beautiful with her freshly painted makeup. She had scarlet red lipstick and coconut brown hair which curled and shimmered. She wore a two-piece rose-patterned dress that followed her from the Soviet Union which began to show its age with the odd loose thread and faded flower. Her thin body lowered to one knee. She places one hand on my broken nose.

"Ready?" she asked.

I stared off into the distance at some far corner of the church, where dust was piled high and odd scatterings of papers and church equipment had gathered. I puckered my lips. Took a deep breath in and made a subtle nod.

The crunch of my nose being snapped into place caused me to almost jump out of my seat.
I yelped like a dog being kicked by its master and gently held my now-fixed horn to signs of further bleeding.

"There!" She exclaimed. "All better."

"I don't feel better." I remark.

"Then you had better stop fighting." She chastised. "I don't want Grigori to keep finding his priest of a father with new scars."

She moved aside the medical kit and sat beside me, cradling my still-raw arms. My wife leaned beside me and rested her head on my shoulder. She extended her hand before me and repeatedly curled her fingers.

"You have enough." She said coyly.

I smiled. I gave her my still-smouldering pipe and let her take it from me. She raised her head upright and put the pipe bit in her mouth. She inhaled, held her breath more a second or two, and exhaled the smoke. It surrounded her and danced lazily beside her before dispersing into nothingness. She was radiant. She was beautiful.

She gave me back the pipe and rested her head on my shoulder again.

This was peace.

"I need to quit." She spoke with a soft numbness. "I don't want Grigori to see."

"Smoking?"

"Yes. The Union fell. We live in a different country now, so we need to have different standards."

"And yet, we're still speaking Russian." I smiled.

She smirked.

"My English isn't the best at the moment." She softly chuckled.

We sat and held each other for a moment. The smoulder of burning tobacco and the occasional gust of wind entered the building and gave a decrepit life to the place. I felt my nose for any mistakes but there were none. She had done a good job.

"You were born to be a nurse." I spoke with pride.

"I might go back to it if my English gets better. Although I might have to work on my accent."

"We've been in this country for only six months. You've done well."

"Thank you." She said. "In the meantime, I'll have to keep fixing you up. So please, keep me work-free." She teased.

I smiled. "You have your hands full with Grigori."

"He idolises you; you know."

My smile turned into a frown and sank straight into the darkest pits of my guts.

"He shouldn't." I muttered.

"No." She raised up her body from me, remaining seated. "He should, but he should also learn from you. Your worst nightmare is the same as mine. I don't want him to follow in your steps."

I inhaled my pipe and let out a deep exhale.

"What do you want him to follow?" I asked.

"Your example. You need to look after him."

"And what if he does go in the end?"

Olega's face scowled. Her hand flew to the entrance of the church.

"Then I leave, and you never see me again." Her harshness softened. "So don't let him go."

A smile returned to her face. "So, what are you going to do?"

"Be a good father." I spoke like a child being scolded.

"Well, that and?"

"I'll get the Greek a bottle to keep him happy."

"That's my husband." She said joyfully. "But what I meant was, please stop calling him by his surname. You know he hates that."

"I won't see him for much longer if he acts like this. He's an addict." I scorned.

"But he is teaching you your job." She gently squeezed my shoulder. "So, play nice."

I returned her comfort with a smile, but my gaze drifted towards the door. Her threat reverberated in me. Now two people's lives were in my hands. The church was in disorder, but the door was freshly painted. Not a crack or chip in sight. It was freshly painted black, and the iron ring handle was visibly healthy.

I closed my eyes and its perfect image evaporated. The holes returned and the fractures showed the broken soul of the church before me. Here was my soul in all its material nature. A rotting carcass waiting for carrion to pluck its splinters clean. Here was not my ticket toward everlasting divinity or paradise but to an eternity of failure and damnation.

My son was dead, but he lives here. My wife is gone but her presence lingers. My brothers are dusted in the sand but the small comforts they brought remain. I looked at the bowl of my now extinguished pipe and saw my name carved into it. It was almost faded from years of use but there it was. I am reminded of those I loved and lost. Reminded of sins committed long ago.

"Can we please get back to the questions at hand?" A voice sternly requested.
I retracted my attention from the door and saw a male police officer there in front of me with a young woman officer beside him. It was two against one. Two authoritative figures against one simple priest.
"We can." I spoke.
The woman officer continued taking notes and held her place by the altar.
"Good." The male officer spoke. He sat on the altar, carefully avoiding any sacred relics of our church, and folded his lean but muscular arms, showing the full extent of his tattoos. I recognised military markings when I saw them, even if they were from a different nation.

I felt the itch of my injuries heal. I stroked the bridge of my nose and felt its slight crookedness real me to reality. This obviously did not make me look innocent, but this could be explained away. It just depends on if they believe me.

"Now these kids might have been causing trouble, but I just wanted to have a quick search of the place. I want to find out what caused that loud bang that people described."
"Did the children you captured not say anything?" I spoke.

"They did! And they're adamant that you had a gun in your possession. You know what the penalty for unlicenced firearms is right?"

"I'm a bit slow." I coyly remarked. "Remind me."

"Five years on the spot." He leaned his armoured upper body closer. "*Minimum*." He stressed.

"Do you usually strong-arm people?" I coldly asked.

"Only people I think are up to something."

"And if you find nothing?"

"Then I'll send cake and flowers to you." He remarked sarcastically and dryly. "Those stitches on your face—" He pointed. "They don't make you look innocent."

"I fought with a friend." I spoke.

"Some friend huh?"

"I tolerate him."

"Are you sure that the friend wasn't a teenager?" The officer inquired.

"I don't remember teenagers coming with wrinkles and grey hairs."

"Hmm." The officers' voice turned low. He was interrogating me, but he had little way to apply the pressure.

No one said a word a moment that felt like eternity. Two opposing forces battled each other to see who would crack first. I puffed on my pipe and slowly eyed him.

"When did you serve?" I questioned.

My words pierced through his tough façade. His grizzled face weakened if only for a split second.

"Two tours in Afghanistan. Two thousand and nine"

He finally recognised what kind of person he was speaking to. He stared at my hands which did not ache as much. But I could see the lightbulb in his head emit radiance through his ears.

"What about you? Russian I'm assuming by your accent."

"Yes… USSR. Same place. The nineteen eighties. Motor Rifle Division."

The officer slumped on the altar and deeply exhaled.
"I assume you got a purple heart out of it."
"What is that?"

The officer was momentarily stunned. Trying to eke out a word but stopped at the last moment. He finally found himself again and showed me his left cheek, presumably from the realisation of the difference in our militaries.
"Never mind." He dismissed.
He pulled his head down. The girl meticulously takes notes, audibly scratching away the leather-bound notebook with freshly scribed ink.

"Can we get back to the matter at hand?" I asked. Staring him down like a watchdog.
I didn't want them in my church for a moment longer and I was eager to be rid of them.
"Fine." The officer agreed.

I leaned back in my seat and scoured him for his appearance. He was in the profession for a long time. He found his own method of work. I respected this, but his young and eager protégé with her obsessive notetaking would prove to be a problem here.
A problem I would exploit.

"My question is, why is this being investigated a week after the incident? This would have been forgotten about by now."

The officer pandered his thoughts for a moment in search of an answer. The girl stopped and stared. She withdrew from her note-making but the subtle twitches in her diamond cheeks would give away her nervousness.

"We—"

The officer was interrupted by his female colleague who blurted out information like a kicked puppy.

"We got called for another job." She spoke with anxious haste. "We had to deal with a bunch of drug addicts who got attacked."

The male officer shot her a disapproving look. His eyes narrowed like daggers and his cool posture broke. His original thoughts of the appropriate answer were now directed towards damage control of leaked information.

He cleared his throat with an exacerbated volume in an attempt to shut her up.

It was too late. I got what I needed.

"The ones in the news?" I feigned innocence.
"Yeah." She answered. "We still haven't recovered all the victims and perpetrators."
"How many are left to find?"
"Some girl. The main ringleader of the attack was a coal miner. He was the father of a prev—"

"Constable!" The male officer yelled. His desperate but deep voice echoed in the church halls. The voice shocked the spirit out of this girl and sent her jumping backward out of fright.
"Outside!" He demanded, pointing to the entrance of the door.
"This isn't finished." He said, directing his attention to me.
He stormed off from the church, dragging his newly shamed rookie. The fractured door slammed behind me and left me alone once again.

Bern
1:42pm
288 days post exam

The office stank of rancid smoke and spilled vodka. The world was not to be trusted. Not even my own flesh and blood could be trusted. I sat hunched over my books keeping this month's

294

payment of five hundred British sterling tucked away in an envelope. My hands were sweating and became clammy. The ink on the newly scribed pages bled away if I touched them too soon. The sun flowed its vibrant rays into the office, exposing the dust in the air that surrounded the room.

The door creaked open, and I looked up. Lev stood in the door arch with a foul mood scrawled across his face. His moustache twitched and his tightened fist shook.
"What's the matter?" I asked meekly.

His words spoken the week before clouded the air like a malevolent shadow haunting a darkened closet.

"Fedor." He spoke with frustration. "He has the police skulking around."
"I know."
"You know?!" He erupted. "What do you mean you know?"

The volume sent a shock wave which blasted me out of my seat.
"They came asking about him earlier." I whimpered out.
"And you knew?" He yelled out. Slowly approaching me. His hand extended and fingers retracted like poised claws.
"Yeah, I knew, I thought you were told."
"I should kill you and your priests. Do you know the danger you have put me in?"
"What danger? You've done nothing."
"No?" He pointed to the window outside. "Go look in the bins and see what I mean."

I trembled but I followed his command. I walked outside and saw the giant black metal skip bin. I lifted the top open and saw what Lev meant.
Inside was a body. Inside was someone I recognised.
Inside was Lisa. I felt a rush of guilt. I lost control of my limbs. I collapsed onto my side and felt the bitter, jagged embrace of the concrete and the surrounding trash with took me in as one of their own. One pile of refuse to join another.

The lid slammed shut and fell on its metal cradle metal with a resounding acoustic clang.

I was in shock. This was the end of the world for me. The girls I knew were both dead. Coming to the realisation. I felt my eyes begin to well up with tears, but I couldn't cry anymore. I felt empty but I did not feel sadness. There was nothing that surprised me about death when I faced the ugliest parts of it. Two of the people I knew were closest, and they were gone.

I rotated my body. Showing my soft belly to the world. I stared into the sky and saw the clouds drift lazily in the sky. They called for me to join them. Their shifting shapes and the shadows of Payne's grey tucked into the white virtuous clouds. They were like performers dancing on a set. A gathering of soft cushions on the inviting blue sky, surrounding the sun was at the centre of attention. I reached my hand to join them, but a dark figure heeded my call. He ripped my hand and lifted me up from the ground.

The interloper and his clumsy movements yanked me up, forcing me to face them.
Lev who took me away from my trance saw what was happening. He struck the side of my head and awakened me to the world through a sharp stinging pain, and the harsh slap of abused flesh.

"This is your mess!" Fix this!" He demanded in a hushed and gritted tone. He didn't want the public to know there was a body on his property, but he made the effort to make me know.
Still recoiling from the hit. I covered the side of my face and felt the sorrow flood, refilled by hate and despair. Not for the death of the ones I knew but for the offense Lev committed.

"How long have they been there?" I responded glacially.
"I don't know." He dismissed. "That thing turned up today. Most likely from some band of nomads or idiots. I don't care!" He bellowed. He waved his hands up and down as if to shrug off the questions. "Fix this!"

296

"She…" I responded through gritted teeth.
"What?" The Russian yelped with a raised eyebrow.
"Not *that*. She!"

"I don't care if *she* was the Virgin Mary." He pointed his forefinger into my chest. "Fix it!"

My manager left me there to fester with the trash and the dead.
He re-entered the building to
once again man his command station of over and under-aged workers.
I looked inside the bin once again and stared at the face of death.
Or what was left of it to observe. She was lying there in state.
Covered in what once was a pristine white dress. Now black with decay.
The smell, however… The smell stuck with me. Rotting flesh and sweetly sick of decomposed meat and bone, sloughing hair, and cracked nails.
In her hands, I saw something. A faint dim glimmer of something. I used a spare rag from the bins and reached down to grab it. The silvered chrome case was carved with the initials of her and her now-dead friend.

"I'm sorry it came to this Lisa." I whimpered. I could not cry anymore. Not after this.
This once amazing girl I could call my friend was now lifeless.
I pocketed the lighter. This might be seen as evidence tampering but I don't care.
Thoughts of the past flooded into my mind upon touching the cold steel. Our time, though turbulent was healing to me. If only it would be a simpler time without the interference of manipulators and murderers. If only I could sit on the metal gazebo with her and have my first cigarette. If only that dream died with her in this container.

I don't know how much longer I would be in this place, but it felt like even prison was an improvement.

I slammed the lid shut. I walked away from this place with my head held high. My resolve now bitterly strengthened. In my mind the once great burning star of white and red was now a fading memory, fuelling a macabre emotion. In that moment I realised something. In this past year, I knew my life was a path I would walk alone.
I was isolated with nothing left to lose.
I feel around for my tobacco pipe and then I realise.

I almost had nothing left to lose. A small smile lifted my face before being washed away in a wave of hate.

I dialled the police and waited for a connection with the operator.

"Police. What is your emergency?" The female voice asked calmly.
"Hello..." My voice trembled for a moment. I sobered up nearly instantaneously when I felt the raw mark made across my cheek.
"I found a body hidden away by a takeaway shop."
"Can you please give me the location?"

I gave them the location of the takeaway shop and the church. I would not let this go unanswered. This would be his punishment for sins old and new.

I stormed into work. Bypassing all the workers and the customers that filled the restaurant. I grabbed a plastic bag from the front of the counter and moved from there. I marched into the office with fire in my footsteps that hadn't been seen since time immemorial. I threw the door open and saw the old man sitting there. Unimpressed and slouching in the chair. He still thought he was in control.
"Well?" Lev asked.
I didn't respond. I started shoving my things in the bag with haste. Notebooks, textbooks, pens, pencils, everything!
Everything scattered on the desk I used flew into the bag as if it were weightless.

This was it!

"What are you doing?!" He demanded, but his plea would go unanswered.

This was it! This is where I make my first stand!

THIS IS WHERE I FIGHT!

I rushed out. Lev following me like a bear chasing quail. I ran. Faster and faster with the weight of my things carried in the sticks, I call arms. Closer and closer to my goal.

And there it was. The main room. Filled with about thirty customers. Enough to get the word around. I was safe here. Lev stood there by the front desk. He knew he could not touch me. Not in front of all these people who regarded him as a hero.

"Everyone!" I beckoned. "Listen to me!"

I had drawn their attention. My heart was racing. The room was spinning. The mass of onlookers who numbered the tens was projected in my mind to number the millions. The masses looked to my preaching and heard my cries.

"This man is crooked!" I screamed, pointing at the man who would soon be my ex-employer.

I needed to choose my words carefully. These at the end of the day were residents in a working-class town. I needed to appeal to them.

"He does nothing but hire underaged people to staff the place. He has a few ancient people, but he only keeps them to trick you."

Now the employees were looking at me. They mostly made crew of underaged crew teams with their overaged crew chiefs.

They lined up by the counter to observe the show, and what a show I would make.

I marched towards one side of the counter and began to list off their ages.

From one side to the other. My finger of doom moving from one person to the next.

"Thirteen."

"Fifteen."

"They're thirty-four but god knows why they're working in a place run by kids."

"Fourteen."

"Fifteen."

Finally, my accusations reach Lev.

"This man right here. Is forty to fifty years older than most of the people here. So, I don't know what he does with them."

Now my accusations turned to lies. Now I wanted to make him suffer and take his business down with him.

"Maybe he does something in the back with them when people aren't looking." I sneered.

"Is that why you kept Bern in office for all this time?" That one comment. That one question followed with uproar. I looked to see who spoke and saw it was a teenager, barely a few years younger than me who felt revolted at the revelation of figment of my imagination. A young girl who now felt not drained from her work but in danger from her manager. "Why was he getting special treatment?"

The crowd dropped their meals and made a stand. Some left whilst others crowded to the front. This was orchestrated to look like a lynching. The story span and his reputation was ruined. Lev backed away and tried to calm the crowd but the moment he tried they became more and more agitated. I escaped the building and left them to have their monster.

Sidorovich
15:43

"How are you feeling Fedor?" Samara asked.

"I'm fine." I spoke. I feel the soft sting of my stitches. I lied of course. I was the furthest thing from it. Not when I struggle to control myself. "How are you feeling?" I asked back.

"Oh…" He grimaced leaning back on the pew with a tumbler in his hand. "Like I'm twenty-five again." He cracked a small smile. "But I feel like I'm thirty years too late."
"Age is a state of mind." I quipped.
"In that case, I'm eighteen and still a hot stud, and you're ready for the retirement home."

We laughed. We joked for a while, but this was all we could do whilst we waited for this investigation to cease.

I readied my pipe and began to start smoking, whereas Samara started to make another drink for himself. He offered me one, but I swiftly waved it away.
There was little we could do here except talk and continue like nothing had happened.

The conversation turned grim when Samara upon his fourth double of aged whiskey.
"I'm scared Fedor."
"Scared of what?"
"Dying."

I rested my hand on his shoulder and leaned in a little bit closer.

"Why do you say that?"
"I just feel like I've pissed away my life." He said with a slight slur. "I don't have too much to give the world except for—" He pointed to the office. "That cabinet."
"Are you scared that you didn't do enough?"
"I'm scared that I didn't leave something here." Samara took a sip. "I never had a child, and I don't plan to give that cabinet away."

Samara's left hand starts to shake.
"I felt like my stupid ass hasn't done enough."

I softly hold him by his shaking wrist and feel the vibration myself.

"What's it like?" He asks.
"What?"
"To die?"

I paused and collected myself. I tried to think of an answer, but nothing came to mind. Any comforting lies I could muster faded in the smoke I spat out.

"I don't know." I said softly.
"Nobody does. It was a stupid question to ask." Samara rubbed his yellowed scalp. A few stands of his now fully greyed hair rested on his hand. "Everybody wants to go to heaven, but nobody wants to die."

"I think you would get bored of it up there." I compassionately jested.
"Yeah!" Samara snorted. "They probably would have less than eighty proof alcohol up there."

Samara put his glass down on the floor.
"Can you do me a favour Fedor?"
"Anything."
"Get me the grey bottle from the cabinet. It'll have a wax seal on it."

I nod and walk to the office. I procure the bottle with a creak open from the cabinet.
The bottle itself was made from ceramic. It was tightly sealed by crimson wax which had been touched by no master except time. Even he, however, could not erode the seal.
There was a small tag dangling on rotting twine. There was no label on the body of it. No markings of any significance except the wax seal. The stamped wax held a royal queen in an opulent and patterned dress. She held a sceptre and a crown. There were minute details that were eroded but the overall design stood against the age. The label was mostly faded out but the writing on it was cursive. It was illegible due to the age, but this was a relic of a bygone age.

302

I returned the bottle to my friend, and he sat me down.

He cradled it like it was his firstborn and held it on his lap.

"This bottle is older than both you and I put together." He said.
"This bottle is from the American Revolution." He gave a small
but shamed chuckle. "You don't know what I had to do to get
this."

Samara paused for a moment. His expression turned to sadness,
weighed down by a crushing realisation.
"This bottle Fedor..." He stammered. He took in a deep breath
and quickly sobered himself. "This is my death bottle. I want this
to be buried with me."

My heart sank. Now my friend needed to plan his departure from
this world.
"How long have you had this?" I asked with crushing pain in my
voice.
"I got this as a joke when I joined the church. I thought I could
go and party with God." His lips parted as if he would laugh but
no sound exited them. His feelings would sink back into despair.
"Now... I don't know anymore."

Samara emptied the rest of his tumbler down his throat and
placed the crystal on the floor.
"Can you do me one favour Fedor?"
"Anything."
Samara laid back in his seat. His lip quivered and his forehead
wrinkled.
"Be there at my side when I die. I don't want to go alone."

His request touched me but saddened me greatly in more ways
than one. Here my oldest friend was on his deathbed, asking me
to watch him die.

"What about your wife?" I asked in concern.
"I don't want my wife; I want my friend."

I nodded and then gripped his shoulder fiercely as if to never let him go.

Samara exhaled and then wrenched himself up from his seat. "I need a drink." I grimaced.

Upon the trickling of alcohol and the charring of tobacco. The church door creaked open.
We turned around and saw the boy there.

He was angry. But this was an anger never shown to us before. He marched into the holy site carrying a plastic bag of heavy books and stationery. He shut the door behind him with enough force to project his frustration but not so much to break the wood further.

"Keep Lev away from me!" The boy demanded. He threw the bag out onto the floor, letting the odd spattering of papers and pens spread out across the uneven floor.

"Why?" I asked. "What has he done?"

"He smacked me and showed me the body of my dead friend." Mine and Samara's shock was on display. This was disgusting, even by his standards. I didn't half believe it. It felt supernatural or tortuous to show the body of a close friend. I helped my friend up, careful to not break Samara's bottle. We stood to talk to the boy and gave our full attention.

"What happened?" Samara asked.

"That girl I brought in here."
"Which one?" I asked with concern.
"The one that liked Samara. The one that dressed in white."
"I remember."

This was low... Even for Lev.

Dark thoughts raced through my mind. I did not know if he took this girl's life. That if this old killer had turned murderer. The news soured the lingering taste of tobacco.

My brow furrowed. I took another smoke of my pipe and prepared myself for the unwelcome news.

"She isn't dead, is she?" Samara asked his voice along with his heart falling to pieces.

"She is." The boy confirmed.

"Did Lev kill her?" I asked with anger in my tone.

The boy's response disgruntled us. "I don't know." The boy said in a mix of uncertainty and fury.

Me and Samara looked at each other. Something needed to be done.

Something soon.

"*I Don't know*', likely means he did." Samara accused. "I wouldn't put it past him."

"I called the police on him." The boy interjected.

"You did what?" I gasped out.

"They'll find the body, but I don't know if they will be able to pin it on him."

Samara and I looked at each other. It was a look of pride. A small smile crept on our lips. This was different from the boy that first entered our church. My child knew how to fight for himself. I staunched my pride and returned my focus to the boy. I nodded my head. This was no game now. I cannot protect this boy anymore. Now I need to get him to safety.

"When do you finish school?"

"In a couple of months but I think I can do my exams early."

"Are you certain?"

"Pretty certain."

I took another puff and thought about how to get him out of there.

Samara beat me to it.

305

"Then we get you on that bike and we get you out of here."
"And go where?" The boy questioned.
"We'll send you to a different church."

A sudden moment of brilliance appeared in my head. Suddenly I knew what Samara wanted to do.
"You'll be sent to Batushka Kasparov" I explained.
"Be warned though." Samara inputted. "He is nothing like us. He is a bit of a shit."
"But he's a good shit. He'll help you but he's mean." I explained further. "But there is a catch."
"Which is?" Said the boy.
"He'll be hard on you, but he is fair."

I scratched my arms and Samara refilled his drink. We both thought of our way to get this boy out. If the police did not lock him up, then the fury of Lev would come, and it would not be found wanting.

The boy's tone had softened. He released his anger and started to plan with us.

"But I need a place to stay." He stated.

"If you don't have much, then you can stay in the office."
Samara offered.
"I never had much to begin with." The boy stated with tamed sorrow.
"Then it is settled!" I roared. "Gather your things and bring them. Here study, sleep, do whatever. But practice on that bike otherwise you won't be able to get out."

I turned to my fellow priest.
"Samara!" I place my hand on his shoulder once again. "We have work to do for our son."
The other priest patted his arm on my back. His face beamed and his broken posture straightened as if he was reinvigorated with life.

"That we do!" He bellowed and filled the halls with a boastful laugh.

Finally, his life was given purpose. Finally, he could leave his mark on the world.

"You get the place set up." Samara ordered me. "I'll see if I can scrap some money together."
"Money?" The child asked. "Money for what?"
"Your motorbike of course."

The boy's face blushed with shock. He stood still but his eyes betrayed him when they welled up with a small glimmer of ecstatic joy.

"Ha Ha!" Samara roared. He began marching to the office to work on his plan. "Just you wait boy, we will—" Samara stopped in his tracks and turned back to me. "What do you mean when you said, *'our son'*?"

The question would not be answered as there was a knock on the front door which stole the opportunity from us.
The three of us had our attention drawn to our unexpected guests. We turned to our typical reaction and fell back into our innocent facades.
I extinguished my pipe and carried the bottles to the cabinet.
"Boy!" I ordered. "Help me here."
The boy collected his things from the bag and carried the tumblers to the office with me. Samara hobbled to the brass censers to blame any smell of smoke on them.
Another knock on the door.
"Please wait!" Samara cried. He overextended his voice, matching the effort of his failing body. "I'll be there in a moment."

After our task was complete and the boy left his things on my side of the office, I shooed the boy from the office. I slammed the door behind me, and we got into position. My boy who stood beside me, was processing all sorts of emotions. But there was an anticipation to him. As if it was a child who held a terrible secret from his parent.

My friend opened the church door and there stood the officer with his partner.
Samara took one glancing look at him and bitterly said, "We don't what you're selling."
The law enforcer jammed his black boot in the door before it was shut.
"Move your hoof, you donkey."
The officer pushed the door open and forced himself into our sanctity.
"It's not a good idea to call your only hope in this situation a *'donkey'*." The officer chided. "I got called here."
"Well, I didn't call you." Samara pointed to the door. "So, get out!"
"I called them." The boy interjected.
He was the centre of attention now. Samara exhaled a sharp frustrated breath. He rapidly shook his head in small rotations and theatrically gestured to inside the church. "Come in then." He said spitefully.

"No need for that tone." He said calmly. He turned his attention to me as he proceeded to the front of the church, the girl officer scampering behind him. "Good to see you again soldier." He taunted.

"*Idi Nahui*" I sneered back, with narrowed eyes.
"I'll pretend to know what that means."

The officer sat on the altar once again, this time moving the artifacts around so he could fully place his backside onto it. The show of respect was gone. Now this was a spitting match.

"What did you call us for lad?" He said with clasped hands.

"Let me go and get it for you?" The boy said. He opened the office door with a creak and clack and vanished from us.

"While we're here—" The officer folded his arms. "Anything you two would like to say?"
"I met someone who you might know." Samara said. "They had some good things to say about me."
"Yeah? Who's that?"
"Your Mother after I slept with her."

The officer leaned back and shook his head.
"Finished?" He said unimpressed.
"Well, I made her finish."

The officer's lips puckered; his grip tightened around his triceps as if he tried to pop them. The little girl beside him was more timid than ever. Now she was not so much taking notes but more standing in the corner quietly.

"Can we stop?" The boy demanded.

He wandered from the office holding a stack of papers. He gently but casually placed them on the altar. The officers' eyes grew like a fly, hungry for the latest information.
"Gladly." He spoke with fresh relief. He snatched up the papers and skimmed them thoroughly.
"Bank statements?" He asked with confusion.
"Proof."
"Of what?"
"I'm being extorted officer."

The enforced rested the evidence onto his lap.
"By who?" He gestured his forefinger to me and my fellow priest. "By these two?"
"No. By my own dad."

He pondered his thoughts. He scratched his forehead and bit his lip, hoping some sort of stimulation would give him an answer.
"This won't be enough proof to get him done for anything. Have you got anything else?"
"Yeah," The boy said. "Speak to David at the Bailiff's office. He should fill you in more."

The officer nodded his head and stood up.
"Then we're off." He announced. He directed his ire to me again.
"I'm not finished with you—" He pointed to Samara. "Or him.
I'll be back."
"I can't wait." I spoke sarcastically.

The two intruders made their way out and proceeded to leave.
The male officer opened the door and the two exited their stage
with a slam from an abused piece of ancient wood.

"Fuckers." Samara snapped. "Look at what they're doing to my
door!"
"Forget about the door." I whined. My tone softened and turned
to the boy. My grasp tightened around his arm, marking my
bandages with his grease-soaked clothes. "Get your things and
get back here. I'll get you set up with motorbike lessons but only
if you learn how to use the push bike."
"But what about you guys?" The boy asked.
"We'll be fine my boy." I grab him softly by both arms. "We
will be fine. Now listen to your father and go."
I tap him on the shoulder and release him.
He jogged to the door and opened it frantically.
"Be careful!" Samara pleaded.

Once again, the door was met with a violent force. Another
crunch follows through, and a new streak of cracks follows. This
door became more and more brittle by the day. Eventually
leading to its death. I was proud to see the boy make a life for
himself. As proud as any father would be but I felt saddened by
the realisation that this would soon be over.
The end would come.

Michael
About six-ish

Today was pay day and today is when I get the time to finally
rest and relax. I left me youngest upstairs to play whatever

games he wanted on his computer, while I sat on me leather sofa in the lounge and watched a soap opera.

I left the lounge door open to keep an eye out for Bernard and lo and behold, he walked through the front door.

"Ah, I was waiting for you." I called out.

He was different though. He just stared at me and said nothing.

He ran upstairs, thumping his steps along the way.

"Where are you going?" I demanded.

He didn't respond. I pull myself up. I put my stuff aside and then go after him.

I see him racing down carrying bags and bags of clothes. This took me by surprise.

"What the hell are you doing?" I demanded further.

Still no response. I moved in front of the door and outstretched meself to block him.

"Where are you going?" I asked.

"Away." He grumbled.

"Ah. So, it speaks." I joked. "You need to pay me."

"For what?"

I was flabbergasted by the gall on this lad.

"For staying under my roof!" I yelled.

"I'm not staying here for long."

"What do you mean?"

"I'm leaving."

I lean on the door and fold my arms.

"You're not. You're paying me first."

"For what?"

"You need to look after your brother. I can't support him by meself."

"Don't you care about your family?"

"No." He said deadpan.

"Then you're a selfish bastard!" I yelled again.

311

"You say that, but most of the money you spend either goes to whatever Jason wants or whatever is shoved down your face."
"What?" I cried innocently. "Am I so bad to have a reward for meself?" I shoved him by the shoulder. "Where are you going anyway?"
"Don't touch me." He said.
"I can do what I like." I shove him again. This time he takes a few steps back. "You live in my house. So where are you going."
"Somewhere you'll never see me again." He continued with no emotion.
"Where are you going?" I asked.
"Church."

I felt like he was lying. I did a little laugh in disbelief.
"A little late for it isn't it? I didn't think you believed in that rubbish either."
"Get out of my way."

I leaned forward.

"Make me." I spoke horridly.

What this lad I kept in me house did, was he kicked me straight in the gonads. I collapsed to the floor, and he ran out the door. He tossed his key onto the tiled floor and left. I was on the floor for a moment before I could get up. I chased after him and then he just ran off into the night.

He was gone.

My blood raced. I felt my blood boil and me skin turn red with rage. I brought him into this world, and I will take him out from it just the same.

Sidorovich
16:23

"Where do I go from here?" I asked myself. "Where should I go?"

312

I addressed the air like it was a friend. Like it was something I should care for. Something I should long for. Like a brother's embrace or the soft caress of a loved one. Instead, the brightened void said nothing and left me alone like a vacant lover who disappeared into the dark. The church said nothing. Not even Samara could answer, he was too busy asking those questions himself.

I bowed over the altar and said a few compassionate words. There was no response, nor did I expect one. They were faint whispers to a deaf preternatural ear. I look beside me and see my black bible. I open it and see the old memories in there. I see the ancient photos and I gently caress them. This gesture, while futile to most, sparked at least a little life in me.
I itched my bandages and felt their need to be changed. This could wait, at least for a moment. Tucked away in another page is an envelope. An official thing that was not meant for me but for another.

I hear the main door open. I leave my things and I stand up to meet who entered it and see the boy in his school uniform. "How did it go?" I asked.

The boy sighed and collapsed on the nearest pew. "Good, I guess." He began lighting his tobacco pipe. "I'm just glad it's over now."
I walked over to the boy and joined him smoking.
"What do you want kind of grades do you want to come out of it?" I asked.
"I don't care. Just as long as I pass."

I exhale smoke and put a compassionate smile on my face.
"Good." I stated. "Because I'll still be proud of you."

The boy returned a smile and breathed out tobacco through his nose.
"Thank you." He said.
"Don't thank me yet. We have a surprise for you."

I stood from the pew and went to the front of the church.
"Samara!" I called out. "Get in here."
My friend entered the hall from the office and greeted the boy.
We both held gleeful grins and happy hearts.
I procured the envelope and gave it to the boy.
"Well done!" I said.

The child's eyes darted between the envelope and me. He
snatched it from my hands and ravenously ripped it apart.
"Well?" I asked.
My child's face brightened. He dropped the paper before him
and hugged both me and Samara.
"Woah!" Samara gasped out. "Not too tightly." He jested.
The boy released us.
"Sorry." They muttered happily.
"That's OK." Samara said. "Come around the church, we have
something for you."

The three of us walked outside and to the rear of the church.
There sat the boy's iron steed, glossed in red and black. Behind it
were the bright fields where crops and plants began to bloom.
Not the full glistening gold but enough yellow to coat the
landscape with illuminating beauty. Their shining sparkle and
lively presence gave us the world we dreamed of. A stark bright
contrast to a dark horse who made their own path.
Beside it was his essential equipment. A black and white helmet
full face helmet, decorated in a paint splatter pattern. An olive-
green Kevlar jacket that looked rough to the touch but the lining
I was assured, would be comfortable to wear all day. Finally,
black military boots and a bike chain lock. We guessed his size
again, but I feel like Samara's eye for fashion had helped here.

Samara and I stood like proud parents with each other. Our boy
was in awe, trying to pick his jaw up from the floor and find
words to express his joy.
There was none. Instead, he could only cry out a desperate
"Thank you!"
He hugged us tighter this time. This time we could not complain.

He released us and said words both me and Samara could agree to.
"We need to celebrate." He cheered.
"Now you're talking." Samara returned. "I'll get the good stuff out."

18:32

There was peace around us. It was not sober, and it was not quiet, but it was us. Music played from the old CD player I kept. We gathered in the hall and sat on whatever furniture we could spare, less concerned by comfort and more by camaraderie. There was calm in the night, but there was darkness still clouding us in the dim church lights. Each man held a crystal tumbler filled with an ancient cognac and drank leisurely.

"How was your stay in our hotel?" Samara asked.
For the week I've been here?"
"Yeah."
"I'd give it three stars." The boy teased.
"Three stars?" He outraged. "Why not five?"

A shape in the corner caught my eye. I don't know what it was, but it held the faint shape of a man. I thought my eyes deceived me as the figure warped like ink in water. I stared at it for a moment to adjust my eyes and figure out what it was. To see if it was a threat or a mishap of my shattered mind. I felt my hands shake. I placed my glass down on the floor and took a puff of my pipe. The taste of char and ash fixing me to this earth.

"Minus four for the space but plus two stars for the hotel managers."
"Add another for the hotel drinks and we'll call it square." Samara winked.
"Deal." The boy grinned.

The two clinked their tumblers together.

My attention was on the floor and the object in my hand. I looked down and saw my pipe there. Bandages still tightening. They needed changing desperately as they were now more than a day old.

"What about you Fedor?" I heard.
"What?" I asked dumbfounded.
"What will you do when you get out of here?" Vasya asked.

The room was dishevelled but still had markings of a holy site foreign to us. The room was dark except for the makeshift bonfire we created. Vasya sat to one side, still clutching his now worsening stomach wound. There was nothing we could do for him. Nothing except wait. To the other side, sat Arseny. Smoking his last cigarette. Each of us sat on the cold stone floor. I could feel whatever presence in this place wished me out as the patterned artwork under our backsides gave a sharper bitterness than winter.
Before us was a feast of whatever we could find. The odd scraps of bread and water we rationed between us. We were so hungry though and so tired. We had not found any sort of rest in days and now the debt was to be paid on our bodies.

Once we were filled with the energy to fight an army and escape with our lives, now we battled the urge to sleep for fear of being killed in our sleep.

I once again looked at my pipe. It was new and fresh. Without smoke or use. I pocketed the memento and drank some water.

"I don't know." I said grimly. "I didn't think we would make it this far."
"Oh, come on." Arseny groaned. "There must be something."
"What will you do then?" I asked.

The soldier inhales his poison and leans back, splaying his limbs on the ground and releasing the extinguished tar into the air.
"I'll go to school." He said. "I think I've had enough of the soldiers' life."

"You say you want to learn but we're burning books." Vasya chided.

Silence clouded us for a moment more, allowing the licking flames and burning scripture before us to do the speaking. My gaze reached the corner. There sat Lev, banging sand out of his boots. He felt my presence and met my gaze.

There was no fight left in him. There was just defeat. I felt the pain in us. We knew we had done unspeakable things, but it was too late to turn back. He broke his gaze and continued with his task.

I returned to the conversation and bit into a small scrap of bread.

"What about you Vasya?" Arseny asked.
"I don't think I'll make it out." He revealed the fresh stitchwork on his wound. The cut was developing into something fetid. The rust and dirt of the thing that stabbed him will kill him without intervention. The question is when will that intervention come?

"Well, how long did the army say they would take?" The boy soldier asked me.

I swallowed and tried to search for hope, but there was none. "They said they'll be here in the morning. But the problem is that the rebels know we're here."
"So…" The medic grimaced. "It's a race to see who gets here first."

We all stared into the fire. Holy words and things that gave people comfort disappeared. We burned history in selfish favour. Scrolls and books crumbled and broke. Inside the fire, I suddenly found my answer to the question.

"You asked what I wanted to do if I got out." I felt my hands shake. "I want to atone. I want to do right."
"How long will that take?" Vasya asked.

317

"I don't know. As long as it takes."

The three of us couldn't think of a word to say to each other. We carved our path and placed ourselves in this situation. We asked for this, we just did not know this mosque would be our answer. I continued to stare into the fire and felt the death of something. In my mind, I felt a plague riddle me. A burning question I needed to ask its killer.
"Why?" I murmured.
The two heard but I did not understand.
"Why what?" Vasya asked.
"Why did you call out to Kars?" I accused bitterly.

The man was taken aback. He tried to think of an excuse but did not come. Instead, he spoke the damning truth.
"Those men were…" He quivered. "They were about to shoot him anyway, so I called to warn him." His tone turned defensive. "What difference does it make why I did it? He's dead now!"

"It matters to me." I hissed.
"So, you blame me for his death when he was gunned down?"
"That and more?"

Vasya looked at his worsening stab mark. Pus and white fluids began to leak from his belly.
"I might die soon." He stated.
"Good." I spat hatefully "Do it faster."

In that conversation, something pure I had before the war died. My compassion for man. My innocence. My friend that I could call brother.
I clutched the prayer rope Mikhail gave me and felt myself slip. I thought about throwing the thing in the fire but instead, it called to me. It beckoned for something from me.

"Here lies our souls." I whispered to the cross. "Built from the murder of the pure and those who believed they were better."

I wrapped the holy cross around my neck and let the necklace hang from me. I cradled the cross with my forefinger and thumb and then I looked up.

I blinked and heard a voice.

"What about you Fedor?" Samara threw his arm my way, careful not to spill his drink. "What would you give us?"

It took me a moment to recognise the situation, but I remembered myself and where I was. My eyes fluttered and my head shook.

"Are you ok?" Samara asked.
"Yes." I dismissed. "I'm just tired."
"Tired?" He blurted. "Apparently, the boy says that I am worth a star. Do I need to check you into our hotel?"
"I'd give you no stars and kick you out." I joked.
"Keep talking like that and I'll hide your tobacco."
"Fine then." I submitted. "A single star."
"Better." Samara smiled.

The boy laughed. His joy was stolen from him when he realised that he would have to leave.
"I'll miss you guys when I go." He muttered with sorrow.

"We won't be far." Samara comforted. "You're welcome to call."

"He deserves something from here though." I spoke, understanding the boy's sentimentality. "He needs something from us."

"He has the motorbike." Samara blustered.
"But not a piece from us."

I roam to the back of the church and disappear into the office. I reach into the locked metal box that keeps my cursed objects and possessions. In it, I see nothing fitting to give. Not due to the

strangeness or the lack of trinkets I kept but because this would hold no purpose to him, only to me.
Nothing except for the bible that rested in there. It was mine. I had marked it as so, but this was the only thing to give.

I reach for a note and scribble a personal message of mine. The time was not right though. He will read it when he leaves, not before. I stick it to the back of the old crumbling holy book. I pick it up with speed, but something stops me.
A small clatter of paper on cobbled steps. The photos of my past. Laid to bare.
I quickly reach for them, as if my guts were spilled onto the floor, and scoop them up the same way.
There was a pause a whisper as I stared at the man in front of me. The failure that plagued my time on this earth. They accompanied this bible since their inception but have not seen other eyes except those who were close to me or those who were dead to me.

"Fedor!" Sarama beckoned. "Where have you gone?"

I heard the call to action, and I answered, not with words but with a hasty decision.
I tucked the pictures back inside. Parting them would feel inappropriate.
I unlocked the cabinet and quickly grabbed the first bottle I saw.
I reached for a bottle of 'Black & White' scotch whiskey and revealed another behind it.
Samara behovely labelled his 'Death Bottle'.
The object of his mortality locked its gaze on me. A reminder of his time soon approaching. I now felt the judging eyes of my bible. The objects of our demise now coming to fruition, accompanied by a cruel realisation. We are helping this boy, but he is learning from our very worst and absorbing it.

I close the cabinet and re-enter the hall. Bottle and bible in hand. I gave the poison to my friend. I was enabling him and still, even though he says it, I feel like I'm killing him.
I handed the book to the boy.

320

"This is yours now." I stated kindly.

The child was taken back for a moment. I don't know if it was the alcohol in my stomach compelling me to do such a thing or if I wished rid of this thing, but he took my burden as if it was freshly carved gold.
"Are—" He stammered. "Are you sure?"
"Yes." I smiled.
"There is something I wrote in there but please don't open it until you get to the new church."
He embraced the artifact with care and placed it on his lap.
"Thank you." He said with composed gratitude.

In that moment I felt a weight lifted. I don't know if I have just cursed him, but I wanted this boy. My boy. To have something that would give him at least a good memory of us.

Bern
9:43am
The first day of the new life.

In this moment... I felt free.
I felt relieved.
I felt alive for once.
This time I was ready to leave this accused town behind for all the problems it has caused me. I gathered my things in bags and sacks which would be slung across the new bike. I threw on my Kevlar jacket and boots.
I tried the patterned helmet on and forced my head through the padded interior. It was tight, it pressed against my jaw and crushed my blonde hair.
I took it off and felt the air rush to comfort my released skull. I walked out of the office and saw my two mentors there. One was smoking, the other hobbling on a cane.
They stared at me and felt a newfound pride.
Here they were, my fathers.
"This is one hot guy here!" Samara inputted like an ecstatic parent.
"Agreed." Sidorovich reinforced.

321

I felt a small blush come across me. This felt right. This felt pure.

No more slaving away for pennies. No more time looking after my brother and no more abuse. Freedom at my grasp and the end to suffering.

"Thank you." I returned.

Sidorovich waved me over to the door.

"Come on." He beckoned. "Get your bike out to the front. I'll help you push."

The Russian walked halfway out the door. He held it open for me and turned his attention to the Greek.

"Watch the place while I'm gone." I asked.

He returned, partially sober. "Yes wife, I'll behave."

The child and I walked to the rear of the church. We saw the bike still standing there, with some bags slung over the side of it. We secured any remaining loose things and tied them down with zip ties.

"Can you manage with these?" I asked the boy.

"We'll find out." He nonchalantly spoke.

We tried to push the crimson iron horse to the front of the church. We achieved the side with moderate effort until we heard screaming inside.

"I'll be back." Sidorovich spluttered.

He ran into the church and left me to push the bike to the front. I pushed this hunk of metal and petrol out to the street. I quickly tried to put on the lock to protect it from the possibility of an ambitious thief.

I wrapped the lock around the front wheel, but I could not secure it. Not when something was more deserving of my attention.

A single crunchy pop and a whistle past my head. I looked over the bike and saw a small crater on the tarmac. Inside was a little metal pellet that had crushed itself from the impact.

I was horrified. Battling the questions of if I had just been shot at or if Sidorovich was once again back in time. I looked at the ancient building and saw the door was left wide open. The priests were not in eye shot but I did a fat man wearing a white vest.

When my ears adjusted to the screaming, I could hear the difference in the accents. The unfamiliar one is English.
I dropped what I was doing and rushed back into the church. I approached the stranger, but he sensed my presence.
The man was my father. He grabbed me by the collar of my new jacket and threw me into the nearest wall, forcing his body weight against me.
"This is where you've been huh?" The attacker blared. "I had to go knocking on every church in the county until I finally fucking found you!"
"Let him go!" One of the priests demanded.

The bastard who held me gripped me by the neck and began to squeeze. I felt his meaty fingers dig into my scrawny neck, trying to pop my neck like a chicken.
Another shot rang out, this time beside his foot. The invader moved back into the waiting arms of another intruder.
Lev threw a punch to the back of my father's spine, putting him on one knee.
The predator circled his prey like a wolf waiting for a chance to strike.

The veteran bared his teeth and readied his fists to land like meteors. I moved away from the conflict and caught my stolen breath.
"Why are—" I gasped before sputtering a cough. "Why are you here?"

The questioned kicked his opponent to the floor. He spat on him before turning his attention to me.
"I came for you—" Lev pointed to the armed priest. "And him."

My dad tried to scurry away through the church door like a frightened rat, but the old veteran turned business owner caught this action. He marched to him at a mocking pace and kicked him in the face. The force sent him reeling onto his back and clutching his injury.

"You're not leaving." Lev spat.

He slammed the door before him. Trapping him in the church with us.

I looked to my two mentors. Samara was stood, but wobbly. Moving side to side like a branch in the wind, there as Sidorovich remained vigilant like a stone. He held his posture, not budging his hands or his weapon of war.

Lev walked to us, keeping one eye on the man he imprisoned here with us.

He sat on the backrest of the closest pew and lit a cigarette.

"Do you know what this boy did?" The veteran asked.

"I do." Sidorovich spoke.

"Do you know what type of damage he did to my business?" Lev accused. "I'm tempted to grab that gun from you and shoot him with it."

Sidorovich turned his weapon to Lev for a moment. I could see the look in his eyes. He was battling a war on two fronts. His hands shook and his thoughts were not his own. It was hard to tell where this man was but so far, he dwelled in a place of violence.

"I hate you all." He spat. Lev flicked ash in the direction of my dad. "But I hate this man more."

My progenitor rose and assessed the situation. He knew he was in an impossible situation that could result in his death.

"Kill him." Lev hissed.

"No!" Samara begged. "Don't do it!"

Sidorovich was pulled in different directions. The call of both worlds took a toll on him.

324

"I don't…" Sidorovich murmured.
"Do it Fedor!" Lev Exhorted. "If you did not hesitate on the difficult decisions, you would not be wearing those bandages."

The priest's gaze drifted to his arms. His eyes widened like he uncovered a lost secret.
"Why are these here?"
He lowered his weapon for a moment and started unwrapping his bandages, revealing the old scars for the world to see. The discomfort on his face was visible. To him, it must have felt like peeling off his own skin. The matured marks of stretched skin and chunks of missing flesh were now visible. He raised his weapon again. Confused as to what was happening. This was too much for the old man.

Lev smiled and approached the old man.
He was winning.
The old squad mates stood before each other.

The veteran opposed the priest.
I quickly realised what was going on. This was revenge for my actions. If he could not punish me, he would take away the ones close to me.
Samara approached his friend in crisis. Sidorovich extended his one free arm to hold the old man upright.
"Don't kill him!" Samara begged.
"Shut up!" Lev spat.
"Don't do it Fedor. I'm begging you." He spoke, gasping for any air his weak lungs could capture. "You'll be in more trouble than you know."

"I don't care Vasya." He whispered.
The battle was lost. He was already gone, but Samara was still defiant and eager for the return of his friend.
"I do!" Samara flapped his outstretched hand in front of his chest.

Lev leaned against one of the pews with his arms crossed, seeing the situation as a minor inconvenience. "Just kill him, Fedor. Get it over with."

"No!" Samara swung his cane as if to hit Lev. However, he was too far, resulting in the wasted effort to topple him, forcing Samara to catch himself on the polished wood. He clutched his hand on his stomach as if to hold his rotting guts from spilling on the cobbled floor.
"Don't do it." He begged further with more desperation in his voice. The dying man on the floor sat himself upright, holding himself up by the mid-section of the cane.

"You can't kill him. He's lost. No job. No family. On the run." Samara's breath shuddered. "He's lost. Killing him won't do a thing. It will hurt you more instead and I can't see you in prison."

Samara forced the last of his remaining energy to look Sidorovich in the eyes, but the killer kept his eyes on the target.

"Look at me Fedor." Samara asked with a heavy breath.

The request was ignored.

"Hey!" Samara screeched. "Piece of shit, look at me!"

His voice was finally heard. The Russian's eyes drifted to the dying man on the floor.

"I can't lose you." Samara's voice broke slightly. "I can't lose the only friend I have. The only one that was there for me. I don't care about this." The Greek swept his hand through the air as if spreading the ashes of a loved one. "I don't care about the booze, or the women, or even the shit I used to shove up my nose." He weakly pointed his cane at the veteran. "I want my friend back."

The old man's eyes eased. They lost their killer instinct and replaced them with a small glimmer of compassion and brotherly love.

"Ok." The Russian said.

He pathetically dropped his weapon onto the floor. It landed with a clatter and then erupted in a pop. The pistol shot itself across the church.
The conclave hid and ducked for cover as the crack of gunpowder echoed through the church. The force of the small weapon carried it to the front door, close to where the father stood. He was eagerly eying up the weapon and its power as it was tantalisingly close but still inside the church. It was one last way to assert power. To gain dominance. Lev and Sidorovich saw what had happened and glanced at each other for a moment. They made a quick dash to the door to block off the attacker.
The father did not waste time. He saw the gun in arms reach and reached forward to it.
The two soldiers used the force of their bodies to block the door from the attacker.
The father bolted through the door, but the two soldiers barricaded the door with their bodies.
Small gaps exposed sunlight into the church due to the years of damage and abuse the ancient wood had suffered.
"Boy!" Samara called. "Help me up!"
I ran over to help him and pick him up. His bones rattled and his stomach groaned as he left the embrace of the floor.
"Hold the door!" Sidorovich called.

Sharp bangs and clatters cracked the ancient arboreous flesh, causing chunks to break off as if were a victim of rotting tissue being flayed by swords.
"Let me in!" The father screamed. "Let me in or I start shooting!"
"Get the police boy!" Samara pleaded.
The wounded priest hobbled closer to the door to help hold off the intruder until reinforcement arrived.

327

The two forces battled against each other, shouting expletives and foul insults at each other. Some in English and some in Russian.

The war at the door ceased for a moment. Lev ran to push a pew to the door. He attempted to drag it along, but his old bones prevented him from doing such. Lev bowed over and clutched his back. He pushed his weight against the door instead. The two soldiers barricaded against the door and pushed harder, as if more men were about to come.

Lev rotated his back to the door and forced himself up with his legs now that his back was decommissioned. "Idiot!" Lev hissed at Sidorovich as if he were a serpent biting his victim with venom. "That thing better have run out of bullets."

The was silence for a few tense moments. The men's muscles had activated every part of the sinew and tissue that had not been used in years which was not helped by their age. Their lungs both charred from years of abuse finally put to extreme conditions, causing them to breathe with great exhausted effort.

A small click was heard in between the sharp gasps of air.

Their breathing stopped. Silence was in the air again. The men knew what sound that was. A shot rang out, hitting the door and whistling past the two men's heads. A second hit the door. This time there was a blood-curdling scream.

Lev lost the power in his right leg. A small trickle of blood pooled on the floor and streamed down his trousers. His body landed on the floor. His voice singing an agonising song with intermediate grunts and winces. He shuffled away from the door holding his leg and trying to staunch the flow.

I sprung to action and dialled the number and waited for the buzz tone to put me through to an emergency operator.

"Police, what is your emergency?" a male voice asked pleasantly.

"I've got someone shooting at us?"

Another shot broke through the door. The men at the door flinched and covered themselves from the flying splinters. She must have heard the noise as she immediately lost the nice attitude and became attentive to the situation.

I looked to the door and saw Sidorovich standing defiant. But I could see it wasn't him, it was his monster. Bearing fangs and blockading the door as he was pushing against a monsoon. The rest of us ran for some kind of shelter. Except for Samara who joined the fight with his friend and barricaded the door.

Sidorovich

"Hold The door!" I bellowed to Vasya.
"I'm trying!"
An angry mob of the local militia was trying to break down the door to the mosque. We invaded their sanctity, and they wanted it back. Lev took a firing position against a window. Bullets of varied sizes and calibres smashed against the body and flesh of this stone building.
We were tired. The final stretch was here, the final fight before freedom but our time was running out.
Vasya and I held against the door, taking cover, and flinching at any shot that flew too close to where we stood.
"How much longer till they get here?" Lev cried.
"They'll be here as fast as they can be!" Arseny replied, terrified.

Cracks of splinters and ricochets deafened us. There was little we could do for safety except wait for rescue.
"Then we wait!" I bellowed.
"Wait for them to kill us you mean." Lev called in a dry tone.

Another barrage of steel and lead roared in the air. Vasya was hit. He lay broken, clutching the gushing holes which now rearranged his destroyed organs. Only I was left standing against the door.

"Vasya!" Arseny cried. He rushed over to pull his carcass aside from the conflict. There was little he could do, he was dead. But he did not believe that.

The mosque doors finally broke, and Vasya's side was little more than fragments of ruined wood that would not even be enough to fuel a fire.

I retreated and matched the first man in with my fists. I felt weak. I drew it up to the extended fighting sapping our will but there was still adrenaline in my veins and a hope to go home.

I gapped with the man whilst Lev secured the door beside him, shooting anyone who dared to try and enter. The rebel in front of me wore a vest carrying bottles of petrol, capped with soaked rags. Most of them broke and soaked his clothes but one remained. One was all he needed. He was unarmed and lost his weapon in the struggle, but he looked at the man being dragged off and saw his opportunity. He grabbed the remaining bottle in his pouch, lit it, and then threw it to the vulnerable.

The bottle cracked open with a sickening crunch and sprayed thousands of ravenous licking tongues all onto Vasya and Arseny.

The screams. My God the screams a young man could give. The first few seconds saw his voice in excoriating agony before the smoke entered his lungs and began to choke him.

I struck the rebel in the face and knocked him back, letting Lev handle him.

I ran to the men and saw Arseny rolling around in the burning puddle. The smell sickened me, it was like burning steak over a coal fire. I could see his childlike face melt away and the muscle and bone char from the heat that he dwelled in.

I saw no other alternative. To save his life, I reached in and pulled him out of the fire. He still squirmed and his flesh peeled like rotten fruit. I felt my skin boil, my hands burn, and set in place. I dragged him out of the fire, but he was still now. I grew more preoccupied with myself now. The flames spread to me. They burned my hands and spread to my elbows.

I screamed. I screamed like hell had finally reached me.

I rolled around in the church, still feeling my bones cook and my skin sizzle. I feel a hand grab me by the collar and douse my burns in water. They ceased but the man in front of me which I could call my saviour wore military gear. He wore a black helmet not of Soviet issue but of another time.

"He's ok!" The man called.

The mosque was gone. The sand was gone. I looked at my hands and saw they were not on fire but still held the aftereffects of one.
The boy rushed to me and started rolling fresh bandages on my hands.
My child rushed to help me.

I looked at his forehead and saw a small leak of blood trickle down his forehead.
"What happened?" I asked.
"That bastard!" He spoke with a spiteful tone. "He ran out of bullets so instead he threw the pistol at my head."

I was still in shock as if I had been ripped from the womb.

"Are you ok?" He asked.
"I'm fine." I lied. "I just need to get up. Where is Samara?"

The boy's head sank. His face broke from a sorrow I was not aware of.
"He's…" The boy quivered. "He's dead."
"What?" I gasped in shock.

"He shot him."

I did not wait for the bandages to finish wrapping. I bolted up from the floor.
I scanned the room rapidly and saw a swath of armed police officers, carrying rifles and dressed in black.

The father out of sight. My friend, however, was surrounded by paramedics. People came to pick up his corpse so they could assess the cause of death.

His body was face down, revealing a small bloody hole in his clothes. The wound only just stopped sucking blood.

He was murdered. My child would go. I was alone.
"I'm so sorry about this." The boy wept.
I wrapped my arm around his shoulder.
"It is not your fault." I consoled. "You did OK."

I released the boy and moved to the office. I opened the cabinet and saw his bottle stare at me. The final bottle of my friend.
I reached in for it and held the ancient liquor in my broken, half-covered hands.
It felt wrong. Like a world that was hostile. A world that stripped and whipped from any notion of goodness.
This was grief in its fullness. But I had a promise to keep.
I marched back into the church and quickly pulled the boy to one side, away from prying ears.
"Go from here." I whispered.
"But they'll want to ask me questions."
"They can ask them, but you will go to the new place. Live with the new priest and be gone from here."

"What about you?" The boy asked.
"Read the note in the book I gave you."

There was a silence between us. There was little to be said in a moment like this. No words would feel appropriate. The boy instead embraced me as a father. We held each other for a few precious moments, knowing that it would be the last time we heard from each other.

We let go of each other and I saw a tear running down his face. I wiped it from his cheek.
"Where is Lev?" I asked.

The boy sniffled and tried to steady himself. He struggled but managed to eke out some words. "He was taken in an ambulance."

"Then he won't trouble you anymore."

"But what about you?"

I felt a dark pit in my gut. A difficult time would arise and this time I would not hesitate.

"I'll be ok." I lied. "Go. Live your new life."

The boy nodded and walked off. He wiped his face with his jacket sleeve and walked out of the church.

I turned to the altar to assess the damage of the church but instead, I felt a sort of pride.

Three spectres sat on the altar with smiles on their faces. Three who gave me more power than the ground I walked on.

My wife, my son and Samara. They held smiles on their faces and held out their arms in welcome.

I looked back to the crime scene and saw the officers take photographs of the crime scene. There someone pulled the old pistol into an airtight plastic bag. The shadow of war hovered over me, and my loved ones called.

I walked to the altar, approaching my wife. I felt her hand on my face. She felt more real to me than flesh and blood. I left the bottle on her lap ready for the time I would use it.

Her lips moved but no sound was made. None was needed to understand what she mouthed. Words I waited more than twenty years to hear from her.

"Thank you."

My son was dead. But my boy is alive, and he escaped.

"Are you ready to talk now?" I heard a voice call.

I turned to meet it and saw the tattooed officer in front of me. He folded his arms unimpressed.

I looked at the weapon in the distance again and felt its call.

"I am."

333

I looked to the end of the church door and saw it in pieces. I muttered the final words that I wrote in the bible to myself. I knew I would not see him again. Not after this.

But those words, even now gave me some small hope to be reunited.

"I will miss you, boy. I will see you in heaven."

Writers Acknowledgements:

To Jason, Alex, Ryan, James, JJ, and Mel.

May God bless you for the help you have given me through this project. I couldn't have done it without you. Your support from turning this dream to a reality has shone brightly and I do appreciate it.

To Candice.

I'm so glad we met over this. You were my biggest cheer leader and I thank you every day for your kind words.

Printed in Great Britain
by Amazon